GW00507408

F

As the result of a cataclysm[...] North Polar ice cap that has caused the melting of the bergs, swollen water, crossing the North Atlantic, has inundated the low-lying areas of Britain. Virtually only the Cotswolds and some of the Welsh mountains together with the Pennines and the Scottish hills remain free of the floodwater. While a shattered central government and the local authorities do their best to cope with an unparalleled situation of disease and death on a gigantic scale a number of families make for comparative safety in such craft as are available, and head for the now vastly over-crowded high areas through scummy waters polluted by all manner of debris including putrefying corpses. Not families alone: looting gangs, killers and rapists are making such hay as they can as they too make for what land they can find; while a mobile brothel aboard a commandeered London double-decker bus rumbles north ahead of the rising waters, its madam hoping to establish her trade in the Yorkshire Dales.

SURREY COUNTY COUNCIL
WITHDRAWN FROM STOCK
AND OFFERED FOR SALE
WITH ALL FAULTS BY
SURREY COUNTY LIBRARY

By the same author

Whistle and I'll Come
The Kid
Storm South
Hopkinson and the Devil of Hate
Leave the Dead Behind Us
Marley's Empire
Bowering's Breakwater
Sladd's Evil
A Time for Survival
Poulter's Passage
The Day of the Coastwatch
Man, Let's Go On
Half a Bag of Stringer
The German Helmet
The Oil Bastards
Pull My String
Coach North

Featuring Simon Shard
Call for Simon Shard
A Very Big Bang
Blood Run East
The Eros Affair
Blackmail North
Shard Calls the Tune
The Hoof
Shard at Bay
The Executioners
Overnight Express
The Logan File

Featuring Lieutenant St. Vincent Halfhyde, RN
Beware, Beware the Bight of Benin
Halfhyde's Island
The Guns of Arrest
Halfhyde to the Narrows
Halfhyde for the Queen
Halfhyde Ordered South
Halfhyde and the Flag Captain
Halfhyde on the Yangtze
Halfhyde on Zanatu
Halfhyde Outward Bound
The Halfhyde Line
Halfhyde and the Chain Gangs
Halfhyde Goes to War
Halfhyde on the Amazon
Halfhyde and the Admiral

Featuring Donald Cameron
Cameron, Ordinary Seaman
Cameron Comes Through
Cameron of the Castle Bay
Lieutenant Cameron, RNVR
Cameron's Convoy
Cameron in the Gap
Orders for Cameron
Cameron in Command
Cameron and the Kaiserhof
Cameron's Raid
Cameron's Chase
Cameron's Troop Lift
Cameron's Commitment

Featuring Commander Shaw
Gibraltar Road
Redcap
Bluebolt One
The Man From Moscow
Warmaster
Moscow Coach
The Dead Line
Skyprobe
The Screaming Dead Balloons
The Bright Red Businessman
The All-Purpose Bodies
Hartinger's Mouse
This Drakotny . . .
Sunstrike
Corpse
Werewolf
Rollerball
Greenfly
The Boy Who Liked Monsters
The Spatchcock Plan
The Logan File

*Featuring Commodore John Mason
   Kemp, RD, RNR*
The Convoy Commodore
Convoy North
Convoy South
Convoy East
Convoy of Fear

Non-Fiction
TALL SHIPS: THE GOLDEN-AGE OF SAIL
GREAT YACHTS

FLOOD

PHILIP McCUTCHAN

ROBERT HALE · LONDON

91-523759

© Philip McCutchan 1991
First published in Great Britain 1991

ISBN 0 7090 4381 3

Robert Hale Limited
Clerkenwell House
Clerkenwell Green
London EC1R 0HT

The right of Philip McCutchan to be identified as
author of this work has been asserted by him
in accordance with the Copyright, Designs and
Patents Act 1988.

Photoset in North Wales by
Derek Doyle & Associates, Mold, Clwyd.
Printed and bound in Great Britain by
WBC Print Ltd,
and WBC Bookbinders Ltd, Bridgend, Glamorgan.

ONE

In the beginning no one had really taken it seriously; or anyway, few had. The man in the street scoffed, safe in Britain, where such things didn't happen. When the first tidings had come even the scientists, even the meteorologists and oceanographers, had been unable to agree as to what might happen. Just local, some of them said, very regrettable for Alaska and parts adjacent – there was a good deal of concern in Canada and parts of the northern United States – but really it was unlikely that Great Britain or the Continent would be under much threat. Others had sounded the alarm bells: some years before there had been concern about a glacier, about eight miles long and four hundred feet in height, that had come loose in Alaska and was moving seaward at around fifty feet a day, a record sprint for anything so vast. There had been believed to be a potential in that, a potential threat to the lands across the North Atlantic, the sudden surge of melting water adding so greatly to the sea levels that even London could lie beneath the waves when they came. The scientists had been unsure of just why that glacier had moved, but there had been a suggestion of a build-up of water beneath, thus destroying the friction that kept the huge edifice of ice in its place, so that it had got on the move.

John Rushworth, would-have-been medical student living in Cambridge, now sitting in the open deck abaft the midship superstructure of his father's power-boat that had been kept on the Norfolk Broads, sitting and staring across the featureless floodwater – featureless now that they had moved well away from the isolated towers of Ely cathedral and the high points of the Cambridge colleges – thought about the day tragedy had come in fast across the North Atlantic and the scoffers had panicked with all the others.

Charles Rushworth, John's father, was a lecturer in Computer Technology and thought entirely in computer language to the extent that normal, or even abnormal, matters passed him by; he was the present-day equivalent of the absent-minded professor of Greek. In the beginning he had been neither a scoffer nor a believer: he was nicely neutral until after the BBC Six O'Clock News had been broken into with a report of a surge of water coming in from the Atlantic and already resulting in some remarkably high tides in the Channel and along the western and southern coasts of Ireland. He had had words the next day with Alan Watson, who was professor of Geophysics at the University.

'Watson's worried,' he said to his wife when he got home that evening.

'What does he say?'

'Quite a lot.' Charles Rushworth poured himself a gin and tonic. He stared out of the big drawing-room windows at his garden. The house was a big one, on the north-western outskirts, near Girton. His garden was his pride and joy, his one relaxation from computer technology. A shame if it flooded, all that mud and debris, and nasty scum afterwards ... if there was an afterwards. Rushworth gave a sudden shiver of apprehension: Alan Watson was not normally a gloomy man, but that lunchtime, over a glass of dry sherry, he had been alarming.

'*What* does he say?' Mary Rushworth, at thirty-eight some years younger than her husband and very attractive with dark hair done in a halo around a wide forehead, spoke sharply, since she had sensed her husband's worry and knew that Alan Watson was no alarmist. 'Tell me, Charles.'

'All right.' Rushworth, clasping his glass tight, turned away from the window and went across the room to stand with his back to the empty fireplace: it was summer and a warm one, and in two days' time the colleges would be done for the long vacation. 'He talked about glaciers. Their normal characteristics, not this dreadful affair. I really didn't understand it all ... he quoted authorities on the movement of glaciers – Croll, Thomson, Tyndall, Helmholt and some modern ones. Rivers of ice, moving very slowly normally, but if speeded up so that all the ice comes down and melts in one big thaw, then the sea levels really could rise enormously. He says that's already happened, that it's on its way.'

'Is anyone doing anything about it?' Mary asked.

Rushworth shrugged. 'They're still wrapped up in the laying of blame. Watson believes the authorities still don't really see the danger – or if they do, they know there's nothing to be done about it. You can't hold back nature, after all ...'

'And us, Charles? Cambridge? The Fens?'

'The first to go, I suppose.'

Mary gave him a quizzical look. 'You don't really believe it yourself, do you?'

'Well, it's hard to imagine, certainly. Our life here, the University, the house. It can't just all vanish. And us ...'

'There's always the Gog Magogs.'

Rushworth gave a harsh laugh. John, who had just come into the room, had heard both the laugh and his mother's remark. In the days that followed, his reflections led him to believe that it had been that remark, probably facetiously uttered, that had all of a sudden made his father see things plainly and horribly: just the thought of the only hills in East Anglia becoming the mecca of all Cambridge and its surrounding villages, those who could crowd aboard a boat all making for the Gog Magogs to wait, like Noah in

his Ark, for the floodwaters to subside. Whether it was
that remark or not, Charles Rushworth had come to a
fast decision: the moment term was down, the family
would drive over to Breydon Water near Great
Yarmouth and live aboard the boat for a while.

'We'll take your parents,' he said to his wife.

'There's not a lot of room. You know what Daddy's
like in anyone else's house, too – let alone anyone else's
boat.'

'Room,' Rushworth said, and again laughed. 'Soon
there won't be any *room* anywhere!'

Radio and television had played it down by direction
from Whitehall. The press was not so reticent: doom lay
ahead and it was time the government took action,
though it didn't suggest what action. Condemnation of
the superpowers filled the newspapers' opinion
columns: as yet the blame had not been pin-pointed.
Just the facts as known, or as picked up by the sensitive
defensive instruments of NATO – there had been
nothing but denials from both Washington and
Moscow. London wasn't likely to be involved, other than
as a victim – the innocent victim of a nuclear blow-up
that had either not gone as planned, or had gone off too
soon, or had never been expected to go off at all short of
Armageddon. The one undoubted fact was that a vast
nuclear explosion had taken place beneath the glacier
system of Alaska and that this had sparked off a
sympathy shift in the glacier systems of Greenland and
the North Polar regions and all the ice in the area had
melted and was pouring down into the northern waters
which were now reaching out towards Britain, the
Continent and Scandinavia. And then, as though some
evil manifestation, or the simple wrath of God, had
determined to pile one disaster upon another, there
came a serious of cataclysmic earthquakes in South
America and, unbelievably, in Greenland – the result, it
was believed, of some huge object from space striking
the earth near the North Pole – and these had been

followed by a massive tidal wave, more a tidal surge when augmented by the fast-melting glacier systems, that had borne down with savage speed and ferocity and seemed to have carried all before them.

As the Rushworth family drove out of Cambridge with as many valuables and as much food and spare clothing as could be crammed into the big Volvo Estate, with the McNaughten parents-in-law, Mrs McNaughten severely disabled, with their cat in a wicker basket, the panic had started nationwide. All along the south coast the waters had encroached, rising so far as even almost to spill over Beachy Head and the White Cliffs of Dover, so that you could step from the summits directly into the English Channel; long-drop suicides were out at Beachy Head. A number of towns and villages inland, not there behind the various cliff formations but there where the land was close to the sea-level, had been inundated, among them Hove, Shoreham, Worthing and Littlehampton. This was the medical profession's Costa Geriatrica, and from the nursing homes, rest homes and hospital wards an apparently unending stream of old persons had, with great difficulty, been evacuated ahead of the rising waters, taken north of the South Downs to what for a time would be safety. Road vehicles had been used until the waters had risen further, after which a conscripted fleet of waterborne geriatric ambulance boats had carried them.

Most of them, that was: the old people living in their own houses had been the really recalcitrant ones, many of them disbelieving but determined at their great ages to remain *in situ* and take it if it came. Those mostly drowned. Worthing, as an instance, was not an old town and few of the houses had basements, but some did, notably along the sea end of Heene Road, and in these basements, long since converted into one-bedroom flatlets, a number of elderly corpses floated and bloated. Within a matter of days the water-level had increased alarmingly and, where the beaches had once been, ships of the Royal Navy stood off, sending their small boats inshore as far as the Downs, picking up people clinging to wooden makeshift rafts and so on. Farther along, around Portsmouth and Southampton, the Army assisted with boats manned by the Royal Corps of Transport from Marchwood on Southampton Water. Such merchant ships, largely great tankers and container ships, as had been alongside the berths in Southampton or lying at the Fawley oil refinery, became besieged by the safety seekers and found themselves taken over as accommodation units or refugee camps. Every part of the southern seaboard counties that stood clear above the water was crowded with the displaced, homeless population. The local authorities, after a period of dally and indecision, turned their minds from local politicking towards succour for the multitude and did what they could to distribute such items as blankets and warm clothing and food and water drawn from the so far flood free regions. This was no easy task, for the boats bringing this succour were in many cases attacked by the survivors and taken over as personal transport and out of the afflicted areas; in a number of cases there was looting and killing.

The Rushworth car had reached Breydon Waters ahead of the worst but only just. The low-lying, reclaimed fens were wide open to the immensely high tidal encroachment and the Volvo had been unloaded only minutes before it was engulfed. Rushworth's power-boat, a cabin cruiser named *Hilda*, was dragged down by her moorings until Charles's father-in-law, a retired naval commander, shouted at John to let go for'ard while he cast off the ropes aft, after which the boat righted herself with a nasty rocking motion.

'Where's the cat?' Commander McNaughten asked.

Rushworth said, 'Oh, damn the bloody cat!'

'That's no way to talk.' MacNaughten had served in the last war, if only as a midshipman at the tail end, but throughout his service life the cat had been a vital part of any ship's company. He scrabbled about, calling for the cat, a fat tabby. As it happened, the cat was still in its basket, which just then toppled over into the water. McNaughten made a successful grab and then subsided, purple-faced, the bedraggled animal staring with terrified eyes through the wicker.

Rushworth began stowing away the food and water, and the valuables, the latter consisting of some family silver, photographs hastily snatched up, family shots from past holidays and such, share certificates, National Savings certificates, premium bonds, top-up pension policies, house insurance policies, all in a steel file, plus credit-cards, cheque-books and cash. The parents-in-law had brought their own valuables, these consisting largely of a case of Glenturrent single malt whisky, the Commander's nightly tipple. There was also tobacco: the Commander was adamant that he would never give up smoking. He had no time for the futile waffle of the British Medical Association. He always kept a stock of cigarettes made from cigar tobacco by Dunhill and called cigarlettes. These were, he maintained, good for him. He had often been heard to remark that he objected strongly to people eating when he was smoking. And no flood was going to stop him until his supply ran out.

'You there, boy!'

John looked round. 'Yes, grandpa?'

'Better get under way.'

'Dad's –'

'Never mind your father, *get under way*. Look!' The commander waved an arm. Along what had been the roadway the roof of the car was still visible and so was something else: a number of persons half wading and half swimming, all of them with determined faces that said they were intending to board. Some had shaven heads, some had spiky hair of various colours starched into shapes like Roman legionaires' helmets, or cockattoos, or Red Indian braves. They wore an assortment of leather jackets, sleeveless, with vests beneath in some cases, others being bare chested. Here and there a female breast drooped.

The Commander said, 'The navy's always had a reputation for rescue, but this is too much. Only a bloody fool permits overloading.' He turned as Rushworth came out from amidships. 'Where do you intend to head?'

'I don't know.'

'I suggest you find out.' McNaughten was a big man, with big hands which he waved when angry, and a loud voice, the voice of authority. 'I further suggest high ground –'

'There isn't any. Not here.'

'Quite. We should head west. I don't know how long the fuel will last. Do you?'

'No.'

'Well, we have paddles when it does run out. Head west, Charles.' McNaughten paused and narrowed his eyes. 'Know how to get there?'

'Er – no. No, I don't.'

'No damn use when you're not held to the straight and narrow by the Broads? You have a compass. Use it! Any fool can do that.'

Something happened in Rushworth's head: there had been so much worry, and university lecturers were not doers, nor men of action. He felt harassed. He snapped, 'Including you, I suppose?'

'Don't be impertinent, Charles.'

'But you were an engineer. Not a seaman.'

'I was also an officer of some intelligence and one who was given some training in seamanship as a snotty. Don't argue, Charles. Head west and don't take too long about it. Good God almighty!' The Commnder staggered and fell to the deck of the after cockpit as something struck him very hard, a flying object that had taken off from a floating baulk of timber, one of the 'leather jackets'. As McNaughten struggled back to his feet, furious, his son-in-law started the engine and the *Hilda* drew away fast from the rest of the would-be boarders. McNaughten faced a young woman with a painted face, now streaked by the floodwater, and variegated hair, crimson, green, orange, blue with the Roman helmet shape. She had made it aboard: the knife in her hand said she intended to stay.

TWO

The whole land was at a standstill now. The waters spread wide, deepening as the great melted ice masses flooded in from Alaska, the North Polar regions and Greenland. Now there was one area of sea from North America, across much of England to France and the low countries. The agricultural land was devastated, the corpses of sheep and pigs, horses and cows floated abominably near the surface. So did countless human bodies. It was no longer a flood; it was the sea, and it would stand open to the primeval forces that had always afflicted deep-sea mariners – gales and heavy seas.

Clear above the waters rose the high parts of Britain: the tops of the Downs in the South, parts of the North Downs, the Chilterns and the Berkshire Downs, the Cotswolds. In the West Country Dartmoor, Exmoor and Bodmin Moor stood largely though not entirely clear, as did some of the higher coastal points. Wales had plenty of mountains, now with their clustered hordes of survivors. The highlands of Scotland had become a mecca, the boatloads converging from the lowlands that might come under threat suddenly. It was the same in the north of England, in the Cheviots, the Lake District, the Pennines that stretched from Northumberland to Derbyshire.

In those districts a kind of life could be carried on: the dales of the North Yorkshire area had been well above sea-level to start with, and so far they had not been reached though all the links with the South had gone. Fish swam over the M1 and the A1, hurrying through the drowned service areas where all the fittings were

intact, and much food still in the freezers and store-
rooms. Both in those service areas and along the once
great highways leading north a number of vehicles had
been trapped by the surge of water and now lay beneath
it, abandoned in the nick of time, the articulated lorries
still with their loads aboard. Some of the drivers had not
made it in time, had stayed too long with their vehicles,
and now swirled back and forth along what had been the
roads, corpses at the mercy of the water's movement.

In the capital, the government no longer existed.
London lay beneath the floodwater, which had laughed
at the Thames Barrier at Woolwich, over-running it and
outflanking it at one and the same time. High-rise
buildings and cathedral and church spires stood free, as
did the top storeys of some of the larger houses on
higher ground. The Post Office Tower rose, a lonely
sentinel with Big Ben and Nelson over what had been a
teeming city. The members of the government, along
with the royal family, had gone north towards Scotland
in the royal yacht *Britannia*, and would probably remain
aboard. *Britannia* was currently both the Palace of West-
minster and Buckingham Palace itself. And not one of
HM's ministers had the least idea as to what they should
or could do. The Home Secretary put it in a nutshell.

'There's damn-all we *can* do. No posts or telegraphs …'
All communication had gone, the police were as helpless
as anyone else, all authority had vanished. 'It's worse
than a nuclear attack – *something* would be left working.
Now there's nothing.'

No one could put the plug back in and get the pumps
working. It was a case of waiting, waiting to see if the
great icebergs re-formed in another freeze, or if other
areas of the world would take up the slack.

In that lay perhaps the only hope.

It wasn't only the fully flooded areas: those above the
flood also had their problems.

'It's a bloody influx,' old Tom Braithwaite said.

'Townspeople and half o' t' boogers Southerners. Tourists and picnickers.'

'Not now they're not.'

The old Yorkshireman glowered at his wife. 'Maybe not,' he admitted grudgingly. 'But there'll be litter all the same.' He moved to the window and looked out from his cottage towards the green, the green he'd known all his life. He'd been born and bred in Bainbridge in Wensleydale, a shepherd tending the sheep on the fells. Bainbridge had always been a quiet, peaceful village, at least until the tourists had come, pouring from detestable coaches, with their ice-cream wrappers and their discarded cigarette packets and their Coca-cola tins, staring at Yorkshiremen as though they were exhibits in a zoo, or a museum. They had filled the pub, driven out the regulars, sat on the green surrounded by picnics and occasionally a man who had had too much to drink would relieve himself against a wheel of his coach. Now they were back in full force, not as tourists but refugees, and the implications were worse, much worse, for they obviously meant to stay as long as the flood did, and God knew how long that would be. Unlike the tourists, who came only in the summer months, they might stay a hell of a long time. Tom Braithwaite gave a chuckle, thinking of the winter. All those people on the green, out in the open or in their cars, so many already you could scarcely see a blade of grass, some of them with tents – they weren't going to like the North Yorkshire winter when it came with its snowdrifts and its biting winds and its ice.

His wife raised another fear, one that Tom had kept at the back of his mind. She said, 'Before long they'll be billeted. We've got a room to spare. We can't refuse.'

Braithwaite snapped his teeth but didn't say anything. Too true, they couldn't refuse. Not out of charity, for charity began in an unbilleted home, but because the local council would say so. North Yorkshire was still in being as an authority, as an entity. So far anyway. the waters could come to Bainbridge yet, old Tom Braithwaite reckoned, and then what?

He gave a shiver. Of course that would be worse than the refugees, a lot worse. They would have to become refugees themselves, he and Edna, going somewhere in a boat. No doubt boats would be provided: boats were never part of a shepherd's equipment and Tom Braithwaite had never so much as set foot on one. As for Edna, she was a very bad arthritic, all doubled up, and how would she fare in a bloody boat even if she could be got into it? One thing: they wouldn't have far to go. The fells were close enough and if needs be they could row across country in a direct line to the heights above Bishopdale Beck.

He said this to Edna. 'Summat like that ... plenty of high ground.'

'And what when we get there – eh?' Her voice had risen high and her face was twisted with pain and anxiety. 'Starve, that's what. Get soaked through when it rains, no shelter. And for how long? Till winter?'

'I don't know –'

'I'd sooner die in my own house than up there ont' fells, Tom Braithwaite, I would really. I mean it. You remember that when time comes, eh?'

'If it comes. It won't, old lass. We're reet high.' He went across to her and laid a hand on her shoulder, a protective gesture, but he was aware of the shake in his hand as he did it. He said bitterly, 'Those bloody Yanks!'

'How d'you know it was them Yanks, eh? Could have been the Russians. BBC said so an' all.' There had in fact been no BBC now for some days, or ITV either. No TV, no radio. Everything was a flummox, no one knowing what was going on. No newspapers. 'Why blame the Americans?'

'Why bloody not?' Tom Braithwaite asked sourly. 'It's just like the boogers, I reckon.' He'd overheard something in the bar of the Rose and Crown before the refugees had come: a man in a city suit, some sort of politician from York, Tom believed from the conversation, a man in the know, a man who looked authoritative and referred to some of the cabinet ministers by their

first names. Apparently it was being whispered around
that the Americans had made a boob while attempting
to install a nuclear device deep beneath the sea between
Alaska and the tip of the Russian land mass opposite,
across some strait or other the name of which
Braithwaite couldn't quite get. Neither had he picked
up the reason for what the Americans had done, but it
was clearly nefarious and look what the result had been,
a proper sod. As the old shepherd ruminated darkly on
America his country sense told him rain was coming, as
though there wasn't enough water around already.
Later that day it came, heavy cloud spreading over
Wensleydale and the rain coming down in buckets. It
shifted the hordes of people on the green. Those
without tents or cars, and in fact most of them had cars,
dashed for the Rose and Crown and any other shelter
they could find. A group of them banged at
Braithwaite's door. He didn't answer the bang, just
stared grim-faced from his window, king of his own
little castle, as neat and trim as constant work and love
could make it. He was looking out when a man came up
close, a young man with a shaven head and a nasty
expression. This man had a heavy stone in his hand and
with it he smashed the window, showering Tom
Braithwaite with glass.

James and Karen Lockhart lived, or had lived, in the
Blackmore Vale. The beautiful Blackmore Vale as the
estate agents' blurb had it. James Lockhart had been an
estate agent himself, but now all the land and house
property on his books had vanished beneath the flood
and he and his family – Karen and the two children,
David and Rosemary – were floating over it in the boat
that he used to tow on a trailer behind the car to the sea
at Poole, around thirty-five miles south-east of Mere
where his home had been. Mere was a low-lying place, a
long straggle of houses and shops that had flooded with
the first onslaught. Not many people had got away: both
James and Karen assumed their parents, who had also

lived in Mere, were dead. Now their worries were for
the children, aged ten and seven and currently
shivering because they were wet. As in Yorkshire, there
had been rain, and the boat, just a sailing dinghy, had
no comfortable cabin as the Rushworths' power-boat
had. Neither did it contain much beyond its human
freight: there had been so little time. Food had come
first, but panic hadn't helped selection: Karen had
grabbed up tins of coffee, peas, carrots, soups, meat
roll. She had brought nothing with which to open tins.

'Starving in the midst of plenty,' she said, attempting
a smile.

'Don't know about plenty.' James Lockhart rubbed his
eyes, which stung behind his glasses. It hadn't been just
tins, in fact: there was a loaf of bread, now soggy, and a
large carton of fresh milk from the supermarket. That
had to be strictly rationed; it would have to last for they
knew not how long, even when it went off. The boat was
heading, or James hoped it was, for high ground to the
north-west, the Mendip Hills. If the visibility had been
clear they could have seen the hills, seen their way, but it
was far from clear. The cloud base was very low and the
rain was heavy. All they could see was what was close,
and that was death: human and animal bodies, floating
at random before an increasing wind that made
matters worse. The flood, the sea, was becoming rough.
They had seen only a few other boats, one or two
coming close enough for verbal contact, but this had
been no more than an exchange of misery. They were
all at sea now …

Rosemary was crying. 'Mummy, it's cold.'

'I know, darling.' They were cuddled up but it didn't
help much.

'And hungry, mummy. Mummy I want some Rice
Krispies.'

'I expect we'll get some food soon,' Karen said, feeling
desperate.

'Where from?'

'I don't know! A shop somewhere, where it's dry.

We're bound to find land soon, darling.' She thought: a terrible way to be talking, finding land when they were over the Blackmore Vale.

Rosemary wailed. 'Mummy-mummy-mummy ...'

James snapped at her, all tensed up. 'Stop moaning for God's sake!'

'James!'

'Oh –' James rubbed again at his eyes. 'I'm sorry, but she goes on and on.'

'She's only a child,' Karen said protectively.

'Nothing like stating the obvious, is there?'

Karen didn't respond. there was nothing to be gained from getting ragged. She was convinced they were all going to die and she wanted them to die on good terms. A moment later Rosemary started again. 'Mummy, I want to wee.'

'All right, darling. Over the side.'

'Daddy won't look, will he?'

'No, Daddy won't look – he didn't before, why should he now?'

They went through the procedure. So much easier for men, Karen thought ... and David, she saw, *was* having a good look, quite deliberately to annoy his little sister. Meanwhile the dinghy, somewhat incongruously in the present circumstances named *Good Hope*, sailed on. James was a pretty fair sailor and handled her well. If only he knew where he was going they could get there quite soon, for the *Good Hope* was bowling along before the wind very nicely. If only they knew.

More bodies drifted. Karen kept her eyes away, terrified that she might see her mother or father. She believed that if she did, she might not be able to fight off an impulse to jump in and join them.

A boatload of a very different character was also at sea inshore of Portsmouth. In Portsmouth's Commercial Road there was, or had been until so recently, a public house named the British Empire. When the water of Spithead between Portsmouth and the Isle of Wight had

risen and inundated the low-lying city, a local gang
largely wearing metal-studded leather jackets hung with
chains and covered with badges had happened to be in
this pub. Half drunk, they had stayed behind when the
other customers beat it following the police warning – a
patrol car with flashing blue light and a broadcaster.
The gang, known as the Big Clout, using knives and
fists and coshes, and bicycle chains with each link filed
to razor sharpness, had stopped a car making its way
down the already water-slopped road, smashing in the
heads and bodies of the occupants. While three
members of the gang stayed to guard the car, the rest
nipped back to the British Empire and laid hands on as
much booze as could be carried to the car. Bottled beer
and lager, plus whisky, gin, vodka and one bottle of
crême de menthe. Loaded thus, the car had driven off
north for Cosham and Portsdown Hill, just about
beating the rising water, which was halted by the high
ground just north of the Queen Alexandra Hospital, a
kind of natural sea wall would cause it to deepen fast
before long.

The car took the turn for the main entrance to the
hospital grounds and there it packed up. Just stopped
dead and there was nothing to be done about that. The
water, presumably, had entered the engine. On passing
the hospital entrance, the gang leader had seen
something that interested him.

'All out,' the gang leader said. 'With the booze, right?'
His name was Wayne. The others were Roxy, Kevin,
Leroy, Tracy – the gang was of mixed sex – Clara, Dean,
Lee, Sharon and Gemma. They followed Wayne's
strikingly coloured head into the hospital grounds,
wading through five feet of water, carrying the booty
from the British Empire while the flood deepened,
coming back on them as it were from the blocking point
of the rise of Portsdown Hill. Wayne seemed to know
what he was doing, or they supposed he did, but no one
else seemed to know. They followed, burdened as they
were, like sheep.

Then they saw what Wayne had seen.

A large boat, a power-boat, on a big trailer behind a lorry. Doctors were rich, they had rich men's hobbies. Maybe some top medic had taken precautions along with him when he reported for duty, cutting people up or something. Round the lorry and its trailer were several men, two of them in long white coats with stethoscopes dangling from the pockets. They were quite young; the rest were older and instead of white coats wore jeans and singlets or oddly-coloured shirts.

'Right,' Wayne said. He indicated a high bank surrounding a car-park, a bank still standing well clear of the water. 'Put the booze there – make it fast, right – then come with me.'

Leroy asked what Wayne intended to do.

'What d'you fucking think? There's a boat. It's going to be ours, right?'

'Right,' Leroy said.

The booze was deposited, fast as Wayne had said. Wayne was big, thickset, huge-shouldered, swung a good bicycle chain, and was handy with his knife. The Big Clout boarded and attacked as a team, efficient, done similar things before, no stopping the Big Clout. The medics didn't have a chance and no one interfered from the hospital, being too much concerned with their own coming predicament. 'Now what?' the man called Leroy asked.

'Get the boat off the trailer. No.' Wayne corrected himself. 'Just wait. Untie it and just wait. It'll float itself off, all right? Get the booze brought over.' He ducked down into the wheelhouse, went for'ard and found a store cupboard. The medics had prepared well: food in plenty, and water in tanks. A full load of fuel, too. And something else: a young nurse, cowering in a small cabin. The Big Clout was in luck.

Violence was an inevitable part of panic and tragedy, along with the better instincts of kindness and Samaritanism in times of great stress. Violence came to

Tom Braithwaite and his wife in the shape of the man
who had smashed in the window of their little cottage, a
man who had come up to Bainbridge from the vicinity of
Leeds ahead of the waters.

Old Tom had made an attempt to bar the man's
way but had been thrown aside when the man had
cleared away the glass and come through into the living-
room. Behind him came more people, men and women.
The Braithwaites were knocked down and trodden on
and no notice was taken of the arthritic old woman's
screams of agony. The cottage filled up with refugees
escaping the rain, which was exceptionally heavy even
for North Yorkshire: something seemed to have happened to the weather, sharpening it, following upon the
nuclear-assisted ice melt. The skies over Wensleydale
held a curious light, a light of evil and of immense threat.
There was the same light a long way south of Wensleydale, where inshore of the Holderness Peninsula a
middle-aged country parson and his wife, together with a
number of parishioners, all of them boatless, had taken
refuge of a sort on the tower of the church. Daniel
Matthews, rector for the last year, did what a person
should: he said prayers, asking God to lower the waters,
asking for forgiveness, fearing that the flood was in fact
sent by God – a second flood and no ark.

'Have mercy upon us, miserable offenders,' Matthews
said, kneeling in his soaked cassock, his bowed head bare.
He uttered the words of prayer and supplication earn-
estly and genuinely but somehow he didn't believe they
would be answered. The world had grown wicked, more
wicked in fact than before the last flood in Noah's time,
and really there was no reason why God should withdraw
His punishment just because sinners asked Him to …

'Rector –'

Matthews looked round: the speaker, his voice excited,
was the people's warden, a farmer, Old Josh as he was
known in the parish. Old Josh was pointing: Matthews
followed the outstretched arm.

'A boat! Thank God, thank God! All of you – wave and

shout!'

They waved and shouted. There were a dozen people on the church tower, which stood some twenty feet clear of the roof but only some ten feet clear of the water. Nevertheless, it was very visible and the stranded villagers made plenty of noise. They stared across the scummy water, over the inevitable floating corpses, the driftwood, odd bits of clothing, the general debris washed out of the flood wave. The shouts became angry. It was no use. Slowly, the boat moved away.

Daniel Matthews gave a deep sigh: God was not ready yet. He said, 'They must be overloaded already. We couldn't expect to put everyone else at risk.'

At his side he was aware of his wife crying. He put his arm around her and held her close, openly cuddling. She said, 'They'll all be the same, Daniel. All full already.'

He had no words to offer: she was probably absolutely right.

Away south of the marooned church tower dwellers, the Rushworth family in their power-boat headed west under the direction of Commander McNaughten, and made the best they could of their unwelcome passenger, the young woman with the spiky hair and the knife. The boat's own speed, brought up to full by Charles Rushworth in the nick of time, had ensured that the young woman was the only gatecrasher.

She had been easily enough disarmed once she'd seen that she wasn't going to be thrown overboard. McNaughten had said simply, 'Give me that knife, you stupid girl.'

'Okay.' She had handed it over. She had quite a nice face, though the jaws were moving on a piece of chewing-gum. John Rushworth asked her name.

'Victoria,' she said. 'Vicki.'

'Where from?'

'Norwich.'

'Your home?'

'Flooded,' she said. 'Flooded out.' She was quite calm about it. 'Home, it was just a room over a chippy.'

McNaughten asked, 'Your family?'

She shrugged. 'Don't have any. I had a feller … but he bloody left me. Just – well –'

'Deserted you?'

'Fucked off,' she said without embarrassment. 'Just like that. Never know who you can trust, do you, eh?'

McNaughten, listening, cleared his throat. He said nothing but he was thinking a lot. He hadn't much time for today's young, and none at all for those with spiky, coloured hair. While his grandson continued talking to the young woman, McNaughten went into the wheelhouse for a word with his son-in-law.

'That girl, Charles.'

'Blasted nuisance. She'll have to be fed, I suppose. That shortens the rations.'

'That's not my chief worry.' The Commander's tone was ominous. 'Do I have to be explicit?'

'Yes,' Charles said, glancing sideways, 'I think you do.'

McNaughten frowned. 'You know girls like that. She spoke of a – a *fellow*, she called him. I'll bet any money he wasn't the only one. You see what I'm driving at.'

Charles Rushworth stared ahead, through the windshield,. over the rain-pocked water, stared at unending water. By a kind of dead reckoning by compass and road map, assisted by a sight of Norwich cathedral spire, he fancied they were probably somewhere over Wymondham on the A11. He responded to his father-in-law. 'A number of sexual contacts. Promiscuity. Yes, I do see.'

McNaughten drove the point home. 'AIDS. We'll be sharing cooking facilities, cups, knives, forks. Lavatory, the lot. I don't like it, I can tell you.'

'What d'you suggest we do? Chuck her over?'

'Not exactly. No, but we'll have to land her at the first opportunity. It's a deadly risk, Charles.'

'If we find land,' Charles said, 'that's no doubt what I'll do. If we don't … well, there won't be any point in worrying, will there? The AIDS germs'll starve along with all of us, won't they?'

McNaughten glared. 'I call that defeatist talk. One more word of advice: watch that son of yours. If you don't, I will.' He added, 'I'm simply not having any hanky-panky.'

'A nice old-fashioned expression,' Charles murmured.

THREE

The rain had come everywhere: James Lockhart, heading north-westward from above the Blackmore Vale, had collected rainwater, the milk being the only other thing they had to drink. He had collected it in the spare sail rigged across the body of the dinghy, and they all drank. Earlier, being thirsty, young David had leaned over the gunwale and gathered a cupped handful of the floodwater.

'Brackish,' he'd said, sounding consciously grown-up.

James had been furious. 'Just don't do that again. Want to poison yourself?' He hadn't been in time to stop the boy.

'But what –'

'Bodies,' James said shortly. He was going to add something further but didn't: he thought of both their sets of parents, maybe trapped in Mere, maybe floating. There had been no time to go to their aid; it had come very suddenly, a swirl of water with an immense build-up behind it. There had of course been advance warnings issued by the government, but no real preparations had been made. No one had any idea of what those preparations might have been, for a flood was a flood was a flood and the Mere area had seen flood many times in the past if not very recently – until now. You might, if it was bad, have to move for a while to

higher ground, you might even have to sit for a while on
the roof of your house until you were picked up by a
boat, probably manned by the police or the army, and
eventually the waters would go down. There was no
point in fussing – that, at any rate, had been the view of
the Lockhart parents and in-laws and when it had come
they had been inundated with most of the other
inhabitants.

And now, as he peered through the torrential rain,
trying to find the Mendips and believing that he must be
heading in any direction but the right one, James
Lockhart reflected that nothing was ever going to be
the same again. True, the waters would one day subside,
but what would be left? Total ruination, soaked
buildings, waterlogged fields, agriculture brought to a
standstill, power stations useless, mines flooded and
almost certainly the greater part of the population
drowned or starved or dead from the diseases that must
surely strike in such a situation. No hospitals, no
services, no transport, no anything but water. No real
estate for an estate agent and no one to buy it if there
were. What about money, afterwards? Very possibly it
wouldn't exist. A waterlogged City of London, banks,
insurance companies, building societies – all the
financial records gone if the floods lasted any length of
time. Savings gone, in effect. A lifetime's effort to date.

What about the children, David and Rosemary?
Currently the first concern was for their physical safety,
their survival. That was obvious. But James Lockhart
was a man who had always thought ahead, looking
ahead for security, and the habit stuck even now. What
of their future, in a broken country, their education
interrupted by the general chaos, and most of the
teachers dead? They would have to start all over again,
find new ways.

'No bad thing either,' McNaughten said. The conversation aboard the Rushworth craft, as it made westerly
and left behind the spires and towers of Ely Cathedral

and Cambridge University, had happened to follow broadly some of the thoughts of James Lockhart so many miles ahead to the west. 'We'd got into a rotten mess in this poor old country. Look at your mother-in-law, Charles.'

Rushworth nodded sympathetically. Mrs McNaughten, not so long ago a pretty woman still, charming, kindly, had been brought aboard from Cambridge with much difficulty and was now lying on a bunk in the midship cabin beneath the wheelhouse. Eighteen months earlier, walking home across Jesus Green after a late winter evening's shopping at Eaden Lilley's, she had been mugged. She had never seen her attackers and they had never been caught. They had got away with two five-pound notes, some loose change and the usual handbag clutter of scant value. They had tried to pull off her engagement and wedding rings but had given up when they refused to come off over the somewhat swollen knuckles of age.

They had left a wreck behind. There had been serious head injuries and she hadn't been expected to live. When she did pull through, she had a permanently stiffened left arm and leg and she had lost her speech. None of that came back: she had had a stroke among other things. And her spirit had gone with her speech. She was no longer a woman, no longer even, really, a human being.

It was no wonder McNaughten was bitter.

'A filthy, rotten world,' he said. 'If it wasn't for the deaths of the decent people along with the others, I'd welcome this whole business, damned if I wouldn't! A fresh start is just what's needed.' He ruminated as the rain came down on the roof of the wheelhouse, rattling almost like machine-gun fire. 'You wouldn't remember my old mother, of course.'

'No.'

'Well, she was something of a moaner, you know. Always thinking the worst – always saying everything's awful now, a sort of parrot cry. It used to irritate me, although I could understand, of course. Then one day I went to a funeral and met an old friend whom I hadn't seen for years and he asked me how my mother was. I said she wasn't as bad as she thought she was ... and was always saying everything's awful now.' McNaughten stopped.

'Well?'

'Well, this friend of mine ... he put a hand on my shoulder and said, and this I always remember, "But Humphrey, everything *is* awful now." '

Rushworth laughed. 'You began to see more point in what your mother said?'

'Yes, I did. She was only expressing, rather too often perhaps, what so many people were starting to feel. Now, of course – before all this happened, I mean – it's worse than ever. Damn rudeness, lefty trendies, buggery taught as a subject in the schools –'

'Oh, come! Not quite!'

'Don't interrupt me, Charles. It very nearly is – those frightful London councils or whatever! Those pamphlets, child in bed with a couple of pansies. Poofs. It's utterly revolting. No *safety* anywhere, either. Streets, tubes, trains, aeroplanes being hijacked every five minutes, even the cross-Channel ferries. Those frightful football mobs. Corrupt police, slackness in the Civil Service, no one pulling his weight, no one being able to be sacked however blasted useless or work-shy he or she is. Harassment of those who do try to put in a decent day's work and keep up proper standards. Look at some of these lunatics in charge of education – the appalling people who refuse to put children to the test as it were, denigrate competition, take away the motive to win or excel, just in case the dimwits get their feelings hurt. Everyone dragged down by order to the lowest level, the lowest common denominator.'

'Yes,' Rushworth said, nodding. 'I agree with a lot of what you say, but –'

'There aren't any buts, Charles. None at all. Everything's gone downhill now. I often think, what's the point of going on at all? That's to say, I did think that. Until now.'

'You're seeing a way ahead? A way of turning this to some sort of good account?'

'That's it, yes.' McNaughten slammed a bunched fist into his palm. 'That fresh start. It's a godsend in many ways, if we handle it right when the time comes.'

'There's a snag, isn't there?'

'What snag?'

Rushworth said, 'It depends a lot on who comes through. The baddies often have a habit of being survivors while the goodies go under.'

'Oh, nonsense.' McNaughten waved a hand dismissingly. 'There's going to be enough of us to take charge. The useless ones won't survive anyway, no guts basically. Where's that awful girl?'

He looked round. She was close behind him, entering from the open deck. 'Mean me, granddad?' she enquired.

'Yes. Kindly don't call me granddad, I don't like it.'

'Why ever not?' Big eyes with lurid colour, now running, around them stared at McNaughten in surprise. 'You are a granddad, aren't you?'

'Grand*father*.'

'Same thing, innit?'

McNaughten didn't answer: there was no point. Girls of that sort always came back with something that threw you, made you look a fool because their outlook was different from your own and provoked situations that your own sort wouldn't. But the girl was persistent and stood her ground, staring at McNaughten's back, since he had turned away with a frown.

'Didn't like what you said just now.'

'I'm sorry.'

'Don't sound it. It's not fair. just 'cos I got the sort of hair-do you don't like.'

'I don't like gatecrashers,' McNaughten snapped.

'This your boat or the other bloke's?'

Charles Rushworth stepped in; his father-in-law

seemed on the verge of a stroke. 'Never mind the niceties of ownership,' he said. 'We're all in this together now. Just don't let's fall out, it won't help. All right? Happy and peaceful and one day we'll get somewhere.'

'It's still not fair,' the girl said. She said it passionately but they took no notice and she turned away and looked over the stern, tears sparkling in her eyes as she looked across the apparently endless water covering East Anglia, joining it direct and without hindrance to the North Sea, reaching over Cromer, the Wash now vanished beneath the water that stretched over Lincolnshire and Norfolk. The tears were for herself and her predicament, not for anything left behind in Norwich or anywhere else for that matter. She had been one of the unfortunates, the losers, the no-hopers really, done-for from the start.

For Vicki the start had been in Brighton, in a sleazy basement flat in what had once been good property but which had gone very far down in the world. Not that Vicki had been aware of how awful it was until she'd left it, since to her in infancy her surroundings were normal: wallpaper blotched, damp and hanging, overall smell of gas leaks and frying chips, cracked loo with no seat, minimal heating – just an electric bowl fire that should by rights have been thrown out years before. Washing hanging on wooden chairs in the living-room, hardly any bedclothes to cover her at night, but newspaper had helped a little.

And mum and a succession of men ... Vicki had learned early some of the facts of life and she knew her mother had never been exactly a prostitute, not on the game as such, but was a kept woman, kept by a succession of men. In short, mum was a slut: drooping boobs, curlers, fag dangling constantly from her lips, dirty skirt and jumper or sometimes jeans and a tank-top when she was on the look-out for a new man, the last one having deserted her. Vicki had never known who her father was and she guessed, later, that even mum, who had been clever or lucky enough to have had just the one child, couldn't be sure. And mum was not only a slut, she was sadistic from being worn out and having had no luck in *her* life either. She cuffed Vicki constantly, almost wrenched her arm out once when flinging her across the room in a sudden rage. Vicki, as a baby seldom having had her nappies changed, always seemed thereafter to have wet knickers ... she remembered a lady visiting, a bossy lady from the welfare or something, and she remembered all the lies mum used to tell the lady, who was very busy with all the other problem families and just seemed to accept the fibs, which were largely concerned with what a tiresome child Vicki was.

At the age of seven, just over, Vicki was interfered with by one of mum's men friends. Vicki had no one to tell, to talk to. No use telling mum, she wouldn't believe it and there would be more cuffs. After that first time, she was interfered with again and at the age of ten finally she ran away. She was found by a policeman, huddled in an empty shelter on Worthing sea-front, crying, her heart thudding in her narrow, scrawny chest. The policeman sat beside her for a while, and talked quietly. When he had the story he took her hand and walked her to the police station. When they took her home all mum said was, 'Oh, so it's you back.' That was all. But the policewoman who brought Vicki home had seen the set-up, and after that there was a very long hoo-ha with more policemen and more ladies from the welfare or whatever it was, and then a number of important-looking men in expensive suits and grave faces, and ultimately Vicki found herself removed for good from home, mum and the men friends and placed in an institution with other girls, some of whom were bullies, and some of whom taught her a good deal more about the world and its ways, and the ways around the ways of the world. At sixteen she got a job helping out in a caff and six months after that she left the institution, having found a room of her own at a low rent because it was virtually unliveable in; but at least it wasn't an institution and she had freedom for the first time in her short life. At seventeen she became pregnant and with the help of the father induced an abortion at an early stage. She was desperately ill for weeks, during which time the father decamped and the landlady of the room grumblingly pulled her through, and threw her out as soon as she was fit.

Soon after this she decided to get the hell out of Brighton, started walking north along the A23 to London, and was picked up by an artic driver who was going through to Norwich.

Thus she came to Norwich, the room over the chippy, the floodwater and the Rushworths' power-boat.

Away to the north Daniel Matthews, rector of his parish, was now inside the church tower, shivering with his wife in his arms and a feeling of hopelessness in his heart. No other boat, after the one that had turned a deaf ear, had come within distance and now it was night and a cold one for the time of year: everything was against survival, it seemed.

What could they do?

No boats: there was only one alternative and that was to swim, which was obviously a non-starter since there was nothing visible to swim to. When the flood had come Mollie, his wife, had for the first time expressed regret at his having sought a change of living from his previous parish, which had been in Liverpool. There would surely have been any number of boats there, and also municipal services that would have laid something on for the salvation of the citizens. But Matthews had not liked Liverpool and Mollie had liked it less. So much dereliction, so much crime, so much violence, so little employment, so little hope. Just looking at the queues at the Jobcentre had depressed Matthews utterly … Thinking about the past in Liverpool, Matthews felt his wife stir in his arms. 'What are you thinking about, Daniel?' she asked.

'My grandfather, Mollie. I've an idea he'd have known what to do.'

'The one who'd been a sea captain? Even he couldn't have done anything with no materials.'

'He used to say a seaman was never at a loss, Mollie. You could always improvise and if you couldn't you were no bloody use.'

'Daniel! In church, too!'

He gave a humourless laugh. '*On* church. Anyway, I was only quoting.' He gave a sudden sneeze: the bell loft was still cold in spite of the fug from so many parish bodies clustered together beneath the big bells. Although the ends of the bell ropes were dangling down into the flood that filled the church itself, they had managed at intervals to get the bells swinging to send their mournful peals across the watery wastes in the hope that someone might hear and come to the rescue. But there were not enough good Samaritans – or there was no one left to hear. Daniel said, 'There must be something. There really must. God doesn't leave His people in the lurch, Mollie. He – He puts something in their hands.'

'Not this time, dearest Daniel.'

'Well, I don't know. Remember what old Josh suggested – I've been thinking about that –'

'You turned it down, didn't you?'

'Yes. Because I was so sure someone would come along. A boat. There must be police, or army or navy, or so I thought – hoped, anyway. No doubt they're busy elsewhere, the larger centres of population. Quite normal and proper, of course.'

'Princes and bishops?'

'What? Don't be cynical, Mollie. Princes and bishops first, yes, but only in terms of the larger groups of people – *they're* the princes and bishops in the scale of priorities now.'

'And the devil take the little, isolated pockets. Well, go on, Daniel. What have you been thinking?'

He said, 'Old Josh –'

'Timber.'

'Yes. The floorboards up here – it'll mean everybody going back to the outside, up top, of course. I know Mrs Ames isn't well, but one has to make a decision, and if we do nothing she'll die anyway. We –'

'You know very well the floorboards wouldn't take a man's weight. You said so yourself.'

'Yes. But if we could get something more substantial – use the floorboard just as extras – cut the bell ropes and use them to bind something together. Do you see?'

'What sort of something?' she asked.

'Well – a pew, perhaps. The chest with the parish records. Chairs.'

'Yes. How do you get them up, for heaven's sake?'

'They'll be floating most probably –'

'How do you get them *up here*?'

'I don't know unless we try, Mollie.' He was sounding desperate now. 'I think they could, might, be got up the ladder and through the hatch. Not the chest, I suppose, but the – the other things.' He paused. 'I really think someone should go down. I was against it when old Josh suggested … but now I've changed my mind.'

Mollie was silent for a while: there was a good reason why her husband had been against old Josh and his suggestion. Below, in the body of the little church, were floating bodies and by this time they would be a nasty sight. A number of bloating corpses, fathers and mothers and grandparents of some of the people in the tower's comparative safety, old folk who simply hadn't made it up the ladder when the sudden surge had come over the flat lands, across the Holderness peninsula, across Spurn Head. They had panicked, not surprisingly, and it had simply not been possible to reach them and bring them to the ladder and the hatch – one had almost made it but had fallen back from the top of the ladder and that had been that. It would be too terrible to see them again, bobbing about, eyes wide with the death terror, mouths agape.

Daniel said, 'The living must come first, Mollie. I hope

that doesn't sound ... pompous. Or unfeeling.'

'No,' she said. 'No, it doesn't at all. You're quite right, but –'

'Someone must go down.'

'You mean, you must. Don't you, Daniel?'

'It may be the only hope. And it's my responsibility. My church.'

'Over my dead body!' she said energetically. 'You're thinking too much of your old grandfather. Captain of the ship ... the last to leave if it sinks!'

'I have to do something, Mollie. I've thought for a long time now ...' His voice tailed off.

'What?'

'Oh ... never mind. Look, I'll wait for daylight. It might be better then, a little light filtering down.' No more was said; Matthews listened to heavy breathing, snoring, movement of restless bodies. He felt the thump of his own heart, was aware of Mollie snuggling her head down on his chest. His arm went round her again but he was not thinking of her. He was going back in his mind to Liverpool, the parish he had left behind so gladly. All those hopeless people – some of them, not many, used to come to his church for reasons other than marriage or funerals. Some of those who did come were young and he had managed to establish some sort of rapport with them so that now and again they would come and ask his advice and help. Mostly secular help, of course, any port in a storm perhaps, even the vicarage. Anxieties about love, sex, jobs, debt, crime. He believed that on some occasions he may have been of use, though he seldom got any follow-up or any subsequent thanks. Their problems sorted, they often forgot about him and his church. Even so, he had done a lot of heart-searching over the last few months. He had deserted, he had let the parish down, he couldn't take it as a man of God should have done. He had failed, he had proved himself a coward.

Something had to be set right.

FOUR

The waters had moved a little farther north now and
the city of York lay partially submerged. York was not
unaccustomed to flood when the Ouse rose and burst its
banks but it had never been remotely like this. The
Lendal Bridge, the other bridges, lay beneath the water.
The Railway Museum was inundated and the great,
gleaming old steam engines, lovingly cared for until
now, were submerged; the ornate drawing-room coach
used by Queen Victoria a hundred years earlier was
filled and desolate.

The towers of the Minster rose high above the water
but the body of the building lay half under, scummy,
foul with street refuse and the corpses of vermin. The
regimental chapels of the King's Own Yorkshire Light
Infantry and the West Yorkshire Regiment lay with
their banners weirdly floating and their Books of
Remembrance ruined. Beneath them the undercroft
was a place for fish alone. Elsewhere in the city the
Jorvik Centre, the reconstructed Viking village beneath
the once busy streets, evoking York's early settlement,
would have looked as though it had joined forces with
the sewers had there been tourists left to see. The little
shops – Scottish wool and tweed, the specialist shirt shop
in High Petergate, Anderson's for fine gents' clothing in
Blake Street, the card and gift shops, all the others –
were nothing now but containers for ruined stock. Some
people had drowned; as elsewhere in the country those
who had obstinately refused to heed the official dictum
and wouldn't leave their homes had become victims; but
these were not very many, for in York the warning had
come in good time and everyone knew by the horror in
the south. There had been a massive evacuation by road
and train, from the whole of the Plain of York, until

those links were cut; thence by boat, in the form of a fleet organized by the military authorities at Catterick who had sent in the amphibious transport of the Royal Engineers and the Royal Corps of Transport.

Wensleydale was still above the waters and was becoming more crowded as more refugees poured in from the south. Some of them moved on through the market town of Hawes towards Sedbergh, standing high to overlook Dentdale and across the Barkin Beck and Barbon High Fell and Scales Moor to Ingleborough where, with so much rain, the cave systems had flooded and water was pouring from the mouth of White Scar cave across the road running from Hawes to Ingleton on the verge of Lancashire.

Bainbridge had grown worse.

All the cottages had been invaded by now and usually the refugees were mannerless and demanding: they had been degraded by panic. They had lost everything, and the people of Bainbridge had lost nothing.

Except their privacy and their sole possession of their homes.

Old Tom Braithwaite had watched his wife die. He didn't know why she had died, she hadn't seemed ill as such though she was obviously in pain from the arthritis and shocked by the rough treatment of the louts who had swarmed in through the broken window and then, as it was opened from inside, the door. After being thrown to the floor, Edna Braithwaite had lain with eyes wide and haunted as she watched her home desecrated. She had whimpered with pain. To her it was as though war had been declared and the Russians had come. All of a sudden, as it seemed, she had died. Shock, broken heart, sheer terror – it had to be something like that.

Old Tom was numbed, unbelieving.

He had tried to rouse her. 'Coom on, lass! Coom on! Say summat, do.' He had seized her hand; it was cold and lifeless. One of the louts pushed him aside and looked down.

'Dead,' he said.

'No ...'

'Get used to the idea, granddad.'

Tom Braithwaite knelt on by her side. In a trembling voice he said, 'Married fifty-two years, we were.'

'She can't stay here now,' the lout said. He was big, hefty, fed with chips and plenty of beer that showed in his gut. His face was pimply behind the stubble, and he had mean pig's eyes, red and small. 'Can't have corpses around.' He bent and lifted.

'You leave 'er be!' Tom Braithwaite shouted.

'You leave *me* be,' the lout said.

They were too much for the old man. The body was lifted and taken out to the small garden behind the cottage, and left there. Old Tom went out, once again a kind of shepherd, looking after what was his, guarding to the end.

The louts were just one group of many such. This was a time to look out for oneself if ever there was one, if you were that way inclined. There was a good deal of looting in Bainbridge before the refugees, or some of them, moved on for Hawes and other places even farther from the floodwaters. Money, food, jewellery were stolen; and a few girls and married women raped. One of the rapists had nasty-looking lesions on his body, like small slugs, purplish. The girl whom he raped had done some reading: she recognized the sign of AIDS and knew her life was finished. Her father and mother, who also saw the signs, were forced to watch. Afterwards the trembling girl went outside, hiding her face, out into the rain that was falling still, as though it would never stop. Her father tried to follow but he had a leg in plaster as the result of an accident on the fells, and she gave him the slip easily enough. She ran until she was exhausted, then she walked, chest heaving, eyes wild, part of the straggle of displaced on foot or in cars heading for Hawes. Before Hawes she turned off the road to the right and went across country. She knew the district like the back of her hand; she climbed high ground towards

High Shaw above Hardraw village and next day her body was found below Hardraw Force, smashed and mangled from the impact of the 100-foot drop.

The rapist had moved on by this time, going to Hawes, a bigger place than Bainbridge but equally full of refugees and equally at the mercy of the looters. Many people had become looters by now: professional people among them. They had to survive somehow, that was the excuse they gave to their own consciences. By this time there was a complete breakdown of law and order. the law-abiding inhabitants met in secret, gathered together by word of mouth, and discussed the setting-up of vigilante groups. Plenty of the farmers in the area had sporting guns and a few still had antiquated pitchforks gathering dust in outbuildings. A pitchfork's prongs – through the throat, or in the gut, or up the bottom – made for a formidable weapon.

Some 300 miles south the Big Clout moved on in their murderously acquired power-boat as the waters continued to rise. At first, as the flood had lifted the big boat clear of its trailer, the man called Wayne had headed south across Cosham and North End, making for what had been the open sea beyond Clarence Pier and South Parade Pier – Spithead, between Pompey and the Isle of Wight. It was manifestly no use attempting to go north direct since Portsdown Hill with its old fortresses, built in the 1860s by Lord Palmerston against the possibility of a French invasion, stood in the way, as yet above the rise of the water; but north was the ultimate intent of the Big Clout. That was where the best of the dry land lay.

After nearly bumping the Isle of Wight's higher ground they altered westerly: Kevin had recently been discharged from the navy and he could read and use a boat's compass. He set the course towards Southampton.

'Know when we get there, will you?' Wayne asked.

'No … not unless I recognize a landmark, something sticking up.'

'Like the town hall.'

'Yeah, I reckon.' Kevin waved an arm and pointed towards where the Fawley oil refinery had been, the Fawley Flame. Or was. Out now. But the stack's there, see it?'

'No, I bloody don't.'

'Not much of it above water, but I reckon that's it.' Kevin indicated again but Wayne was not particularly interested in what had been the Fawley Flame, a tongue of smoke and fire continously flaring as the excess gas from the great refinery escaped to the open air. It had been visible for miles around Southampton, but now it was extinguished, maybe by design before the refinery had been evacuated, maybe by some action of the water. Anyway, Wayne now said, it gave them some idea of where they were. No real need to identify Southampton beneath the sea, they could head north now and he said so, and Kevin moved the wheel, watching the compass.

'Used to be big tankers at Fawley,' he remarked. 'All gone now.'

'Where to, eh?'

Kevin shrugged. 'Don't know, do I? Buggered off … Rotterdam, maybe. Probably not, though. Rotterdam'll be submerged too. Up the Gulf maybe, or the Plate, or a Texan port, Galveston. I heard a buzz in Pompey that those at the Fawley berths were kind of invaded by a mob looking for out. Could have been forced to sail anywhere.' He grinned. 'Maybe we'll find 'em at anchor in the Pennines.'

'Fuck the Pennines.'

'That's where we're going. Mountains, see.' Kevin didn't press against ignorance; Wayne was a tricky customer: Kevin had the idea Wayne had never even heard of the Pennine Chain. The power-boat moved on, going across the submerged land between Stokes Bay and Lee-on-Solent to leave Southampton docks away on the port side, the docks with all their cranes and gantries

and railway lines and container terminals, where now
the fish drifted in and out. After a while Wayne left
Kevin to it and squeezed his big bulk with difficulty
through the door into the cabin where the young nurse
cowered. There were two cabins, small but neat, each
with two bunks, one above the other. Nice fittings,
Wayne noted, the boat's owner had had plenty of gilt.

The nurse stared up at him.

His face twitched. 'Who was the boyfriend, eh?'

'What do you mean?'

'Like I said. The boyfriend. The donor of this here
bloody boat.'

'Donor,' she said flatly. 'He was … one of our doctors.
A consultant.'

'One of the nobs.'

She was silent, still staring at him, obviously terrified,
dreading the next move but doing her best not to show
it. He asked, 'What's your name?'

'Nothing to do with you.'

'Okay. Where you come from?'

'Does it matter?'

'No, it don't.' He began to take off his clothing, stood
there in a dirty vest and flashy socks. 'The doc knew
how to pick the birds.'

'He was my father,' she said.

'Bad bloody luck.'

Her face was stiff but only by an effort of will. Then
suddenly it crumpled, tears came and her eyes
reddened. She sobbed wildly, the control gone. Wayne
reached for her, fought her, grabbed for her clothing,
wrenching and pulling. When enough was off a hand
groped horribly and he lowered his gross body, the
stomach coming down on her like a suet pudding. As
this contact was made she was sick, a surge of vomit that
spewed out over his back. He came upright, mad.

'You – dirty – little – bitch!' he yelled at her, each
spaced word accompanied by a stinging slap across her
face with a horny hand. Then a punch from a balled fist
that mangled her lips against her teeth. Blood flowed

and she panted. Wayne went to the door of the cabin and yelled out for someone to come and clean up. Turning back to the girl he made an obscene promise for the future.

The power-boat moved on at around ten knots and two of the female Big Clouts went into the galley to prepare a meal. There was a good stock, mostly tinned stuff, but there was also a refrigerator and a small deep-freeze, both crammed. Bread, butter, eggs, frozen vegetables, cheese, minced beef, steak, fish. The boat was carrying more persons than intended, but it would be a while yet before the Big Clout would need to worry about starvation.

'It's an ill wind,' Commander McNaughten said aboard his son-in-law's boat, now well to the west of the M1 motorway, having crossed it somewhere between the service areas at Toddington and Newport Pagnell. As they'd crossed it – at least McNaughten said that by dead reckoning he thought that was where they were – Charles Rushworth's mind had gone back some years when the M1 had been his holiday route to the North, along with John. When John had been a boy they had often gone north together, just the two of them. In those years he had worked in London University and he and John, taking the M1 from its start, had always turned off into the Toddington service area, calling that first cup of coffee and chocolate biscuit the start of the holiday. Sometimes it had been Scotland and the Highlands, sometimes it had been North Riding of Yorkshire – as Charles even now thought of the county of North Yorkshire – staying on a small farm and driving around the dales and the moors and farther north as well, into Durham and Westmorland and Cumberland – covering an area from York to Middleton-in-Teesdale and High Force, from Carlisle in the West to Robin Hood's Bay in the East.

They had been good years; now they were in the past. Charles would have liked to head north now, since most of the North would presumably be free of the flood ... on the other hand it would be pretty awful to see the lower-lying areas inundated, York itself no doubt, and of course all the way up until around, say, Ripon, immensely sad to see the once familiar route all gone, all somewhere beneath. In any case, his father-in-law had favoured going west where there was also high ground, because it was nearer and it was vital to touch land as soon as possible. Charles had seen the point: the food and water wouldn't last for ever, and less long now that that hippie girl had come aboard. Charles, at the wheel, looked down as he felt something soft rub against his leg. The cat, seemingly cheerful: Mary had remembered to bring a number of tins of cat food and some biscuit.

Even the cat had a Yorkshire connotation: 'Pontefract' had come into Charles' mind as a suitable name the moment the then tiny kitten had come to their home in a basket from a pet shop in Cambridge. Pontefract, or Pomfret as the older generation of Yorkshire people pronounced it, had soon become Pum. Pum was a tabby, a tabby of character with fine markings. Pum was a family favourite, much loved. Charles picked him up for a brief cuddle then called for his son.

'Take him below, John, will you? Better be safe than sorry.'

'Cats don't like water.'

'I know. But there can be accidents. He won't have got his sea legs yet, so –' Charles broke off, becoming aware that his father-in-law had said something. 'What was that?'

'I said, it's an ill wind.' McNaughten had loomed behind John and was blowing his nose.

'What is?'

'All this.' The Commander waved a hand around the desolation of the rain-pocked water. 'As I think I've already said – it's going to sink a whole lot of crap. Hooligans, vandals, lefty trendies, queers. They'll all have died. Thank God. I mean that, by the way. I shall thank God.'

'Uh-huh. You see all this as His work?'

'I do indeed. He's had enough and now he's sent us a lesson.'

'A lot of other people will have gone too.'

'Yes, I know. So they must have done in the days of the Ark. And in the plague, the Black Death. And other apparently natural catastrophes. I say *apparent*. There's been a good deal of God's hand visible over the centuries if you ask me.'

Charles said, 'I didn't know you were a Holy Joe. You never have been to date. I didn't even realize you had a belief.'

McNaughten gave an angry snort and turned away without responding. John grinned at his father and said, 'I don't think he has, Dad. Not really.'

'Just getting in well with God, in advance?'

'I think so.'

'It's a little late and it won't wash. We have to admit he may be right – and one thing he mentioned struck a note. The plague. I don't know if that was God's hand or not. What I'm pretty sure of is that there's going to be epidemics where any number of people gather. That's inevitable. No sanitation in the high parts, almost bugger-all food, ditto medicines and medical services.'

'The surviving medics'll get something going, Dad.'

'Oh, they'll do their best, of course. But it'll be a losing battle. A battle largely against those poor people who've drowned.'

'How d'you mean?'

'Use your imagination, John. Thousands, probably millions – certainly millions – of bodies. Floating everywhere – you've seen 'em for yourself. Coming to the surface after going down for a spell, rising and floating and bloating and eventually impacting on the dry areas, the high ground. There'll be no clean water supplies anywhere I shouldn't wonder. All the reservoirs either flooded or suspect. There'll be a crying need for corpse disposal as they hit the land.'

'Mass burial …' John gave a shudder.

'Mass cremation more like. Like they did in North Africa during the war. Not the army or the German Afrika Corps – the Arabs. Typhus ... I remember my father saying he'd driven from Bizerta to Tunis, past bloody great mounds of burning corpses. He said he'd never forget the smell.'

An hour after the dawn had come with a threatening red light in an angry sky over the church tower west of the Holderness peninsula, the Rev Daniel Matthews, seeing his tiny congregation beginning to stir, called them together to tell them what he meant to do. 'It was Josh's idea,' he said. 'I've been thinking. We have to try it. There's nothing else. There's no one around apparently.' Throughout the night a watch had been maintained on the roof of the tower, the men and women taking turns like look-outs aboard a ship, watching for any passing boat that might come within hailing distance, but none of them had reported anything at all.

'Who's going down?' someone asked.

'I am,' Matthews said.

Old Josh spoke up. 'Reckon I'll come too. Seeing as it were my idea int' first place, like you said, Rector.'

Old Josh, as his sobriquet implied, was old – too old to be of much use down there in the floodwater. 'Thank you, Josh. I appreciate that,' Matthews said. 'A hand at the hatch, perhaps – that would be a great help.' He coughed. 'Now let us join together in a prayer, asking God's blessing on what we are about to do.'

He said a simple prayer, head bowed in the lee of the great bells, cast in the previous century. They all joined in the Amen: Old Josh, loud-voiced as any people's warden had a right to be; Mrs Rackstraw, widow from Hull; Jimmy Brook who kept the village inn, patronized predominantly by young people from Hull and more local towns, the village inhabitants being remarkably few; Mr and Mrs Renton from the one thatched cottage in the vicinity, it having been 'improved' into something

of a showpiece and never mind that the thatch didn't
really go with the Yorkshire stone of its walls, it didn't
matter any longer anyway; Andrew Malton and his wife;
Bill Taylor and his wife and two children – both men
being employed by Old Josh as hands about the farm;
Sherrie Tait and her illegitimate, fatherless baby.

Oddly enough, perhaps, it was Sherrie Tait who
suggested, tentatively, that they might sing a hymn.
Daniel Matthews, delighted, agreed wholeheartedly.
Without accompaniment they sang. It was Old Josh who
chose the hymn, not the rector: Old Josh, who had lost a
son at sea in the Second World War, chose with a fair
appropriateness. They all knew the words; they were not
all that far from Hull and its seafaring tradition.

> Eternal Father, strong to save
> Whose arm doth bind the restless wave …
> Oh hear us when we cry to Thee
> For those in peril on the sea.

As the hymn came to an end Matthews took his wife's
hand, drew her to him and kissed her. Her face was pale
and her body shook: she had been unable to dissuade
Daniel, and in fact she was a little ashamed of having
even tried, but it had been human and she was
desperately afraid for him. He was not the sort to do
what he proposed: he was not especially strong. He was
no Royal Marine commando, for a start. He was a
country rector who looked more like what he had been
– a town vicar, accustomed to city streets rather than
farmyards and fields, never having to lend a hand with
even the rescue of a cow from a pond.

His wife kissed, Matthews moved for the hatch,
opened it up, and started down the ladder with Old
Josh standing by at the top. There was little light, only
what came through from the tower's embrasures. No
one had thought of bringing a torch.

FIVE

Somebody, somewhere, was at last trying to do something about the situation, although there was still a high degree of non-coordination. From off the east coast of Scotland, after the Royals had been put ashore to be driven to Balmoral on Royal Deeside, messages had gone to those parts of the country that could still be contacted, messages from the embarked cabinet ministers. Regional governments were to be set up in Edinburgh Castle, in Durham for the North-east, Richmond in North Yorkshire, in Buxton for the Midlands, in Brecon in Wales, in Cirencester for the South and West, and other places standing clear, so far anyway, of the flood. In each of the regions the chief executive of the named town council would take charge and be responsible for health, food supplies, water, security and so on over a very large area. No guidance was issued as to how in fact they were to cope with anything in a situation where everything had broken down. All they were told, rather belatedly and unnecessarily, was that they must prepare to receive an influx of refugees by boat, raft or anything else that floated: men, women and children in much distress, all of them hungry and many of them sick.

'As though we didn't know! As though we haven't got enough already!' This was Bentwood-Jones in Cirencester, where you could scarcely move along the streets and where all the food shops and all the hotels and public houses had been looted and stripped bare, and where, as in Bainbridge in Wensleydale, private houses had been broken into and taken over by the mob rule of desperation. 'I get the idea, very strongly, that the cabinet hasn't a clue what to do and is just handing it to us to think something up and get them off the hook.

What are we to *do*, for God's sake?'

No one seemed to know. It was a similar story all over. Prepare for the sick, the message from the cabinet safely at sea had said. There were plenty of sick – the hospitals where they still existed were crammed to full capacity, largely with the old persons among the refugees but also with the younger sick: in Brecon, for instance, there had been dysentery, probably as the result of drinking flood-water, infected by all sorts of nasty things. There was a worry about the spread of AIDS, for one thing, and these worries grew as the crowds of refugees thickened in the high-standing parts.

In the various areas aircraft began to overfly the water, photographing and reporting back. All the RAF airfields in the eastern part of England had gone underwater very quickly, and most of those elsewhere. The planes that now appeared had come down from Scotland, where some airfields were still serviceable. These planes swooped low, making a frightening noise but yet bringing a hope that when they returned to base they just might get something down. What they could achieve as a result of just photographing floodwater no one could say, but, as ever, hope sprang eternal and the mere fact of the aircraft presence did some good. They hadn't all been forgotten and somewhere there was normal life.

The sorties brought cheer of a kind to those still moving on the waters. Temporarily they lost some of their aloneness. The Lockharts, for instance, growing hungrier in their sailing dinghy. Thanks to that earlier rain and the extraordinarily low visibility, James Lockhart had missed his target of the Mendip Hills and was starting to feel desperate when his small boat was over-flown by a big aircraft with the RAF roundels on the wings and fuselage. They all waved and yelled, quite uselessly; Rosemary, sitting in the stern wrapped like a parcel in warm clothing and looking terrified, called out that David was about to fall overboard. The boy was prancing about in high excitement, and James grabbed him by an arm just in time.

'Calm down, can't you?'

David wriggled; Karen took him over. She asked, 'Do you think they'll send someone?'

'What for?'

'Well ... to guide us to land.'

James let out a long breath. 'Unlikely. We're just one of thousands.'

'Not around here.'

This was true: earlier they'd seen other boats, but now they were alone on the waters. When the aircraft vanished, flying very low, towards the north, they felt more alone than ever. Rosemary, very white and forlorn in her protective wrappings, began to whimper.

James said, 'Shut up.'

After a startled moment, Rosemary whimpered more than ever. Karen said, 'There's no need to speak like that, James. Can't you understand –'

'Can't you bloody well keep her quiet?' James' voice had risen; he had become a bag of nerves, anything could rile him now. How long was this going to go on? Sometime, surely, it had to end, the world had to return to normal, not that it would be fully normal, as he had reflected earlier, for a very long time. He peered ahead, desperately seeking land. The visibility was better but now the dark was starting to come down and soon there would be no light anywhere. No lighthouses with their friendly beams, not in the heart of the English countryside. However, there was one thing: if they did spot a light, it would have to mean dry land. Or would it? It might be a boat showing a navigation light. If a boat was small enough, it needed just the one white lantern, ready for showing as and when required. It was strange to think of navigation lights being required somewhere north of the Blackmoor Vale, somewhere over – where? Somewhere north of Shepton Mallet, Warminster, Frome? Weird to think of the places that would be submerged. Downside school, the Marquis of Bath's great house of Longleat which the Lockharts had visited a number of times over the years.

He spoke of this to Karen. 'Longleat – just think of it. All those treasures.'

'All those poor animals. The lions and tigers ... giraffes, monkeys.'

'They won't have had much chance,' James said. Rosemary began to cry, the whimper being insufficient to express her concern for the animals. Hastily James said, 'Of course I expect they can swim. They'll be all right.'

'They haven't got a boat,' Rosemary said between sobs.

'No, they haven't got a boat.' James thought, but didn't say so, that the animals were perhaps luckier not to have a boat; at least the end would have come quicker.

Earlier in the day helicopters with Royal Naval markings had appeared, overflying the saturated area inshore of the Holderness peninsula. They had come from an aircraft carrier that had been returning from a world cruise, showing the flag and encouraging trade. Bound for Devonport dockyard, she had been diverted by wirelessed orders from the Ministry of Defence operating from the royal yacht. She was to steam up what had been the east coast, making for the sea area north of the Firth of Tay to rendezvous with the *Britannia*, take off the various member of the cabinet and their staffs and act as the seat of government during the emergency. On the way she was to fly off her helicopters on sorties westwards over the submerged countryside, the helicopters taking photographs and rendering reports as to numbers of boats observed and of points of land still above the waters together with some estimate of numbers of survivors clustered on these points of dry land.

There was no dry land for a long way inshore of the Holderness peninsula. There were a few protuberances, factory chimneys and church steeples and so on, but nowhere likely to hold survivors; not until the helicopter's crew came in sight of the church tower with its solitary look-out. A woman, currently: Mrs Rackstraw, the widow from Hull. All the others were below, standing by the hatch down which the rector had gone and was splashing about seeking loose wood, coming up to report at intervals.

'It's a helicopter!' Mrs Rackstraw shouted down in much excitement. 'Someone tell the rector.' She began waving frantically as the machine approached, her heart pumping. This was salvation, the manifest answer to prayer. As the helicopter eased its speed and circled the tower, then went into what Mrs Rackstraw fancied was a hover, her waving was returned by a big man holding on inside a side hatch, a bearded man who grinned down and gave her a thumbs-up. Mrs Rackstraw shouted down again, urging them all to come up. The pilot would want to know how many people were awaiting rescue, she said.

But by the time they had all reached the open tower, the helicopter had flown away. The man in the side hatch had shouted something down, but there had been so much din and such a gale from the rotors that Mrs Rackstraw hadn't caught a word. There had been another thumbs-up, however, which was encouraging, and Mrs Rackstraw had liked the look of the man who had given it.

'They'll be back,' she said stoutly. 'Stands to reason … they couldn't take a lot of people, and there's not just us, there's all the others, everywhere else.'

'What they call a recce,' Old Josh said.

'Aye, that'll be it reet enough.'

'I'll go an' tell rector … next time he comes oop,' Old Josh said, and sniffed. 'Fat lot o' good he's doing down there. Best if he'd let me.' He went down again, his legs stiff on the ladder. They were all desperately hungry now, and thirsty, and soon their strength would go. Somebody had to do something mighty fast, Old Josh knew. That there helicopter: their position might have been noted and rescue might come, but they had to

remember the facts, that they were just one group out
of the Lord knew how many others. Old Josh stood by
the steps going down from the belfry into the body of
the church, waiting for the rector to come up again, but
this time he seemed to be down quite a while.

The helicopter that had overflown them turned north
and then east, setting a course to rejoin the parent
carrier on her track for the Firth of Tay. The orders
had been very clear: as Old Josh had surmised, they
were for recce only. No rescues; it was cold and
calculated but it was logical and inevitable. There was no
knowing when the supply of aviation spirit would run
out – fuel for the carrier's main engines too. The
refineries in Britain and on the Continent were under
water. The supply was virtually limited to what the
carrier had aboard in her fuel tanks. When later the
carrier captain received the reports as the crews were
debriefed, he wondered why the hell the MOD Ministry
had ever bothered with reconnaissance at all.

Aboard the power-boat ex-Queen Alexandra hospital at
Cosham in Hampshire, now somewhere above Cran-
borne Chase, there had been a sudden lurch as the bows
hit. Wayne, the boss of the Big Clout, was at the wheel
and when the way came so suddenly off the boat he was
thrown forward violently, with the binnacle thrust into
his stomach like a battering-ram. It was dark now, which
was why he'd seen nothing ahead. All over the boat
things flew through the air, coming off shelves in the
cabins and out of the store cupboards in the small
galley.

The boys and girls sorted themselves out. Pleasure in
most cases had been interrupted, rudely and painfully.
There was a good deal of swearing until one of the girls
ticked over.

'Land,' she said. 'Bloody land, unless we've gone and
hit another boat.'

They went up on deck as fast as possible, thinking
they might be about to sink. Wayne was groaning.

Someone flashed a torch ahead. It was land right enough, not much, but it was dry. There was grass and a hard surface, possibly a road. The boat seemed stuck, its bow a little up, so that the deck slanted towards the stern.

Kevin asked if there was any damage.

'Go and bloody look,' Wayne said angrily. 'Go up to the bows and look over. You're supposed to be the one what knows.'

Kevin, ex-Navy, went for'ard with the torch. He flashed the beam down to the waterline. He couldn't see any damage but there would have to be an inspection of the boat's forefoot below the water. He went back to Wayne and said as much.

'I reckon it'll be okay till daylight, Wayne.'

'Right, then, leave it for now.'

'Better have as little movement as possible.'

Wayne looked blank, the heavy face totally bovine. 'Movement? The boat's bloody stopped, innit?'

Kevin explained. 'Don't shake her about, that's what I mean. Keep everyone as still as possible. If there's any vibration – you know – she can be shaken off, see, and if there's damage we could sink. Right now – if there's a hole – what we hit is kind of plugging it.'

Wayne shrugged and said, 'OK, you tell 'em all. Lie down and keep still till morning.'

When morning came, the power-boat was still fast on whatever she had hit and the people aboard were able to see that they were stuck fast on some high ground, not much of it, with a much larger piece of land some way ahead, a town built on a hill, the floodwater having left quite a lot of it free. With Kevin, Wayne jumped ashore for an inspection of the damage. Kevin got into the scummy water and felt around the hull. No damage, he reported.

'Bloody lucky. How come, eh?'

'Hit soft earth, that's why. We're just jammed, like, you know.' Kevin looked round the horizons. He stared towards the town, saw other hummocks intervening but only just above the water and none of them large. There was no life on them, but obviously the town ahead would be crowded.

Wayne asked, 'Know where we are, do you?'

'I reckon it could be Shaftesbury.' Kevin, once he was out of the Navy had driven pantechnicon before the floods had come, and he used to get around a lot, moving people's homes. 'If it is ...' he looked around their present billet: the water had left a curve of roadway, not in very good condition, with a couple of waste-disposal bins; there was the feel of a lay-by. 'If that's Shaftesbury, we could be on Zig-Zag Hill, I reckon. Must be, in fact.'

'So what, eh?'

Kevin said, 'So nothing in particular. But it doesn't hurt to know exactly where we are.' He walked away.

'Where you going, then?'

'Check the litter bins. You never know ... something to give us a clue whether that's bloody Shaftesbury or not.' Kevin went across, opened the first bin, rooted about in an assortment of discarded coke tins, ice-cream wrappers and so on. No clues. He went to the second bin. Still no luck.

Wayne came across. 'Never mind, sod Shaftesbury, mate. Go too near other people and we stand to lose the bloody boat, right? Besides ... there could be disease. Better orf on our own, we are. Got a boat, got enough nosh for quite a while.'

Within ten minutes the boat had come astern on its engine and was clear of Zig-Zag Hill. Wayne took her in a wide sweep, well clear of Shaftesbury, before setting his course northerly again.

Shaftesbury, like Cirencester, was chock-a-block with refugees from the adjacent areas and some from farther off. One boatload had come from Dulverton in Somerset – an old-timer, a genuine Thames sailing-barge belonging to a retired master mariner who had kept her at Barnstaple and spent most of his time

aboard her. She was named the *Ethel Margaret* and
Captain Wilson, a widower, was virtually in love with
her. For crew normally he had his sister and her
husband and their two sons, Peter and Harry Henschel.
His nephews had come with him when the waters had
risen, but not his sister or her husband, who had lived in
Bridgwater and been swept away when the flood had
surged up the Bristol Channel and poured inland across
Bridgwater Bay and the low-lying coastal areas to north
and south.

Captain Wilson's original intention had been to sail
towards Exmoor or further north into Wales, to make
for the mountains over the Welsh valleys, what was left
of the mines now flooded, the valleys gone finally and
the waters carrying the coal-dust from the slagheaps to
the surface, reminding the survivors of the great days
when coal had been king, long ago now of course, and
the little chapels had been full of fine song on Sundays.
Merthyr Tydfil, Tredegar, Ebbw Vale, Pontypool below
the distant shadow of the Black Mountains and the
Brecon Beacons. Now those and other mountains could
be the best refuge, for there was a big extent of them.

But other matters had intervened: he had a niece in
Shaftesbury, working as a management trainee and
currently in reception in the Grosvenor Hotel. Elizabeth
Henschel's brothers, knowing how she would be feeling
if she was still alive pleaded with him and he had given
in.

'All right, I understand. But I warn you, there's no
space, or there won't be, in a town like Shaftesbury. But
I suppose we can take her off, and then head for the
Welsh mountains. Mind you, I can't guarantee we'll find
Shaftesbury standing clear – it must depend on how far
the floods rise, obviously.'

He and the nephews were by no means the only
persons to sail for Shaftesbury aboard the *Ethel
Margaret*. Wilson was not the man to take an almost
empty boat to safety. He picked up some thirty persons
all told: men, women and children and in one case a

Welsh sheepdog that scrambled aboard willy-nilly with its master from a big log of wood, half a tree by the look of it, that had come from Exmoor. Others were the Thomas family from the port of Barry in Glamorgan, who like Captain Wilson had intended making for the mountains to the north of them but whose rowing-boat had lost its oars. They had been swept across the Bristol Channel and had been picked up by the *Ethel Margaret* more or less at their last gasp, for they were landspeople and very scared, and they had nothing with them except for thin summer clothing. They had been so many that the boat had become overloaded: four grandparents, an aunt and uncle, the Thomases themselves, two plus three young children, two girls and a boy. Mr Thomas – Evan Thomas the younger – had worked for some years at Butlin's on Barry Island until it had pulled out, and then he had worked for too many years at being unemployed. His father, Evan Thomas the elder, had also lived all his life in Barry and had worked in the docks, just remembering the good days when Barry had despatched good Welsh coal, which was acknowledged as the best for ships' engines when they had been coal-fired.

The best in all the world, despatched it to coaling stations all over.

That, of course, had been a very long time ago, before the Second World War, which changed everything.

He talked about it to Captain Wilson after he and his family had been dried out, fed and given clean clothing so far as could be provided from Wilson's own wardrobe. He had some of his dead wife's gear aboard and was pleased to see it used again so appreciatively by people in distress.

'The war, now,' old Evan Thomas said. 'You'd not remember that, I expect?'

Wilson smiled. 'I was an apprentice then, a cadet new to the sea. Yes, I remember.'

'Well, in the war the Royal Navy took over Barry from the start … Barry Roads, it was used as an anchorage for the merchant ships waiting for the convoys to form up. In the docks there is still the building used by the Navy for the control and routeing of the convoys. The Navy was everywhere. And the Army too, and later the Americans. There was a great armament depot at Sully close to Barry, an ordnance depot, and there are still the slipways where the warships and landing craft took their ammunition for the invasion of Normandy. You see, a great part of the invasion fleet sailed from Barry docks, including the big headquarters ships with the admirals and the generals. And after the war was over, and the Navy and the soldiers left, well, there was nothing comparatively speaking. Few ships used coal any more, for one thing. The coaling stations had closed down. And then gradually things got worse and worse, and our docks became a dumping ground for old railway engines until they took even them away too. And in the end scarcely a ship entered and it became very sad …'

'And now this.' Wilson waved a hand across the Bristol Channel that, in effect, had ceased to exist.

'Yes, now this. Perhaps, in a sense, apart of course from the loss of life, it is for the best, since it has all gone anyway.'

'Not for ever, Mr Thomas.'

'Not for ever?' The old man looked at him straight. 'Yes, for ever. What will be left when the waters go down again?'

'I'm afraid it's no use,' Daniel Matthews said, short of breath as he surfaced from the flooded body of his church, hanging onto the treads of the ladder into the belfry. 'I'm very sorry.'

'Did yer best, Rector, can't do more than that. What's it like, eh?'

'Terrible,' Mathews said, and pulled himself higher up to stand, dripping water on the belfry floor. He had made several sorties, coming up frequently for air, before he had realized that he was doing no good at all. The pews were much too heavy – not so much too heavy, for he been able to push them along, but too big, too unwieldy to be brought up through the hatch. There was no other loose wood that he could find. Some light had come down from the tower, and as the day lightened there was a faint sort of luminosity behind the stained glass windows, just enough to make the whole place thoroughly eerie, and he had seen the altar, with the cloth washed away somewhere and the candlesticks fallen down ... it had been terrible to see it all. There had been the corpses: he shuddered. He had swum past the marble tablets, the memorials dating back some three centuries in the case of the big landowners, the family that had produced the village squires in the old days – not since Matthews' own short time as rector, for the hall had been empty for some years and had finally been pulled down to make way for road development, and a four-carriage-way trunk road now ran where there had been parkland and ponds and a gracious garden around a fine house.

'What about that helicopter, Mrs Rackstraw?'

'Never did come back. There's time yet.'

Matthews nodded and looked at his wife's face: it seemed quite haunted, he thought, though there had been a momentary relief showing when he'd come up to confess failure. She knew what he knew, what they all knew but didn't want to put into words: there was no hope for them short of rescue, and that would be a miracle. On the other hand, they had been spotted by that helicopter's crew. The miracle might come, would surely come. Daniel Matthews said as much, doing his best to sound confident. His flock listened, and heads were nodded. The helicopter had borne naval markings, and the Navy never let anyone down. It was, really, a matter of speed now. No food and no water, no drinkable water, that was the problem. And there was that poor mite, Sherrie Tait's single-parent family problem. The baby was crying now, a monotonous wail, and was thereby encouraging the other two children, the Taylor children, to emulate it. The sound got very much on the nerves, Matthews found.

SIX

Aboard the Rushworth boat, *Hilda*, making westward, John Rushworth talked to the girl Vicki from Norwich.

He tried to draw her out: this was a hard task because his grandfather was glaring balefully all the time and the girl herself seemed not to want to communicate. She sat on the seat in the stern of the boat once the rain had stopped and the day brightened, sat with her legs drawn up and her hands clasped around her knees, her long hair falling across one eye, the one nearer to John so that he was unable even to read her expression.

'Have you always lived in Norwich, Vicky?'

'Bloody seemed like it sometimes.'

'Oh.'

'Not long, no.'

'Where were you before?'

'None of your business, mate.'

'Sorry.' John Rushworth flushed: the tone had verged on venom. All the same, he believed there had been a hint, just a hint of tears. The girl intrigued him. She wasn't exactly pretty but she was attractive, she had personality and she exuded sex. John wanted to help her, make her feel wanted now that she had projected herself into their lives. One could scarcely, he felt, do less. She was now a fact of their environment. They would have to feed her, live with her, look after her if she was ill, so they might as well get to know her.

John said, and, even as he spoke, knew it sounded false, 'We're very glad to have you with us, you know.'

'Oh.'

'I really mean that.'

'Sure,' she said, and laughed. 'Bloody likely! Did your best to shove off before I got on, didn't you? Call that a bloody welcome, do you?'

'Well, I … it wasn't me who shoved off.'

'No. No, I'll give you that.'

'So can't we … sort of get to know each other?'

She turned her head and stared at him, right into his eyes. Her own held an unreadable expression. She asked, 'Why?'

He was nonplussed at the sharpness. 'Why?' he repeated.

'Yes, why. *Why?*'

'Well, I …'

'*I'll* tell *you*: you want to fuck me – right?'

He stared, stupidly, aware of shock on the part of his grandfather. He said, 'Of course not.'

'Why not? Plenty have wanted to, plenty have, come to that. You a gay, are you?'

'No!'

'Glad to hear it. OK, carry on getting to know me if you want. If I were you, I wouldn't though. Not unless you want to get up against that old grand-dad of yours.' She turned her head again, and leaned forward, stared back at McNaughten, glowering still. Vicki raised her voice, loudly. 'Silly old fart, thinks I've got AIDS, he's scared stiff. I'll bet he thinks everybody's got AIDS except himself. Right, grand-dad?'

'You're an impertinent young woman,' McNaughten said angrily, 'and I suggest you come to terms with the facts, which are that you're in the sort of company to which you're not accustomed and is not accustomed to you. I suggest you learn some manners, and learn them fast.'

'My arse I will,' the girl said, grinning. Oddly, John thought, she's cheered up a bit now that she's riled the old man. McNaughten, looking speechless, turned his back and went into the wheelhouse where he stood glaring through the glass screen. He was champing his jaws, a sign of age he knew, and stopped the moment he thought about it. He didn't like growing older: for one thing, there was no longer any respect for age. When he'd been a boy, his father and grandfather and their friends had been held in immense respect, their word being law. No one was ever cheeky to them, or more correctly no one was ever cheeky to them twice. The first punishment had been quite enough for a lifetime, a real lesson. It wasn't like that now, hadn't been for some time, and McNaughten detested the deterioration. Girls like that young urchin ... was she perhaps a junkie as well as being promiscuous? She didn't look very fit, McNaughten thought. His reading had told him that AIDS patients were usually constitutionally unwell. The girl was spotty, and the medics had written about such things as seborrhoeic dermatitis, folliculitis, acne vulgaris, xeroderma, fungal infections, herpes, impetigo ... an endless list of dirty horror.

She ought to be landed as soon as possible – of course she should But where was the land, for God's sake?

The Lockharts in their sailing dinghy raised a small vessel hull down to the east. As it came nearer it looked like a coaster: single funnel rising from the after superstructure, flush deck, one mast.

James Lockhart stood up in the boat, stripped off his shirt and waved at it. Karen and the children waved as well, too excited to wonder at the curious thought of a coasting vessel, probably in normal times trading between east coast ports and the Brest–Elbe limits, making its way across England's fields and forests and downs.

They all shouted, the children too.

'She's altering!' Lockhart said in immense relief. 'Thank God.' He put an arm around his wife. 'It'll be all right now.'

She nodded, tears of relief running down her cheeks. The coaster came nearer: they could see the crowded decks now, people everywhere, staring down at the little boat as they approached closely. The vessel slowed and a man called down from the bridge.

'Where are you heading?'

'Wherever there's land,' Lockhart called back. 'Or we were. Can you take us aboard?'

The man waved an arm for'ard across the cargo deck. 'Sorry. Very sorry. We're overloaded as it is. I can't risk taking any more. We're down below our marks.' He paused. 'If you continue on your present course, you'll pick up high ground, around the Cotswolds.'

'Can you spare some food?' Lockhart shouted urgently.

'Sorry. Very sorry.'

The coaster's engines started up again and the little dinghy rocked to the wash as the larger vessel moved away. Tears of anger and frustration came to Lockhart's eyes and he shook a fist. 'Bastards!' he called after the retreating coaster. 'What do bloody MOT regulations mean now!'

It was every man for himself in the catastrophe. Once you were OK, you wanted to stay that way and the devil take the rest. Soon they were alone again on the wide expanse, more deserted now than they had been before. The Cotswolds ahead ... well, that was perhaps something; but James Lockhart wondered after a while what good it would really do them to reach the Cotswolds. What would they find there?

Aboard his old Thames barge *Ethel Margaret* Captain Wilson was approaching Shaftesbury, sailing across Somerset, over Glastonbury and Castle Cary, with a reasonable wind ruffling the foul water and filling his sails. As a seaman all his life, the oddity of the situation struck him perhaps more forcibly, more incredulously, than a landsman. He had sailed the world's oceans in storm and calm, beneath hot suns and beneath the lash of wind-driven rain and snow. He had sailed as an apprentice with Smith's of Cardiff, then as third officer in the cargo-liners of International Freight, advancing over the years to master. He had covered the seas from UK to America, from Hong Kong to Sydney and New

Zealand, from Japan to Chile and Peru and the
Argentine. He had commanded a ship roped in for
service during the Falklands War, and he had seen the
terrible end of the Royal Fleet Auxiliary *Sir Galahad*,
carrying men of the Welsh Guards. He had seen the
heroism that day.

He spoke of it to the Evan Thomases, both of them,
elder and younger. They for their part spoke with
personal sadness: it turned out that a son who was also a
grandson, had been lost with the Welsh Guards.

'A terrible waste of life,' Evan Thomas the elder said,
and paused, frowning. 'Do you think the waters will
have risen down there, Captain?'

Wilson shrugged. 'I can't say. This is an entirely new
situation, quite unprecedented –'

'Not quite, no, Captain Wilson. There was the Ark,
you remember.'

'A rather different story.'

'Yes, perhaps. Perhaps not. Perhaps there was
something similar then, a natural phenomenon, but at
that time God gave warning to Noah. This time there
was no warning. Or not to speak of.'

'The trouble was,' Wilson said, 'that too few people
were prepared to listen, they thought it could never
happen. I don't know if that was the case with Noah, or
not. Anyway, there wasn't much room in the Ark!'

Evan Thomas looked at him quizzically. 'Are you a
religious man, Captain Wilson?'

Wilson paused before answering. The question had
been asked seriously. He said, 'No one who's spent a
lifetime at sea could fail to believe in God. Or what for
convenience we call God. We don't know anything
about Him, not for sure, that is. But I've no doubt at all
that there's a superior being in charge. You've only to
see the elements at work. There's a majesty out there on
the deep oceans, something that makes a man very
humble.'

'Even a captain?' There was a twinkle in Evan
Thomas's eye.

'Yes, even a captain.'

'Captains not being noted for humility.'

'Perhaps not. But – well, amazing things happen that make you believe.'

'The hand of God, Captain Wilson? Let us hope that God has His eye on all of us at this moment, indeed to goodness …'

It was soon after this conversation that a hump of land came up ahead and Wilson studied it through his binoculars. 'A town on a hill. By my reckoning it should be Shaftesbury. I wonder what we'll find.'

'I think I shut your grand-dad up,' Vicki said. She trailed a hand over the gunwale and brought up a feather of water. Something else as well: unnamed scum, something rotten that could have been part of a body, either human or animal. She withdrew her hand violently and looked sick. *Had* it been a body? There had scarcely been time yet for drowned bodies to disintegrate, but there would have been injuries when the waters came and everyone fought for out, injuries that could have involved torn-off arms and legs, even murders in the panic. She knew there had been one murder back in Norwich, which was one reason why she wasn't saying much about her life there. She had good reason to know about that murder, though she disliked the word in the context of what had happened. Justifiable homicide was much more fitting.

By chance one night, not long before the flood had come, she had encountered a man she had known in Brighton – years before, one of mum's boyfriends. One of the men who had interfered with her. The encounter had taken place outside the café where she worked part-time, now shut for the night. He'd lurched into her, a little sloshed, and made a grab at her. Of course she was a lot older by this time and so was he, but she'd recognized him instantly beneath the street-light and because of her memories she'd done something stupid, something she'd regretted the moment it was done.

Instead of shoving him away she'd flared up at him. 'You bastard,' she said. 'Just like bloody Brighton!' She'd slapped his face, hard, and he'd seized her wrist and twisted her arm behind her back, and hoisted her up until her face was level with his, and then he'd recognized her.

'You. You little slut, like your mum.'

She had looked round desperately but there was no-one about. She kicked out, took him right in the crutch, and when he let go with an oath she ran, her usual short-cut along by the river bank, which was daft but she wasn't thinking straight. The man followed. Some way off the road, heading towards a bridge, he began to overtake, panting and blowing because he had a big gut. She had turned at bay, eyes blazing, heart going like anything, and had taken up a heavy piece of wood that happened to be handy on the ground. She swung it as he reached her, using all the strength and determination of desperation, and brought it across the side of his head. He went down without a sound and rolled down the bank and into the river. She stood petrified for a moment, saw him go under, his body all limp, then she ran. She reached the road, slowed down so as not to draw attention, went across the bridge, looked along the river and saw nothing. That night, trembling and afraid in the loneliness of the room over the chip shop, for by this time her boyfriend had done his disappearing act, she didn't sleep. She calmed down during the day and that evening she went to work as usual. Next day the paper reported a body that had been snagged by a bush or something, down river. The body of a middle-aged man with the side of the head smashed in and a large nail embedded – she'd not been aware of the nail.

The police had no clues. There was nothing whatsoever to connect her with it. She felt reasonably safe and she began to be glad about what she'd done. It had been deserved: he was a molester of small girls, and the chances of time and coincidence had given her

revenge. She just wished she'd asked him about Mum,
though she had in fact no conscious wish ever to see
Mum again. A few days later the floods had come close
to England and the flat lands of East Anglia and then
there was no time left to bother about looking for
murderers.

The helicopter had not returned to the lonely church
tower. The pilot had been ordered to rejoin the parent
aircraft carrier, now under orders to close the
Britannia as soon as possible. After landing, the crew
had attended the pilots' ready room for debriefing and,
along with other sightings, had reported the people
marooned on the tower. All this was noted: but for now
there were more urgent considerations: the British
Government, now no longer able to rule through the
proper procedures of Parliament, was to be taken
aboard from the royal yacht which might be needed
independently for the royal household currently at
Balmoral. And because the carrier had guns and
helicopters it would prove a better seat of government.
A State of Emergency had of course been declared from
the start, but now matters had gone beyond that, and
any governance that could henceforth be applied at all
would be by means of decree, even though it was
acknowledged that the chance of notifying the
population at large of any decrees might be so remote as
to be virtually non-existent.

'The main thing,' the Home Secretary said to the
captain of the carrier when the cabinet was transferred
on the warship's arrival off the east coast of Scotland,
'the main thing is that we are a government in being.
That's obviously the first essential, that we're *here*.'

'Yes, indeed. At the same time, if nobody knows it –'

'Oh, they'll assume it, they'll know they'll never be let
down,' the Home Secretary said with complete
assurance, the stock-in-trade of any politician. The
captain kept his thoughts to himself for the time being:
everything was in a state of flux. The ship was

beginning to feel like Downing Street. They had their WT installation, powerful transmitters capable of reaching as far as Australia, good receivers, and a highly trained staff of communications ratings. The trouble was likely to be that the surviving population of Britain would be much more distant, in a sense, than Australia. A few may have saved their radios ... and of course there were some official radio stations still standing above the flood-waters, so it might be possible to maintain some kind of a network for the transmission of orders and decrees. But that would be dependent on the maintenance of the power supply, which was in itself doubtful. Very doubtful.

Meanwhile the aircraft carrier was being taken over by the Whitehall men: ministers and their staffs, senior civil servants from all the ministries, secretaries of varying grades, public relations officers ... the Department of the Environment alone like an anthill with people from Planning, Local Transportation and Roads, Regional and Minerals, Local Government, Water, Highways, Systems Analysis Research Unit. It was amazing how they had all escaped the rising waters. The royal yacht, the carrier captain thought, must have burst at the seams. A lot of paper had come with the government departments: sacks of it, file after file after file emerging to be strewn about the ship's offices and other requisitioned spaces. Sleep was going to be extremely difficult: nothing like enough cabins or bunk spaces. But they would have to make the best of it. For how long? As the Home Secretary remarked to the captain, there was absolutely no knowing. There were no experts now: such a situation had never been faced before. In due course news would no doubt filter through from North America. But so far there had been nothing, which was itself far from reassuring. It had been known from the start that parts of Canada at any rate had suffered. It was possible there had been widespread flooding further south.

SEVEN

A different sort of London had come north to
Yorkshire and its so-far safe fells and dales. It had
fetched up in Bainbridge: an unlikely place in normal
times to find representatives of Soho. Admittedly
Madame Smith, née Mocatta, had not come direct from
Soho, where some years ago she had been landlady of a
public house; she had progressed from there to an
establishment of a different sort in a London suburb.
She had come chiefly, of course, to escape the flood, but
also she had seen the main chance, the chances of
carrying on a lucrative trade amongst displaced
persons, perhaps of a different class from what she had
been used to, but still clients. Being something of a
prophetess, she had come north in good time, while
there was still an M1 and still petrol and diesel available,
travelling in an old double-decker London bus which,
while the panic was in its early stages, her strong-arm
boys had nicked from its currently projected occupation
as part of that summer's hippie convoy. It was not much
of a vehicle, and the hippie junk had had to be cleared
out and the whole interior scrubbed down, but it was big
and that was important. Madame Smith, dressed as for
London in gloves and a big flowery hat, was travelling
with her staff of girls, maids and a chucker-out.

She had spent a while outside York before moving on
ahead of the rising water and entering Bainbridge, not
long after old Tom Braithwaite had watched his wife
die, seen her almost literally thrown out into the tiny
back garden by the yoboes and soon after that had died
himself. He had died of terror, anger and a broken
heart, his whole life's experience upended. So he never
saw the strange vehicle, still looking like a hippie
conveyance outwardly, coming over the narrow bridge

across the River Ure.

The girls were looking out of the window but they were behaving themselves and appeared almost prim. Madame Smith had run a strict house and although there had been plenty of abandon in the bedrooms, the atmosphere elsewhere had been that of respectability, as befitted suburbia. Madame Smith's was not at all like some other places, or as some other places were said to be. She had never wanted to attract the wrong sort of attention, the attention of the fuzz, policemen in drag pretending to want sex but really there only to pounce and besmirch a respectable woman's home. So Madame Smith was very careful about the behaviour of her young ladies, some of whom were very well connected, one or two even having titles, real aristocrats. It was they who tended to enjoy their jobs the most. Gentlemen paid very well indeed for their services and Madame Smith, originally from Malta but now to all intents and purposes a dyed-in-the-wool cockney, had grown rich. Gentleman of all sorts came to her house: city tycoons, solicitors, judges, highly placed civil servants, clergymen, members of parliament, even a chief constable or two from the provinces. Madame Smith always liked having the Old Bill as genuine paying clients, since this tended to keep the nasty, prying sort away. She imagined there was some sort of a grapevine that informed the nasty part of the Old Bill that so-and-so would be having his oats and they'd do better to lay off.

Madame Smith, very large in the front near-side seat, looked out of the window and into the rear-view mirror on the passenger side. There had been a lot of hooting: the hippie vehicle was slow and large and the A684 was narrow in places.

'Some people,' she said tartly, "ave no bleeding patience. What's the bloody 'urry might I ask?'

Her driver, the chucker-out, said, 'It's a council van. Something about North Yorkshire County Council on its side.'

'One o' them, eh. Important buggers.'

'Think they are, yes.'

'That's what I meant, Albert. Block 'im.'

'Right.' The bus went slowly on, came clear of the bridge and on to a road running across a wide village green, crowded with people and cars and other vans. The bus came to a halt. The road itself was jam-packed. There was the slam of a door behind and a man appeared, looking officious and dressed in a collar and tie.

He stood by the door, his hand on the sill of the wound-down window. 'Who's the owner of this object?' he asked.

Madame Smith got up and leaned through the cab to speak across the driver. 'I'm the possessor. So what?'

'Got an MOT? I'd like to see it, please.'

'It's in London, innit?' This was the driver. Madame Smith didn't tell lies herself.

'I don't know. You tell me.'

'Just 'ave.'

'London, eh.' The man from the council was irresolute.

'Out of touch, like.'

'You'll have to get it sent up.'

'Don't talk daft,' Madame Smith said, still leaning across. 'London's under water. Don't you know there's a flood on?' She cackled.

'You'll have to stay here,' the official said, 'until you can get another MOT locally. There's a garage back beyond the bridge, the way you came in.'

'Silly prat,' Madame Smith said angrily. 'The country in the state it's bloody in, and you stand there and –'

'This part of the country is *not* flooded. This part of the country is still in a state of law and order, and everything is still enforceable. I'm just telling you, that's all.' The man vanished, took a walk all round the bus, peered beneath, poked a sharp instrument into some rust, kicked at the tyres, looked in at the window. The girls stared back and then dropped their eyes demurely. The man went back to the driver's door. 'Vehicle's about to fall apart, as you must well know. I'll be having my eye on you. Who're all those young women?'

'Young ladies,' Madame Smith said.

'What is their purpose?'

'Fuck all to do with you, mate. Just confine your interest to the bloody bus itself. This is their bloody 'ome, see? We're all 'aving to make do. Tell the daft bugger who they are, Albert,' she said to her driver.

Albert said, 'Chorus from *Dead End Charlie*.'

'What's that?'

'Musical, playing in the West End.'

'Oh. Well, just remember what I said, and pull off the road.'

'No bloody room.' By this time the traffic in front was on the move again and a chorus of hoots and shouts was coming from behind. Madame Smith's driver clicked his tongue and got moving, but something had happened, not for the first time, to the gears, and the double-decker moved backwards. The council van was right behind; there was a heavy crump and the official ran back, cursing savagely. The bus moved again, this time forward. The driver looked in his mirror and laughed. 'Bust radiator,' he said.

'Well, that settles 'im, daft prat. We'll go on. What's ahead?'

'A lot of Yorkshire.' Albert watched while Madame Smith, first removing her town gloves, studied the road map.

''Awes,' she said. 'Next town. Let's get there.'

'Well named,' Albert said. Madame Smith thinned her lips. She didn't like that sort of joke.

The *Ethel Margaret* approached Shaftesbury under the careful guidance of Captain Wilson, with one of the nephews taking soundings for'ard in the bows. A lot of the town was under water; Wilson wasn't going to risk coming to grief on somebody's submerged roof. He was not using his sails now. Not long ago he had had an auxiliary petrol engine fitted, and although the conservation of fuel was important this was one of the times when the use of the engine was essential to safe pilotage.

Moving in, Wilson glanced from time to time over the side: visual soundings, where possible, were a useful aid in the circumstances. The water was scummy and littered with debris but now and again something other than filth and decay could be seen. Roofs, skylight windows. Wilson believed he saw a human form in one skylight, drifting backwards and forwards as the water moved. The dead arms made patterns. The *Ethel Margaret* drifted on; Wilson was heading her for the edge of the floodwater, not to put her on the beach or even alongside anything, but so as to find some projection where he could pass a line and hold the old barge for long enough to get his nephews ashore to look for their sister. She would presumably be in the Grosvenor Hotel, which Wilson could now see fine on his starboard bow, standing nicely clear of the water, a tall old building. Wilson knew the hotel: he had stayed there on a couple of occasions and found it an excellent and very comfortable hotel.

The report from for'ard was good: no bottom.

'Report continuously,' Wilson called. He looked down, could see nothing except, on his port side, what could have been roofs but he couldn't be sure. Right beneath, looking down close to the side, nothing at all and the reports still said no bottom. Wilson had a hunch he was coming up over a road, and if so, that was the place to stay until he found that secure line-holding point. A couple of minutes later he believed he had: As he began to come past buildings only half submerged, buildings that now gave him a positive fix over a street that climbed a hill beneath the flood, he saw quite close to the water's edge ahead of him an iron bollard protruding, a bollard set in the roadway at the entry to a side street so as to keep traffic out. Men and women had looked out from the upper windows of the houses as the boat passed along, some of them cheering, others jeering, others looking like zombies who had lost all hope and interest. As the securing lines were sent across to the bollard, people gathered by the edge of the water at the high part of the street, hundreds of them as it seemed, dirty and haggard and somehow threatening.

'Quick as you can,' Wilson said to his nephews. 'Sooner we're away the better I'll like it.'

They jumped ashore. They pushed through the crowd. They were not impeded but a curious sound came from the massed humanity, a kind of subdued sound of hate, Wilson believed. Men and women were being turned by the pressure of events into near animals – it was an animal sound. Some of them splashed into the water, making to board.

Wilson called out, 'Stand away there, please. I've got all I can safely take.' He knew that in fact he could take perhaps a half-dozen more but this crowd was not far off being a mob and the smallest concession would lead to an avalanche and that would be the end of the *Ethel Margaret* and her present passengers. By his side stood the Evan Thomases, father and son.

The elder man said, 'Captain, I have a revolver. I shouldn't have, but I have. And ammunition. And now I think the police are no longer effective. Do you see a policeman in that crowd?'

Wilson shook his head. 'No.'

'No more do I. The revolver is yours if you wish it. It may be the only thing that will preserve order.' Evan Thomas brought the revolver from the pocket of what looked like a poacher's jacket and handed it to Wilson.

'Perhaps as a last resort,' Wilson said. He waited for his nephews to come back from the Grosvenor Hotel, prayed for speed on their part.

By now there had been contact with other parts of the world, notably with the United States of America. It seemed that something had gone off the beam until now, the cataclysmic upheaval caused by the nuclear explosion below the ice having had its effect on even the communications satellites spinning around in space as well as on the land-bound transmitters, but now some sort of radio link had been established again. The news was bad: not only had a large part of North America, and South America too, been unundated but there was a big nuclear cloud, the fall-out, spreading over Alaska and Canada and the eastern regions of the USSR.

Depending on the winds, this cloud could come across to Britain and the Continent, currently suffering floods as severe as in Britain. Aboard the aircraft carrier now standing off the Firth of Forth the cabinet was more than ever dismayed, seeing less and less hope for any kind of future. The opinion from Washington seemed to be that it might be many weeks or even months before the water-levels fell back. If that did prove to be the case, there could be few survivors. Never mind the fall-out possibilities: what would bring them all down would be water. Not the floods, but drinking water. Virtually the only clean water lay in the big reservoirs of the North and in the mountainous parts of the West. The others were now simply part of the flood itself. The chief water engineer from Environmental Protection and Water Engineering saw nothing but doom. The regions had reported most of the West Country reservoirs gone, likewise all those around London and the South-east and the Midlands, while of course East Anglia was totally under flood, the Broads and the Fens and the dams of the drainage system near Downham Market all gone. Aboard the carrier there was no worry: The ship simply sucked up the sea-water and the condensers turned it into fresh water. With so many extra persons aboard rationing would be strict, but that was all. They would survive if no one else did.

'So what do we do?' the Prime Minister, who had taken over the captain's day cabin and sleeping cabin, asked blankly. 'About the marooned persons?'

The chief water engineer said he would be in touch with the regions, telling them to use their best endeavours to provide clean water.

'Yes. I suppose that's really all we can do.' The Prime Minister passed on to other business. It was never-ending and the answer was always the same: nothing to be done other than try to pick up survivors wherever they were found and ferry them to the high ground in the North and in Scotland. Which, of course, was already being done so far as was humanly possible. Once the government machine had been embarked off the Firth of Tay the carrier had moved a little way, not far, south; and action was being taken on the report of the helicopter sorties earlier. The pilot who had spotted the church tower had identified it as such and was confident of finding it again from his map references and bearings and so on and he believed, and said as much, that where there was a church tower you might well find a parson among the survivors, and there was something about the cloth that made you not wish to let a parson down. When questioned about this, the pilot couldn't quite put his feelings into words and gave the general impression that he was playing safe with God at a time of great danger. His rescue mission was approved and the helicopter located the church tower and took off all the clustered persons by means of the winch. On arrival back aboard, Sherrie Tait's single-parent baby went down well with the ship's company but was nevertheless a nuisance aboard an aircraft carrier, even though much of the seamen's sleeping and ablutions space had been taken over by the women of the various departmental staffs and a baby could be, as it were, absorbed into the system.

The Big Clout in their power-boat had moved a long way north by now. The young nurse had remained in the cabin where she had been constantly visited by the leather-jacketed male members of the mob. She lay inert, no longer caring, knowing she had scant chance of living anyway and that if she did survive there would be nothing worthwhile to survive into. Not now: she had adored her father; and the young doctor she had hoped to marry had been killed in a road accident just a few weeks before. Until then life had been happy enough; when both were off duty together they'd gone around the countryside in his car, searching out the decent pubs where you could have a drink and a snack by yourselves, even though in the evenings the pubs were crowded. They had ranged mainly into West Sussex, where the pubs were better than around Portsmouth and Cosham. Friendly places; now they were all gone, all beneath the water, the old beams and stone floors and the cosy winter fires, the camaraderie, the memories. The latter came back, like the floodwaters themselves. Her young doctor had left an unfillable gap.

The man named Kevin, the ex-naval rating, came to her. He wasn't as bad as the others: she'd been gently treated by him. Now he read the look in her eyes, the wild animal at the end of its tether look. He stood there at the end of the bunk, looking down at her, not speaking.

She said, 'Well? Why don't you get on with it?'

'It's all right,' he said.

'Is it?'

'You know what I mean.'

'You mean you're not going to –'

'No,' he said. 'No, I'm not.' He went on standing there, looking sorry. He seemed different from the others, cleaner, less vicious. She believed he was ashamed of himself and his mates. He was.

She asked why he'd come down to the cabin.

'Just to see you were OK.'

She stared back, felt tears run. The first bit of decency, of kindliness ... Suddenly he moved, sat on the bunk by her side, reached out and began gently stroking her hair. 'It won't go on for ever,' he said. 'Nothing ever does, see?' She didn't respond; once, he'd thought that things did go on for ever, that there would never be any hope for people like himself, the unfortunates, the unloved. In some respects Kevin had been the male counterpart of Vicki aboard the Rushworth boat. Not quite the same, but there were definite similarities. Kevin's father had left his mother five years after he'd been born and Dad had never been heard of again. Mum had gone on the bottle after that, and to keep herself in drink she'd started fiddling the Social Security and doing a bit of shoplifting on the side. Mum had gone to prison and the young Kevin had been taken into care, eventually being farmed out to a family in Portsmouth where he'd seen the warships in the port and had formed an interest in the Navy. But again tragedy had struck and the foster parents had both been killed in a road traffic accident. For a while after that Kevin had gone back to an orphanage. He'd hated that after a taste of family life and, like Vicki from Brighton, he had run away and gone to London, the Big Smoke where all the opportunities lay.

Or so he'd thought. That was the fiction; the truth was different.

Having no money, or none to speak of, there had been no question of train or coach. Kevin had hitched, walking north through Cosham and on to the old London road that ran through Waterlooville and Horndean. Just before Horndean he'd been picked up by a lorry driver and taken as far as Petersfield ... he'd made the outskirts of London in a succession of lifts, and tired and hungry had made for Piccadilly Circus, about the only place in London he'd ever heard of apart from Buckingham Palace and the Houses of Parliament, trudging along the dreary streets and asking the way at intervals.

The lights of Piccadilly Circus and Leicester Square had been bright and welcoming, fascinating to a youngster on his first visit. They held a lot of promise – gaiety, glamour, girls, easy money – in a place the size of London there just had to be plenty of work and he would have no difficulty. He started the great adventure by going into a café in Shaftesbury Avenue and spending nearly a quarter of his capital on a meal of bacon and eggs, sausages and chips and a bottle of coke and then he felt fit for anything. The one snag was he had nowhere to live, nowhere to spend the night. He knew it would be no use going to a hotel, not with only about six quid of saved-up orphanage pocket-money in his possession. Why, they might even charge all that for just the one night, and he would have more nights to worry about than just the one before he found a job. So he slept rough.

From then it was not easy. Next day all his small store of cash had gone. No one wanted to employ him: he tried very hard but got nowhere. There were, it seemed, too many people in London and all looking for work. The replies were mostly the same:

'Sorry, son, no vacancies.'

'Sorry, lad, it's end of season.'

"Oo the 'ell d'you think I am, Croesus or Jesus Christ?'

'Sod off before I call the cops.'

After a week he wasn't looking presentable, far from it. Dirty tank top and jeans that had never been off him since he'd scarpered from Portsmouth, wild eyes, haggard face, lank and dirty hair – no wonder the bastards talked about the cops. He'd nicked food when he could. When he couldn't, he searched through the night's dustbins for scraps, like a scavenging cat. Nicked other things too, including cash when an easy mugging job showed up. He wouldn't risk going to the Social Security because they would dig out the truth and send him back to Pompey and the orphanage. He continued to sleep where he could, slept very rough amongst the litter and the empty tin cans, covering himself with newspaper or sacks, or dossing in doorways, car parks, stationary railway trains at the big termini, or just huddled up on a pavement somewhere.

Not much of a life. But it had come to a merciful end when he'd been found by the Salvation Army. He'd been fed, given a night in a hostel, given a load of advice. With the Sally Army behind him, things had changed. He got a job, not much of one but something to tide over: the Army told him he was in fact too old now to be sent back to the orphanage so that was no longer a worry. They soon found him somewhere to live, a room shared with another youth. He didn't look back. One day he passed a naval recruiting office and that got his mind working again along the lines of an old interest. He applied to join and was accepted. Things were going right at last. They stayed right until at the end of his enlistment period he came out of the Navy and met up with Wayne and the Big Clout ...

Wayne's shout came down from the deck. 'Kev! Up 'ere.'

'What is it?'

'Boat.'

Kevin got up from the bunk, bent quickly and kissed the girl's hair, then left the cabin.

EIGHT

'It's a boat,' Lockhart said at the same time as, across the water, Wayne yelled down to the cabin. 'A big one, a power-boat.'

Karen said, 'Like the others, it'll just pass us by without a care in the world.' She spoke bitterly. The food had all gone now and they had no strength left. They were just drifting: Lockhart had been unusually cack-handed with the sail in a heavy gust of wind and it had torn in half. It hadn't been at all new; now it was useless. They had very little idea, too, whereabouts they were. They must have missed the Cotswolds like the Mendips.

'It's altering,' Lockhart said. 'It's coming towards us!' Excitement gripped: salvation, just about in time. They couldn't have gone on much longer. So far as he could see, the approaching boat didn't look overcrowded, just reasonably full ... surely they would find room for two adults and two children?

The big boat came nearer, moving fast, looking as though it was about to hit them amidships rather than reduce speed to take them off. Karen said in a suddenly scared voice, 'I don't like the look of them, James.'

'Beggars can't be choosers.'

There seemed to be some argument going on aboard the power-boat, a lot of arm-waving and loud shouts that came down onto the Lockharts, along the wind. Argument there was: Wayne was after sport. The collision course was intentional and was his idea. He wanted some action, was going to have himself some fun. There was a strong smell of beer in the wheelhouse. The bar had been well stocked. Wayne had been sloshing it, spilling almost as much as he drank, after a while. There was a mad look in his eyes as he gripped the wheel like a vice, heading for the dinghy.

'What are you at?' Kevin demanded.

'Chase the fuckers.'

'They're bloody stationary! Sitting ducks, Wayne – for Christ's sake –'

'Fuck off,' Wayne said. He swept a heavy arm sideways, took Kevin off balance. Kevin lurched and fell over the step leading up to the wheelhouse and somersaulted to the deck. Wayne held the wheel steady. No one else interfered; some of them cheered Wayne on. There was something hilarious in the dead-scared, almost unbelieving looks of the people in the small boat. With Wayne in full control the power-boat took the dinghy slap amidships and carved through like a knife through butter.

In Shaftesbury Captain Wilson's two nephews had reached the Grosvenor Hotel more or less without incident, pushing through the mob. Just a few days ago these people had not been a mob at all. They had been following their trades or professions, their love lives and private interests, and then disaster had come to bring an end to law and order and they had reacted. Their one interest now was to remain alive until the waters receded and that meant they had to eat and drink. When the town had been virtually out of food and water other than what could be boiled, a helicopter lift had come in with supplies, little enough for the survivors but it would have to suffice. More would be on its way, the crew had said. The supplies had been lowered on the winch, in a number of metal containers, along with two men from the RAF Regiment armed with quick-firing rifles. The food had been basic: bread, dried milk, dried fruit, that sort of thing. The Wilson nephews were told this by their sister, whom they found intact in the hotel. She said the supplies had been landed in the car park just along the road, and four of the townspeople had volunteered to be responsible for the issue of minute rations. One was a retired colonel, one a local butcher, another a bank manager, and the fourth a solicitor. The food had been taken under guard to the hotel kitchens: the Grosvenor was now the seat of such local government as existed. It was also in use by the police.

'Was there any trouble?' one of the nephews asked.

'The RAF chaps had to aim their guns, that's all. It did the trick.'

'And now? Since they left?'

'Touch and go,' the girl answered. 'Luckily there's some sensible people around. The fact that we've been promised more supplies is helping. They'll wait and see ... for a while, anyhow.'

The nephews, Peter and Harry Henschel, exchanged glances: they had already told Anne they had come to bring her to safety aboard their uncle's boat but she had been non-committal. Now, she had spoken of 'we' having been promised further supplies. Peter asked, 'Well?'

'Well, what?'

'Coming? Uncle Bill doesn't want to linger. The situation's nasty.'

She shook her head. 'No, Pete. I'm staying. I can help here ... what you've told me – about Mum and Dad. I don't want to see the *Ethel Margaret* again now. And I want to be busy, I want to help. I'll be all right. As a matter of fact I'm acting as the colonel's assistant and I can't let him down.'

'You're a beleaguered fortress, Anne. The hotel is, I mean.'

'Yes, but –'

'Have you any means of defence? Any guns?'

'There's some sporting rifles, shot-guns.'

'Every time a helicopter comes in with supplies, you'll get a riot.'

She nodded: that couldn't be denied. She said, 'We'll cope. They're not all loonies, as I said. We've got several policemen, too.'

'Not much use against all that lot.' Harry Henschel swept an arm around towards the roadway outside the hotel. The entry to the courtyard, where the supplies had been taken through to the kitchens, had been barricaded but the crowd was milling about and had that threatening look they had all noticed when the *Ethel Margaret* had made its approach over the flooded streets, up the hill that lay beneath.

'It'll be just the same everywhere else,' Anne said. 'Wherever you go, wherever there's survivors. Every survivor will have been … washed up to the higher ground with no food or water. They'll all be the same. We just have to cope, that's all.' She added, 'Water's just one thing. We're getting by by boiling the floodwater and rationing it out. Everyone with a kitchen above water, including the hotel of course.'

'What happens when the power supplies give out?'

She shrugged. 'Same as I just said. The whole country's in it. Shaftesbury's nothing special. We'll all find a way.'

Harry and Peter once again exchanged glances: Anne had always been one to find a way and when her mind was made up that was it, right from early childhood. She was tenacious, though she didn't look it. Physically she was on the frail side, thin in face and body, with a pale skin made paler by thick dark-brown hair. She had a defenceless look that was wholly deceptive. The Henschel brothers could remember the times she'd turned the tables on childhood tormentors, boys and girls intent on taunting as boys and girls were. At school she'd held her own with equanimity; and she had won out in her choice of a hotel career although the Henschel parents had been dead against it, seeing it as an unsuitable career for a girl who'd got nine O levels and three A levels, all at good grades, and whom they'd seen in a profession such as medicine or the law, or even the diplomatic service. Anne had stuck to her guns; and she was doing so now. It was in her face, in her straight blue eyes.

Peter said, 'Righto. It's your decision.'

She kissed them both, hugged them. They had always been a close family. Her distress at the news of the parents had been obvious but she had controlled it. Peter and Harry knew the reaction would come when they had left her, or anyway when she had a moment to think, to revert to the news which in fact must have been more than half expected. No families would have been left unbereaved. 'We'll be back,' Peter said. 'Just a word with Uncle Bill first.' They would stick together. They knew that their uncle would agree wholeheartedly. Really Shaftesbury was no worse a place to remain in than anywhere else, and Uncle Bill, though he'd wanted to reach the Welsh mountains, wouldn't leave Anne behind. The way back to the old Thames barge was aided by the arrival overhead of another helicopter presumably bringing more supplies. The crowd surged towards the car park, leaving the main street uncluttered.

The little dinghy named *Good Hope* was no more than a scattered jumble of shattered woodwork and strips of canvas from the already split sail. James Lockhart was gone: the knifing bows of the power-boat had smashed directly into his body and then he had been cut up by the blades of the screw as the power-boat passed over him. His body was somewhere beneath the floodwater and the scummy surface had been reddened with blood. Karen was screaming in the water; Rosemary clung to her, screaming too. David, his face white and terrified, hung on to what was left of the dinghy's stern section, which held him just above the water.

The power-boat swept on and away, then seemed to turn in a half circle as though it was coming back for a pick-up. But it didn't come all the way back. Its course veered, leaving a twisting wake behind, and a moment later somebody fell from it and vanished beneath the water. Whoever it was, he or she was left behind as the boat steadied and went away at full speed. Karen Lockhart, now not screaming but red-eyed from the dirty water and the sudden total shattering of her life and a feeling of utter desolation and desperation, saw something else.

Another boat, also under power, coming in quite fast.

She waved an arm, treading water, Rosemary's weight beginning to pull her down. There was an answering wave from the boat: she had just to hang on for long enough. It seemed an eternity. She was aware of someone swimming towards her, from where the first power-boat had been when it had started to turn about, where the body had gone overboard.

The second boat came in close, stopping its engines and drifting up alongside. Assisted by his grandson Commander McNaughten leaned down over the gunwale with a lifebelt and words of encouragement. 'Ups-a-daisy, then, gently does it. You're all right now. Children! My God. Who were those buggers – do you know?'

He had addressed Karen. Through her tears she said she had no idea. McNaughten didn't ask further questions. He shook a frustrated fist at the now distant power-boat: a chase would be quite useless; compared with the other boat, the *Hilda* was a plodder, no speed to speak of. Vicki went below with Karen and the two

children. Vicki got their wet clothes off, found a
dressing-gown for Karen and blankets for the children,
and got Karen on to one of the bunks. McNaughten
came down, said there was no hope of pursuit. 'Bloody
shame we can't *shoot* them,' Vicki said, sounding vicious.
She'd suffered in her own young life from people who
found cruelty funny. People who just used you.

McNaughten asked where the *Good Hope* had been
going.

'I – I don't know. We'd lost our bearings ... and the
sail split, and – and –' Karen started crying again, big
sobs that racked her body. She held the two children
tight against her; they cried as well.

McNaughten looked baffled, helpless: he was no
hand with crying women. His daughter-in-law Mary was
in the galley, preparing hot drinks and food for the
three castaways. Vicki took over. She gathered up the
children, pulled them away from the bunk. 'Now, look,'
she said, 'your mum needs rest, see? She'll be all right,
so will you if you come with me. We've got a pussy ...
d'you like cats?'

David said yes, he did. 'Where is she?'

'It's a he. Come outside and we'll find him. His name's
Pum.'

They went with Vicki on deck. A long tabby tail was
visible, stuck out from behind a ventilator. As they
approached the tail disappeared and a face was seen.
Big wide eyes and long white whiskers, a somewhat fat
body behind it. A friendly cat. As David reached out a
hand a deep purr started up. The eyes closed and the
neck extended, the face rubbing against the boy's hand.
It was almost as though the cat understood.

Madame Smith alias Mocatta (or the other way round,
no one had ever really known for sure), had reached
Hawes and, still huffy and sensitive about her driver's
play on words, had passed on along the A684 in the
direction of Kendal. The ancient bus, lurching and
noisy, passed a number of stragglers on foot and was in

its turn hooted at and passed by a large number of cars, the exodus still making its way as far north as possible to keep well ahead of the waters.

En route they got some news: a man who'd passed them and was found again farther on, standing by his overloaded car that had boiled. Clouds of steam came from the radiator. In the car were two old people, a younger woman, three children and a Rottweiler plus a bootful, the lid being open so full was it, of food and water containers, plus one suitcase. There was a rise in the roadway just where the car had stopped, and the bus came to a halt alongside as Albert wrenched at the gears, seeking first and not finding it.

Madame Smith leaned from her window, hat at odds with the Yorkshire Dales. From the windows behind her the young ladies looked out, eyelids fluttering professionally. Madame Smith bowed as best she could in the circumstances and said, 'Good-morning.'

'Good-morning.'

'Them as speed,' Madame Smith said grandly, 'them as *belt* past other people what haven't got fast cars, gets what they deserve.'

'D'you mind?' the man said wearily. 'Do me a favour, eh?'

Madame Smith leaned the other way, towards the driver's cab. 'Common as dirt,' she said, and turned back again, heaving her bosom. 'Where you bloody from, may I ask?'

'London. Clapham.'

'I'm from London too. The –'

'What's that lot? A circus?' The man was staring at the young ladies.

'There's no call to be rude. If I might ask a civil question and 'ope to get a civil hanswer, 'ave you any news of 'ow things are down south?'

'Bad. Very, very bad. Nothing functioning. Flood's getting worse, so I've heard. Past York now. Place called Boroughbridge and going father north up the A1. I reckon –' The man broke off, gave a shout and a whistle: the Rottweiler had broken free, scrambling out over the geriatrics' knees, and was beating it towards some sheep the other side of a stone wall that he'd cleared with ease. The animal took no notice of its master, made a beeline for the nearest sheep and clasped its jaws around its neck.

'Goodness gracious me!' Madame Smith said. 'Fancy letting it do that to a defenceless bloody sheep!'

Albert got his gears in at last. 'Nice meal for someone,' he said as the double-decker ground on again, up the hill. 'Be a lot more o' that I shouldn't wonder.'

They had Sedbergh ahead of them according to the road map. 'Sedbergh,' Madame Smith said reflectively. 'Remember Lady Whatsit, do you? Come from a big 'ouse somewhere up this way.'

'What 'appened to her?' Suddenly Albert seemed to remember. 'Was it 'er what 'ad that Gyppo bloke –?'

'Yes,' Madame Smith said. "*E* 'ad a big 'un an' all. Whopper. *Too* big. Peritonitis. Took a lot of getting out of, that did. Anyway, point is, she used to talk about the big school in Sedbergh. Public school, young nobs. What they used to get up to! During the 'olidays it was, no hanky-panky in term time she said.' She fluffed out her blue rinse. 'Term time, the 'ead teacher was too bloody fly.'

'So?'

'Use your loaf. Ready-made clientele and all of 'em decent young blokes. We stop in Sedbergh, see what 'appens.'

The mobile brothel moved on, a bus of ill repute. The day began to darken, the high fells casting their deep shadows over the dales. It grew colder and the girls huddled together, two to a seat. Madame Smith turned in her seat and spoke in a loud, carrying voice to the girls on the lower deck. They were to be ready to start work again in Sedbergh, make what cash they could to carry them all on until the floods subsided and they could resume a more normal routine. The clientele would be different up here, Madame Smith said, but they mustn't complain and they mustn't show their feelings. After the pep talk the young ladies, intrigued, giggled about schoolboys and fell farmers, young innocents and rough men who would smell of beer and cow dung, wear hob-nailed boots with mud half-way up their gaitered legs, displaying long-johns made of flannel once the trousers were off.

It would make a change.

NINE

The Minister for Health, safely aboard the aircraft carrier, had had endless discussions with his various under-secretaries, with other departments, and with the PM. The health of the survivors was naturally of paramount concern. According to reports from the regions virtually all the country's hospitals south of a line drawn from Ripon in North Yorkshire south-westerly to Preston in Lancashire were under water. There had in fact been time to evacuate the great majority of the patients and staffs before the inundation had come; the result was unbelievable over-crowding of the hospitals in the areas still free of the water. Makeshift accommodation had been found in such places as empty warehouses, in rows of sub-standard housing awaiting demolition, with gaping, glassless windows boarded up. The surroundings were unpropitious to say the least and the doctors were fiendishly overworked in doing what they could, which wasn't much, to stem the spread of disease. Everything was rife: bacilliary dysentery, typhoid, children's diseases of measles, chicken-pox and mumps, all added to the normal run of the medical wards and the geriatric wards.

Advice poured from the medical experts: do this, do that, do the other. Above all improvise and don't lose your nerve. The Government, still in being, was in control and all possible help would be provided as soon as proper arrangements had been made. Food was of course a basic problem in the flooded areas: so much had been lost either growing in the rich fields of the South and in East Anglia or lying in tins and deep freezers in the flooded homes and supermarkets.

Shoals of fish were swimming across the land: herring from northern waters, displaced perhaps by the cataclysmic ocean upheaval, sole, hake, dace, skate, haddock. Fishing was not advised: the fish were swimming in contaminated water. In any case thanks to cuts over the years in the extent of the seal cull, seals had proliferated and had, like the herring, been diverted south and they were seen everywhere, hundreds of them, devouring the fish before the human survivors would have had much of a chance. Nature was in the throes of total upset.

Shaftesbury was one of the areas to be hit early by typhoid. Dr Hannington, one of the general practitioners working around the clock, believed this could have come from the fish. Either that or some people hadn't been conscientious enough over boiling their drinking water. You always had to suffer the fools. Hannington, who had not long completed his GP training, was faced with apparently endless cases of headache, constipation changing later to diarrhoea, nose-bleeds, rising temperature, abdominal pain and rash. The supplies of chloramphenicol began to run out. And there were far from enough nurses to go round. Good nursing was the first essential after the chloramphenicol. One of those who volunteered to act as a kind of auxiliary nurse was Anne Henschel. As the days had passed since her brothers had so suddenly appeared, she had seen that the sick were of more immediate importance than her self-imposed task of acting as secretary to the colonel in charge of food supplies. Peter and Harry, coming back to her from the *Ethel Margaret*, had joined in the food guard. They had told her that Uncle Bill had sailed on, out of Shaftesbury, but had told them they must take their own decision as to themselves.

'He's got a load of people to think about,' Harry had said. 'Gatecrashers really, but still survivors. He's going to head for a less crowded spot – if he can find one.'

'Top of a hill?'

'I think that's the general idea.'

'Lonely! No food. No means of boiling water.'

'You know Uncle Bill. He'll improvise. Basically, he'll still be living aboard the old barge. He said that was a better prospect for his passengers than sending them ashore here, where they wouldn't be wanted to swell the numbers.'

Anne thought about that when later she did what she could for the typhoid cases, bringing sips of boiled water, precious water, smoothing brows, listening to rambling discourses emerging from high fever. Uncle Bill had been right: there were too many people here already, clustered in what was left of the town. And Uncle Bill had weathered plenty of storms, plenty of fraught situations, in his time. He would make out: her one regret, really, was that she had been responsible for stopping her brothers from going with him. Yet, all said and done, that too had been their own decision …

'You've done very well,' Dr Hannington told her at the end of the first day of patient care. He looked at her critically. 'You're tired out. Go and get some sleep.'

'I'm all right,' she insisted, but felt herself sway a little.

'I say you're not. Look, I'll see you back to the hotel.' He took her arm firmly and propelled her along the street. 'I'm going to get some sleep myself as a matter of fact.' Hannington, young and single, had lived in a flat in the lower part of the town; this together with the GP Medical Centre had been under water since the start of the flood, and he'd been found accommodation, as one of the town's essential persons, in the Grosvenor. 'But first I feel like a drink. You could do with a shot of whisky yourself. How's the supply?'

She said, 'I can find some. For you. Not me.'

He grinned. 'It's a prescription. I'm going to need you. It'll help you to relax. All right?'

'Oh, all right,' she said, and when they reached the hotel she went to find the bottle. There was not much left: bottle in the singular was about right.

The man named Kevin, who had tried to stop Wayne ramming the Rushworths' boat and had been knocked over the side as a result, had not been found. He had gone over the side away from the boat approaching from the general direction of Norwich, and having been knocked out by Wayne's fist he had sunk immediately without a struggle. Karen Lockhart had been too distressed to say anything of what she had seen. Later, she remembered; but by that time it was too late.

She didn't care in any case. She was numbed by the sudden, so cruel loss of her husband. A vicious act, mindless, inhuman ... the sort of thing Britain had grown used to in the days before the flood. Every time you picked up a newspaper: rapes, muggings, murders, dreadful violence for absolutely no gain, just the satisfaction of some terrible, bestial desire to hurt. That was what made it so terrible: you could understand the ordinary criminal, the thief, the house-breaker, the hot-head who hit out during a dispute and did his opponent grievous bodily harm. But who could ever even begin to comprehend the outlook of a mugger, a vandal for the sake of wanton destruction and the urge to fulfil a blood-lust? The anguish that they left behind them ...

Lying on the bunk she had been given, in a cabin shared with the old lady, McNaughten's wife, who lay like a zombie clasping and unclasping the fingers of her right hand and staring with dulled eyes at the white-painted deckhead above her, she was not to know that she was looking at a mugger's victim. No one had told her; she had tried to speak to the old woman but there had been no response and when she'd said

something to the girl Vicki she had been told who she
was and that she was doolally.

'Just save your breath. Poor old thing. Just senile, I
s'pose. Better to die really, don't you think?'

'Yes,' Karen said, thinking of James who was, or had
been, years and years away from dying. She closed her
eyes and tears ran from below the lids. Vicki said
something she didn't catch and she heard the girl going
back on deck, up the two steps that led through the
wheelhouse. Soon after that she seemed to have drifted
off to sleep despite her sorrows but when she woke, and
it was dark, and the boat was still moving on for she
knew not where, it all returned to her again, the whole
nightmare, and she called out frantically for David and
Rosemary, half believing something terrible had
happened to them as well as to James. Mary Rushworth
came to her and said they were asleep. She would or
course bring them, but wouldn't it be best if they slept
on?

'Yes,' she said dully. 'Are they all right?'

'Yes, they are. Don't worry about them.'

Karen's lips trembled. 'You've been very good.'

'Nonsense,' Mary Rushworth said briskly. 'You're
very welcome. We were getting bored with our own
company.' She paused. 'If you want to know where
we're going, it's North.'

'North?' Karen repeated vaguely.

'Yorkshire, perhaps farther north. We've been
heading west so far, but now my father thinks we'd do
better to get as far north as possible. Even Scotland,
perhaps.'

'It's a long way, isn't it?'

Yes, Mary said, it was. She looked down shrewdly at
the girl on the bunk. There had been something extra
behind the words, not merely an expression of a long
journey by boat but something deeper. Mary Rushworth thought of her own home in Cambridge, and that
of her parents. What would it be like beneath the
waters? Fish, nameless horrors that dwelt and crawled

on slimy stomachs in floodwater, oozing through doors and windows that could have been smashed by the weight of water, crawling over the flooded Wilton carpets, over antique furniture, some of it handed down over many generations, some of it bought in auctions and antique shops ... She pulled herself up. No point in thinking about what was gone – her whole life had gone, or at any rate had changed so suddenly and dramatically, and would never be the same again. Coffee mornings, afternoon teas in the many Cambridge cafés filled in term time with undergraduates, when term was down, by hordes of tourists of all nationalities; American, French, German, Scandinavian, Italian, Indian, Chinese, Japanese, all drifting along slowly, blocking the narrow pavements as they gazed up at some architectural splendour or other or crossed from the market square to bring human inundation to King's College chapel. University functions, mainly quiet affairs consisting of a little sherry and some excellent food, and dusty-dry professors and masters of colleges not quite so dry. And affairs of another sort: Mary Rushworth's heart seemed to turn over as she thought of a lecturer named Tom Chase. Lecturers and their wives, however academic their environment, however discreet they had to be, were as human as anyone else. Where was Tom Chase now? She didn't know if he was alive or dead. In the panic that had struck Cambridge as the low-lying Fens began to come under threat, she had met him for what might prove to be the last time, met as if by chance on the quadrangle at St John's and walked together over the replica of the Bridge of Sighs, an appropriate enough place for a parting. It was now, he'd said, a time for husbands to stand by their wives and children. She couldn't argue against that: she knew the total inevitability, and for her own part she was fond of Charles if only from long association and shared memories.

Seeing that Karen Lockhart was becoming more

aware, Mary was about to sit down on the bunk beside
her and get her to relieve her mind by talking if she
wanted to, when she was interrupted.

There was a commotion from outside, on the after
deck. A shout from Charles, an oath from her father,
and a child crying.

'What is it?' Karen asked in alarm.

'I'll go and see. You stay right where you are.'

'My children –'

'They'll be all right. My husband and father – they
know what they're doing.'

John was in the wheelhouse and the boat was turning
in a circle. Mary asked what was up. Her father was in
the stern with Charles and Vicki and the two Lockhart
children. John said it was the cat. Pum had gone
overboard. Mary asked, 'Overboard? But for God's
sake, how? I mean, a *cat* –'

'We don't know, mum. Dad says the water's
dangerous for anyone to go in. I'm bringing us up
alongside, and they'll grab from aft where the
freeboard's lower.'

Mary, looking anxiously ahead said, 'I can't see
anything.' Then, as they came closer, there was a
curfuffle in the water, a distraught face, whirling paws.
'Oh, now I've got him ... poor old Pum!' She was almost
crying. She clutched at John. 'John, he's gone under!'

John was about to say something when there was a
sudden movement in the stern, a splash, another oath
from his grandfather. Vicki had gone in and was
swimming for where the cat had last been seen. She
went under herself, surfaced with a pathetic, struggling
bundle that opened its mouth to emit hopeless,
strangled cries.

'Damn silly thing to do,' McNaughten said, his face
red with anger. Not all of it for Vicki: there would be an
enquiry, and McNaughten reckoned one of the
Lockhart children would be found guilty.

'She's done it, anyway,' Charles said. He and his
father-in-law stood by with a lifebuoy and a strong line.

Dripping water, cat and girl emerged and were hauled over the gunwale. Both were shivering.

'Stupid girl,' McNaughten said, but he said it gruffly and without blame – almost, for him, kindly. He was as fond of the bloody cat as anyone, he told himself. But it was still a reckless act. The water was appallingly filthy: both girl and cat stank like sewers.

The policeman in Sedbergh lifted his chequer-banded cap to scratch his head. 'I don't rightly know and that's a fact, Mr Blundell,' he said.

'Well, if you don't, Jack, then I bloody well do!' Blundell spoke energetically: he was an energetic man, never still, barrel-shaped and red in the face with a bluish nose. A member of the North Yorkshire County Council. Blundell was a regular chapel goer and was one of those, and there were not a few, who firmly believed that the flood was indeed the work of an angry God who had decided that the time had come for another lesson on sin. And the crowded, semi-derelict double-decker bus that had wended its way into Sedbergh from somewhere south – had borne every evidence of the devil's work.

He said, 'It'll have to be turned back, that's what.'

'I've no reason to do that, Mr Blundell.'

Blundell stamped a foot. 'Just use your bloody eyes!'

PC Slatterthwaite looked again and rose and fell on the balls of his feet, his hands clasped behind his back. Mr Blundell was in a rare old state. Never had he been heard to swear before, to use the word 'bloody'. Obviously, he felt very deeply about the vehicle. Up to a point Slatterthwaite could understand: they certainly didn't want trouble, they had enough already with all the people converging on the small town and its one long main street of shops. But what could he do?

'No crime's been committed,' he said.

'You can get them on summat!'

'I don't know as I can, Mr Blundell, the law –'

'Causing an obstruction! Look at the size of it!'

'They're all causing some sort of obstruction, Mr
Blundell. Times like this, you have to accept –'

'I'll not accept that bus, never! I'll not! Just bloody
look at it! It yells sin! Those women. Paint and goo-goo
eyes. It's obvious what it is. It even *smells* like a brothel!'
Mr Blundell aimed a thick forefinger at Slatterthwaite
and stuck it into the uniformed chest. 'You watch, right?
Watch and pounce the first time you see anything that
seems unlawful. Day an' night, right? Day an' night.'

'I can't be everywhere at once, Mr Blundell. I'm the
one and only police officer in Sedbergh just now, you
know that. There's a lot to see to. Possible vandalism for
one thing ... churches and chapels, private property,
homes and shops –'

'All right, Jack, all right. I take the point. I'm not an
unreasonable man, never 'ave bin. I've got friends
who'll help out, take turns to watch –'

'Vigilantes, Mr Blundell, you know as well as –'

'Not vigilantes. Men what know sin when they see it
and report the observed facts. They won't take action on
their own. That'll be up to you. Don't you worry about
vigilantes. I'll 'ave a word with the Chief Constable, put
it all on a proper footing, all right?'

Blundell turned away, bounced along the crowded
street, pushing and shoving, a busy and self-important
man. PC Slatterthwaite sighed and blew out his cheeks,
the healthy cheeks of a man who had spent a lifetime in
the open air of the North Riding. One thing Blundell
hadn't mentioned as a sanction against the double-
decker bus was the state of the vehicle, which was quite
something to see. Worth pursuing, or was it? If you
pronounced the vehicle unfit, then you could hardly
move it on and Sedbergh would be stuck with it.
Blundell wouldn't like that. Slatterthwaite mounted his
bicycle and moved along slowly, making up his mind. If
he'd been Mr Blundell he'd have turned a blind eye:
there was more to worry about than a busload of women
with possibly doubtful morals, a damn sight more.
True, it was difficult to turn a blind eye and not look as

though you were doing so: the bus was eye-catching right enough, couldn't be avoided. Entering the one-way system from the South, it had parked where there was an open space on its left, and well-to-do house property on the right. There might well be complaints and if there were, well, then he would have to deal with them.

Better just take a preliminary look.

The fast power-boat carrying the Big Clout (bar Kevin) was now also moving north, as far north as it could get was Wayne's idea now. That other boat had come at a dangerous moment, and its occupants would have seen the ramming. Some of the rammed dinghy's crew could have drowned. And there was Kevin – that might have been seen too. With so much sea around them, it made sense to scarper from the scene of two crimes, not that there would be much law around, but Wayne knew from experience that a clean get away was the first line of defence.

Wayne hadn't always made a total get away; mostly, though. Muggings were easy, sometimes very profitable, and muggers seldom got caught provided they made themselves scarce and didn't do it too often in one locality. Anonymity was a good safeguard. It was, in a way, like a murder in which the pigs couldn't find a motive. Motive was just about the only thing that could start the pigs off. Robbery, greed, passion, jealousy, plain enmity, advantage of one sort or another to be gained from someone's death. Of course it did depend on not being seen, but anyone with his head screwed on could guarantee that. Wayne had gone beyond theory; liking killing, and wanting to prove his theory to himself, he had found a totally anonymous youth at a bus-stop one night, late and in dirty weather with no one else around. That had been in London, or more accurately a suburb of London ... he'd knifed the youth, left him dead and disappeared. He'd gone back to Pompey and read it all in the papers and the pigs had never come within a hundred miles of bothering him. How could you get a bloke who'd done a bloke he didn't even know?

What eventually he'd gone down for was beating up a mate so badly that it very nearly was murder. Wayne had gone to the Moor. He wondered now, as the power-boat headed up the backbone of England towards Derbyshire and its peaks, what things were like currently in Dartmoor gaol. Princetown stood high up, it could be above the floodwater, but of course cut off, the screws isolated from help if there was any trouble. Trouble there well could be, the cons taking the opportunity of a break-out, chancing survival afterwards. Of course, if the flood was that deep, the Moor *could* even be right under and would have been evacuated presumably. Funny to think of the cells all flooded, and the workshops and that, and the screws' mess down the road ...

By now Captain Wilson had found the Welsh mountains that had been his original goal. Approaching what had been the Welsh border with England he had found shoaling water, probably over the Malvern hills since he had moved north-westwards from the Shaftesbury area. Then he had come to what he estimated to be the Black Mountains with the Brecon Beacons a little to the south.

'Can't be sure,' he said to Evan Thomas senior as the hills loomed up, distantly ahead of his course. 'Take a look yourself – you should be better than me at recognition.'

Evan Thomas had looked for a long while. 'It is hard to say, Captain. They look different now, surrounded with the water. And I am not in fact very familiar with that part, though certainly I have been there.'

Wilson nodded. 'Well, anyway, it's dry land.'

'And crowded, I think.'

'That was always to be expected.'

'You have my revolver, Captain Wilson.'

Wilson laughed. 'I don't propose to turn this into a shooting-match!'

'Not if it can be avoided, no, of course not.'

'We all have equal rights in this situation. There'll have to be give and take on all sides.'

Evan Thomas was silent for a while, then he said tentatively, 'Do you not think, Captain, it would be better to keep going? There is likely danger in joining a community at this stage, I believe. They were not friendly in Shaftesbury. And one day the flood will drain away.'

'Not before we starve. Look at the numbers! I've not food or water to cope.'

'We can boil the floodwater as we have been doing –'

'The galley fuel isn't going to last.'

'And for the food, fish. There are the fish.'

'We've been into that, Mr Thomas. It's not safe. You've only to see the debris. The chances are the fish'll have been feeding on corpses. We have to face it.'

'Yes.' Evan Thomas looked around the empty horizons astern and to port and starboard, the hills now growing larger before them as they neared sanctuary of a kind. Again now there was a hint of rain – heavy cloud coming up towards them from the South-west, borne along on an increasing wind. A threatening day it looked to be, with the sun going down now and the edges of the cumulus formation tinged with bright light, and below it the water with a curious purple look as though it had been steeped in strong dye, and there was an unearthly green along the horizons beneath the clouds. Evan Thomas gave a sudden shiver. There was evil around, he was convinced of that. It was as though the flood had put out the lights of God and substituted for them the darker lights of the devil.

'I do not like it,' he said.

Wilson felt irritated. He recognized the dangers but knew he had no real alternative. Wherever he touched dry land in isolated places, the tops of the hills, the danger would be the same. It was true to say that

greater safety would lie far to the north, where it was at
least possible the flood had not yet reached and there
would be room for survivors, but the North was a long
way – he had no means of knowing for sure just how far
north the floods reached – and he simply hadn't got the
food to last, however minute the ration. As he had said
to Evan Thomas, there was not much galley fuel aboard.
It had not in the first place been his intention even to go
as far as Shaftesbury. And in any case, they couldn't
float around for ever and a day.

But he compromised, to satisfy Evan Thomas. 'We'll
carry out a recce,' he said.

TEN

'A recce,' Evan Thomas said. 'Yes, that is a good idea. In
my view, you know, the top of a mountain is at best no
better than being aboard a boat. There will be no food on
the top of a mountain any more than here, and so long as
we are floating we can at least move on farther.'

Wilson grunted. What the Welshman had said made
plenty of sense and as a seaman he should himself
prefer to remain out on the waters. But some instinct
propelled him on: he believed there would not be just a
mountain-top; behind the peaks themselves would be
high plateaux, standing high enough to be above the
flood, and with space, and something eatable, where
with any luck they could survive, eke out an existence
until the floods subsided. He looked with a seaman's eye
at the cloud formation, and the wind's direction, and
the weird light. By now the rain had started, was in fact
lashing down, and the day had darkened as the curious
colouring began to go.

There was a flash of lightning, a brilliant streak –
forked lightning, jagging down from the heavens to
touch the high ground ahead. On its heels the clap and

rattle of thunder, a sound of tumult and doom in the circumstances of their approach to the mountains turned into islands.

Evan Thomas, now joined by his son, was looking more and more apprehensive. He asked how Wilson meant to carry out his recce. 'Will you anchor, Captain?'

Wilson shook his head. 'Doubtful, unless the soundings show gently sloping ground on the approach. I don't think they will. The high points'll be sheer, too sheer to make a holding ground. If I can't find something to make a line fast to, as we did in Shaftesbury, I'll have to lie off and put a party ashore to take a look around.'

'Ashore,' Evan Thomas the son said wonderingly. 'Ashore, on the Black Mountains! It sounds funny, does that. To talk of landing-parties, in the middle of Wales!' He shook his head, as gloomy as his father. He thought about Barry to the south-west, Barry under water, and Barry Island – Butlin's, where the families from the valleys had enjoyed themselves without having to pay through the nose for their pleasures. The atmosphere had been very good, everyone determined to enjoy themselves for their brief week away from the daily chores and the sadness of the valleys, mostly lying silent with the pits closed down and the great wheels of the winding gear motionless and always the great slagheaps looming above, a constant source of anxiety in case they should be dislodged by heavy rainfall, and slip. Now all those slagheaps would be gone, their bases eroded first and then all the great edifices flattened and the valleys under layers of ancient coal-dust floating on the water, the mines themselves flooded, the winding gear like rusted metal skeletons standing useless guard.

'The water is rough,' Evan Thomas senior said. 'A rough sea, over the Welsh borders!'

Wilson nodded. The *Ethel Margaret* was pitching and water was slopping aboard. The clustered passengers hung on tightly, faces becoming green, bodies and clothing soaked with foul water. Wilson said, 'We'll lie off farther out. I'll not attempt a landing while this lasts.'

The Evan Thomases had been assisting with the handling of the sails after Wilson had left his nephews in Shaftesbury: anticipating just such an emergency at any time, Wilson had given them brief instruction; the elder at any rate, having spent his working life around the ships in Barry docks, was handy enough and quick to learn. They loosened the sheets of the mainsail, gathered in the folds of canvas and secured them along the boom as Wilson once again brought his auxiliary engine alive and turned the barge away from the hilltops. Looking over the side he saw bodies, bloated and horrible. They had seen bodies all the way along – there would be literally millions of them over the flooded parts as a whole, the speed and suddenness of the massive tidal surge would have seen to that – but now the water seemed thick with them. The effects of the wind and the disturbed water ... and, swimming among the dead, seals could be seen, their shiny black humps or puppy-like whiskered faces nudging and pushing and carving a path, the seals that had been displaced from their normal habitats. It made a terrible sight.

What would the end of it all be? Wilson could see nothing but more horror. After the flood, disease would take over. That was inevitable. All those bodies, left behind by the receding waters, strewn across the land.

Illness had struck the Rushworth boat: Vicki from Norwich, on whose body strange slug-like excrescences had already been noted, complained of headache, tiredness and a sick feeling.

'What is it?' Charles Rushworth asked his father-in-law.

'How should I know? Of course, I can make guesses.'

'Your guess would be AIDS.'

'Yes, it would. I've already spoken about –'

'It could be anything. Typhoid, dysentery, even

cholera, I suppose.' The Rushworths, like those aboard the *Ethel Margaret*, had seen bodies in plenty, and for all Charles knew there could be some sort of connection between bodies and cholera, though he had no idea how it was transmitted. His ideas on illness were pretty vague. His father-in-law, who knew everything, or gave the impression that he thought he did, now expounded.

'Headache and a sick feeling, and those discolorations, those blemishes. All right, feeling tired and sick could be any number of things, I agree. We don't seem to have a damn thermometer aboard or I'd have seen to it she took her temperature and reported back. Temperatures mean fever, and fever's always a pointer.'

'What to?'

'Oh, a number of things,' McNaughten said impatiently. 'I don't propose to itemize them all –'

'Because you've already made up your mind, already made a diagnosis: AIDS.'

Breath hissed down the commander's nostrils. 'Now look here, Charles. I've read a booklet called *Medical Briefing on AIDS* or something like that. Very well authenticated and very clearly put –'

'I've read it too.' Charles shifted the wheel a little, to avoid running down a heap, a bundle of clothing head down in the water. Some sort of fish, a big one, seemed to be pecking at it, making runs at it then swirling its tail and going away, only to return for another attack. It wasn't the first time he'd seen something like that, and fishing for food was right out, his stomach simply wouldn't be able to take it.

McNaughten was going on. 'More blemishes! That's the nub, Charles. The matter's deadly serious –'

'I agree, it may be. The point is, there's nothing whatever we can do about it. I believe I've said that before. We're stuck with it, at any rate until we find land somewhere.'

'You're taking it too damn lightly,' McNaughten said. 'One would have thought you'd worry about your wife and son, for a start. And that poor damn girl we picked

up, and her children. Something'll have to be done to
protect them.'

'We can't isolate aboard a small boat.'

'At least we can keep her out of the cabin. And we can
disinfect. I don't believe what the medics say about not
being able to pass it on via lavatory seats and so on,
cutlery, plates, cups. One should play it safe.'

Charles said nothing, just let his father-in-law ramble
on. Of course, the girl *could* have the virus; plenty of
people had, according to the latest figures issued before
the flood, but it was pretty clear that it wasn't all that easy
to catch. The defence was to keep your flies zipped up. If
God had sent the disease as a scourge, then he'd aimed it
very precisely for the at-risk groups, the sleepers-
around. McNaughten could blast off as much as he liked
about lavatory seats and the rest; Charles was content to
believe the medics. Like anyone else with the opportunity, he'd discussed it in college with the medics and
scientists and bio-chemists and they'd all seemed to agree
that sexual intercourse was about the only way you
caught it and anyway there was scant chance of anybody
having it off unseen with anyone else aboard a small
power-boat.

Steering north, Charles kept his eye on the chart.
There were no more recognizable landmarks thrusting
up from the water now; they navigated by dead reckoning. And by dead reckoning Charles believed they
should sight high ground within about twelve hours. The
southern end of the Pennines, in Derbyshire. There they
might get some news of how things were farther to the
north, in Yorkshire perhaps. The boat's radio had in fact
picked up part of a broadcast made on government
authority the day before, transmitting source unknown –
the broadcast was very overlaid with static and they were
able to get very little – but Charles believed it was saying
that the northern part of England was so far largely
untouched.

A long way ahead of the Rushworth boat PC Slatterthwaite had taken the preliminary look at the double-decker bus that he had decided upon.

He could smell it as he approached: scent, very largely, strong scent. Also diesel and oil, the latter having dripped from the sump to leave a spoor behind it.

The windows, those along the lower deck, were curtained. The curtains were drawn across. Slatterthwaite approached from behind, found a lifted corner and peeped. He couldn't see much but what he could see appeared innocent enough: a young lady reading a paperback and looking bored. Slatterthwaite was about to withdraw when the young lady turned a page and in so doing shifted a little in her seat, which was next to the window, and saw his red Yorkshire face looking in.

'Oooh!' she said loudly. 'You dare!'

Somewhat flustered, PC Slatterthwaite straightened and clasped his hands behind his back. At the front of the bus a door opened and a man got down and approached Slatterthwaite. Behind this man came a large woman in a black crêpe-de Chine dress beneath a large hat, a string of pearls and a number of rings and earrings.

The man began speaking but was cut short by the woman. 'All right, Albert, I'll deal with this.' She spoke to Slatterthwaite. ''Oo are you, might I ask?'

'Police –'

'That I can see for myself.' The woman peered ostentatiously at the metal number on Slatterthwaite's shoulder, making a mental note. 'I am Madame Smith. What do you bloody want, eh?' Before Slatterthwaite could answer she went into a tirade. 'Peeping in on my young ladies! Whatever next! Hoping to find bare bloody flesh, what you wouldn't if you knocked proper! I never *'eard* of such a thing, not on the part of the bloody law I 'aven't. Peeping bloody Toms in uniforms, I never did! You just wait till I've made a report to your superiors. I got connections, see, down in London. They're not *all* bloody drowned. I've 'ad cabinet

ministers –' Madame Smith felt an urgent nudge from
her driver and stopped before she became indiscreet.
She placed her hands firmly on her hips. ''Op it! Go on,
'op it!'

She was too much for PC Slatterthwaite: redder in the
face than normal, he turned and mounted his bicycle.
He pedalled away, cursing Mr Blundell: no crime had
been committed – except possibly by himself, at any rate
in that woman's eyes, and she looked the sort who could
put up a good story.

Behind him Madame Smith was laughing, her bosoms
heaving about. She said, 'That's the bloody way, Albert.
Best defence is bloody attack. The fuzz'll think twice in
future. Let's get back aboard. We got some plans to
make. About clients.' Behind Albert, Madame Smith
heaved herself up and sank back in her seat with a sigh.
This would be her first experience of carrying out trade
from a bus; though there had been other unlikely
places, early places when she'd been new to the game,
operating solo and gradually building up her empire.
Backs of cars, of course; behind bushes in parks; in a
vast section of drainpipe by a roadside waiting for the
workmen to join it to the system and bury it; a church
vestry – the organist, that had been; in a stuck lift at the
Inland Revenue, in an unlocked mattress store at St
Thomas's Hospital; in a gents' toilet in a deserted car
park in Bishop's Waltham, Hants; in a fitting room at
the British Home stores; in a beach hut at Worthing
during a working seaside holiday. None of them
perfect, but all of them easier than trying to organize
fifteen young ladies within the confines of a double-
decker bus with all its seats. The clients might prove
difficult: in small communities – Madame Smith had
heard about Yorkshire from Lady Vera – they wouldn't
be keen to share bus seats. When Northerners sinned,
they liked to be in a position to issue strong denials.
Madame Smith would have to use the aisles, and only
two clients at a time, one up and one down.

She swivelled in her seat and addressed the young

ladies. 'Remember this is bloody Sedbergh, not London. Remember all I said earlier. They're going to need warming up ... though my guess is, they won't show much finesse. If bloody any.' She gave a sniff of disdain for Northerners. 'Straight up, the moment you're lying flat. And don't expect no bloody rush. It'll take time for the word to spread. One more thing: we watch out for the law. They'll snoop tonight, bound to, even though that fuzz did get a flea in 'is lug-'ole.'

Around the *Ethel Margaret* there was now a raging thunderstorm; the forked lightning, red, jagged and threatening, acted as lightning usually did at sea: it struck the old barge's masthead, or more strictly the lightning conductor. The resulting clap was immediate and terrifying to the survivors; the boat seemed to lurch sideways, seemed as though the timbers must split and send them all into the foul water. After that, another and another; it was like the ending of the world, a time of uncontrolled fury, violent noise and movement and that red flickering light.

Wilson shouted above the racket, calming incipient panic as best he could. 'Nothing to worry about. I've weathered plenty of storms like this. Out at sea ...'

Out at sea, he thought, having spoken. Where were they now, for God's sake, other than out at sea, the shoreline being the mountain-tops of the Welsh borders? They were joined now to all the great seas, they were one with them, the land gone. For the time being he must wait. He had words with the Evan Thomases, sensible men, asking them to circulate around the overloaded barge and assure the passengers that they would come safely through. By now the water was more than ever disturbed, the wind growing stronger by the minute, the waves increasing in size. As far as the eye could see there were wave-crests, rank on rank, with spume blowing from them to give the appearance of a cloth laid over the water.

Wilson thought about his nephews, left in

Shaftesbury. If trouble came, and despite his reassuring words trouble could come, for the *Ethel Margaret* was taking the battering somewhat badly in her old age, he was going to miss their expertise, their trained knowledge of the barge's capabilities and idiosyncrasies.

Across the water in Shaftesbury, where soon the disturbed weather reached, Wilson's niece Anne Henschel carried on the work of nursing the sick and the injured: there had been a riot when the last helicopter had come in with supplies and a number of people had been hurt, some seriously, when the guarding cordon had been attacked by men and women using anything that could be found as weapons: iron bars, lengths of timber, knives, bricks, stones, plus an assortment of implements belonging to a group of Hell's Angels that had been caught by the flood and marooned in the town. Metal-studded clubs, filed bicycle chains, swinging iron balls with spikes were just a few. There would have been a bloodbath had Anne's colonel not used his sporting shot-gun, first over the heads of the mob and then point-blank into them.

'No damn choice,' he'd said briefly afterwards. And it had worked: the mob had scattered, yelling and screaming. By a stroke of luck none had been killed; but the mob left eight of their number on the ground. With Paul Hannington Anne went out amongst them, at risk of her life. The colonel mustered a party of helpers and the wounded were carried into the Grosvenor Hotel and laid out in the bar and lounge for treatment. Hannington removed the shot and Anne, under his direction, cleaned and bandaged the wounds. In the mean time people were dying from the prevalent typhoid, mainly the old, dying really for want of enough chloramphenicol.

The question arose, how to dispose of the dead?

There was nowhere to bury them, nowhere now to cremate them. The only possible solution was the water, already polluted. A few more corpses would make no difference to the level of pollution as they circulated through the broken windows or doors of the abandoned houses down the hill, like wandering fish.

ELEVEN

By now McNaughten had held his inquiry into the events leading to the cat's immersion, potentially fatal if actually with a happy ending. The boy David was given away by his sister and in floods of tears made an admission.

'Bad lad,' McNaughten said gruffly. 'A defenceless animal. You deserve to be damn well whacked. Don't ever do anything like that again.' In truth he was desperately sorry for the boy, who had seen his father drown as a result of a callous and vicious act; there could even have been a connection of some sort: taking it out on the cat, treating it in the same sort of way? Understanding perhaps, but a rebuke had had to be given. The boy had to know right from wrong if ever they came out of all this; not fair to his character development to let him get away with it entirely. Although in the end it might not matter: McNaughten was growing more and more unhopeful that the waters would ever recede. If the great ice masses didn't refreeze, then certainly the flood wasn't going to go away. He wished he knew more about these things so that he could form some sort of estimate …

The small inquiry over, he found Vicki looking at him and he didn't like the look. He said irritably, 'Do you have to stare like that?'

'No,' she said, shrugging.

'Then kindly stop.'

'I'll stare if I want.'

'You're a very rude and uncooperative girl. I might remind you, you owe your life to us.'

'Maybe. Maybe not.'

'Oh, don't be –'

'There would have been other fucking boats, mate.' She spoke in the sort of tone that she was speaking to a child. McNaughten ignored both the four-letter word and the tone, and turned his back in disgust. But now she wouldn't let him go. She called at his back. 'Think I've got AIDS, you do.'

'What?'

'You've got a loud voice. It carries. I heard all you said.'

McNaughten turned back to face her. 'Now look here, if you've got AIDS –'

'I never said I had.'

'You have the symptoms. One of the symptoms, naturally I don't know about the others –'

'No, you bloody don't. I may have AIDS. Or I may not.'

'You've been exposed?'

'May have. Look, I'm *young*, aren't I? When you're young you do things. Maybe *you* didn't ... not in your day, bloody centuries ago. Anyway, what d'you expect me to do about it now?'

McNaughten said coldly, 'Keep yourself to yourself, don't touch anyone else. We'll find land shortly, that's certain. So until then, and –'

'And after?'

'You'll leave us. But I shall see to it that you're handed over, not just let loose to be free to infect other people.'

There was a glint in her eye and an angry flush had spread over her face. 'Handed over, eh? Just what does that bloody mean, eh? Just tell me.'

'It means what it says. Handed over.'

'No one's handing me over, mate.' She hesitated, eyes fearful: she was in the Rushworths' hands and she knew it. 'Who to?'

'Police –'

'There won't be any bloody law now. And AIDS isn't a crime.'

McNaughten said, 'The whole country hasn't flooded.

Since you're so good at eavesdropping, you might possibly have heard what came over the radio: the North is free so far. Not everything will have collapsed. As to AIDS not being a crime, you may be sure there'll be a pretty rigid control of those likely to have got it. In the circumstances of what everyone's faced with.' He added, 'If not the police, then a hospital. You'd be better off there in any case.'

'Bollocks.' She put her tongue out at him.

'What else would you do? Just answer me that, young woman.'

She didn't answer; she put her tongue out again. McNaughten, worried as they all were, at the end of his tether with Vicki, reached out to give her a cuff. To his astonishment he found his wrist grabbed from behind and looked round into his grandson's face.

'Don't, grandpa. Don't make things worse.' John still held on to the wrist. McNaughten's face was deeply suffused: mortification at being rebuked by his grandson, mortification at having lost his temper, mortification at being made to look a fool. He shook the hand off without a word and went into the wheelhouse, lips quivering with anger. John sat beside Vicki, on the seat in the stern below the gunwale.

'Don't mind him,' he said. 'Bark's worse than his bite.'

'All wind and piss?'

John grinned. 'Yes, largely. Don't blame him too much. You've seen my grandmother. He's never been the same since, has it in for anyone young. You can't really blame him.'

She jeered. 'I've had it tough all my bloody life.'

'You've got plenty of time yet to … let it go into the past. My grandfather hasn't.'

'There's no future for any of us, far as I can see. What's it going to be like after?' When John merely shrugged, unable to answer the question, she went on, 'Can't be bloody worse than before, I s'pose. For me, I mean.'

'Was it that bad?'

'Yes,' she said, 'it was an' all.' She paused, looked into his eyes. 'Want to hear? Or not?'

'If you want to tell me, yes, of course.'

'No "of course" about it,' she said. 'It's sordid. That's what it is, sordid.' That was a word she'd picked up long ago, when the police had escorted her home to Mum in Brighton and had seen how they lived, and the word had also been used in her hearing many times by the Social Security. She told John about it all, the words pouring out in a torrent once she got going. But she didn't say anything about the Norwich killing, the body in the river. She was trying to force that from her mind and in any case if ever the grandfather got to hear of it the old bugger would make sure she was done for the moment they reached dry land.

John heard her out, not saying a word. She sensed his sympathy through his silence and impulsively she reached out to him and the skin of his forearm touched against one of the purplish patches and he flinched away instinctively. Seeing that, she burst into a torrent of tears.

Later that day Karen Lockhart became ill. Mary Rushworth heard sounds of distress and went down to her, watched by the flickering eyes of her stricken mother-in-law, a shapeless huddle on the opposite bunk. Karen said all her limbs were aching and her throat was very sore. There were swollen glands in her neck and her breath was foul. Nobody knew what was the matter with her, but Mary suspected typhoid – that immersion in the water, the filthy, stinking water. But surely the incubation period was a matter of a week or more? No one knew the answer to that, either.

The Big Clout from Cosham in Hampshire was now well to the north, in fact – although this they didn't know – they were moving over Stoke-on-Trent towards Leek and Upper Hulme and heading for the town of Buxton in Derbyshire. Later that day, beneath a black and angry sky, they found the town ahead, a lump on the horizon. They moved in closer; like Shaftesbury, the lower parts of the town lay under flood, the higher parts stood clear. There were big buildings, solid, once prosperous, looking like hotels or council offices or insurance offices. Them, and a lot of people milling about. Closer yet, and then, when they came within range, Wayne shouted from the deck.

'Where's this, eh?'

'Buxton –'

'What's it like?'

'What does it look like?' The voice was surly. A number of people gathered, staring, not looking helpful.

'Friendly lot I don't think,' Wayne said. Coming in closer he called again. "Ow about taking a line? We've sailed far enough. Got any water, 'ave you?'

The man who had called back waved a hand around. 'All you want. No fresh. Little enough food, too many people.'

'Are you saying –?'

'I'm saying you're not welcome, that's what I'm saying.'

'Look, we –'

'You're not wanted here. Go on farther north. There's plenty of land … the flood's held where the rise to the Yorkshire Dales begins. That's where we're going, soon as more helicopters come in. Some's gone already.'

'Well, can't we –'

The voice rose almost hysterically. 'It's taking too long as it is, we don't want extras. You've got a boat. Go on using it. You can come in to take off what people you've room for, and that's all.'

'Sod you for a start,' Wayne shouted. 'You can all fucking drown for all I care, mate.' Angrily he shoved the motor lever into astern, and came away, backing out into the wide waters, the waters that everywhere were scummy with debris. He wasn't going to risk making a fight for it, the numerical odds this time were dead against the Big Clout. Watching the compass, once clear of the tip of Buxton, he set a course northerly. For much of the way along the Big Clout found high peaks, the peaks of the Pennines, but they were isolated, and as unfriendly-looking as what was left of Buxton. No future there, Wayne thought. He would take the man's advice, and go on and on until the water petered out into a nice big stretch of dry land where there was room and scope for living. During that night, in the early hours, he found it some miles to the south of Skipton in North Yorkshire, that part of it that had once been the West Riding. By the time the boat grounded it was dark, and the grounding was sudden, throwing the Big Clout off their feet and jarring the girl, the nurse, lying in one of the cabin bunks. They had grounded at speed and the bows were stove in, and leaking. The boat had had it now, their temporary home really gone.

Wayne shouted for them all to get ashore. There were no other people about, which was encouraging and spoke of plenty of space. It seemed they had grounded on a dry-stone wall edging a field. As the Big Clout moved the boat shifted and lurched sideways, and filled more. There wasn't far to go, but they had to swim for it. They made it in safety and one of them asked about the girl in the cabin, the daughter of the murdered owner.

Wayne said, 'Leave 'er, there'll be others.'

Like sheep, behind Wayne, they moved away from the water's edge. They reached a road and trudged along it in the darkness. Later they found the signpost for Skipton: north of Skipton lay Settle and Giggles-wick. They went that way. There was a smell overall, a dank smell from the floodwater behind them, following them with its stench of sewage and corpses. Next day around noon a police water patrol came upon an abandoned power-boat sagging into the flood from the top of a dry-stone wall and they investigated. They entered the wheelhouse, dropped down into a cabin where they found deep water and a young girl dead and floating about. The door had been shut and clamped.

'Murder?' a constable asked.

The sergeant shrugged. 'I don't suppose we'll ever know.'

The PC thought that was likely enough the truth: there were so many other things to worry about for the foreseeable future. In the mean time there was little that could be done about the power-boat. The police sergeant noted the name and other details, and the girl's body was brought up with a certain amount of difficulty and transferred to the patrol boat. One day, perhaps, forensic would have time to take a look at the boat, search for fingerprints. For now, a report would be made and that was all.

By the time the boat had been found the Big Clout had reached Skipton, a place seething with refugees from farther south. You could scarcely move. A lot of people were in fact moving on north, but there wasn't much road transport left for those, such as the Big Clout, without their own cars.

Wayne called a conference outside a public lavatory in a deserted car park. He said, 'No use staying put. Gotta get on north. Less crowded the more north you get, right?'

They said yes, right. They'd taken a look around the town: most of the shops were shut and there seemed to be nowhere to eat, not that they were starving, far from it, thanks to the erstwhile owner of the power-boat, but they hadn't been able to salvage any food in the panic disembarkation and they would need to eat before long. The members of the Big Clout didn't take long to hoist in one simple fact: refugees, survivors, were not popular. What food there was, was being conserved for locals or near-locals. The password, of course, was the Yorkshire accent, though Lancashire would do almost as well, the Wars of the Roses forgotten in the interest of presenting a united front to Southerners. The North had ganged up.

'They're a lousy lot of bastards,' Wayne said in disgust. 'And there's more of 'em than there is of us.'

Leroy asked, plaintively, 'Where do we go?'

'I just said. North. Follow the road signs out.'

'Walk?'

'For Christ's sake, what else? Maybe we'll find something along the road.'

They left the car park, followed the signs for Giggleswick and Settle, a straggle of thugs and tearaways without quite the confidence they'd had down South in Pompey where they were known and feared by the others, the rival mobs. Up here, in the general horror that had solidified the population, they didn't count for much. Wayne, Roxy, Leroy, Dean, Clara, Lee, Sharon, Gemma looked in fact deflated. But they would recover once they'd found somewhere to re-establish their identity and someone to kick around. And if things didn't go according to plan, there might have to be changes in the leadership. It was the law of the jungle. Leroy, behind Wayne as they trudged along in single file, passed all the time by northbound traffic with nothing moving south, stared at Wayne's thick back and mane of black hair, bear-like. Leroy was pale and thin, with a shifty, dangerous expression. He slunk along, almost like a snake's progress, right and left buttocks rising and falling alternately, keeping his torso straight as he went along. Wayne, Leroy believed, could be losing his grip: he'd taken Skipton a shade too easy. Leroy wasn't going to argue the toss, not just yet, but the time might come. Left to Leroy, the Big Clout would have established itself right there in Skipton.

The helicopter squadrons embarked aboard the carrier off the Firth of Forth couldn't hope to cover the whole of the flooded areas. The pilots, having flown around the clock, were dead-tired. But by now the sorties, the relief operations, were being flown largely by the RAF from their airfields in Scotland and the free parts of the northern English counties. All the helicopter crews attending upon the North Sea oil and gas rigs had been conscripted into the relief operation and all of them,

like the Fleet Air Arm, were flying almost all the hours
available, caning themselves and their aircraft, lifting
groups of survivors from isolation, dropping supplies of
food and medicines on places such as Shaftesbury. A
number of places remained without help: there was a
limit on range, a limit set by the exigencies of fuel
capacity.

In those places there was starvation. These were
mainly in the South and West. On the high parts of
Bodmin Moor, Exmoor and Dartmoor men, women
and children clustered together with sheep. The sheep
were eyed as potential food; but there was no means of
making fire to cook the meat, so it would be a very last
resort. If ever it happened: thirst would get them before
that. Of water there was none but the flood, though
some had been gathered in hands and hats whenever
there was rain – gathered and quickly drunk. And now
the rain had stopped in most parts, though not on the
Welsh border near the Black Mountains, where the
Ethel Margaret, having come through the thunder and
lightning, had come to land on the heights above what
had once been the Afon Honddhu. Unused to
navigating over the top of the Forest of Dean, and
Monmouth, and the land north of Abergavenny, and
not having the experience of his nephews handy to take
soundings from the bows, Captain Wilson had
grounded sharply on a jag of high land and, like the Big
Clout farther north, had damaged the barge severely
and had been forced to abandon. Thereafter, again like
the Big Clout, they were faced with having to walk.

'Damn lucky to be able to,' Wilson said, doing his best
to sound cheerful in the rain-filled darkness of the
Black Mountains, with a strong wind, almost gale-force,
blowing the rain into huddled bodies in whom there was
little real hope. 'We have a fair expanse of ground, I
believe.' There had been, still was, fitful moonlight as
the clouds moved across the moon's face, and not only
the stark bleakness had been seen but also the fact of a
sort of valley, a kind of depression behind which the

Ethel Margaret had touched ground, a depression ringed
with higher ground, much as Wilson had expected if his
landfall had been the Black Mountains. 'We'll push on
and look for shelter. Then we can start making plans. I
say again, we're lucky. Right, Mr Thomas?'

Evan Thomas senior said, 'That is very right, yes.
With luck we shall find food and shelter in the villages –'

'Depending on where the floods have reached. I
imagine the village settlements are in the valleys.'

'Well, that is right, yes. There is also a reservoir, I
believe, high up – the Grwyne Fawr, near Capel-y-ffin.
But I do not know how far we are from Capel-y-ffin, do
you, Captain?'

'No,' Wilson said. 'But we won't be the only ones up
here in the mountains, that's for sure. All right – let's
move out.' He went past his clustered passengers taking
the lead along a path that could be presumed to lead
somewhere.

Aboard the ex-hippie bus in Sedbergh, the young ladies
waited. Madame Smith was patient; it was early days,
and the people of the North were slow to adapt to new
ways, and there could be no doubt about it that a brothel
in Sedbergh was a novelty of the first order.

'Give 'em time,' she said. 'They'll come flocking like
their bloody sheep. You see. All said an' done … it's
yuman nature.' Madame Smith's fortune had been
founded on human nature and it was quite a
respectable, if such was the word, fortune; but it was all
behind her now, all in the past, all beneath the
floodwater that swirled over and through the London
suburban streets, the smart shops, the cafés, the public
houses, the gentleman's residences, the parks and
public libraries, the conveniences – Madame Smith
thought fleetingly of those who might possibly have
been trapped in a cubicle, what a way to die – the bingo
halls and cinemas, her own premises on which she had
lavished both care and money and which were her
pride. Nothing sordid. Madame Smith had proper

mattresses made by Slumberland, and orthopaedic at that, because you didn't want clients to roll down into a hollow from which they might find it a struggle to emerge; so many of them were geriatric. Lumbago, sciatica, arthritis and replacement hips had all to be reckoned with, though many of the old grand-daddies had the agility of monkeys plus the legendary sexual propensities of rabbits. You had to admire them ... and they paid well, especially for the satisfaction of their oddities. One of Madame Smith's clients, a judge, had been prepared to pay £500 in cash for his particular fetish. What that must have cost the judge in a year – whenever he was on heat but not on circuit he paid a visit and seemed to enjoy it enough to keep on coming. *Visiting*, Madame Smith corrected herself mentally. No need to think vulgar thoughts.

But now, no money. Plenty invested – and what good was that? – but no ready. If that went on for long it would become serious. The girls had to eat. And the first night they had drawn a total blank. No one approached, though a vague figure moved furtively at the end of the road and even he, or she, didn't come any farther. Madame Smith had an idea it might be the fuzz in plain clothes, acting as a dick. No lights came on in the front windows of the houses opposite the double-decker but there was movement of the lace curtains and Madame Smith knew she was under observation for one reason or the other: either the habitants were watching so as to report and complain or they were watching in the roles of voyeurs, all steamed up behind the curtains' anonymity.

Or maybe both.

Madame Smith, waiting in her seat throughout the night, hat and gloves discarded. had sighed and commiserated with herself. Always antagonism, suspicion, people out to stop anyone else enjoying themselves. She'd had it most of her life really, even in her London suburb, although she'd always managed to survive and smile. So much fuss about nothing; it wasn't

as though any of it was done in public, and what went on
in private was no business of anyone other than the
participants. And all the girls were so nice; Madame
Smith was really fond of them. Young, pretty,
co-operative with the clientele, never talked dirty unless
by special request and never talked shop off-duty, like
doctors. The conversation was always far removed from
sex: knitting patterns, pop music, fashion, diets, that
sort of thing. If only the bloody fuzz could be made to
realize what decent girls they were, just doing a useful
job. Why not make use of what you'd got?

In the end, that first night, they all slept in their seats,
very uncomfortably, some of them snoring. At about 2
a.m. Mr Blundell emerged from the darkness and
moved in on rubber-soled shoes. He crept around the
bus: all quiet. All the curtains were drawn and unlike PC
Slatterthwaite he was unable to find a chink. He listened
carefully for sounds of sex even though his vigil had
been attentive and he'd seen no one entering the bus.

TWELVE

The Rushworths had suffered an engine breakdown, or
rather, as it turned out after a lengthy stripping-down
of the power unit, an obstruction to the screw which
had caused the engine to stop. Someone had to go over
the side and clear the obstruction. McNaughten said
he'd go if he was younger: his son-in-law took the hint,
ungraciously.

'You're supposed to be the marine engineer.'

'Clearing propellors,' McNaughten said, 'is a deck job.
Not that I'd shirk –'

'All right, all right.' Charles Rushworth made ready,
stripping himself to his underpants: no use mucking up
clothes they might have to live in for months. It was
dark, and the job wasn't easy. John brought a light on a

wandering lead connected to the electrics, and dangled it over the gunwale aft. The water was turgid and as scummy as ever, filled with all kinds of muck, and it stank. McNaughten had prophesied that the sea, joining forces with the floodwater, would soon clear it. So far he had been wrong. Probably there was too much debris to hope for quick cleansing by salt water and what they needed was a full gale.

Charles leaned down as far as he could go, with his father-in-law hanging onto his legs. He couldn't see anything through the scum. He reached a hand down, felt around. His fingers touched the tip of one of the blades. He tried to shift it, but it was stuck fast.

He said as much.

McNaughten said irritably, 'You'll have to go over.'

'I'm not keen.'

'Don't argue, Charles. You know –'

'It's not your bloody boat! It's mine.'

'If you want to split hairs ... or do you propose to keep us here forever?'

'We'll drift and end up somewhere.'

'Not necessarily where we want to go, which is north. The sea'll be doing all sort of capers with the tides and currents. Get on with it, for God's sake!'

Charles let out a long breath; it had to be gone through with. He heaved himself up on to the gunwale, sat for a moment, turned and let himself down gingerly, down into the filthy water lit by the electric light, a single bare bulb. This reflected back from the surface and didn't penetrate. It had to be a case of feeling around, and Charles felt. He contacted the obstruction quickly enough: something that gave a little. His flesh crawled; he ran his hand along the obstruction. It was long, thicker at one end than the other. It was cold and, had it been clear of the water, he believed it would be clammy.

There was little doubt as to what it was. At the thinner end he made out a hand. He said in a shaking voice, 'It's an arm ... a human arm.'

'Get rid of it,' McNaughten said. 'You've got a knife.'

'Yes.' The knife was on a lanyard secured to his waist above the underpants. Feeling sick Charles got to work, blindly, raking and slashing with the knife. Pieces of flesh came to the surface, stinking. There was a lot of it and the job took some time. When the flesh had been cut away, Charles dragged and pushed at the bone. He twisted and wrenched, using all his strength, desperate to be finished. The arm seemed to have been caught between the screw and the rudder, jammed tight by some malignancy of fate. But when it came free it came very suddenly, and Charles lurched forward, lost his one-handed grip on the gunwale, and went head under. He emerged gasping and choking, a few yards off.

'Don't swallow it,' McNaughten called.

Stupid old bastard, Charles thought. He'd swallowed plenty, caught off guard and not closing his mouth in time. A lot had gone up his nose. He swam for the boat and was hauled over the gunwale and lay for a while being sick on the boards of the after section. Dead arms, corpses … he felt like death himself, wondered what he might have caught. He went on retching; Mary wiped at his head and face, her own face white and strained. Vicki went forward and brought hot water from the small galley, and a towel, and helped clean him up, then went down to the cabin and brought up his clothes, and, trembling, he got dressed.

'I'll try the engine,' McNaughten said. He did so, and all was well. The boat headed north once again. The delay had been lengthy but by dawn they were not far off Rotherham, over where the M1 motorway joined the M18 leading off towards Doncaster. Below and astern lay the Woodall service area, eerie now, the home of fish and corpses, rotting food, submerged with its petrol pumps and its car parks, its police post, the AA and the RAC, its shopping area and restaurant. Now they were coming to higher ground and the roof of the main building was not so far below the surface: they had skimmed over it unknowingly, a place John and his father had often stopped at in past years.

In the cabin below Karen Lockhart twisted and turned in the bunk, sweating as she had done throughout the night while the old lady, McNaughten's wife, stared and made gobbling motions with her lips, a geriatric chew on nothing. Vicki was there as well; she had taken no notice of McNaughten's strictures not to enter the cabin: someone needed her and that, for Vicki, was a new experience. She knew nothing of nursing but she did her best: some things were obvious, such as keeping the face and forehead cool with wiping, and giving sips of precious water from a bottle given her by John Rushworth, who came down from time to time to see how Karen was.

'Not too good I reckon,' Vicki said each time he appeared.

'I wonder what it is. Mum thinks it's typhoid.'

'I thought you were a medic,' she'd said the first time he visited the sick girl. They'd talked together a lot since Vicki had come aboard, quite friendly in spite of the black looks from McNaughten. She'd learned a bit about John's past but, being more concerned with other matters, hadn't really listened.

He said, 'Hoping to be. I hadn't even started the pre-clinical course. But I doubt if it's typhoid – too fast, unless she'd been brewing it for more than about a week before we picked her up.'

'She may have, for all we know.'

'Yes. But I think it could be diphtheria, though it's rare for adults to get it.'

'Kids' disease?'

He nodded. 'Spreads at school – you know. Droplets on the breath, that's the usual way it spreads.'

'You know quite a lot, don't you?'

'Not really,' he said. 'It's just that being interested – wanting to read medicine – I've done a fair amount of reading already. That's all.'

'What about those two kids, then?'

'They're at risk, of course. That's why I've suggested to Dad they're kept on deck or in the wheelhouse.'

She nodded, seemed absorbed in her own thoughts as she continued to mop with a soaked cloth at Karen Lockhart's forehead and cheeks. Then suddenly she spoke again. 'Know anything else, do you?'

'What about?'

'About being a doctor ... knowing what's wrong.'

'No,' he said. 'Why d'you ask?'

"Cos I could be pregnant. That's why,' she said in a flat voice.

John was startled. 'Oh, my God! Don't let my grandfather hear you say that –'

'Sod your grandfather. It wouldn't be his kid, anyway.' She laughed, a slightly hysterical sound.

As the dawn broke over submerged Wales and the Black Mountains, Captain Wilson halted and looked ahead. The path he had taken had proven a good choice, though in fact all such paths could have been presumed to lead downwards towards the valleys. This one gave a good prospect. Wilson, with the Evan Thomases, looked along towards what they had hoped to find: a broad stretch of land below the level of the peaks, a small piece of Wales that offered freedom from the immensity of the waters.

'We're not going to be alone,' Wilson said. There were hundreds of people ahead, people who had made a kind of camp, or a series of camps. Smoke arose from wood fires: some of the refugees had evidently taken the precaution of bringing matches, or knew how to coax fire by friction, like a bushman or a boy scout. 'It's pretty crowded.'

'To be expected, Captain,' Evan Thomas the elder said.

Wilson nodded. 'Of course. Well – let's get on.' He paused. 'Do we expect a warm welcome – or the opposite?'

'You are thinking of Shaftesbury.'

'Yes –'

'So am I, Captain. Times like these, they change men. We still have the revolver.'

'And will be heavily outnumbered. Overwhelmed – the moment we use it. Which I wouldn't want to do anyway. Besides, this isn't Shaftesbury, the simile isn't really very good. There's space. There's room for more.'

Evan Thomas didn't answer, merely shrugged and looked long-faced. Wilson went forward again, the straggle from the *Ethel Margaret* following behind. The sun edged farther up; it was a splendid dawn, red and green, purple and gold, striking off the high peaks and the plateau, glinting on the floodwater beyond. To Wilson, there was something not quite right.

Evan Thomas the elder asked suddenly, 'Should we be seeing the water, Captain? Do you think we should?'

Wilson looked sideways. 'Why do you ask?'

'Because I have a feeling ... we should not, if the depth –'

'Are you thinking the same as me?'

The Welshman nodded. 'I believe I am, Captain. I believe I am. That is, if you are thinking that the water-level is going up.'

'I believe it is,' Wilson said. 'We shall know ... before much longer. But whatever happens, we can't sail the *Ethel Margaret* any farther.'

'It's a disgrace,' Mr Blundell said, his face quivering with his indignation. 'Nobbut a disgrace to Yorkshire –'

'I understood you to say, Mr Blundell,' Slatterthwaite said, 'that no one had made an approach.'

'Made an approach?'

'Went to the bus. Or from it either, I take it –'

'From it?' Heavy-faced, the county councillor stared.

'Soliciting, Mr Blundell. There hasn't been any soliciting.'

'Well no. No, I suppose there hasn't.' Blundell was grudging about that. 'Not that it makes any difference.'

Slatterthwaite scratched at his cheek. 'It makes the

difference that there's still nothing to charge them with.
They've created no disturbance. I can't charge them
with obstruction, not in a road that wide. They haven't
exhibited themselves – if they 'ave, then no one's
complained about it, and I reckon they *would* 'ave –'

'Do you, eh?'

'Well.'

'There's some as might not and you know that as well
as I do. We're not all alike, more's the pity. Some
people, they let t'side down.' Mr Blundell brooded for a
moment, looking round him at Sedbergh and its grey,
stone buildings that, like himself, seemed to brood out
across towards Calf Top and Castle Knott. A good
county was Yorkshire. Clean – clean in its open
countryside, in its small dales towns; clean in its living
and its thoughts. A mobile brothel was far from being a
clean thing. It wasn't just the morals of the issue: there
were even firmer, even harder considerations, and Mr
Blundell voiced them. 'Diseases,' he said, keeping his
voice low and looking around again before speaking.
'Other things. Pox an' clap. 'Erpes. All very nasty, very
spreadable. Times like this, coming up from London …
London's a mucky place. We know there's been typhoid,
all the mucky water. Not reet for Sedbergh, it isn't.'

'Aye, that's a fact, Mr Blundell.'

'You agree?'

Slatterthwaite said cautiously, 'I agree, yes, o' course I
do. Stands to reason … but still doesn't mean I 'ave
grounds upon which to act, grounds upon –'

'Now look, PC Slatterthwaite,' Blundell interrupted,
digging the officer in the ribs with his stubby forefinger,
'just look. Don't keep on about grounds – I've given you
grounds and you know it. So just you get on with it. This
situation's not normal and it's no bloody good quoting
normal routines and what-not. Doesn't work any more.
What's wanted is action, not words. I just spoke of
disease. What about 'ealth in general? Eh? Sanitation.'
Law or not, Mr Blundell was going to have the bus out
of Sedbergh before next nightfall. They could go on to

Kendal, say. Kendal was big enough and it wasn't in Yorkshire, it was in Cumbria, and Mr Blundell wasn't at all fussy about what happened outside Yorkshire.

Reports worldwide were scanty still: all the communications systems had been upset and in any case the facts were still in the process of being gathered. When reports did come in to the receiving station aboard the aircraft carrier all they indicated was total chaos, particularly in the low-lying areas of Europe and North America. So far as could be made out the floods had not reached all that far into the southern latitudes: most of the African continent was presumed clear, likewise South America. The Mediterranean had greatly extended itself, however, lapping up against the North African mountains; Gibraltar rose above the water still, but had been reduced to two isolated peaks, crammed with the local inhabitants and the tourists, plus the famous Barbary apes, who had scampered from their viewing platform to the heights very early on, possibly alerted to danger by some primordial sense not available to humans. The report about the Mediterranean and Gibraltar had come in from a visiting frigate now crowded with refugees and homeward bound in the absence of any orders to remain on a largely vanished station. On receipt of her signal aboard the carrier, she was given radioed orders to join the main body of the fleet disposed around Britain to take part in the massive rescue operation. There was, in fact, not much Navy: a handful of frigates and mine-hunters, plus submarines. Past cuts had been heavy. What was left was hopelessly inadequate to the task.

Aboard the command carrier the daily routine went on as usual: the British Navy was a service of strict routine that allowed no interference with its age-old customs. The pipes were made over the tannoy in their proper sequence, ordering the day for all aboard other than the tight-packed secretaries, heads of Civil Service departments and the cabinet and other ministers sandwiched each day between Both Watches and Stand Easy, was a form of Divine Service, in which the carrier's Church of England chaplain and the Rev. Daniel Matthews, assisted by the Roman Catholic chaplain, said prayers over the tannoy, asking for God's intercession at a time of great tragedy. By personal order of the Prime Minister, all work was stopped during the broadcast prayers, and men joined in with bowed heads, at their various stations throughout the ship. Some were heard to remark that it was a waste of breath: it was, presumably, God who had sent the flood in the first place, and He was scarcely likely to change His mind that fast.

Daniel Matthews was inclined to a similar view: God had turned against the world, perhaps not surprisingly, though He had possibly relented in regard to Matthews himself and his wife and parishioners, allowing them to be rescued and brought to the safety of the aircraft carrier. There was doubtless a reason for this, and Matthews, cogitating as to what it might be, decided that he was meant to bring cheer to the ship's company by moving about the decks and working-spaces below, speaking of his faith in a happy outcome, trying to assure the men that many of their families would be safe. This he had done diligently but had realized he was mostly not being listened to.

He spoke of this, sadly, to his fellow clerics; and admitted to his current failing, the one shared with some of the sailors, the horrible suspicion that God, having started the flood, would be unlikely to disperse it.

Father O'Donovan, a portly, red-faced man of good humour, laughed and dug a finger into Matthew's ribs. 'O ye of little faith,' he said. 'We all know the unholy state of the world. When God's purpose is accomplished, He'll relent. Not before.'

'Then praying –'

'Pray we must,' Father O'Donovan said briskly, 'for that is what God will be expecting, sure. And as soon as we pray as though we mean it, then the relenting will come.'

Daniel Matthews nodded uncertainly. They, the clergy as well the laity, had at least gone along with so much that was wicked; they had connived and they couldn't deny it. Abortion, divorce, people living together before marriage and then coming to church to be joined together, sullied, by God; a current and spreading disbelief in the basic tenets of Christianity – the Virgin Birth, the Resurrection, disbelief handed down from high places; the empty churches, the desecration of the Sabbath, the awful antics of the trendy clergy.

Was it any wonder God was annoyed, and had sent down His wrath? These were difficult times for the clergy: Daniel Matthews himself had been responsible for bringing an illegitimate baby with him aboard the carrier. Naturally, no blame attached to the innocent child itself. But perhaps Matthews, as the mother's parish priest, should have taught her better than that. His own personal example was good, but his ministry had lacked thrust.

Later that day it was confirmed that God had not yet relented: there had been reports that the water was deepening and there was a belief among the carrier's meteorological experts that more of the glaciers were melting.

THIRTEEN

In Sedbergh a few clients had come at last, discreetly and nervously. They had come singly, a dour-faced middle-aged dales farmer, a youth of around eighteen years of age, a shepherd, an old man with a stick and a dog, and a younger man who looked like a bank clerk or a solicitor. Madame Smith, who kept the log herself, made the appointments, nicely spaced, and allocated the particular girl who would satisfy the particular need: basically they were all general practitioners but each was a specialist as and when required.

First in the appointments book was the farmer, who wore heavy tweed trousers covered with mud and supported, pessimistically, by both belt and braces.

Doris, the allocated specialist, commented on this.

'Like to be sure, do you?'

'Aye.'

'Good cloth.' She felt it.

'Aye.'

'Ugh!' She had laid a hand on the mud. 'Cow shit!'

'Aye.'

The remainder of the appointments list was unlucky; the farmer's tweed trousers, with the rest of his working clothing, were dangling over the back of a seat, and he was hopping about in the nude trying to get his socks off because Doris was particular and had said they smelt, when the door at the back next to the Elsan, the door constructed by the hippies, the previous owners, to make the rear platform into habitable quarters, burst open very suddenly. No approach had been heard; but there stood Mr Blundell, in the van of his vigilantes.

Madame Smith came down the aisle while the farmer tried to hide behind the seat. 'What's all this, eh?' she demanded.

'It's us,' Blundell said.

'I can bloody see that, thank you very much. 'Oo are you, and what the –'

'Come to get you out of Sedbergh, that's what. Whores, harlots –'

'Don't you dare say that again! This is a respectable bus.' Madame Smith stood with hands on hips, glaring. There was a strong surge of scent and face-powder. 'Them as thinks otherwise, 'as dirty minds. I –'

'What's that chap doing without his trousers?' Blundell demanded, pointing. 'You,' he said, naming the mortified farmer, whose attempt at hiding had no been successful. 'A disgrace to Yorkshire, you are! Best get out before I lose my temper.' He looked round at his cohort, most of whom carried pitchforks or sporting guns. 'Or my chaps lose theirs. I'm just warning you.'

Wordless, red-faced, trying to look decent whilst gathering up his clothes, the farmer accepted the warning. He scuttled off the bus, hastened by a threatening pitchfork. The vigilantes advanced into the vehicle, each man doing his best to look as if he was closing his eyes against sin. Some of the girls were ready for bed and had almost nothing on. A pitchfork was held against each of them, and a shotgun was laid against Madame Smith's breast. Murder was being threatened by the look of it, and the Yorkshiremen all had determined faces. They were not play-acting.

Definitely.

Blundell issued the orders. 'I'm North Yorkshire County Council and I'm serving notice to quit. Best get out of Sedbergh before there's trouble. You're not wanted here. This is a respectable place.'

'Look, just leave us bloody alone ... anyway till morning.'

'You'll get out *now*. I don't want any argument. We'll leave the bus now and wait outside till you're on the move. If you don't move, we'll set fire to the bus.'

In Wales the water was undoubtedly rising, and quite fast. Another tidal wave was Captain Wilson's verdict, great pressure building up across the Atlantic, sending another surge against Britain and the Continent. So far, however, the level was still a long way below the higher ground and Wilson had hopes that the mountains would go on shielding the plateau where so many people were gathered.

Wilson and his followers continued ahead, coming down to the flatness between the peaks, behind the last rampart between them and the floodwaters. The people ahead seemed apathetic rather than belligerent, just

sitting about with a look as though they were awaiting
the end.

'I doubt if we'll need the revolver after all,' Evan
Thomas senior said. As they reached what seemed to be
the forward line of refugees Evan Thomas called out to
them.

'I am Evan Thomas from Barry Dock. Is there anyone
who knows me?'

There was no direct response. After a while a small,
thin man got to his feet and called back. 'From Barry
Dock, is it? How did you get here? The roads are
flooded, the whole land is flooded to the south, almost.'

'We came by boat, from across the Bristol Channel,
but the boat is useless now –'

'The bridge … is it still above the water, bach?'

'I don't know,' Evan Thomas answered. 'Why do you
ask?'

'I helped to build it, see. I lived in Newport then. I
moved after, to a village down there.' The small man
jabbed downward with a thumb. 'Now that has gone,
and my wife and family with it.' He burst suddenly into
tears; his face streamed as he turned it upwards and
clasped his hands in prayer, talking silently to God.
When he had finished, Evan Thomas called out again,
loudly, saying that the good times would come again,
the flood would not last forever. His friend, he said, the
owner of the boat, was a master mariner, a seaman of
wide experience, and he had said as much. But he could
see they didn't believe him; what, the nearer faces
mutely asked, did any man know of massive flood, flood
on such a disastrous, devastating scale?

The faces lacked all hope, so far as Wilson could see.
Not even the children played; they sat watchfully by
their parents or other accompanying adults. Here and
there there was a cry of a baby. A woman sang softly to
one of the babies close by, some traditional Welsh
lullaby, but it failed to soothe the baby whose cry turned
to an angry yell.

The crowd seemed after a while to be turning to

Wilson as a leader: there was talk of Noah: Wilson was a man of obvious authority and the way he had come, as if from nowhere, from beyond the floodwaters and over the mountain, gave him, as it were, a kind of Noah-like aspect, a figure of hope and salvation even though his own Ark had been shipwrecked. And even so, Noah's Ark too had grounded on Mount Ararat, hadn't it, so the simile held.

Well, Wilson would accept the mantle if that was how they felt. First he asked questions, establishing his whereabouts as precisely as possible, asking about food and water stocks, if any — there was little enough it turned out — and sickness among the refugees. There was as yet no sickness, but it could not be long in coming if they were left as they were, with no helicopter lift. They had been passed by so far, nothing coming within sight at all. Wilson enquired about wood: he had seen those fires. They must make all possible smoke, and hope to attract some attention. And they must build some sort of shelter against the wind, which was starting to blow again from the South-west. If that wind rose, it could make a build-up of the floodwater and send it buffeting against the shield of the mountainside.

The Rushworths came to dry land in the vicinity of Harrogate, south of the town and on the fringes of a small, grey stone community, a typical Yorkshire village. The name of it was Stainsby. The boat grounded gently, no damage, but there was no point in remaining aboard indefinitely. In it they could go only south, back into the flood, and land had all along been their objective; now they had found it, they had to go north on foot or in such transport as could be found. McNaughten organized things: they could carry between them all the remaining food, or most of it, just in case of local supply difficulties. Water would presumably be no problem as they went north. There were other problems: McNaughten's disabled wife, and Karen Lockhart, whose condition was if anything worse.

'A doctor,' McNaughten said. 'And a hospital. They'll have to accommodate the children as well.'

Charles Rushworth said, 'We'd better wait around. The hospitals will be crammed full. We can't just leave the three of them.'

'Well, we'll see. A doctor's the first thing, obviously.'

'What about mother-in-law?'

'Yes, I know. A wheelchair, if there's such a thing to be found.'

'Another reason for staying a while. I think we should stay aboard till we've made arrangements.'

'The whole idea was to land ... but I take your point. All right, we'll base ourselves aboard, but we'll leave the boat as soon as we can find transport –'

'And a doctor.'

'Yes. Go ashore and make enquiries. And don't be too long. And see what you can find in the way of transport. If you can find something suitable, then we'll not need to worry about a wheelchair.' As Charles stood there looking undecided McNaughten snapped, 'Well, go on, then. In a situation like this, we can commandeer a vehicle, surely?'

'You're not in the Navy now,' Charles said, 'and we're not at war. Anybody with a car will be guarding it with his life, if he hasn't used it to get out already.'

McNaughten gave an angry shrug and turned away, down to the cabin and his wife, and the sick woman. Vicki was having trouble with the two children, David and Rosemary: they wanted to be with their mother. McNaughten had no patience with them, told Vicki to get them out of his sight. 'I'm going off the boat,' she told him. 'Stretch me legs, all right? I'll take the kids.'

'Do what you like.' McNaughten didn't seem to be listening. He turned his back and she put out her tongue at it. She went on deck and told Charles she would go ashore with him and bring the children. He didn't demur; the four of them left the boat, slipping over the side and wading the few yards of floodwater to the dry land of Stainsby. It was quite a moment, to be on

land again. They'd beached in fact around a mile short of
the village and there was no one around, no one to
approach them with questions, no one to offer them help
or tell them what things were like in the region. As they
reached a road and headed towards the village, passing
the name sign on the left, there was still no one about.
The silence was oppressive, the lack of human contact
somehow alarming.

'Funny,' Vicki said.

'Wrong choice of word.'

'Oh, I'm sorry I'm sure. I didn't get much learning.'

'I meant I don't find it funny. That's all. There's just
nobody about, they've deserted the village.'

'Mean they've done a bunk ahead of the flood?'

Charles nodded. 'Gone farther north, obviously.
There'll be a fat chance of finding transport.'

'So what do we do?'

'Press on, search the whole village. There's not a lot of
it. You never know ... we might find something with
wheels, I suppose.' He knew it was hopeless really: anything and everything would have been taken into service
by a fleeing population. They passed a garage with silent
petrol pumps, all the litter of repairs and servicing lying
about, but no vehicles, nothing that could move. They
passed a silent inn, the Stainsby Arms, all its doors locked
and windows curtained, the landlord no doubt hoping to
come back one day. Cottages equally silent, equally
locked and curtained. Narrow cobbled streets leading off
the main through-road to Harrogate, all silent too, all
apparently deserted, not even a cat or a dog. Charles and
Vicki explored narrow alleys between groups of cottages,
looking for they knew not what – a bicycle, perhaps,
overlooked by someone who had got out by car, but there
was no luck. There were shops, when they came back to
the main street, a chemist's, a newsagent's. Professional
people in larger houses in another road leading off, a
solicitor, a vet, an accountant according to the plates. No
doctor; and if there had been, Vicki said, he'd probably
have scarpered with the others.

They came to a village green, an oblong of well-kept turf with more cottages beside it. At the far end a goat was tethered, moving around its pole on a long length of rope, munching. There was little grass left within its reach, mostly bare earth.

'Poor sod,' Vicki said. 'Got left behind ... too smelly, I s'pose. Fancy leaving it tied up like that.'

'They had other things on their minds.'

'Yes, but still, wouldn't have taken a minute. Look, you got that knife on you?'

'Yes,' Charles said. 'But the goat won't appreciate being cut loose. He'll just butt whoever's handiest.'

'Well, I'm not going to leave the poor sod like that,' Vicki said with determination. 'You going to help, or not?'

Charles sighed. 'Oh, all right.' They made a joint approach, Charles with his seaman's knife ready for a fast cut, but it was no use. The goat was not co-operative; Charles turned in the nick of time and took a butt on his rump. Vicki fell and was saved only by a goat-deflecting yell from Charles. They had to give it up; the goat was a lot faster than either of them and they would never have got clear in time. There was a wicked, red look in the goat's eyes; the Rushworths could afford no more people on the sick or injured list. They went on, north along the green, and they found a bus-stop next to a post office. They stopped to read the notices.

'There,' Vicki said, pointing.

'What?'

'Doctor.'

Charles read; county bus times that fitted in with surgery hours were indicated, and something about picking up prescriptions. There would be no buses now and the nearest doctor was in Harrogate, and Harrogate was seven miles away.

'Bugger,' Charles said, feeling desperate. A fourteen mile walk, and no knowing if or when the doctor could see them, when he would be able to make the journey to the south of Stainsby and the edge of the flood. Even if he were willing: the Rushworth ménage was nowhere near his list and he would be having his work cut out already. Charles said, 'My father-in-law'll be doing his nut if we take all that time, and him not knowing the score.'

'So what? It's your boat.'

'You'd never think so,' Charles said feelingly. 'But he's got his good points and I don't want to worry him. He's got enough on his plate.'

'The old lady? Your John said something about that. Muggers, he said.'

Charles nodded. 'Upset a lot of lives ... just for some bloody gratuitous cruelty and nastiness.'

'I know. That's why I was dead upset about that poor bloody goat, see? I –'

'For God's sake, where's the connection?' Charles was looking blank.

'Look,' she said defensively, 'I don't say the old lady's same as a goat, it's not that. But I seen helpless bloody animals tortured by vandals. Down near Brighton. Bad as muggers in their own way. All sorts of things you'd never believe. Cats skinned alive, or petrol poured on them and then lit ... gerbils flushed down lavatories. Tethered horses and donkeys ... eyes put out with iron spikes. You name it, some sod thinks it and does it. See what I mean? It's not just *people*.' Suddenly she changed the subject. 'Look, you go back to that pompous old fart – sorry – and keep him happy. I'll go on to Harrogate and find the doctor bloke. All right?' Her eyes seemed to search his face; looking back into them, Charles read honesty. As if that were in doubt, she asked, 'Trust me, don't you?'

'Yes –'

'I won't desert the boat and I'll do me best with the doctor. Get him to bring me back in his car.'

'Well –'

'Look, it's me who needs the doctor as well as that Mrs Lockhart – not you. All right?'

'If you think that's best –'

'I do, mate, I do. You take the kids back, it's too bloody far to take kids, and they'd only start creating.'

'My father-in-law –'

'Sod your father-in-law, mate; if you won't stand up to him I bloody will.'

'All right, all right, no need to shout. Anyway … why do you need the doctor? Is it the –'

'Not the raised bruises, no. Not the bloody AIDS that your pa-in-law thinks I've got. I told John … I could be pregnant. If so, I want to know. See?'

There was a pleading look in her eyes now and they glistened with tears. Charles said it was all right, he did see, and she'd better start right away and get back before dark and he wished her luck. He took over David and Rosemary and they watched Vicki as she turned away and walked north.

David asked, 'What's pregnant, Mr Rushworth?'

Rushworth searched for words; before he'd found them David's question was answered by Rosemary, with a giggle. 'When you get a bun in the oven,' she said, then, meeting Charles' rather shocked eyes, she blushed furiously. Children, Charles thought, they know too much, overhear too much, are allowed to read too much unsuitable matter. But the days of innocence were long gone now, which was perhaps something God was taking into account … Charles pulled himself up sharply. God was God and Charles didn't disbelieve but it was a scientific – in the broad sense – problem that was posed now by the flood, not one of religion. All the same, you couldn't help thinking … things had got into a very bad state one way and another, what with the senseless cruelty Vicki had spoken of, and so many other things.

Charles went back through deserted Stainsby towards the power-boat. He was evidently seen approaching, the Lockhart children each with a hand in one of his: his father-in-law clambered over the side and waded through the shallows.

'You found that doctor? Where's that wretched girl?

We've all been worried about the children. You've been a long time, I must say –'

Charles cut in with explanations. McNaughten didn't seem to be listening. He said in Charles' ear. 'Don't bring the children aboard just yet. They can play.' He turned to David and Rosemary, his voice brusque. 'Off you go, you two, you've been cooped up aboard too long. Don't go far, mind – not out of sight from the boat.' They went off happily enough, and McNaughten said to Charles, 'Too late for the doctor. She's dead.'

FOURTEEN

When the end came to the declivity in the Welsh mountains it came fast, very fast. There was an overspill of the deepening water, coming through in a dip between two higher peaks. Its sheer force, its weight and its terrifying speed broke through like the bursting of a dam, carrying debris and earth and rock, plunging across the land towards the refugees and their handful of camp fires, irresistible and lethal.

The Evan Thomases stood as if transfixed, standing fast beside Captain Wilson. Everywhere men and women ran before the onslaught, carrying children, ran this way and that like tormented rabbits. There was nothing anybody could do. Wilson watched in horror as the flood took the first of the crowd and hurled them along the rock-strewn ground to be smashed to fragments of bloody flesh.

Evan Thomas the elder said, 'God's vengeance is at hand now.'

'Yes,' Wilson said. The heights were some miles behind them now. To run from before the onrush would be useless, would only prolong the agony. As a seaman he had faced the prospect of death many times before, and it had never been his practice to run from it.

When death came, it came. He had seen men die in war, seen them die screaming in agony as tankers had gone down to the German torpedoes or gunfire and the stricken ships had been immersed in a sea of flame from the burning oil cargoes spilled out from the shattered tanks; he had seen them blown to shreds by high explosive as the dive-bombers had come down on them out of the Mediterranean skies over the Malta convoys; he had seen them die quietly, with serious wounds and their senses dulled by the pain-killing drugs.

Those men had been seamen, and all had known the risks inherent in their calling, in both peace and war. The men, women and children now dying before his eyes as the rushing waters came closer, so fast, to himself had never been prepared for what was happening now. Their lives had been peaceful, ordered, their daily routines not upset by thoughts of tragedy until the time when the floods had started.

Evan Thomas the elder stirred. 'What do we do, Captain?'

Wilson said, 'You're a Welshman. Why not – sing a hymn?'

Evan Thomas nodded. 'Yes, that is a good suggestion.' The two men, father and son, side by side, began singing. Wilson joined in. They sang loudly, defiantly, beneath the angry sky as the waters rolled closer.

> Guide me, O thou great Redeemer
> Pilgrim through this barren land;
> I am weak but Thou art mighty,
> Hold me with Thy powerful hand …

All three were still singing as the waters closed and hit, and took them and flung them bodily away. The flood surged on, filling the declivity, turning the plateau into broad ocean.

Alone now, Vicki had gone on along the road to Harrogate, tired but walking with dogged determin-

ation. The land seemed orderly but was as deserted as
the village of Stainsby had been. She went along a road,
a main road without any traffic moving on it. It was
thoroughly weird; not so long ago this would no doubt
have been a busy road. Now the traffic had passed along
it for what might have been the last time. The
inhabitants had been on the brink, would have been the
next to suffer. It made sense to get out.

She passed fields empty of animals. Vicki was no
country girl but she had some sort of awareness from
the television and so on that fields usually had animals
in them unless they were corn or vegetables or
something. It seemed as if the local farmers might have
driven their cows and sheep to safety with them, though
they would be a funny sight in the towns they passed
through on the way to wherever they were going.

She whistled to keep her spirits up, a discordant
sound that tried to reproduce something from Top of
the Pops, her favourite programme in the days before
the flood. The boyfriend in Norwich had liked it too.
She thought about the boyfriend, without anger now
over his desertion: if he was still alive, he too would be
facing the end of everything he had known, and the
knowledge of shared tragedy seemed to make her
attitude humbler and more understanding. Maybe she
had been a pain in the neck, always at him to get a job
instead of lying around all day in the room over the chip
shop. But he had got well and truly on her nerves and
she hadn't been able to stop herself nagging. His
thoughts, actions and ambitions had been few and very
basic: sex in plenty, fish and chips, stay in bed nearly all
day and then down to the amusement arcade until the
boozers opened in the evening.

Her money it was that kept them; what she earned in
the café, which was little enough. The rent was always in
arrears and she had to guard the money for the gas and
electricity meters, slipping it in whenever she had it
before the boyfriend knew. Sometimes, when she'd
done that, and had been forced to confess, he had hit

her and sworn at her, calling her all the filthy names he could think of, which was plenty. She wondered, as she walked on for Harrogate, what he would have done had he still been living with her when she'd committed that murder not so long ago.

And as to that murder, had she really got away with it? It was a worry that nagged.

Resolutely now, she put it behind her. There were other worries, and she had to do her best for the people aboard the boat, to whom she owed her life so far.

For what her life was worth. *Was* she pregnant? She believed she was; there had been tell-tale signs and in all conscience it couldn't be considered unlikely. And what about AIDS? That was something else again: had she contracted it? Those bruises that wouldn't go away ... but she felt all right. So far as she knew, the boyfriend hadn't been bisexual, but of course he'd had other women and they could have been infected, and she had had other men, though not for some while before shacking up in Norwich, since she'd stayed faithful thereafter.

And if there was a baby?

She looked around the quiet landscape, crossing a bridge over a river in a village named Overby. Overby, too, was deserted so far as she could see. Some world to be born into, she thought; maybe it would be kinder if the baby died fast.

She went on, through the village. She jumped a mile when there was a metallic clang away to her right, down an alley, a sound that might have meant anything. It turned out to be a cat, scavenging for food in the dustbins.

She stopped and called. 'Puss, puss.' The cat, its tail in the air, spat at her, glaring with fearful eyes. Feeling rejected, Vicki walked on.

In the boat just to the south of Stainsby, they waited. McNaughten had gone ashore to see what he could rake up; he had no clear idea of what he was going to do, but not trusting his son-in-law to have done a thorough job of search he was going to take a look for himself and if necessary break into a promising-looking building. These were not times for over-observance of the law; it was a case of survival and he was going to survive. Another reason for making himself scarce had been to avoid emotional scenes with the two children, now orphaned. His daughter could best cope with that. In the mean time he had to think about how to dispose of the body, although that could wait until the girl came back with a doctor.

He went on through the village, peering, prying, rattling at doors, looking through windows. There were the good houses of the professional people, hurriedly abandoned – quite possibly too precipitate an abandonment, for the floodwaters might not rise further, even though word had come through the radio that the experts believed they would.

While her father probed, Mary Rushworth broke the news to the Lockhart children. They had become bored with compulsory playing along the shore and had called from the waterline that they wanted mummy.

Mary turned in despair to her husband and son. 'What do we *do*?'

'Tell 'em,' Charles said briefly.

'It's all very well for you to say that, Charles. Who's going to do the telling?'

'You are. It's obvious –'

'Is it? Because I'm a woman?'

'Yes. Look, we can't keep up the pretence, can't possibly, and you know it. They *must* be told, and the sooner the better –'

'Why exactly, the sooner –'

'Disposal,' Charles answered briefly. 'We can't keep a body … and there's your mother to be considered too. You've been down there, you've seen –'

'Yes,' Mary broke in, shivering. It had been a harrowing experience. The dead woman, little more than a girl, was pretty even in death when Mary had drawn back the sheet that covered the face, even though the signs of suffering, of sadness were there still.

And in the bunk opposite the dead that shouldn't
have been was the life that would be better off dead: it
was always a cruel world. Mary's mother, staring and
staring and almost certainly not seeing – Charles having
talked of her mother to be considered had been
rubbish, for her mother was most likely totally unaware
– with her lips folding and unfolding in the everlasting
chew, as though holding a grotesque mouthful of
spearmint, had seemed to heighten the horror of it all.
Mary came back to the present: the children were
calling again. She stiffened herself and asked John to go
across and bring them aboard.

The ex-hippie double-decker bus, ejected from Sedbergh, was making slow progress: all the way along
Carsdale from Hawes the road had become very narrow
and twisty and now it was more so, a lot of climbing out
of Sedbergh, a river running alongside and looking
dangerous, narrow bridges and all, the bus only just
able to scrape through, and to cap it all the top gear had
gone and Albert didn't know why. He did know that in a
lower gear they would use more diesel once they were
able to increase speed and there was no knowing when
they would find a fill.

'Kendal, maybe,' he said.

'Bugger Kendal.' Madame Smith had been restive all
the way from Sedbergh and was changing her mind.
'Too much bloody law around there, if you ask me.'

'We're on the road for Kendal right now, aren't we?'
They had just passed over the top of the M6 and were
making more speed where the road was wider and
better surfaced.

'I know that,' Madame Smith said snappishly. 'Get us
bloody off it. Turn around and –'

'Go back through Sedbergh? They'd 'ave our guts for
garters they would – them farmers.'

'I didn't bloody mean that. I meant find another
bloody road, a side road.' Madame Smith took up the
road map herself and identified where they were, just

beyond the M6. 'Look, there's a left turn ahead. New Hutton, Millholme, looks like. Comes down to a B road.'

'Not much point.'

'I'll decide that, thank you very much.' Madame Smith's voice was sharp.

'Oh, sorry I spoke, I'm sure. Let's 'ave a gander, eh.'

Madame Smith passed over the road map and the bus slowed still further as Albert studied the proposed route. 'Narrow,' he said. 'Single track by the look of it, could be tricky, thing this size –'

'Don't make bloody difficulties! We'll manage. Depending on the flood, of course, we might head for Barrow-in-Furness.'

'Why there, for God's sake?'

'Seaport. Sailors. Not so bloody *moral* as farmers. Much more sex-orientated.'

'Low-lying and all,' Albert said after another look at the map. 'Won't be anything left there by now.'

'Oh well,' Madame Smith said crossly, 'we'll think when we get to that B road. Just bloody get there, that's all.' She turned in her seat and called along the aisle. 'All right back there, are you, girls?'

There was a chorus of dissent, mostly; life aboard the bus was not really comfortable and one of the young ladies had been bus sick before she could reach the Elsan, not the first time it had happened since leaving London. At the start it had all been a change, but boredom had soon set in. Looking out at crowds of refugees, returning cheeky stares when there was a traffic hold-up, rude hand signals, suggestive remarks shouted through the windows. Fields and cows and that, and then when they reached the North the dry-stone walls and the distant, rearing fells, very different from London. A lot of mud from the rain, and mud-covered locals, and sheep, funny-looking sheep with horns, even the lady ones, and scraggy coats with long trails of wool dangling along their sides and backsides, covered with shit. Their faces looked different, too from the sheep some of the girls had seen on the South Downs and thereabouts on days

off; they were somehow crosser, less contented.
Yorkshire was a cold place, even in summer. The bus
took the left-hand turn off the A684 past a sign reading
'UNSUITABLE FOR HEAVY GOODS VEHICLES', and
Madame Smith, relieved not to be going to Kendal,
settled back in her seat, and closed her eyes. Time for a
snooze, she told herself.

From Skipton the Big Clout had made good progress
north, passing through Gargrave and Hellifield on the
road for Settle. They had stopped in Gargrave for nosh,
finding a café miraculously open where they got tea and
ham and eggs with lashings of bread and butter. This
they obtained by threat: like the closed cafés in Skipton,
the proprietor wasn't keen to serve refugees,
Southerners. Wayne simply went up close and
produced his knife and stuck it against the man's big
gut. The remainder of the Big Clout surged in, ejected
the seated customers, and smashed a couple of chairs on
the counter, breaking a glass sandwich container as a
promise of what could come. The food was served, and
while they were eating it the proprietor went into the
back of the café and rang the police. The phone rang
and rang in the station and when at last it was answered
a harassed voice said they had more important matters
to attend to and they had their work cut out trying to
cope.
　So that was that. As a parting gesture the Big Clout,
not paying for the meal, took the contents of the till and
then completed the job of smashing the place up. Tears
of anger and frustration ran down the proprietor's
cheeks as he watched the wrecking process: he was no
longer young, and he'd built up a nice little business
which could have survived the flood if it hadn't been for
the Southern thugs. Going out when it was all over,
Leroy in the rear saw the sad face, picked up the one
intact chair, and smashed it over the man's head.
　Then they went on for Hellifield and passed through
it, dead weary now. In a straggling village called Long

Preston they had some luck: behind a big building like a warehouse, set close against the main road with some small houses and an area of grass in rear, they saw a green-painted van with its back doors open.

'See that?' Leroy said. 'Transit. Ready for loading.'

'Keys in the ignition if we're lucky,' Wayne said. 'Don't waste time. I'll go for the driver's seat, rest of you into the back. OK?'

'OK,' they said.

They moved fast; luck was really with them, the key in the ignition all ready to go. Wayne got behind the wheel and started the engine. Before the others could cram into the back, two men appeared from the building, at the top of some steps where there was a door. They had a large dog with them. They yelled at the Big Clout and the dog went into action, growling from a deep throat and jumping one of the thugs, going for his throat. Leroy used his knife in rescue and the dog dropped, howling. The two men from the warehouse were down the steps and fighting but they didn't have a chance. The knives got them. Leaving one warehouseman dead and the other wounded, the Big Clout went off north in the Transit van. Other men had come from the warehouse by this time and a foreman rang the police. The answer was much the same as had been given to the café proprietor in Gargrave: they just couldn't cope with such an influx, they were stretched beyond all limits of personnel and endurance.

'Murder –'

The police voice said there had been any number of murders. 'And as for theft ... there's been thousands of vehicles stolen or hijacked. Yes, we'll circulate the registration number but I can't hold out any hope.'

There was speculative talk about this aboard the Transit on the move. 'Forget it,' Wayne said. 'Pigs just won't be bothering their arses, too busy feathering their own nests, making sure they'll be okay if the flood deepens. Shouldn't wonder if half of them have buggered off already, deserted like, gone north. *In* their bloody patrol cars, too.' He drove on, groping to his left, one of the girls, who'd got in the front passenger seat with him: Gemma, a striking brunette with big breasts. She giggled as Wayne's hand went low. She liked it. Someone else didn't from the back, Leroy protested.

'Cut it out,' he said, his voice savage but cold. 'She's my girl. As if you didn't know.'

'OK,' Wayne said distantly and withdrew his hand. There would be another time, a more discreet time. But Gemma wasn't pleased. She turned in her seat and spoke to Leroy.

'Over-reaching yourself, aren't you?' Her tone was pert. 'Who said?'

'Who said what?'

'That I was your girl, stupid.'

'I did. And I'm not stupid. So watch it.'

'Watch it yourself,' she said spitefully.

Wayne's voice growled out, the voice of the leader. 'Watch it both of you. We won't get anywhere by falling out.' He didn't grope Gemma again but he conspicuously failed to acknowledge that she belonged to Leroy.

McNaughten had gone round the back of one of the bigger houses in Stainsby, one that had been the rectory, now named The Old Rectory. The parson probably lived, or had lived, in a modern flat, even a council one. The church had fallen on sad days: no money, and no servants if there had been the money. McNaughten sighed: times certainly had changed. Now the flood was changing them even more. Total desertion was a sad thing; but perhaps the people would come back before too long. In the mean time they might have left something that could be made use of …

McNaughten went round the back of the house to what had been the stables and other outhouses. Like the Big Clout farther north, he struck lucky. The absent owners had indeed left something behind that could, perhaps, be used. Looking through a cobwebby window into deep gloom, McNaughten made out something with wheels. Four wheels he believed. Wheels were wheels and had to be investigated. McNaughten tried the door: no padlock, but the door was locked and it was strong. He rooted around the yard and found a brick, and used it to smash the window. He cleared away all the glass. It wasn't an easy task for an ageing man but determination won out and he struggled through, puffing and panting and very aware of the thump of his heart when he was finally inside.

The wheels were on a handcart, perhaps used for garden refuse, perhaps as a child's plaything. Uncomfortable for a helpless invalid but if it could be made to transport her, then it would have to be used until something better turned up.

The handcart, of course, wouldn't go through the window. But there was a heavy axe lying on the ground near the sawn-off stump of a big tree, a stump used as a chopping-block for firewood. There was a lot of sawdust around, smelling quite fresh. McNaughten picked up the axe and attacked the door around the lock, which gave way after half-a-dozen blows, and then he wheeled the handcart out into the yard and the road and went back towards the boat.

Vicki was someone else who had some luck, at any rate to start with: along the Harrogate road she was overtaken by a parson driving a very old Mini. Hearing his approach, she thumbed him. He went on past but evidently changed his mind for he slowed and stopped a hundred yards further on and Vicki ran towards him. Like his car, he was old, very old. White, wispy hair and a heavily lined face, and pebble glasses.

'Can I help?' he asked, peering short-sightedly.

'Didn't want to first off, did you, eh? I don't want to be a nuisance.'

'It's no trouble ... perhaps I was hesitant at first, because it's sometimes awkward ...'

'Accusations of rape?' She giggled: he didn't look the part.

'Well –' He gave an embarrassed cough. 'I assume you're going to Harrogate?'

'Yes,' she said.

'I'll take you as far as Knaresborough.'

'Where's that?'

'Close to Harrogate. Jump in.' He held his watch close to his eyes, 'I'm already late.' She got in and banged the door, which nearly fell off in her hand. There was a lot of rust: you'd think vicars got paid enough to afford a better car, living off the fat of the land, in normal times anyway. The old man didn't ask questions, though she saw him glancing sideways at her from time to time, as though summing her up. She felt he could even have sensed that she was pregnant, and no wedding ring, not that he'd be able to see that with his rotten sight, but he ought to be used to that by now and of course that was nonsense – she certainly wasn't very far gone if at all, certainly wasn't showing anything. It turned out he was going to Knaresborough to take a funeral, standing in for a mate who'd buggered off north with his family, though that wasn't quite the way he put it himself. She told him she was going to find a doctor, and she quoted the name she and Rushworth had seen on the post office notice board back in Stainsby, and the reverend knew the doctor.

'He'll be very busy, you know. You come from the South?'

'Norwich,' she said briefly, and then had a moment of deep and penetrating fear. The mention of Norwich … but this old vicar wouldn't have heard anything about bodies found in the river in Norwich, course he wouldn't. Vicki relaxed.

'He'll be co-opted into the overall effort. So many sick, you know. Largely among those refugees from the Southern areas. Dysentery, typhoid. It's spreading and the hospitals can't cope.'

'Yes,' Vicki said, and was seized by a sudden desire to talk to the old priest, to confide in him and through him make contact with God and ask His help as well. But she did no such thing: Vicars were funny; especially old ones: she didn't want to be sermonized at.

They drove on. In Knaresborough the parson stopped the Mini just short of a bridge set high over a river which he said was the Nidd. He gave her directions into Harrogate: over the bridge, follow the road round to the right and then past a golf course. Over a level-crossing and straight ahead until you came to an open space, a park. Turn across the park and the doctor's surgery wasn't far, between Queens Road and Beech Grove, but she'd do better to ask again. Personally, he said, not for the first time since picking her up, she would be more likely to get help from the hospital, though she would certainly have a long wait. This time, she didn't bother to reply: hospital doctors didn't visit homes, let alone boats a long way off.

'Thanks a lot, Reverend,' she said.

'Don't mention it, only too glad to help.' The old man gave her a wave and drove noisily away. Suddenly she was quite sorry to see him go: he had been safe and he hadn't been nosey. Something of a rock, really. 'Rock of ages, cleft for me. let me hide myself in Thee.'

She felt immensely lonely as she crossed the bridge towards Harrogate and looked down at the Nidd so far below. Lonely as one can be in a crowd, much more so than when you were absolutely on your own. The place was packed with people although there had been few cars to slow the reverend's old Mini down. All the cars, she supposed, had gone north, though Knaresborough seemed set high and not liable to inundation. She heard accents from all over: West Country, London, Wales, the Midlands, East Anglia, and there were foreign faces and languages too, many of them American, tourists who'd chosen an unlucky year to 'do' Britain and were now stuck with it. There were plenty of black and Asian people with tones that suggested the Midlands – Birmingham, Stoke-on-Trent. As Vicki crossed the bridge she looked back, hearing shouts, and saw a mob of blacks and whites: the whites seemed to be the attackers. The blacks were fighting back and missiles flew, and she believed she saw knife-blades, reflecting back the sun in flashes of blood and danger. There were no police around and the mob had the arena all to itself.

In the middle of the fighting that was spanning the roadway she saw a car, stopped, surrounded. It was the old Mini. She saw the driver's door start to open, saw it smashed back shut by the heavily booted foot of a skinhead with a tuft of black and yellow hair on top of the shaven portion.

The Mini was lifted by a group of white youths, lifted by one side, and overturned. The rusted roof seemed to collapse inwards, crushingly. The old vicar didn't emerge, and a moment later Vicki saw flame curl round the broken bonnet, and thick black smoke billow upwards, and then the whole car exploded in bright orange flame and a lot more smoke. No one made a move to help; they couldn't with all that flame.

Suddenly, Vicki was sick on the bridge. God what a way to go.

FIFTEEN

The massive rescue operation had continued without cease, co-ordinated by the various regional controllers north, south, east and west, with the overall direction centred upon the aircraft carrier with the embarked brass. In the city of Durham, co-ordination point for the North-east, the cathedral, high above the floodwater, was filled with refugees from the stricken Southern areas. Prayers were being said almost round the clock, led by a succession of duty priests, with the great nave so full of homeless people wrapped in blankets that the priests had to function in a side chapel. The tomb of the Venerable Bede in the Galilee Chapel at the western end of the nave was covered with food brought by the citizens, bread, cakes, hot drinks, pies and so on. The tomb made a handy sideboard. The refugees queued and gave thanks to the Townswomen's Guild and the League of Friends, splendid people who had rallied round even before the bishop's plea had reached them. As well as food they had brought articles of clothing: shirts, blouses, coats, underwear, and the chapel had the aspect of a second-hand clothes stall in a market mixed with a burger bar. Not Bede's chapel, or indeed the cathedral itself, alone: the castle and the university had offered shelter as well, as had many of the city's public buildings, some of them a good deal warmer than the vicinity of the Venerable Bede.

Some of the children complained loudly, shivering between the ancient stone walls, set high between heaven and the River Wear.

'I'm cold, Mum.'

'Yes, dear.'

'It's bloody freezing –'

'Ssssh!' A clergyman had entered through a massive door. 'Not so *loud*. And don't complain.' Mum shook him. 'You're dead lucky to be here at all, you don't seem to realize.'

Far south of Durham in one of the worst of the flood areas, Captain Wilson's niece Anne Henschel, having worked herself to the bone as a kind of auxiliary nurse, had gone down with typhoid like so many hundreds of others who had crowded into Shaftesbury and made conditions insanitary to the point where any improvement while the floods lasted was totally impossible. Dr Hannington said he was putting Anne aboard the next rescue mission, which might be by helicopter or boat. A number of naval craft were now operating, assisted by the water transport companies of the Royal Corps of Transport.

She refused to go. 'There are so many others.'

'Someone has to go, Anne. Why not you?'

There was really no answer to that: it was simple logic. She was of no more value to Shaftesbury than was anyone else, and while sick she wasn't any use anyway, just another encumbrance.

Still thinking about the old vicar in his blazing Mini, Vicki walked on towards Harrogate. It seemed farther than the reverend had suggested. Vicki dragged a weary body past the golf club and went on along a road that seemed to have no ending. But soon the buildings became closer-packed and she came to the level-crossing, open continously now to road traffic, there being no trains running, and walked across. It took her some while to locate the doctor's surgery; so many of the crowds were refugees like herself and no one seemed to know where they were. They were filling the streets and sitting around in the open spaces, in family groups.

When she did find the surgery she went straight in and found more crowds and a frantic receptionist, middle-aged verging on elderly, trying to cope.

Frantic herself now, Vicki banged on the counter, demanding attention.

'You must wait your turn,' the woman snapped. 'For a start, the doctors aren't here. They've other things to do now, and –'

'Listen, I've come from –'

'Wherever you've come from –'

'There's people bloody *sick*! There's an old lady ... and I don't reckon I'm too well either, come to that.' Vicki was yelling now, all her worries and frustrations rushing to the surface in a tide like the flood itself 'There are kids, too, on the boat ... and their mum looks like dying if the doctor don't come. It's not bloody *fair*. Tears streamed down her face. 'All these people – they don't look bloody sick to me. It's us who need the doctor. You know something? I reckon I could be pregnant and – and – and I reckon I may have AIDS.'

For a moment there was silence. The receptionis stared, taken aback at Vicki's display, seeming not to know what she should do. The short, rather stunned silence ended in indignant murmurs from the waiting would-be patients, murmurs that grew louder, angry comments about gate-crashers and queue-jumpers and AIDS spreaders. The sound was threatening and Vicki knew when she was beaten, having had plenty of experience of being beaten. Her head in the air she turned away from the counter and pushed through for the door to the street. Tears ran down her cheeks, which were as pale as death with the raised bruises standing sharply out. Men and women pressed away from her, still loudly critical. As she reached the door a woman held it open, caught the eye of someone behind, and then Vicki felt hard hands going round her body and she was given a bum's rush to the steps outside where she fell headlong to the pavement.

Aboard the power-boat, they all looked back at the handcart on the dry land. Mary Rushworth said, 'You'll never get her into it, Daddy.'

'We can try, can't we?' McNaughten's voice was sharp: he disliked those who gave up before they started.

'You mean get Mummy out for a test run?'

'No need to put it quite like that, Mary.'

'How else would you put it? We'd have to get her on deck, then carry her ashore, and plonk her in it. It's not right. She's not *fit*, Daddy.'

'What do you propose, then? Leave her where she is? She's *got* to be got out – sometime if not now. Surely you can see that, can't you?'

'Yes, but – oh, what's the use! You're just obstinate, Daddy –'

'Obstinate – in trying to save my family, get them to somewhere dry and safe?'

'I don't see why we have to.'

McNaughten let out a sign of exasperation. 'Have to what, Mary?'

'Get out. We're all right here aboard the boat, aren't we? If the flood deepens or if it doesn't. We can live aboard for –'

'For how long? Just think about it.' McNaughten, a

foot raised on the gunwale, ticked off items on his fingers. 'One, the food won't last for ever. You know the position as to that, Mary —'

'Yes, but there'll be food in the village, won't there?'

McNaughten conceded that. 'So long as the water doesn't rise further, yes. Two, the fuel's low — right, Charles?'

Charles Rushworth nodded.

'Nothing we can do about that. A hundred pounds to a penny the pumps in Stainsby are dry as bone.'

'We could check,' Mary said defiantly.

'Yes, we could check. It'd be waste of time. The thing is to move north. We can't do that in the boat —'

'We could find a river,' Charles said. 'Or a canal.'

McNaughten, about to go on with his theme, checked as though hit by a bullet. Of all the people aboard, he should have thought of that one. But he recovered soon enough. 'Damn silly suggestion,' he said angrily. 'Yorkshire — you should know, the times you and the boy have spent up here. Try to a take a boat up the Wharfe, for instance. Or the Ure. Rocks and shallows — oh, we'd get a little way, of course. Nothing like far enough.'

'Canals, then.'

'I'm not too sure about canals,' McNaughten said, sounding huffy. 'There's a canal at Skipton but it's bound to be jam-packed and the fuel's getting shorter, and we'd waste time. That's no good to anyone. No, it's obvious the time's come to go ashore, find some sort of transport when we reach a sizeable town, and then think again.'

'The boat's security,' Mary said. 'Beds for one thing. A roof over our heads.'

McNaughten didn't go along with that at all. The boat, he said, was not so much security as an excuse for staying put. The current conditions could last indefinitely, go on for months perhaps. Something more positive must be done and the fact of the power-boat, useless anyway without its fuel, was giving them blinkered vision.

'Get Mother up on deck,' he said with decision. He looked towards the land, across the shallows they would have to cross with the burden of his wife. 'Where's that damn girl?' he asked. 'Not here when she's needed. I always knew we'd never see her again, she was totally unreliable, you could see it in her face.'

The van with the Big Clout embarked, moving north from Long Preston, passed through Settle, where they continued on north towards Ingleton beneath the shadow of the great peak of Ingleborough. Before Ingleton thirst intervened and Wayne in the driver's seat followed a pub sign, turning off the road for Clapham and the New Inn.

Leroy said they shouldn't risk it: the pigs hadn't entirely vanished off the face of the earth. They were too close yet to Long Preston.

'They won't be bothering their arses,' Wayne said. They had in fact passed two police cars heading south and no notice had been taken of them, which Wayne had found encouraging and far from surprising the way things were, with the roads crowded, everything on the move still. He was beginning to have a feeling that the North would turn out to be jam-packed, the whole surviving population crammed into the north of Scotland or something, so that before long a southward movement would start to even things up a little. All the same, they would go on farther and when they found a propitious place, like a big town, maybe they would stay. Somewhere where there were pickings to be found. Man could not live on a Transit van alone. Behind the New Inn was a car park but it was full: Wayne drove on along a rutted lane and parked right up at the end and they all walked back to the New Inn where the proceeds of the till back in Gargrave paid for drinks. There was hostility as the Big Clout barged their way through the crowd to the bar.

'Fuck off,' Wayne said to a man, one of the hostile ones, next to him as he thumped on the bar counter. 'Or else.' He lifted a big fist. 'Want to be done over, do you, eh?'

The man flinched and turned his back. Wayne laughed. The Big Clout was allowed its way; Leroy and some of the others just let it be seen that they had weaponry: knuckle-dusters, razors, steel spikes. The metal-studded leather jackets alone looked nasty, more Leeds or Bradford than the New Inn, Clapham. A second round of drinks followed the first, then another, after which the Big Clout got on the move again. Wayne led the way out, an arm round Gemma's shoulder. She seemed to like it, and kept giving Leroy superior glances, as much as to say she'd shifted her loyalties and was now the boss's girl. Wayne didn't pay any attention to that, didn't even notice, he was the boss and that was that, his edict held sway and bollocks to what anyone else thought.

When they reached the van Leroy had his say.

'Gemma goes in the back, with me.'

'Gemma,' Wayne said, 'doesn't. Gemma goes in the front. With me.'

'Come here, Gem,' Leroy said. The girl looked from one to the other, excited but at the same time suddenly scared: she knew she'd started something.

Wayne said calmly, 'Stay where you are, right?'

Gemma nodded. Wayne was a good deal bigger than Leroy, who wouldn't stand a chance if trouble came. *When* trouble came: it was on its way, all right. Gemma stayed put beneath the safety of Wayne's strong arms. There was a steely flash of sunlight as Leroy, coming closer, activated a flick knife. Wayne gave an insulting laugh and moved like lightning, going for Leroy and booting the weapon from his hand. Leroy, his wrist almost torn from the arm, spun round in agony and as he did so Wayne got him, swung him round like a puppet, held him at arm's length as though taking aim, and slammed his right fist hard into the pale face which seemed to disintegrate into bloody flesh, like pulp, and four teeth fell to the ground. Tears streamed down Leroy's face.

Wayne laughed again. 'Pick the pieces up,' he said to

his henchmen, 'and shove 'em in the back. Gemma goes in the front. With me.'

Leroy apart, the members of the Big Clout were in good spirits as they left the village and continued north. The drinks helped. They were going to make it. Wayne had ideas of going as far as Glasgow – or if they couldn't for one reason or another make Glasgow, Carlisle would do – and then calling it a day, getting established and making their mark on the local tearaway scene, shifting Pompey to the North as it were, resuming the reins of power. It sounded good. As they drove, they sang the latest numbers of Top of the Pops, an unmelodious outburst of frantic tune hitting the Yorkshire Dales. In front, Gemma preened and shifted her body so that Wayne could manipulate his left hand as freely as possible whilst driving.

Wayne glanced sideways as the van came back to the main road for Ingleton. 'All right, love?'

'Ooooh!' Gemma was all right.

The singing continued.

Aboard the aircraft carrier in the North Sea a fresh series of reports was being studied closely: meteorological reports, seismological reports, less scientific reports from observers in Canada, the United States and the areas around the Caribbean. Some of the reports were from ships at sea, some were from the land. There was a lengthy spiel from Washington: America's capital was back in business, making contact with the world at large.

'Significant,' an assistant under-secretary from the Ministry of Defence said. 'Don't you think?'

Lips were pursed. It was early days, anything could happen and definitive statements were best avoided until there was greater certainty in the air. 'Possibly,' the addressed principal said at last.

'Enough for some cautious optimism, I believe. On the one count, anyway.'

'Are you going to pass it on?'

'A word in the ear, I think – yes.' The assistant

under-secretary took up the telephone on his desk in what had been the ship's commander's office, now acting as Ministry of Defence, and over the next few minutes spoke quietly into several ears: the ears of his own permanent under-secretary, the ears of Agriculture, of Home Office, of the various electricity undertakings, of the Department of Energy, Environment, Foreign and Commonwealth, the makeshift Cabinet Office. In what had been the captain's quarters the Prime Minister was informed: there had been signs, general indications, no more than that, that across the North Atlantic the water-levels were dropping. Only very slightly, but it was seen as a step in the right direction, naturally. Things were steadying up: there had been a very sharp drop in the water temperature in the far North and this was seen as particularly significant.

'Enough to refreeze the glacier systems?' the PM asked.

'Well ...'

'How do glaciers re-form, do you know?'

'I'm afraid not, Prime Minister ...'

'Please find out and let me know, then.' Fingers were tapped on the desk-top. 'Is this ... is this *firm* information, do you suppose?'

'At this stage I rather think not, Prime Minister. But it *is* encouraging, of course. We may be seeing the beginning of the end. At least as regards the flood itself. There's –'

'It'll be the start for us,' the Prime Minister said, sounding grim. 'Getting things back to normal, a most daunting task, most daunting.' He paused, looking up sideways at the harbinger of the news. 'You sounded as though you had more to say, John. You said, as regards the flood itself.'

'Yes, I'm afraid there's bad news as well, Prime Minister.'

'Yes?'

'A shift of wind in the higher layers. Forecast to be a

sustained shift … blowing towards the UK. The fall-out, you see … from that original nuclear explosion.' He added, 'If the wind should decrease at an unfortunate moment, then it's thought likely the fall-out could drop. On the UK, you see. They're not very worried, I gather, in Canada and the United States …'

SIXTEEN

It was quite a business preparing to disembark the old lady. McNaughten and Charles Rushworth carried her from the cabin into the wheelhouse and from there to the deck with not too much difficulty, though she was clearly in pain and was making noises of distress. There was no point in telling her what was happening or what they intended to do: she was taking nothing in; she was just a sack of potatoes but one with the ability to feel.

'Careful,' McNaughten said. When Mrs McNaughten was out on deck, she was sat for a while on the seat in the stern and Mary sat beside her, tidying her up, removing the remains of the last meal which had had to be fed to her as usual. The whimpering noises continued and McNaughten looked terrible. It wasn't that he was unduly hard but he had a lot on his mind and the repetition of the sounds grated.

He vented his anger in once again castigating Vicki in her absence.

'That bloody girl.'

'I thought you didn't want her aboard, Grandpa,' John Rushworth said mildly.

'I didn't, and of course, in many ways it's a good thing she's gone. She was unhealthy, physically and morally. But the way she's —'

'She was an unhappy girl,' Charles said. 'A rotten life.' John had told him a thing or two. 'She had good in her. And we don't know what's happened to her. I suggest we hold our horses, and not criticize.'

'Hear, hear,' John said. 'I liked her, anyway –'

His grandfather rounded on him. 'You would! People of your age have no damn discrimination. However, don't let's argue. Point is, if she'd been here, she could have helped. Now let's get on with it. Where's the cat?'

'He's all right,' Mary said. Pum was sitting on the foredeck, washing himself and enjoying a shaft of sunlight. He would become a problem once they were all ashore, wouldn't like being cooped up in his basket indefinitely while they trudged along the roads north. Mary went for'ard and picked him up, and stroked him, holding him against her breast. Poor God-damn cat, she thought, right out of his element, not seeing himself as a potential problem.

She came back to her father and stood in front of him, challengingly. 'Well?' she demanded.

'Well, what?'

'You're really determined to leave the boat, aren't you? Whatever you do to Mummy.'

McNaughten sighed. 'I've told you. It's the only way. We have to be realistic.'

'I see. So being realistic, how the hell do you propose to get Mummy over into the water?'

McNaughten said, 'She'll be carried. I'll go over first, then she can be lifted onto my shoulders. Easy!'

'And put in that stupid handcart! Haven't you thought what it'll be like for her?'

'It's the best we can do. It's transport. It's only a temporary measure, Mary –'

'Being pushed about … like a penny-for-the-guy outfit! It's horrible!'

'Don't get hysterical about it,' McNaughten snapped. 'I only thought –'

'You only think about yourself, don't you?' For a moment Mary buried her face in Pum's fur, then faced her father again, her expression grim. 'I'm not leaving the boat,' she said, 'and Mummy's staying. We're much better off aboard – especially her.' She turned to he husband. 'Charles.'

'Yes,' he said. He coughed. 'Of course, your father's right about the fuel, but …'

'Yes. But. Remember what Vicki said more than once? I heard her. It's your bloody boat, she said. Well?'

From the bottom of the surgery steps in Harrogate Vicki had picked herself up, her cheeks streaked with tears that mingled with the dust of the long walk from Stainsby and now gave her a muddy appearance. She was at the end of the tether.

What now? Just the one thing: walk again, back to Stainsby. They'd be wondering and she had to get back and tell them what a load of sods and bastards they were in Harrogate, no help there. Would the Rushworths have followed her up when she hadn't come back, some of them anyway, John most likely? Of course they couldn't shift the old lady, that was obvious.

She walked back across the green grass of the park, not much grass to be seen in fact with all the people camped there. They were being succoured by the various agencies, Townswomen's Guild, Red Cross, St John's Ambulance, Help the Aged, organizations for the disabled, Salvation Army …

Salvation Army.

Always in time of trouble turn to the Sally Army: how often had she heard that said? Herself, she'd never troubled them because she'd reckoned her problems weren't the sort that the Sally Army went for. But now, if they could produce transport to Stainsby, accompanied, if possible, by a doctor or failing that a nurse …

She could always try, anyway.

Across the park there were two Sally Army people, a man and a young girl, their blue-and-maroon uniforms like a beacon of hope in a darkening night. She went over, stepping carefully between the mass of people, the distraught mothers and squalling babies and the roaming dogs, either local or dispossessed of home by

the flood. Some of the younger people seemed to be all
right, not too discommoded, radios were playing – some
station was evidently back on the air – and some couples
were all but making love in full view of everyone in the
immediate vicinity if they cared to watch, and some
obviously did, gawping more or less openly and having
a good giggle about it. One old grand-dad's eyes were
almost coming out of his head. Vicki's thought was,
good luck to them; there wasn't much joy in life for
anyone just now. She reached the Salvation Army and
buttonholed the man. He was busy with a middle-aged
woman who was rattling on nineteen to the dozen about
whatever her problem was. He was looking harassed
himself.

'Just a moment,' he said to the talkative women,
turning to Vicki. 'What is it, dear?'

She said, 'It's urgent, mate. Not like some.' She
glanced at the middle-aged woman, whom she didn't
reckon was at all urgent and who had transferred her
harangue to a young woman who looked like a
daughter. 'Stainsby,' Vicki said.

'What about Stainsby?'

She told him, breathlessly, making sure she got it all
out, about the old lady and the sick woman and the
children and her own predicament. The main thing, she
said, was to get back to the boat. Either that, or get the
Rushworths here to Harrogate, which was what they'd
seemed to want basically.

'You said pregnant?'

'Me, yes. Maybe – I don't know for sure. That bloody
woman in the doctor's surgery –'

'Yes, yes.' The Sally Army man was kind, fatherly, but
there were limitations to what he could do in the current
disaster. He said, 'I don't think you're – er –'

She helped him out, rubbing a hand across her
smudged and muddy face. 'Far gone. No, I'm not.
But –'

'It's not an emergency, my dear. Just look at what
we've got on our plate.' The Sally Army man waved a

hand around the crowds of people. 'Stainsby, now. It's a fairish way —'

'I know. I walked some of it.' She thought again about the old reverend and she shuddered. 'Got a van or something, have you, eh?'

He shook his head. 'Out of the question. No transport at all available now. Even if there was, there wouldn't be any petrol or diesel.'

'Bike?'

Again he shook his head. 'I've not seen a bicycle since the floods started. There was such a panic at the start, no one knowing how far the water would extend.'

'What do I do, then? Eh?'

He said, 'I don't know what to suggest and that's a fact. Everywhere's crowded out. Citadel, all the hotels and that, public buildings —'

'I don't want that. I want to get to bloody Stainsby! They're *expecting* me, like I said.' She paused, half expecting him to come up with something, knowing inside that he wouldn't because he couldn't. Everyone was in the same boat, and talking of boats, all the people on the grass of the park would have given anything for the shelter of the boat owned by the Rushworths. 'Oh, well, I reckon I'll just have to bloody walk, won't I? Thanks all the same, mate.'

She turned away. She was beginning to recover her spirits: there was always someone worse off and just talking to the Sally Army man had helped, because he'd been friendly. She'd let that rotten old bitch at the surgery get her down too much. Doctor's receptionists were cowshit, all of them, and no good getting too angry and upset about them, they were just one of life's unpleasant facts.

She started back the way she had come, again picking her path between the family groups and the copulating couples and the gawpers. At one point she was impeded by someone having fainted and those around going to the person's assistance and forming a barrier that brought Vicki to a temporary halt while they sorted themselves out. As she stood there she felt a hand going up her skirt. Looking down, flinching, she saw the leering face, the wet, very red lips, the pale face of a man of around fifty, she thought.

He seemed to think she might be enjoying it.

The impediment to her progress thinned out and she lifted a foot. She drove the heel of her shoe into the leering face and there was a shout of pain. 'Dirty old bugger,' Vicki said, and moved on. Behind her, she heard a flaming row start up: she looked back. Evidently the feeler had a wife and the wife had cottoned on. Looking at the wife, Vicki didn't entirely grudge the husband his grope. Sex, she thought, it's a funny thing, even floods don't drown the urge. About the only thing they didn't.

She came back towards the level-crossing. She crossed the road when she saw the window of a toy shop. It was open: all trade hadn't packed up. But it was dusty and fusty, sad really, with the look that no one ever bought anything there. Maybe too old-fashioned: plastic dolls from the pre-Sindy era, little wooden trucks and so on, and an old lady dressed all in black sitting at the back and doing some crochet work.

The old lady looked up. 'Yes, my dear?'

'Just looking like, thanks.'

'Look all you want, For a baby, is it?'

Vicki thought: not yet anyway. She said, 'Couple of kids. Boy and girl. Lost their mum, see.'

The old lady clicked her tongue. 'In the flood?'

Vicki nodded. She walked round the little shop, here and there shifting the dust of ages. She found something called a Sailor Bunny, a small rabbit dressed in navy blue, with a sailor's cap and collar. She found a clockwork crocodile that when activated moved its head and tail, and went along the floor with a lurching motion on wheels concealed beneath its scaly body. It looked sad and unwanted.

She took both to the old lady. 'How much?' she asked.

'It's marked.' The old lady showed her where. 'Thirty

pence in this new-fangled money,' the old lady said. 'Myself never did change.'

And never did sell much, Vicki thought, feeling sadder than ever. She said, 'I'd like them.'

'Of course, dear. All the poor children, in this dreadful time. Take them. There's no need to pay.'

'I've got some money.' She had ten pounds fifteen pence on her, what was left of the wages from the Norwich café, cash that she'd had on her when she'd done that murder. 'I'd like to pay.' She insisted, and left the shop with the Sailor Bunny and the sad-looking mechanical crocodile, hoping David and Rosemary would appreciate them after they'd waited all those years to be bought.

It was not often that Charles Rushworth had ever stood up to his father-in-law and when, this time, he did so he surprised even himself. McNaughten was the more surprised: the wind had been taken out of his sails by an act of mutiny.

'Oh, very well,' he said huffily. 'I've never suggested it was my boat. I've simply offered advice, that's all. *Good* advice, based on experience. Experience of the Navy. If you care to reject that advice, it's entirely up to you, of course. Just don't blame me when things go wrong – that's all I ask.'

'I won't,' Charles Rushworth assured him. The cave-in had been so fast that it was almost unbelievable. 'It's not that I don't appreciate your –'

'Save the soft soap,' McNaughten interrupted crisply. 'There's things to be done, and quickly. Your job. The first thing's that poor woman. The children's mother,' he added unnecessarily. 'Disposal of the body.'

'Yes. I know. Still no doctor.'

'That bloody girl,' McNaughten said witheringly. 'Can't think how you ever trusted her, *I* wouldn't have done. If no doctor shows by this evening, and that's not long to go now, she'll have to be dealt with – the body I mean. We have to decide how. In my view there's only one way: shore burial. There are implements in that stable where I found the handcart.'

'The sods with our bayonets turning,' John quoted. 'Darkly at dead of night ...'

'At night certainly,' McNaughten said.

'Rather clandestine, isn't it?'

'I was thinking of the children.' After being told by Mary what had happened, David and Rosemary had been kept on deck and young John Rushworth had done his best to find ways of keeping their minds off tragedy. There had been surprisingly few tears; they were in a state approaching shock, their senses dulled, John thought. Now, hearing what his grandfather had just said, he was inclined to agree that after dark would be a better time, while the children were alseep. If they didn't sleep, there were aspirins in the medical outfit and half a one apiece wouldn't hurt them. On the other hand he agreed with his father also: it did have a clandestine feel about it, getting the dead woman over the side in darkness, carrying her ashore like contraband, then digging out a grave and placing her in it, coffinless and without benefit of clergy. It certainly wouldn't do for the children to be present at such a burial whether it took place by night or by day.

McNaughten said, 'Let's get on with it, Charles. The grave, I mean. The three of us. You'll be all right with your mother, Mary?'

She said yes, she would be. Before leaving the boat, Charles and John manoeuvred the old lady back through the wheelhouse and into the cabin and lifted her back onto the bunk. She still seemed totally unaware but there was something in her eyes, some curious inward look, that told her grandson she was seeing something that was a closed book to the rest of them. Back in the wheelhouse he said to his father, 'I don't believe she's got long to go.'

'Why d'you think that?'

John told him. Charles shrugged and said, 'Could be. We don't know much about these things ... but I remember when my old grandfather died. He'd lost a son, my uncle, years before. He had a funny look in his eyes too, and I remember he said distinctly, "Well, Harry old lad, it's been a long, long time". Then he died. He'd seen Harry coming to welcome him – at least, that's what I think.'

'D'you think Granny was seeing someone?'

Charles shrugged again. 'I don't know, John. One thing's certain, she'll be a lot better off, poor old soul.'

They went back on deck and joined McNaughten. They said nothing about his wife and he didn't enquire: his mind was ranging ahead towards grave-digging and ten minutes later the three were walking up the village street towards where McNaughten had found the hand-cart. Once again there was luck around: a couple of useful-sized spades.

'The next question,' McNaughten said, 'is where do we dig it?'

'Plenty of fields around.'

'Yes. And when the inhabitants come back, the fields could be ploughed.'

'That's a nasty thought,' Charles said. 'But if we dig deep enough –'

It was John who broke in. 'There's a church. What about the churchyard? It may not be legal, but so what? It'll be a *fait accompli* ... and these aren't the times to bother too much about the legal bull. After all, she's entitled to a decent burial in consecrated ground.'

McNaughten was dubious. 'How do we know she was C of E?'

'We could ask the children,' Charles said. 'But I doubt if it matters all that much to God.' He hefted his spade on to his shoulder. 'Come on,' he said, taking the lead. 'We'll do this properly.'

They found the church, old stone outside and old oak pews and lectern inside. They had gone in so that they could leave some money in the offertory box, a kind of atonement for guilt. McNaughten murmured, as he made his offering. 'For what we are about to do, may the

Lord forgive us.'

The ground was harder than they had thought likely; the digging was tiring and it was well after nightfall before they finished, working by the light of a torch brought by McNaughten. The father, who had insisted on keeping pace with the others, taking his turn fully, looked about all in. Without speaking, they made their way back towards the edge of the flood and the power-boat riding at its anchor in the darkness, lit by a single masthead lamp above the wheelhouse.

McNaughten stopped at the water's edge. He had been using his torch to signal the boat, to warn his daughter that they were about to embark; and the beam had fallen on the water. 'Funny,' he said.

'What is?'

'There's a tide mark. Since we came ashore. I suppose it's possible the floodwaters have taken up the tidal pattern of rise and fall – I'm not sure about that. All I can say is, there's been no evidence of that till now. It didn't happen this morning.'

'You mean –'

'I mean it could be, and I stress could be, that the thing's coming to an end. The level's falling.'

SEVENTEEN

There had been gangs roaming the streets of Knaresborough. As Vicki came back across the bridge over the River Nidd she saw that the burned-out remains of the Mini were there still. She went past, remembering. If only she hadn't to come through Knaresborough again; but she knew of no alternative route. When she saw the mob ahead, skinheads, she turned aside and went up a narrow street, anywhere just to keep clear of trouble. The mob was howling for blood and from what she had seen after coming off the bridge they were stoned out of their minds, probably raided a pub or something.

It was an animal sound and it seemed to be coming closer. As some of the skinheads appeared at the end of the side street, Vicki pressed herself back into a doorway, her heart going fast, hoping not to be seen if the skinheads came past. As she pressed she felt the door open behind her and she almost fell in backwards. Recovering, she saw a sleazy passage with peeling wallpaper and a smell of leaking gas overlying a kitchen smell of cooking cabbage. An old man stood there, tall, ramrod straight, with a trim white moustache and a totally bald head. He just stood there, saying nothing. Then he reached past Vicki and pushed the door shut. He bolted it. Suddenly nervous, Vicki said, 'Sorry, mate. I pushed me back against it and it sort of gave.'

'It's all right. Those skinheads, I suppose?'

She nodded.

'Scum. Dirty, filthy scum! You're all right here and you're welcome. They'll move off before long. Where have you come from, if I may ask?'

The old man had an authoritative voice. He could be a retired copper for all she knew, something like that. She wouldn't mention Norwich. She said, 'Stainsby, a few miles –'

'I know Stainsby well. Born there I was, lived there till I joined the Army. You don't come from Stainsby.'

'No,' she said. 'Just happened to fetch up there, that's all.' The old man seemed trustworthy: she told him the whole story and while she was telling it he led her along the passage to a small room at the back of the little house, a nicely furnished room with an upright piano in one corner with some framed photographs on it, including one of a solider that she guessed was the old man taken a good many years ago, a soldier with the Royal Arms on the sleeve and a brown leather belt round the waist and across the chest.

He saw her looking at it as she came to the end of her story and he said, 'Regimental Sarn't-Major I was then.'

He named the regiment, not a Yorkshire one. 'Good days. Never come again now. Everyone's rabble now. Life's a misery. Especially since the wife died.' The old man had turned his back to her, looking at himself so many years ago. 'Lonely. And I'm no hand in a house, dusting and that.' Suddenly he turned round. There were tears in his eyes, there was a surge of sound from outside: the skinheads had come along the street and seemed to be congregating at the old man's door, possibly having seen Vicki entering.

Vicki said in alarm, 'They'll break the door down, won't they?' The old man said that if they broke down the door they'd be sorry: he had a shot-gun, ready loaded. He went across to a cupboard and brought it out. 'I'll use it if I have to,' he said. 'There's no law left anyway, not now.' He left the room and went along the passage towards the door. Vicki followed, though not all the way. The old man stood with the shot-gun pointed at the door. Nothing happened: the mob seemed to be drifting away. The old man came back and they returned to the room with the piano and the photograph.

Vicki said, 'I'd better go. They're waiting for me in Stainsby. I reckon –'

'You're safer here, lass.'

She said, 'OK I know what it's like to be lonely. I'll stay till it's safe, though God knows when that'll be.'

'I'll watch out, lass. Tell you what. I'll go with you, me and my gun. See you out of Knaresborough and on the road to Stainsby.'

'You'll be in danger then.'

He shook his head. 'I've got nothing to lose. Not since the wife died. It's a rotten way of living, on your own. Never been on my own till the wife died. Just as soon be dead.'

She talked to him for quite a while until he said it was safe to go out. She felt immensely sorry for him; he walked by her side through the streets, tall and straight, carrying the shot-gun. They came safely through

Knaresborough and he stayed with her a little way beyond till she was firmly out of town. He had put a brown Homburg hat on his head when he left his house, and on parting he raised it in a courtly, old-fashioned gesture. She set off thereafter alone, her heart beating fast. The dark of the countryside was in itself threatening. She had got about half way to Stainsby when she realized she had left the Sailor Bunny and the mechanical crocodile behind in their paper bag. Too late to go back for them. She was sorry, really sorry, about the little toys.

She reached Stainsby while the Rushworths, finished in the churchyard, were starting to wade out to the boat. They told her the news; it hadn't been unexpected, of course. McNaughten was churlish, asked her about the doctor and then turned his back when she tried to explain. She waded towards the boat with John and said, 'I'd brought some things for the kids. Little toys. Got left behind.'

John nodded, told her his grandfather believed the water-level was falling, just slightly. 'Mean all this is going to be over soon?' Vicki asked.

'Don't know about soon. There's a hell of a lot of water around.' John went on to say that his grandfather believed the apparent lowering of the level might be due, not to a retreat on the part of the waters, or a refreeze, but simply that some of it had drained away to parts of the world hitherto untouched. In which case it might not go down all that far for quite a while. If ever it did. John added, 'You've probably gathered he's a pessimist!'

Madame Smith, not far from the junction with the B6254 that avoided Kendal, was in a foul mood.

'I did tell you,' Albert said.

'Tell me bloody what?'

'That the road was narrow. Remember?'

'You never said you'd wreck the bloody bus.'

'It's not *wrecked*. It's still on its wheels, innit?'

'Won't go, will it? I call that wrecked. To all intents and purposes, it's bloody wrecked.' Madame Smith breathed hard down her nose. True, Albert had said the road would be narrow in places and it certainly was. It was fortunate that they'd met nothing coming the other way, because part of the road was so narrow that it became single track with passing places. Currently the double-decker bus was blocking the road totally: taking a corner that had proved sharper than expected, taking it too fast into the bargain, Albert had crashed the bus into a dry-stone wall and the result had been clouds of steam from a broken radiator. That, Albert had said, was somewhat final.

'Get the AA?'

'Ha, ha.'

'One of the girls can go and find a bloody telephone.'

Madame Smith sat and seethed. All this waste of time, when she could be getting somewhere where she could once again be in business. Glasgow, perhaps ... certainly Glasgow was big, far bigger than Kendal where she hadn't wanted to go but now wished she had. She wouldn't be in this mess. Glasgow could be a good spot for trade, cosmopolitan unlike Kendal, and plenty of seafarers as well as tired businessmen with money. They could forsake the bus and set up a proper residential establishment and be a lot more comfortable, and posh again, like London. If only the bloody bus would move.

Well, it *could* move, if slowly. There were plenty of girls to push. Madame Smith turned in her seat preparatory to telling the girls to get out. 'How far to the main road, Albert?' she asked.

'Shouldn't be far. Couple o' miles.'

'Well, then! Get to the main road, find a garage, see what they can do.' Madame Smith turned right round and called out. 'Out you get, the lot of you. Bloody push, all right?' She was busily disregarding Albert's protestations that the hippie vehicle was so ancient and neglected that it would fall apart if interfered with by a mechanic and in any case was far too old for any garage to carry the right parts, let alone a radiator, when she became aware of the radio. With the engine stopped it could be heard without interference and it had never been switched off since the last time.

'Listen,' she said.

'What is it?'

'Something about the water-levels ...'

'What about them?'

'Shut up and you might hear.'

They had missed the beginning of it, but the announcement sounded official and the bloke doing it didn't sound, Madame Smith thought, like those little nonentities of local radio announcers with their rotten diction, unauthoritative voices, and their inability to pronounce names of people and places properly. This one was posh and was quoting some high authority that Madame Smith didn't quite get though she believed it was something American. Yes, there was something about Washington DC that she caught after a few more angry hand-flaps at the young ladies, who were inclined to twitter maddeningly when it was important you heard something correctly.

The voice was saying that in the USA the water-level was subsiding. Not a lot, but the prognosis was quite good: the great surge had retreated and the experts believed the regions in the far North, the land of the glaciers that had melted, were about to return to their normal pattern. A refreeze had begun and there was much more stability. Already the North Atlantic was at a slightly lower level. The voice continued: a small drop had been reported from various points in the British Isles, widely spread. The South of England, Wales and the West, and along the northern edge of the flood in Yorkshire. Similar reports were coming in from the Continent.

After making its announcement, the voice was catechized by another voice, a reporter Madame Smith supposed.

Was the subsidence expected to continue?

The first voice answered circumspectly: caution could be heard in the tone. 'It's possible, but we must not raise our hopes too far.'

Had the Government made its plans to cope with the aftermath, the disease, the distress, the displaced persons, the filth and the damage, the re-establishing of normal life?

'Oh yes. Yes, of course.'

What, precisely, would be the plans?

'It's too early to go into much detail, you'll appreciate that. Of course, announcements will be made just as soon as – as it's thought appropriate.'

What – exactly – did that mean?

'As soon as the levels start *really* going down. As soon as it's confirmed positively.'

The second voice made an enquiry about fall-out from the exploded nuclear device that had started the colossal water movement in the first place. The representative of the Government pounced firmly on that one. He had no knowledge of fall-out: the voice was quite assured. There was no cause for alarm whatsoever. That, although naturally this was not said, had been well thrashed out aboard the aircraft carrier. To alarm the population now would be to induce panic and the flood would end in total chaos. Where ignorance was bliss ... and anyway, if the fall-out did come and did drop on the UK, there wasn't a damn thing anybody could do about it.

When the interview was over Madame Smith was in a state of high excitement: soon they could return south to the metropolis and start drying out the bedrooms.

'Come on, girls,' she called down the length of the bus. 'Let's get us back on the road, all ready for home.'

The young ladies pulled out on to the narrow road and clustered around Albert, who was taking another look at the damage. 'First thing,' he said, 'shove her out of the wall. Back her, see.'

Easier said than done; it was hard to attain full shoving capacity from across the low stone wall, but the girls did their best, tagging on to the sides, using what handholds they could find and exerting themselves to the utmost, with Madame Smith acting as a sort of cheerleader to co-ordinate the combined effort.

'One, two, three ... 'eave!'

Continuing north-west from Clapham, the Big Clout passed through Ingleton close to the Lancashire border and from there went on to Kirkby Lonsdale. In Kirkby Lonsdale Wayne misread the directions for the A6 and shifted on to the B6254. He continued north-west towards Kendal, where he would get back on track for Glasgow. But it didn't work out that way: a little north of Kirkby Lonsdale something unexpected happened.

A police patrol car, coming down from the north, coming fast, slowed and flashed its headlight at a moment when the road ahead of the van was clear.

'Pigs,' Wayne said. 'Bloody pigs!'

His intention was to take no blind bit of notice, just press on and hope the pig car would get holed up in the traffic behind. There was still quite a lot of it and there wouldn't be any hope of the fuzz doing a U-turn, not unless someone slowed and let them in as it were, and not many people were taking too much notice of the law at the present time.

But the pig car, as if its driver could read Wayne's mind, slewed across the road in front of the van. Wayne almost stood on the footbrake, hauling on the handbrake at the same time. That didn't seem to have much effect; the van plunged on and at the last moment the cop car seemed to lose its nerve and pulled back a little to its own side of the road. Recognizing victory, Wayne accelerated. As they reached the police vehicle, the van's off-side front wing took the leading edge of the police bonnet. The van slewed wildly but Wayne managed to keep it on the road, just. He believed there was no damage apart from a crumped wing; but a look in the rear view mirror showed chaos behind. The cop car was on its side, right across the road, and there was a lick of flame starting. All the traffic had been brought to a standstill, rather sharply since those behind the van had accelerated along with Wayne, and there was quite a pile-up.

'Now what?' Leroy asked from the back.

For a start, Wayne said, not the M6. Not now. Pigs could have been killed and the motorway patrols would be on the watch as soon as the word went through on the radio transmitters.

'Where, then?'

'Find a side road and get lost, right? We've got a good start. Then ditch the van and get another.' In truth, Wayne was a shade rattled: it had been a very close thing and he could have been a dead man by now. Also, the pigs definitely weren't going to like it. Nicking a van was one thing, but it had gone beyond that now. In his preoccupation Wayne missed a couple of left-hand turns onto side roads – they weren't all that easily seen anyway and he was moving recklessly fast – and came beneath the carriageways of the M6 before he found another turn, this time to the right.

'Okay,' he said. 'This one.'

He swung the wheel hard; there was a scream from his tyres and another scream as the oncoming traffic braked violently. He noticed that there was no traffic behind him: the block caused by the cop car was still holding things up nicely. He drove fast, reckless still, along a very narrow road with dry-stone walls and behind them sheep-cropped grass with the slopes of the fells beyond. Lonely country, desolate, forbidding to a Southerner, not the place for an accident. Beside Wayne, Gemma manifested fear: Wayne was driving like a fucking lunatic, she said.

'Shut yer gob.'

She put a hand on his arm. He shook it off, angrily.

'Wayne, *please*!' She was screaming now; the van was really hurtling around almost blind corners and something, for all they knew, could be coming the other way. Gemma became hysterical, beating at Wayne with her fists. From the back Leroy leaned through, activated his flick knife, and laid the point against Wayne's thick neck.

'Slow it,' he said in a snarling voice. 'The lady's scared, or didn't you fucking know?'

'Lady,' Wayne said viciously and accelerated, reaching behind himself to clamp strong fingers over Leroy's wrist. The van hurtled on, taking the next corner dangerously and entering a short stretch of straight.

Right ahead, close was a double-decker bus, old and decrepit and trundling slow, with a crowd of girls round it. Wayne yelled out in alarm, and, like with the cop car, crammed on his brakes. Tyres screamed, the van slithered on. When the impact came Leroy once again had his knife where it would do the most damage. The blade went right through Wayne's neck and the point came out the other side, and from behind the body Leroy flew straight through the windscreen and on through more shattering glass into the the lower deck of the bus.

EIGHTEEN

As though by a miracle, Madame Smith had survived: a moment earlier and she would have been in the seat and would have taken the full force of Leroy's hurtling body. As it was, with the Elsan being occupied, and she not being able to wait, and the bus moving so slowly, she had got down in order to go behind the dry-stone wall, properly dressed as ever in the London hat and gloves. She had spotted a gap where the stones had come adrift and she was making for this when the Big Clout hit, whereupon she turned about.

'Oh, my God! My *God*!'

She saw a shambles: the girl Gemma had not gone through the windscreen, but she was dead, a crushed mass of bloody flesh and shattered bone, sandwiched into the crushed front of the double-decker. Wayne's equally dead body had virtually become a pancake as to its lower portion, the waist down. The trunk and face leered horribly, the knife protruding from the throat. The rest of the mob were dead: they had to be and the fact spoke loudly for itself. The van was virtually flattened against the heavy double-decker, little more than crumpled metal oozing blood. Aboard the bus there was a fair amount of blood too: Leroy's head had ben almost severed from his body. He had entered with such force, such impetus that the rest of him had ended up right at the back, by the Elsan compartment. The young lady who had deflected Madame Smith from the toilet felt the impact of the van and heard the thump of dead Leroy and tried to get out, but was blocked by the body. She yelled uselessly. Blood had spurted in all directions and not from Leroy alone: Albert had been in the driver's seat, steering while the girls pushed, and he had been squashed like a fly and all around him the front of the bus was stove in.

'Girls!' It was a brave, rallying cry.

They were all safe and unhurt, every one of them apart from a few bruises sustained when the bus had run backwards and they'd taken a tumble. They clustered round Madame Smith, just the one in the toilet missing but just then they heard the distraught shouts and she was released after Leroy's body had been dragged clear by an ashen-faced young lady.

'Did you ever?' Madame Smith asked shakily, her hat now away. The scene was so terrible; but Madame Smith was tough and knew she had to cope, jolly her young ladies along and not let them sink into anything like hysteria. They'd seen many a sight in their working lives but probably never so bloody a one as this. 'Now we've got to think, like. Eh?'

'What about the bus?' one of the girls asked.

'*What* about it?'

'All that blood. Who's going to clean it away?'

'Not me for a start,' Madame Smith said promptly. 'Anyway, sod the bus. The bus, it's had it.'

'What do we do, then?'

'Walk to the main road. Mr 'Arker,' Madame Smith said in reference to Albert, never referred to by his first name to the girls, 'said we weren't far off the main road and that was a while back.' Just for a moment Madame Smith turned aside and, with a shudder, looked at the mess in the driver's cab. 'Poor bloody Albert,' she said half to herself. 'Oh, my God, poor bloody Albert.' Tears came. She would grieve for Albert, though there had in fact been nothing between them – she wouldn't ever have lowered herself to the level of a chucker-out, but he had been a good man, loyal and useful, if sometimes cheeky. He would be missed and it was such a pity that, if those broadcasts had been right, he would never see the recession of the dreadful floods, dear old London Town emerging from its mud and sludge.

An upright, elderly figure entered Stainsby from the Knaresborough road, riding a bicycle. The old cyclist pedalled through the village, making towards where he would find floodwater. When he saw the shine of it ahead, beneath a bright sun, he dismounted, shoved the bicycle up against the wall of a cottage, and strode down, soldier-like, to the water's edge beyond which he could see the power-boat riding at anchor and the girl sitting on the foredeck with two children.

He cupped his hands and called out; she had already seen him and she went over the side with her jeans rolled up to the knee and waded ashore. She looked astonished.

'You,' she said. 'What the 'ell!'

'You said you'd come from Stainsby. You said there was a boat, and the little children.'

'Yes,' she said. 'A bloody long walk you've had.'

'I bicycled –'

'Never said you had a bike.'

'I hadn't, not then. I – found it, I thought I'd come. You left these.'

From his pocket the ex-RSM brought the Sailor Bunny and the clockwork crocodile. 'I thought of the kids. So I came. I'll get back now.' He turned.

'No, wait.' She put a hand on his arm. 'Look as though you could do with a bite, you do.'

That afternoon the water-level went down more, and before the old man had left to return to Knaresborough the boat had gently grounded. They got over the side to lighten her and they shoved her out a little way, to deeper water, and after she'd drifted far enough they again let go the anchor. Now, the time for decisions had come, and in the mean time McNaughten was glad he'd agreed to stay aboard the boat. They should be able to drop south with the receding flood, and hope one day to resume the old life, pick up the old threads again once everything had dried out. Until then they would have the boat to live on. The problem was going to be the Lockhart children, orphans of the storm as it were. McNaughten had gathered they had grandparents who were probably themselves victims. There was, or had been, an uncle and aunt in Eastbourne in Sussex, another aunt in south-west London. They could perhaps be contacted. Or they, too, might be dead. McNaughten thought the boy and girl were a blasted nuisance really, and was grateful to both the girl and the old RSM for having brought the toys, which seemed to occupy a good deal of the children's attention, as though they were overcome by having something of their own again. McNaughten guessed that neither of those cheap toys would be parted with for a long time to come.

He had liked the ex-RSM too. The old chap had called him sir, unusual enough these days, and McNaughten had been so surprised he'd poured him a whisky from his now slender stock. Late that night, the boat grounded again, and again they had to shift berth farther out.

It was as though some giant's hand had pulled out a plug.

The flood had gone down quite a fair amount in the area around Shaftesbury, and the town and its surroundings, including Zig-Zag Hill, might soon dry out. So long as the rain held off, anyway.

Dr Hannington looked at filth, the awful residue of the recent weeks: bodies both human and animal, refuse of all kinds – the diseases wouldn't go away yet, that was for sure. The stench was terrible, almost overpowering; you needed a gas-mask, but when it was at its worst as the hot sun came up, all you could do was to soak a handkerchief and hold it over your nose. Not much use, but it helped.

From his vantage point near the Grosvenor Hotel, Hannington walked back to his surgery. It had been an uphill fight; and he missed Anne Henschel, now helicoptered out with the other really bad cases. She could die, he knew that; he'd heard nothing since he had waved the helicopter away towards somewhere in the North of England. Dead already? He prayed not. The floods had brought her into his life; he didn't want them, or their effects, to take her away again. She had spoken of her parents in Somerset, known to have died, and of the uncle with the old Thames sailing barge who'd come to take her off but had been turned down because she wanted to be useful; and there had been her brothers, both now dead, victims of typhoid and not enough medical wherewithal to combat it, two among so many.

There had been no news of that elderly uncle and his barge. He might have survived; he might not. If he had, then he was Hannington's only known contact with Anne. In due course, when all this was over and he could be spared, he would start the search.

In Wales the high land was standing well clear now

and like the other places the people counted the cost. So many bodies, left behind by the retreating water … so many bodies and, wedged and grounded in a high cleft of the Black Mountains dangling oddly, a very strange sight so high up in Wales, a broken sailing barge named *Ethel Margaret*, deserted and forlorn, and no explanation at all as to what had happened to the people who had brought her there.

A long way to the north in Wensleydale the villages were starting to empty out and return to more or less normal conditions as the drift back south began in dribs and drabs. The broadcasts had been encouraging and there was hope. People had been advised to stay put for a while longer and not clog the roads, and certain areas, the whole of London among them, were out of bounds until the medical and cleansing teams had gone in and reported and started the massive operation. Those areas would be kept rigorously clear by police cordons and troops, all of them armed. Nevertheless many people had taken a chance and moved closer to their homes in the South. Bainbridge in Wensleydale became a little more civilized and the small cottage that had been inhabited by old Tom Braithwaite and his wife was now mercifully free of invaders, though this relief had come too late for the Braithwaites.

Aboard the aircraft carrier the machinery of government turned over and orders were sent to the various areas, the regional controllers, the police and medical teams, the Army, the naval vessels and the air stations that had carried out the evacuation as best they had been able. Now they were being put on stand-by for the big mop up and the restoration of the essential services; it would be a while before many of the roads were serviceable, it would take many weeks perhaps to get the railways moving again. A full survey would have to be made of all the tracks south of the original flood-line and it was anticipated that they would all need to be relaid; the floodwater would have undermined them, washing away the ballast.

Prayers were still being offered daily by the carrier's two padres and by the Rev. Daniel Matthews from near Hull, the latter worried about his small flock embarked with him from the church tower. Most of them depended in one way or another on the land and what it produced, and that land would be useless for he knew not how long, salted as it would have been from the North Sea sweeping across the Holderness peninsula; but of course they were but few among so many.

After prayers on the day when the reports confirmed that the tide had turned, the RC padre spoke of violence to come.

'Looters,' he said. 'Thugs, taking their pickings. Of course, there'll be martial law, but I'd not like to be in the big cities when the people are allowed back, I'd not like that at all. It'll be every man for himself, I'd say, and the law-abiding people finding their homes ravaged by more than the water and the dirt.'

Matthews came from no big city and was more glad than ever that he'd left Liverpool. But looting could take place in the country districts also, and there was the church plate and the communion vessels, unharmed by the flood but only too susceptible to rapacious hands and minds. And of course there was the rectory, their home, with its possessions, some of them of value – silver, good china, carpets and pictures that could probably be cleaned professionally despite the filth of the flood and the water-effects themselves. Photographs that could never be replaced. So many things that meant a great deal to himself and his wife. Daniel Matthews took comfort from the Bible, or tried to. Lay not up for yourselves treasures upon earth, where moth and rust doth corrupt, and where thieves break through and steal.

It didn't help, really; perhaps his faith was not strong enough. It was a very testing time. very testing ...

The Rushworths, with the Lockhart orphans, proposed to move south after negotiating with the owner of the Stainsby garage, now returned home with the rest of the villagers, for fuel to fill the power-boat's tanks. The garage owner, with good Yorkshire brass-sense, did some profiteering but McNaughten was glad enough to pay up. They would, he said, go as far south as seemed practicable and wait for the city of Cambridge to be declared open once again.

'Could take weeks,' he said. Now was the time, or it soon would be, when the mess would have to be faced up to, and not just the physical mess – the wreckage, the spoil and rot and filth of the actual flood, though that would be bad enough: it was the other things, the intangibles ... McNaughten's mind went back over the time since they'd embarked, to what he'd said to his son-in-law about a fresh start when it was all over. He'd spoken, he remembered, to Charles about a fresh start, a way ahead. He'd felt some optimism then in spite of their predicament, a feeling that good would come out of terror and hardship as it usually had throughout Britain's long history. He didn't feel that any more now; he felt utterly dispirited. As his son-in-law had forecast, the useless ullages, the baddies and the queers and the lefty trendies would have survived and would once again take over because they, as ever, would be the majority. For the others, so many careers would be in abeyance: lawyers, bankers, university professors, even business executives and estate agents and the like – they would have no relevance until the country had been rebuilt and was working again ...

Charles said, 'Penny for 'em?'

'What? Oh – I was just thinking.' McNaughten rubbed at his eyes, feeling very tired all of a sudden. 'Cambridge, now. As I said, it could take weeks before we can re-enter. But at least we've got the boat to live in.'

'Yes,' Mary said, with emphasis.

'All right, all right.' McNaughten changed the subject. 'How's your mother? I thought I heard –'

'She's all right. Thanks to Vicki.'

'That girl!'

'She has a way with her. I wouldn't have thought it a

first, but she has. I think it's because ... well, she's
suffered in her life too. It's given her a capacity to – to
feel, a sort of natural sympathy, I don't know. She's a
good girl, Daddy. I'd miss her now. She's like a nanny to
the children, too.'

McNaughten grunted. Those children ... before he
could speak again, Vicki came up on to the deck. He
told her what they had decided to do.

'Go south? To Cambridge?'

'Handy for there, yes. Or Norwich. I take it you'll
come with us, back to Norwich.'

'Oh, no. No, I bloody won't!'

McNaughten snapped, 'Why the devil not? It's where
you came from, isn't it?'

'Right, but I'm not bloody going back, mate, I'm *not*!'
She wasn't going to risk it. Definitely. She might be
recognized or anything. The past didn't ever go away,
all nice and neat and safe. She said, 'I've broadened my
horizons. I reckon I like Yorkshire. Thanks for
everything, but I'm bloody off.'

Mary said softly, 'Vicki, those little children –'

'Yes, the kids, I know. And the old lady – your mum.
I'm ever so sorry ... I'd like you to tell them that, from
me. But I'm off and the sooner the bloody better. I'm
not one for goodbyes, never was.'

She got up on the gunwale, no belongings to take, no
backward looks but there were tears in her eyes as she
splashed into the water and waded for the shore. The
Rushworths stared after her and McNaughten shouted
for her to come back and not be a little fool but she just
waved without turning and plodded on in her damp
jeans, a forlorn but brave figure going she knew not
where, except not Norwich or parts adjacent. She went
on through Stainsby with its returned inhabitants,
thought for a moment as she passed by the churchyard
of the lonely body illegally buried there, and without
conscious thought took the Harrogate road for
Knaresborough.

Knaresborough was where she had her only friend.

The old soldier had an empty house where once he had lived with his wife. He would give her room for a while. He was lonely. If she did happen to be pregnant, well, it would be a base, somewhere to settle for all the pre-natal clinics and that, an actual address. It made sense.

It had been something out of history, real Victoriana, but it had saved the day for Madame Smith and her young ladies, all now walking south and looking rather tatty. Bugger Glasgow now, as Madame Smith remarked, the reports were good enough to start the trek back to somewhere handy for London. The bright lights would come again eventually, with the soft beds and the wealthy old judges and business tycoons and the occasional way-out cleric who might not have much money but did have class. Past recollections included three deans, four canons and a suffragan bishop.

Trudge, trudge and not a lift offered. Not till the strange vehicle overtook them, slowed and stopped. It was a horse-drawn vehicle, a sort of coach, beautifully kept, really gleaming with polish, swaying behind four horses, no less. Madame Smith had seen pictures in museums … it was bigger than a brougham, she could see that, but at first she couldn't put a name to it, then she realized with a start of astonishment that it was a stage-coach. A fair amount of room inside, more on top. Carrying only the driver, a red-faced, stout man sitting on the box and doing a twirl with a whip.

The driver was calling down. 'You ladies going far?'

'London,' Madame Smith said shortly. 'More or less.'

'Funny, that. So am I.'

'Eh? You what?'

'Going to London. It's my home. Or was. Came up when the first panic started – no use trying to come by car, I said to myself, the petrol'll run out. So I brought the coach. Been in the family for generations. Hop up. There'll be room.'

'Well, I never!' Madame Smith said. 'Take bloody years.'

'Not quite. Of course, we'll do it in stages. Like they used to in years gone by, only slower because we won't get a change of horses. No point in hurrying anyway, they won't let us in yet. Are you coming?'

'You bloody bet,' Madame Smith said.

'You in charge?'

Madame Smith said she was; the coachman told her she could sit with him on the box. Madame Smith hustled her young ladies and first filled the interior; then the remainder got their feet on the step and climbed to the roof, where they sat dangerously, clutching each other and the handrails along the sides. It was a squeeze, but no matter, it was transport, and they would be homeward bound, all the way. Madame Smith hoisted her dress and climbed to the box. She clutched at her London hat as the horses were whipped up and the stagecoach trundled away, stared at by the occupants of passing cars who probably thought they were part of a veteran vehicles' rally, or the Duke of Edinburgh in unexpected company, or a pantomine. Madame Smith's gloved hand clutched the rail for dear life, while the back rail bit into her spine just above her bottom. The seats were very hard, too, as the stout man seemed to recognize.

'You'll have a sore bum by the time we get anywhere near London,' he said. 'The girls, too.' He looked sideways and gave her a wink. 'Quite a bunch, aren't you?'

Madame Smith bridled: the word 'bum' was not a word a gentleman used to a lady, and the man may well have made a good guess at what the party was and she didn't like that either.

'No need to be bloody cheeky,' she said. 'My girls are all sodding respectable, thank you very much. As a matter of fact, we're a finishing school for young ladies what got flooded out.' She sat very upright, largely because she had to anyway on the box but also to show her annoyance. But never mind, she thought, whatever happens to other people *we're* all well placed for survival. Her and the young ladies, they wouldn't starve, there weren't many Sedberghs around, thank the Lord. The world's oldest profession would never allow itself to be overcome; it would go on providing a good and useful service just as soon as everything had dried out; and maybe before, who could tell?

SURREY
COUNTY COUNCIL
WITHDRAWN FROM STOCK
AND OFFERED FOR SALE
WITH ALL FAULTS BY
SURREY COUNTY LIBRARY

WOKING
LIBRARY

STARGAZING
2008

MONTH-BY-MONTH GUIDE TO THE NORTHERN NIGHT SKY

HEATHER COUPER & NIGEL HENBEST

HEATHER COUPER and NIGEL HENBEST are inter-
nationally recognized writers and broadcasters on
astronomy, space and science. They have written more
than 30 books and over 1000 articles and are the
founders of an independent TV production company,
specializing in factual and scientific programming.

Heather is a past President of both the British
Astronomical Association and the Society for Popular
Astronomy. She is a Fellow of the Royal Astronomical
Society, a Fellow of the Institute of Physics and a former
Millennium Commissioner, for which she was awarded
the CBE in 2007. Nigel has been Astronomy Consultant
to *New Scientist* magazine, Editor of the *Journal of the
British Astronomical Association* and Media Consultant to
the Royal Greenwich Observatory.

Published in Great Britain in 2007
by Philip's, a division of Octopus Publishing Group Ltd,
2–4 Heron Quays, London E14 4JP

An Hachette Livre UK Company

Text: Heather Couper & Nigel Henbest (pp. 6–53)
Robin Scagell (pp. 61–64)
Philip's (pp. 1–5, 54–60)

Pages 6–53 Copyright © 2007 Heather Couper &
Nigel Henbest

Pages 1–5, 54–64 Copyright © 2007 Philip's

ISBN-13 978-0-540-09027-3
ISBN-10 0-540-09027-1

Heather Couper and Nigel Henbest have asserted
their moral rights under the Copyright, Designs and
Patents Act, 1988, to be identified as the authors of
pages 6–53 of this work.

All rights reserved. Apart from any fair dealing for the
purpose of private study, research, criticism or review, as
permitted under the Copyright, Designs and Patents Act,
1988, no part of this publication may be reproduced,
stored in a retrieval system, or transmitted in any form or
by any means, electronic, electrical, chemical, mechanical,
optical, photocopying, recording, or otherwise, without
prior written permission. All enquiries should be
addressed to the Publishers.

Printed in China

Details of other Philip's titles and services can be found
on our website at: **www.philips-maps.co.uk**
email: **philips@philips-maps.co.uk**

Title page: Lunar eclipse (Robin Scagell/Galaxy)

ACKNOWLEDGEMENTS

All star maps by Wil Tirion/Philip's, with extra
annotation by Philip's.
Artworks © Philip's.
All photographs from Galaxy.
8 Rob McNaught
12, 16, 29, 32, 36, 62 top, 63 top, 64 Robin
Scagell
20 Yoji Hirose
24 Damian Peach
40, 44–45 Philip Perkins
48 Jamie Cooper
53 Ian King
62 bottom Celestron
63 bottom Meade

CONTENTS

The sight of diamond-bright stars sparkling against a sky of black velvet is one of life's most glorious experiences. No wonder stargazing is so popular. Learning your way around the night sky requires nothing more than patience, a reasonably clear sky and the 12 star charts included in this book.

Stargazing 2008 is a guide to the sky for every month of the year. Complete beginners will find it an essential night-time companion, while seasoned amateur astronomers will find the updates invaluable.

THE MONTHLY CHARTS

Each pair of monthly charts shows the views of the heavens looking north and south. They're useable throughout most of Europe – between 40 and 60 degrees north. Only the brightest stars are shown (otherwise we would have had to put 3000 stars on each chart, instead of about 200). This means that we plot stars down to 3rd magnitude, with a few 4th-magnitude stars to complete distinctive patterns. We also show the ecliptic, which is the apparent path of the Sun in the sky.

USING THE STAR CHARTS

To use the charts, begin by locating the north pole star – Polaris – by using the stars of the Plough (see February). When you are looking at Polaris you are facing north, with west on your left and east on your right. (West and east are reversed on star charts because they show the view looking up into the sky instead of down towards the ground.) The left-hand chart then shows the view you have to the north. Most of the stars you see will be circumpolar, which means that they're visible all year. The other stars rise in the east and set in the west.

Now turn and face the opposite direction, south. This is the view that changes most during the course of the year. Leo, with its prominent 'Sickle' formation, is high in the spring skies. Summer is dominated by the bright trio of Vega, Deneb and Altair. Autumn's familiar marker is the Square of Pegasus, while the winter sky is ruled over by the stars of Orion.

The charts show the sky as it appears in the late evening for each month: the exact times are noted in the caption with the chart. If you are observing in the early morning you will find that the view is different. As a rule of thumb, if you are observing two hours later than the time suggested in the caption, then the following month's map will more accurately represent the stars on view. So, if you wish to observe at midnight in the middle of February, two hours later than the time suggested in the caption, then the stars will appear as they are on March's chart. When using a chart for the 'wrong' month, however, bear in mind that the planets and Moon will not be shown in their correct positions.

THE MOON, PLANETS AND SPECIAL EVENTS

In addition to the stars visible each month, the charts show the positions of any planets on view in the late evening. Other planets may also be visible that month, but they won't be on the chart if they have already set, or if they do not rise until early morning. Their positions are described in the text, so that you can find them if you are observing at other times.

We've also plotted the path of the Moon. Its position is marked at three-day intervals. The dates when it reaches First Quarter, Full Moon, Last Quarter and New Moon are given in the text. If there is a meteor shower in the month we mark the position from which the meteors appear to emanate – the *radiant*. More information on observing the planets and other Solar System objects is given on pages 54–57.

Once you have identified the constellations and found the planets, you'll want to know more about what's on view. Each month, we explain one object, such as a particularly interesting star or galaxy, in detail. We have also chosen a spectacular image for each month and described how it was captured. All of these pictures were taken by amateurs. We list details and dates of special events, such as meteor showers or eclipses, and give observing tips. Finally, each month we pick a topic related to what's on view, ranging from the Milky Way to double stars and space missions, and discuss it in more detail. Where possible, all relevant objects are highlighted on the maps.

FURTHER INFORMATION

The year's star charts form the heart of the book, providing material for many enjoyable observing sessions. For background information turn to pages 54–57, where diagrams help to explain, among other things, the movement of the planets and why we see eclipses.

Although there's plenty to see with the naked eye, many observers use binoculars or telescopes, and some choose to record their observations using cameras, CCDs or webcams. For a round-up of what's new in observing technology, go to pages 61–64, where equipment expert Robin Scagell shares his knowledge.

If you have already invested in binoculars or a telescope then you can explore the deep sky – nebulae (starbirth sites), star clusters and galaxies. On pages 58–60 we list recommended deep sky objects, constellation by constellation. Use the appropriate month's maps to see which constellations are on view, and then choose your targets. The table of 'limiting magnitude' (page 58) will help you to decide if a particular object is visible with your equipment.

Happy stargazing!

If ever there was the opportunity to see A-class stars strutting their stuff, it's right now. Cold though it may be, January is the best month in which to start observing the heavens. The winter constellations are so striking that there's no better time to find your way around the sky. And this year, they're joined by an interloper – the Red Planet **Mars**, which occupies centre-stage in January. It joins the dazzling denizens of **Orion**, **Taurus**, **Gemini** and **Canis Major** to make up a scintillating celestial tableau. Mars hovers just above red giant **Betelgeuse**: which is the redder of the two? This is also the month to catch sight of **Sirius**, the brightest star in the sky. Low on the horizon, it twinkles and flashes all the colours of the rainbow – a result of seeing the Dog Star through thick layers of Earth's atmosphere.

JANUARY'S CONSTELLATION

You can't ignore **Gemini** in January. High in the south, the constellation is dominated by the stars **Castor** and **Pollux**. They are of similar brightness and represent the heads of a pair of twins; their stellar bodies run in parallel lines of stars towards the west. Legend has it that Castor and Pollux were twins, conceived on the same night by the princess Leda. On the night she married the King of Sparta, wicked old Zeus (Jupiter) also invaded the marital suite, disguised as a swan. Pollux was the result of the liaison with Jupiter – and therefore immortal – while Castor was merely human. But the twins were so devoted to each other that Zeus granted Castor honorary immortality, and placed both him and Pollux among the stars.

Castor is an amazing star. It's not just one star, but a family of six. Even a small telescope will reveal that Castor is a double star, comprising two stars circling each other. Both of these are double (although you need special

▼ The sky at 10 pm in mid-January, with Moon positions at three-day intervals either side of Full Moon. The star positions are also correct for 11 pm at the

beginning of January, and 9 pm at the end of the month. The planets move slightly relative to the stars during the month.

equipment to detect this). Then there's another outlying star, visible through a telescope, which also turns out to be double.

PLANETS ON VIEW

Mars opens the year with a dazzling display: at magnitude −1.5, the Red Planet is brighter than any of the stars, and it's visible all night long between the horns of Taurus (the Bull). But the faster-moving Earth is pulling rapidly away from Mars, and it drops to magnitude −0.6 by the end of January.

At magnitude +0.5, **Saturn** shines steadily under the tummy of Leo (the Lion). It rises at around 9 pm at the beginning of January, and at 7 pm by the end of the month.

Venus appears as a brilliant Morning Star, low in the dawn twilight towards the southeast: at magnitude −4.0, it outshines everything bar the Sun and Moon. During January, Venus drops down towards the Sun: at the beginning of the month, it rises three hours before the Sun, but by the end of January its lead is just an hour and a half. By then, it's closing in on giant planet **Jupiter**.

Uranus sets in the southwest around 9 pm, barely visible to the naked eye (magnitude +5.9) in Aquarius.

In the second half of January you may catch a glimpse of **Mercury** very low in the southwest after sunset. The tiny planet is at greatest elongation on 22 January, and on this date and the following evening you'll find Mercury (magnitude −0.5) only

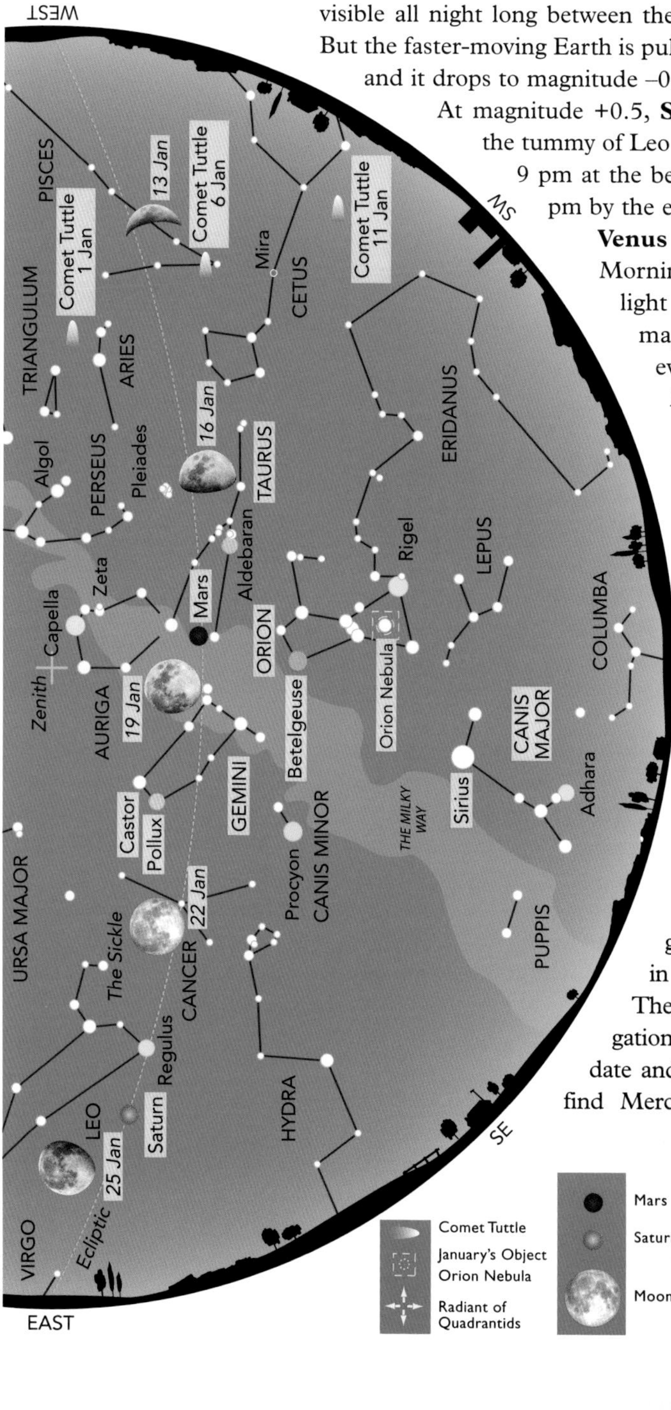

Chart labels: WEST, EAST, SOUTH, SE, NW, SW

Comet Tuttle 1 Jan, Comet Tuttle 6 Jan, Comet Tuttle 11 Jan, 13 Jan, 16 Jan, 19 Jan, 22 Jan, 25 Jan

Constellations and stars: PISCES, TRIANGULUM, ARIES, PERSEUS, Algol, Capella, AURIGA, Zeta, Pleiades, Mira, CETUS, TAURUS, Aldebaran, ORION, Betelgeuse, Rigel, Orion Nebula, ERIDANUS, LEPUS, COLUMBA, CANIS MAJOR, Sirius, Adhara, PUPPIS, THE MILKY WAY, CANIS MINOR, Procyon, GEMINI, Castor, Pollux, CANCER, The Sickle, Regulus, LEO, HYDRA, VIRGO, URSA MAJOR, Zenith, Mars, Saturn, Ecliptic

Legend:
- Comet Tuttle
- January's Object Orion Nebula
- Radiant of Quadrantids
- Mars
- Saturn
- Moon

MOON		
Date	Time	Phase
8	11.37 am	New Moon
15	7.46 pm	First Quarter
22	1.35 pm	Full Moon
30	5.03 am	Last Quarter

one-third of a degree from **Neptune** (magnitude +8.0). This is a great chance, if you have a telescope, to see both the nearest planet to and the farthest planet from the Sun in the same field of view.

MOON

In the morning sky, the thin crescent Moon lies near Venus in the dawn skies of 4 and 5 January. The Moon skims closely past Mars on the night of 19/20 January. On the evening of 24 January, it lies between Regulus and Saturn, and it passes the ringed planet later that night.

SPECIAL EVENTS

During the **first two weeks** of January, look out for Comet Tuttle – the brightest predicted comet of 2008 (an unexpected visitor may put it to shame, though, as Comet McNaught did last year!). Comet Tuttle should start the year as a binocular object, at magnitude +5.5, and fade as it heads towards the horizon (see chart for its changing position); but comets are so unpredictable that it may flare up to naked-eye brightness.

3 January: the Earth is at perihelion, its closest point to the Sun.

4 January: it's the maximum of the **Quadrantid** meteor shower. These shooting stars are tiny particles of dust shed by a now burnt-out comet called 2003 EH1. The solid grains burn up as they enter the Earth's atmosphere. Perspective makes them appear to emanate from one spot in the sky, the *radiant* (marked on the starchart). This is a good year for observing the Quadrantids as moonlight won't interfere.

15 January: NASA's Messenger spaceprobe makes its first flyby of Mercury (see January's Topic).

▲ *Rob McNaught captured this image of his own comet with a 60-second exposure, using a Canon 5D digital camera with a 50-mm f/2.8 lens, ISO 400 setting. It was photographed from about 40 km SW of Dubbo, NSW, Australia, on 24 January 2007.*

JANUARY'S OBJECT

Look at Orion's Belt and, on a clear night, you'll detect a small fuzzy patch below the line of stars. Through binoculars, or a small telescope, the patch looks like a small cloud in space. It *is* a cloud, but at 30 light years across, it's hardly small. Only the distance of the **Orion Nebula** – 1500 light years – diminishes it. Yet it is the nearest region of massive star formation to Earth, containing at least 150 fledgling stars (protostars), which have condensed out of the gas.

◉ *Viewing tip*

It sounds obvious, but if you're stargazing at this most glorious time of year, dress up warmly! Lots of layers are better than a heavy coat (for they trap air next to your skin), heavy-soled boots stop the frost creeping up your legs and a woolly hat really will prevent one-third of your body heat escaping through the top of your head. And – alas – no hipflask of whisky: alcohol constricts the veins, and makes you feel even colder.

This 'star factory' is lit by fierce radiation from a small cluster of newly-born stars called 'the Trapezium', which are beautiful to look at through a small telescope. The Orion Nebula is just part of a huge gas complex in the Orion region which may have enough material to make 500,000 stars in the future.

JANUARY'S PICTURE

The comet of the century, this celestial visitor was a sensational sight in the southern hemisphere in 2007. Brighter than any comet for 40 years, Comet McNaught (discovered by a British astronomer working in Australia) was even visible in daylight. Comets are very unpredictable, and Comet Tuttle – which is visible this month – may put on a great show. Or maybe it won't!

JANUARY'S TOPIC
Messenger to the gods

Mercury – the closest world to the Sun – is putting in an appearance this month. And towards it is heading a NASA spaceprobe with the planet's name writ large upon it. Messenger (standing for ME-rcury S-urface S-pace EN-vironment GE-ochemistry and R-anging mission) celebrates the belief that, in mythology, fleet-footed Mercury was messenger to the gods. This January, Messenger makes its first swing-past of Mercury. The manoeuvre is designed to slow down the probe – as opposed to gravity-assist missions in the outer Solar System which speed up spacecraft – in order that it can enter Mercury's orbit on 18 March 2011. By then Messenger will have travelled almost eight billion kilometres, and made 15 circuits around the Sun. When it arrives at Mercury, its suite of instruments will scan the planet's surface and scrutinize its composition, offering a clue to the origins of this mysterious body. Messenger will also explore Mercury's internal workings – and it could confirm news of the latest discovery from Earth: that the innermost planet has a core made of molten iron. This enigmatic little planet – which may have been born further out from the Sun and later spiralled in – will then be the target for the European probe BepiColombo, to be launched in 2013. BepiColombo comes in two parts: a Japanese spacecraft orbiting high above Mercury to probe its magnetism and a European orbiter circling the planet lower than Messenger, to examine its surface in extreme close-up.

The first signs of spring are on the way, as the winter star-patterns start to drift towards the west, setting earlier. The constantly changing pageant of constellations in the sky is proof that we live on a cosmic merry-go-round, orbiting the Sun. Imagine it: you're in the fairground, circling the Mighty Wurlitzer on your horse, and looking out around you. At times you spot the ghost train; sometimes you see the roller-coaster; and then you swing past the candy-floss stall. So it is with the sky – and the constellations – as we circle our local star and that's how we get to see different stars in different seasons.

In terms of the planets, **Saturn** holds centre-stage this month; but if you're a night-owl, Jupiter and Venus are both lovely morning objects. And talking of mornings – on no account miss the total eclipse of the Moon on 21 February.

FEBRUARY'S CONSTELLATION

One of the most ancient of the constellations, Auriga, the Charioteer, sparkles over-head on February nights. It is named after the Greek hero Erichthoneus, who invented the four-horse chariot to combat his lameness.

Auriga is dominated by Capella, the sixth-bright-est star in the sky. Its name means 'the little she-goat', but there's nothing little about Capella. The giant star is over 150 times more luminous than our Sun, and it also has a yellow companion.

Capella marks the Charioteer's shoulder, and – to her right – is a tiny triangle of stars nicknamed 'the kids'. Two of the stars in the trio are variable stars – but not because of any intrinsic instability. They're 'eclipsing binaries': stars which change in brightness because a com-panion star passes in front of them. **Zeta Aurigae** is an orange star eclipsed every 972 days by a blue partner.

Epsilon Aurigae is one of the weirdest star systems in the sky. Every 27 years, something eclipses the star for a period of

▼ *The sky at 10 pm in mid-February, with Moon positions at three-day intervals either side of Full Moon. The star positions are also correct for 11 pm at the*

WEST

CETUS
PISCES
Ecliptic
ANDROMEDA
TRIANGULUM
ARIES
12 Feb
Pleiades
PEGASUS
CASSIOPEIA
Algol
Epsilon
Zeta
M38
Capella
AURIGA
THE MILKY WAY
PERSEUS
CEPHEUS
Deneb
Polaris
Zenith
CYGNUS
URSA MINOR Kochab
URSA MAJOR
NORTH
DRACO
LYRA
Vega
The Plough
CANES VENATICI
HERCULES
CORONA BOREALIS
BOÖTES
Arcturus
VIRGO
NE
EAST

beginning of February, and 9 pm at the end of the month. The planets move slightly relative to the stars during the month.

nearly two years. This 'something' must be huge – it would stretch beyond the orbit of Saturn if it were in our Solar System. The cool thinking at the moment is that it may be one or two stars with a disc of dust surrounding them, because you get to see the main star peeking out at mid-eclipse. The next eclipse is due in 2009–11.

And when Auriga's overhead, bring out those binoculars (better still, a small telescope) – for within the 'body' of the Charioteer are three very pretty star clusters, **M36**, **M37** and **M38**.

PLANETS ON VIEW

The 'star' of the month is **Saturn** (see February's Topic) which reaches opposition on 24 February. Shining at magnitude +0.2 in the south, in Leo, Saturn is visible all night long.

Mars is hanging in the western sky, and gradually climbing up from Taurus to Gemini. It's above the horizon through most of the hours of darkness, setting at around 4.30 am. During February the Red Planet fades from magnitude −0.6 to +0.3.

In the morning sky, **Venus** is still glorious at magnitude −4.0, though it's now sinking down into the twilight glow. By the end of February, the Morning Star rises only 45 minutes before the Sun.

On the morning of 1 February, the second brightest planet **Jupiter** (magnitude −2.0) lies less than a degree from Venus, making a glorious sight in binoculars or a small telescope. As Venus sinks,

WEST

PISCES
CETUS
ERIDANUS
TAURUS
12 Feb
PERSEUS
Epsilon
Zeta
Pleiades
Aldebaran
M38
M36
Mars
15 Feb
M37
Capella
AURIGA
Castor
GEMINI
Pollux
Zenith
URSA MAJOR
18 Feb
The Sickle
21 Feb
LEO
Saturn
Regulus
VIRGO
24 Feb
Ecliptic
EAST

LEPUS
Rigel
ORION
Betelgeuse
Sirius
Mirzam
CANIS MAJOR
Adhara
Procyon
CANIS MINOR
THE MILKY WAY
PUPPIS
CANCER
HYDRA
SOUTH
SE

		MOON	
	Date	**Time**	**Phase**
Mars	7	3.44 am	New Moon
Saturn	14	3.33 am	First Quarter
	21	3.30 am	Full Moon
Moon	29	2.18 am	Last Quarter

February's Object
Polaris

11

Jupiter ascends ever higher in the dawn sky, rising – by the end of the month – two hours before sunrise.

Mercury, **Uranus** and **Neptune** are too close to the Sun to be easily seen this month.

MOON

On the morning of 4 February the narrow crescent Moon forms an eye-catching triangle with Venus and Jupiter. The Moon lies near Mars on 15 and 16 February. It's very close to Regulus on 20 February, and lies to the lower left of Saturn the following night. On the night of 24/25 February, the Moon passes below Spica, and on the morning of 29 February it's near Antares.

SPECIAL EVENTS

On 7 **February**, the Moon passes directly in front of the Sun, causing an annular eclipse, in which a ring (*annulus* in Latin) of the Sun's brilliant face appears around the Moon's silhouette. It's visible only in Antarctica, though observers in New Zealand and southeastern Australia will witness a partial solar eclipse.

21 **February**: look out for a total eclipse of the Moon, visible from the UK, Europe, western Africa and all of the Americas. The Moon begins to move into the Earth's shadow at 1.43 am. It's totally obscured from 3.01 to 3.52 am, and is free from the eclipse at 5.09 am. It will be interesting to compare this lunar eclipse with last March's: this was unexpectedly bright because of sunlight refracted through the Earth's atmosphere that was then relatively free of cloud.

FEBRUARY'S OBJECT

The Pole Star – **Polaris** – is a surprisingly shy animal, coming in at the modest magnitude of +2.1. You can find it by following the two end stars of **the Plough** (see chart). Polaris lies at the end of the tail of the Lesser Bear (**Ursa Minor**), and it pulsates in size, making its brightness vary slightly over a period of four days. But its importance throughout recent history centres on the fact that Earth's

⊙ *Viewing tip*

When you first go out to observe, you may be disappointed at how few stars you can see in the sky. But wait for around 20 minutes, and you'll be amazed at how your night vision improves. The pupil of your eye is getting larger to make the best of the darkness. Observers call this 'dark adaption', and it also involves the increased production in the retina of a chemical called rhodopsin, which dramatically increases the eye's sensitivity.

north pole points to Polaris, so we spin 'underneath' it. It remains stationary in the sky, and acts as a fixed point for both astronomy and navigation. But over a 26,000-year period, the Earth's axis swings around like an old-fashioned spinning top (a phenomenon called *precession*), so our 'pole stars' change with time. Polaris will be nearest to the 'above pole' position in 2100, before the Earth wobbles off. Famous pole stars of the past include **Kochab** in Ursa Minor, which presided over the skies during the Trojan Wars of 1184 BC. In 14,000 years time, brilliant **Vega**, in Lyra, will be our pole star.

FEBRUARY'S PICTURE

Never as spectacular as an eclipse of the Sun, a lunar eclipse is still a must-see celestial event. In this image of the almost eclipsed Moon, taken last year, the Earth's shadow has almost completely covered the face of our satellite. Look at the curvature of the shadow towards the top of the image: the ancient Greeks – who had figured out how eclipses work – surmised that our world must be four times larger than the Moon.

FEBRUARY'S TOPIC
Saturn

It's Saturn-time again! The ringworld is often featured in February because the giant planet moves very slowly around the sky – taking nearly 30 years to lumber around the Sun. But on 24 February Saturn reaches opposition, when it's opposite the Sun in the sky, and at its closest to Earth. 'Close' is a relative term, though, as Saturn is still 1240 million kilometres away!

Saturn shines at magnitude +0.2 this month. When the planet is exactly in line with the Sun, on the night of 23/24 February, it will appear distinctly brighter. That's because sunlight is reflected directly back to us by icy particles in its rings, like a motorway sign illuminated by headlights.

The rings are Saturn's glory. Visible though a small telescope, they are over 250,000 kilometres across – almost the distance from the Earth to the Moon. Yet they are wafer-thin: less than a kilometre thick. The rings are made up of tiny particles of water-ice, almost certainly the remains of a disrupted moon, which met its gravitationally-challenged fate only a few hundred million years ago. Researchers estimate that – if compressed – the rings would only amount to a moon 100 kilometres across.

On the subject of moons, the total number orbiting Saturn was 47 last year. Now it seems we're up to 60. Keep watching this space ...

◄ *Robin Scagell took this three-second exposure of the 3 March 2007 lunar eclipse on a Canon 10D digital camera at ISO 1600 setting. He was using his Meade LX90 Schmidt-Cassegrain telescope.*

This month, the nights become shorter than the days as we hit the Vernal Equinox. On 20 March, spring is 'official'. That's the date when the Sun climbs up over the equator to shed its rays over the northern hemisphere. Because of the Earth's inclination of 23.5° to its orbital path around the Sun, the north pole points away from our local star between September and March, causing the long nights of autumn and winter. Come the northern spring, Earth's axial tilt favours the Sun – and we can look forward to the long, warm days of summer.

The planets **Mars** and **Saturn** are still in prime position in the night sky, while the new season's constellations – like **Leo** and **Virgo** – are making their presence felt. And don't forget that the clocks go forward on 30 March!

MARCH'S CONSTELLATION

You could be forgiven for missing it, because **Cancer** is hardly one of the most spectacular constellations in the sky. Although it lies in the Zodiac – the band through which the Sun, Moon and planets appear to move – its stars are so faint that city lights completely drown them out. If you do have dark skies, look between **the Sickle** of **Leo** and the twin stars **Castor** and **Pollux** in **Gemini**, and you'll locate the slender little constellation.

According to legend, Cancer is named after the crab which attempted to nip Hercules during his altercation with the multi-headed monster Hydra – one of his 'twelve labours' ordered by the Oracle at Delphi. Alas, Hercules crushed the crustacean under his foot. But Juno (Jupiter's wife) took pity on the crab and placed it in the sky.

At the centre of the constellation, however, there is a gem – the star cluster **Praesepe**. The aptly titled 'Beehive Cluster' is a swarm of about 350 stars lying nearly 600 light years away. It is

▼The sky at 10 pm in mid-March, with Moon positions at three-day intervals either side of Full Moon. The star positions are also correct for 11 pm at the *beginning of March, and 10 pm at the end of the month (after BST begins). The planets move slightly relative to the stars during the month.*

easily visible to the unaided eye, and was well-known to ancient Greek astronomers such as Aratos, Hipparchus and Ptolemy.

PLANETS ON VIEW

Mars lies in Gemini this month, and gradually fades from magnitude +0.2 to +0.8. It's setting at around 4 am at the start of March, and an hour earlier by the end of the month.

Visible all night long, **Saturn** (magnitude +0.3) is creeping along below the chest of Leo towards the constellation's brightest star, Regulus.

Giant planet **Jupiter** is rising in the southeast at around 4.30 am at the beginning of March, and earlier as the month progresses. It shines at magnitude −2.1 in the constellation Sagittarius.

Mercury is at greatest elongation west of the Sun on 3 March, but it's lost in the Sun's glare all this month, as are **Venus**, **Uranus** and **Neptune**.

MOON

On the morning of 3 March, the crescent Moon lies near Jupiter. As it gets dark on 12 March, you'll find the Moon just skimming the Pleiades (the Seven Sisters). The Moon is near Mars on 14 March, Saturn on 19 March and the star Spica on 22 and 23 March. On the morning of 27 March, the Moon passes Antares, and it's near to Jupiter again on 30 and 31 March.

SPECIAL EVENTS

The Vernal Equinox, on **20 March** at 5.48 am, marks the beginning of Spring,

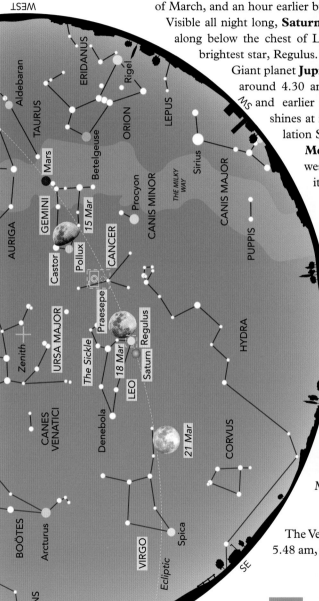

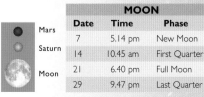

	MOON		
	Date	**Time**	**Phase**
Mars	7	5.14 pm	New Moon
Saturn	14	10.45 am	First Quarter
Moon	21	6.40 pm	Full Moon
	29	9.47 pm	Last Quarter

March's Object
Regulus

March's Picture
Praesepe

as the Sun moves up to shine over the northern hemisphere.

30 March, 1.00 am: British Summer Time starts – don't forget to put your clocks forward (the mnemonic is 'Spring forward, Fall back').

▲ *The stars of Praesepe, photographed by Robin Scagell. This two-minute guided exposure was made on ISO1600 film through a 135-mm f/2.8 telephoto lens.*

OBJECT OF THE MONTH

Regulus – the 'heart' of Leo the Lion – appears to be a bright but fairly anonymous star. Some 77 light years away, it's young (a few hundred million years old), 3.5 times heavier than the Sun, and it chucks out 350 times as much energy as our local star. But recent discoveries have revealed it to be a maverick. It

⊙ **Viewing tip**

This is the time of year to tie down your compass points – the directions of north, south, east and west as seen from your observing site. North is easy – just latch onto Polaris, the Pole Star. But the useful extra in March is that we hit the Spring Equinox, when the Sun hovers over the equator. This means that it rises due east, and sets due west. And at noon, the Sun is always due south. So remember those positions relative to a tree or house around your horizon

spins in less than a day – meaning that it has a rotational velocity of over a million kph. If it were to spin only 10% faster than this, it would tear itself apart. This bizarre behaviour means that its equator bulges like a tangerine (its equatorial girth is one-third larger than its north-south diameter). To compound it all, its rotation axis is tilted at an angle of 86 degrees – which means that Regulus zaps through the Milky Way virtually on its side!

MARCH'S PICTURE

The Praesepe star cluster is at the heart of the constellation Cancer. Its 350 stars are over 700 million years old, and share a common motion through space with the Hyades cluster (which is currently setting in the west). Possibly, both clusters had their origin in the same cloud of dust and gas. In Latin, *praesepe* means 'the manger', but the Chinese had a more prosaic name for the group: 'the exhalation from piled-up corpses'.

MARCH'S TOPIC
Double Stars

The Sun is an exception in having singleton status. Over half the stars you see in the sky are paired up – they're double stars, or binaries. Look no further than the **Plough** for a beautiful naked-eye example: the penultimate star in the Plough's handle (at the bend) is clearly double.

Mizar (the brighter star) and its fainter companion **Alcor** have often been named 'the horse and rider'. But until recently, there was dispute as to whether they were really in orbit around one another, or merely stars that happened to lie in the same direction. Now, the sensitive Hipparcos satellite has pinned down Mizar's distance to 78.1 light years and Alcor's to 81.1 light years. Although this is a gap of three light years, the errors on the measurements could mean that the separation is only 0.7 light years – meaning that the two stars could still form a double-star system. Mizar itself turns out to be a very close double, and is orbited by another close double star – making it a quintuple star-group.

However, there's a down side to double or multiple star systems. The complex gravity of their interactions makes it hard to keep a planet in a stable orbit – which diminishes the chances of life emerging.

Mars and Saturn still continue to grace the evening sky, while early risers will catch Jupiter in the wee small hours.

Constellation-wise, we're now well into spring. Two great beasts stride the sky; **Ursa Major** (the Great Bear), and below it, **Leo** (the Lion). Look for the glorious '**sickle**' of stars – the 'head' of Leo – which is riding high in the south.

The bear and lion are joined by other members of the animal kingdom this month: **Hydra** (the Water Snake) and **Corvus** (the Crow). Hydra is the biggest constellation of all, straggling over 100° – almost one-third of the way around the sky. Despite its sinuous length, it contains only one bright-ish star, **Alphard** (from the Arabic *al fard*, 'the solitary one').

Corvus rests on Hydra's back. According to legend, the crow was meant to deliver water to the god Apollo, but dallied by the pond while the figs ripened. Having gobbled up the figs, he caught a water-snake and returned late with the snake to Apollo, citing it as his excuse for the delay. The god was not pleased – and summarily consigned both Corvus and Hydra to the heavens.

APRIL'S CONSTELLATION

The Y-shaped constellation of **Virgo** is the second-largest in the sky. It takes a bit of imagination to see the group of stars as a virtuous maiden holding an ear of corn (the bright star **Spica**), but this very old constellation has associations with the times of harvest. In the early autumn months, the Sun passes through the stars of Virgo, hence the connections with the gathering-in of fruit and wheat.

Spica is a hot, blue-white star over 13,000 times brighter than the Sun, boasting a temperature of 22,500°C. It has a stellar companion, which lies just 18 million kilometres away from Spica – closer than Mercury's orbit of the Sun. Both stars inflict a mighty gravitational toll on each

▼ *The sky at 11 pm in mid-April, with Moon-positions at three-day intervals either side of Full Moon. The star positions are also correct for midnight at the beginning of*

WEST

ORION
Betelgeuse
8 Apr
Pleiades
TAURUS
Ecliptic
11 Apr | Mars
Mars
MN
Algol
AURIGA
GEMINI
Pollux
Castor
PERSEUS
Capella
URSA MAJOR
M81 and M82
ANDROMEDA
CASSIOPEIA
Polaris
URSA MINOR
Kochab
The Plough
Zenith
BOÖTES
NORTH
CEPHEUS
THE MILKY WAY
Deneb
DRACO
CORONA BOREALIS
CYGNUS
Vega
Radiant of Lyrids
LYRA
HERCULES
NE
OPHIUCHUS

EAST

April and 10 pm at the end of the month. The planets move slightly relative to the stars during the month.

other, raising enormous tides and creating two distorted, egg-shaped stars. In fact, Spica is the celestial equivalent of a rugby ball.

The glory of Virgo is the 'bowl' of the Y-shape. Scan it with a small telescope, and, you'll find it packed with faint, fuzzy blobs. These are just a few of the 3000 galaxies – star-cities like the Milky Way – that make up the gigantic **Virgo Cluster** (see May's Object).

PLANETS ON VIEW

Ringworld **Saturn** is still lording it over the night sky, from its perch in Leo, and just a couple of degrees from the constellation's brightest star, **Regulus**. Currently shining at magnitude +0.5, Saturn is above the horizon throughout the night, setting as dawn comes up.

Mars is still hanging on doggedly in the west, in the constellation Gemini. During April, its brightness drops from magnitude +0.8 to +1.2. At the close of the month, the Red Planet is in line with Castor and Pollux – and at much the same magnitude – so the 'twin stars' will appear to be triplets.

Jupiter is rising in the southeast just before 4 am at the beginning of April, and before 2 am at the end of the month. At magnitude –2.3, it's by far the brightest object in the southern constellation of Sagittarius.

Mercury, **Venus**, **Uranus** and **Neptune** and are too close to the Sun to be visible in April.

MOON		
Date	Time	Phase
6	4.55 am	New Moon
12	7.32 pm	First Quarter
20	11.25 am	Full Moon
28	3.12 pm	Last Quarter

April's Objects M51, M81 and M82

April's Picture Ursa Major

Radiant of Lyrids

Mars
Saturn
Moon

MOON

The crescent Moon forms a lovely sight with the Pleiades low in the northwest on the evening of 8 April. It's near Mars on 11 April, and forms a triangle with Saturn and Regulus on 15 April. The almost-full Moon passes Spica on 19 April. In the morning sky, the Moon lies near Antares on 24 April and near Jupiter on 27 April.

SPECIAL EVENTS

22 April: It's the maximum of the **Lyrids** meteor shower, which – by perspective – appear to emanate from the constellation of Lyra. The shower, consisting of particles from a comet called Thatcher, is active between 19 and 25 April. It's not a very prolific shower, though, and this year the view is hindered by moonlight.

APRIL'S OBJECTS

A trio of galaxies this month – two in **Ursa Major**, and one in neighbouring **Canes Venatici** – called **M81**, **M82** and **M51**. You can just see each of them with binoculars, on a really dark night, though a moderately powerful telescope is needed to reveal them in detail. 'M' stands for Charles Messier, an eighteenth-century Parisian astronomer who catalogued 103 'fuzzy objects' that misleadingly resembled comets – which he was desperate to discover. He did find a handful of comets, but today he's far better remembered for his Messier Catalogue.

M81 is a smooth spiral galaxy, like our Milky Way, with beautiful spiral arms wrapped around a softly glowing core. It's similar in size and mass to our own Galaxy, and lies 11 million light years away.

Lying close by is M82 – another spiral galaxy, but one which couldn't be more different. It looks a total mess, with a huge eruption taking place at its core. This results from an interaction with M81 some 300 million years ago, when the two galaxies pulled streams of interstellar gas out of one another. Gas clouds are still raining onto M82's core, creating an explosion of star formation. For this reason, M82 is called a 'starburst' galaxy.

▼ *Yoji Hirose in Japan captured this classic image of the two bears. The 20-minute exposure was obtained with a Mamiya 645 camera with 55-mm f/4 lens, using Fujichrome 400 film.*

⊙ *Viewing tip*
You don't need a
telescope to bring the
heavens closer. Binoculars
are excellent and can be
flung into the back of the
car at the last minute. But
when you buy binoculars,
make sure to get those
with the biggest lenses,
coupled with a modest
magnification. Binoculars
are described, for instance,
as being '7x50' – meaning
that the magnification is
seven times, and that the
lens diameter is 50 mm.
Ideal for astronomy, these
binoculars, with good light
grasp and low
magnification, don't
exaggerate the wobbles of
your arms. It's always best
to rest your binoculars on
a wall or a fence to steady
the image.

M51 – the Whirlpool Galaxy – in Canes Venatici (the Hunting Dogs) is the epitome of a spiral galaxy, looking for all the world like a Catherine Wheel firework. It was first described by aristocratic astronomer Lord Rosse of Ireland in 1845 as 'spiral convolutions ... the most conspicuous of the spiral class'. It lies 30 million light years away and is about the same size as the Milky Way; it's much brighter, though and is even more glorious for being orientated flat-on. It's accompanied by a smaller companion galaxy, and the two are attached by a stream of stars and gas.

APRIL'S PICTURE

Ursa Major is one of the most recognizable constellations in the sky. This image homes in on its seven central stars (nicknamed 'the Plough' or 'the Big Dipper'). Mizar (second from left) is accompanied by a companion, Alcor; while the two 'pointers' on the right (Dubhe, top, and Merak, below) line up on Polaris (top of image). Ursa Minor (the Little Bear) dangles downward to the left of Polaris. The bright star at the bottom right of the small rectangle is Kochab. It and its neighbour Pherkad served as twin pole stars from 1500 BC to AD 500, but neither was as well aligned with the North Pole as Polaris is today.

APRIL'S TOPIC
Constellations

Virgo, April's constellation, highlights humankind's obsession to 'join up the dots' in the sky, and weave stories around them – even if the shape of the star-pattern bears little relation to its name.

But why do this? One reason is that with the stars on view changing during the year (as the Earth moves around the Sun), the named constellations act as an aide mémoire to the progress of the annual cycle – something that was of especial use to the ancient farming communities.

The stars were a great aid to navigation at sea. Scholars believe that the Greek astronomers 'mapped' their legends onto the sky, specifically so that sailors crossing the Mediterranean would associate the constellations essential to navigation with their traditional stories.

Not all the world saw the sky through western eyes. The Chinese divided up the sky into a plethora of tiny constellations – with only three or four stars apiece. And the Australian Aborigines, in their dark deserts, were so overwhelmed with stars that they made constellations out of the dark places where they couldn't see any stars!

'Now is the month of Maying
When Merry lads are playing, fa la . . .
Each with his bonny lass
Upon the greeny grass. Fa la …

▼ The sky at 11 pm in mid-May, with Moon positions at three-day intervals either side of Full Moon. The star positions are also correct for midnight at the beginning of

So runs composer Thomas Morley's (rather saucy) 1595 account of the delights of this month. And there are delights to be seen in the sky as well. The fourth brightest star in the sky, brilliant orange-red **Arcturus** (about which more later), heads up the constellation of Boötes, the Herdsman, and is a sure sign that summer is around the corner. Hot on the heels of Boötes in the sky comes the tiny coronet of **Corona Borealis**: the Northern Crown. Its brightest star – sparkling in the crown's centre – is appropriately known as **Gemma**.

With **Ursa Major** still riding high this month, look out for the famous double star in the 'kink' of the bear's tail: **Mizar** and **Alcor** (known as 'the horse and rider'). But is this a true double star, with the two components in orbit around one another? The latest measurements suggest that they are separated by more than a quarter of a light year, so the jury is still out. Time will tell!

MAY'S CONSTELLATION

Look up to the south, and you'll spot a distinctly orange-coloured star that lords it over a huge area of sky devoid of other bright stars. This is **Arcturus**, the chief star of the constellation **Boötes**, the Herdsman. Shaped rather like a kite, this constellation was mentioned in Homer's *Odyssey*, and its name refers to the fact that Boötes seems to 'herd' the stars that lie in the northern part of the sky.

The name of the constellation's brightest star, Arcturus, means 'bear-driver' and it apparently drives the Great Bear (Ursa

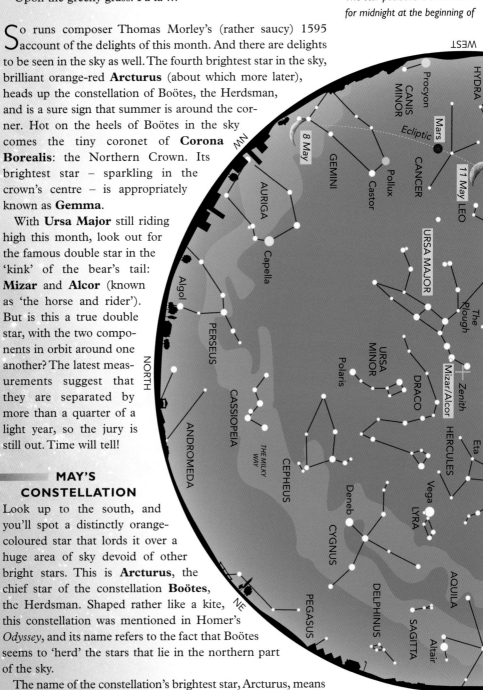

May, and 10 pm at the end of the month. The planets move slightly relative to the stars during the month.

Major) around the sky as the Earth rotates. It's the most brilliant star you can see on May evenings, as the three brighter stars (Sirius, Canopus and Alpha Centauri) are all below the horizon. Arcturus lies 37 light years away, and shines 110 times more brilliantly than the Sun. It's a star in old age, expanding into a red giant.

The star at the ten o'clock position from Arcturus is called **Izar**, meaning 'the belt'. Through a good telescope, it appears as a gorgeous double star – one star yellow and the other blue.

PLANETS ON VIEW

With a clear northwest horizon, you may catch **Mercury** very low down after sunset in mid-May. It reaches greatest eastern elongation from the Sun on 14 May, at magnitude +0.6.

Mars is hanging on in the evening sky, but it's dropping into the twilight by the end of May. At magnitude +1.3, it's faded enormously from its glory days in January. The Red Planet begins the month as a 'triplet' with Castor and Pollux in Gemini, but as May progresses it races upwards to Cancer. On 22 and 23 May, Mars passes in front of the Praesepe (Beehive) star cluster.

At magnitude +0.6, **Saturn** is the jewel in the crown of the celestial lion, Leo, shining twice as brightly as Leo's brightest star – and Saturn's current near neighbour – Regulus. Saturn sets at 4 am at the beginning of May, and at 2 am by the month's end.

WEST

EAST

Mars
Saturn
Moon

May's Object
Virgo Cluster

MOON		
Date	**Time**	**Phase**
5	1.18 pm	New Moon
12	4.47 am	First Quarter
20	3.11 am	Full Moon
28	3.56 am	Last Quarter

23

Jupiter is beginning to make its presence felt, rising before midnight by the last days of May. At magnitude –2.5, it's unmistakeable, despite its low elevation in the southeast.

Venus, **Uranus** and **Neptune** are all lost in the Sun's glare this month.

MOON

The thinnest crescent Moon is near Mercury on 6 May. The Moon lies near Mars on 10 May, and on 12 May it gets together with Saturn and Regulus. On 16 May the Moon passes Spica, and the Full Moon lies very close to Antares on 20 May. The morning of 24 May sees the Moon below Jupiter.

SPECIAL EVENTS

5 May: it is the maximum of the Eta Aquarid meteor shower, when tiny pieces of Halley's Comet burn up in Earth's atmosphere. This year will be good for seeing the shooting stars, as moonlight will not interfere.

Jupiter looks odd at around 5 am on **22 May**: its four bright satellites are invisible, and the giant planet appears alone in space! Europa is in front of Jupiter and Ganymede behind it; while Io and Callisto are in Jupiter's shadow. This rare event occurs around dawn, so you'll need a telescope to view it.

MAY'S OBJECTS

It's 'objects' this month – and big ones, too. If you have a small telescope, sweep across the 'bowl' that is formed by Virgo's 'Y' shape, and you'll detect dozens of fuzzy blobs. These are just a handful of the thousands of galaxies making up the **Virgo Cluster**: our closest giant cluster of galaxies, lying at a distance of 55 million light years.

Galaxies are gregarious. Thanks to the force of gravity, they like living in groups. Our Milky Way, and the neighbouring giant spiral, the Andromeda Galaxy (M31), are in a small cluster of over 30 smallish galaxies called the Local Group.

But the Virgo Cluster is in a different league: it's like a vast galactic swarm of bees. What's more, its enormous gravity holds sway

◉ **Viewing tip**

Unscrupulous mail-order catalogues, selling 'gadgets', often advertise small telescopes that boast huge magnifications. Beware! This is known as 'empty magnification' – blowing up an image that the lens or mirror simply doesn't have the light-grasp to get to grips with. A rule of thumb is to use a maximum magnification no greater than twice the diameter of your lens or mirror in millimetres. So if you have a 100-mm reflecting telescope, go no higher than 200x.

over the smaller groups around – including our Local Group – making a cluster of clusters of galaxies, the Virgo Supercluster.

The galaxies in the Virgo Cluster are also mega. Many of them are spirals like our Milky Way – including the famous 'Sombrero Hat' (M104), which looks just like its namesake – but some are even more spectacular. The heavyweight galaxy of the cluster is **M87**, a giant elliptical galaxy emitting a jet of gas over 4000 light years long that is travelling at one-tenth the speed of light.

PICTURE OF THE MONTH

Jupiter – sans moons! A very rare event occurs on 22 May at 5 am, when Jupiter's four Galilean satellites are either hidden behind, in front, or in the shadow of the giant planet. Usually, you can spot its brightest moons with a small telescope (or a good pair of binoculars).

MAY'S TOPIC
Red Giants

The bright star Arcturus (magnitude –0.04) always gladdens our hearts as the harbinger of summer's arrival. But alas, it is a star on the way out. Its orange colour indicates that it's a red giant: a star near the end of its life.

Arcturus is about 30 times wider than the Sun – even though it is the same weight – because it has swollen up in its old age. This fate befalls humans, too – although the causes are rather different! Stars generate energy by nuclear fusion: they 'burn' hydrogen into the next element up, helium, in their hot cores.

But there's a finite supply of hydrogen in a star's core. When it runs out – after about ten billion years – the core, made of helium, collapses to a smaller size and gets even hotter. The star is now like an onion, with layers. In the centre, the compressed helium switches on its own reactions. And there's a layer around the core, where hydrogen is still turning to helium. These reactions create more heat, causing the outer layers of the star to balloon in size and cool down – hence the baleful red or orange colour of the star's surface.

Eventually Arcturus, like all red giants, will lose a grip on it atmosphere and jettison it into space. Only the dying core will be left: a steadily cooling object, about the size of the Earth, called a white dwarf. This fate awaits our Sun – but not for another 5 billion years.

◄ On 4 March 2003 – from Tenerife – Damian Peach took this image of moonless Jupiter, looking very much as it will appear on 22 May. You can just spot the shadow of a satellite. Damian used a 280-mm Celestron Schmidt-Cassegrain telescope and a ToUcam webcam.

On 21 June, the Sun hits the Summer Solstice – the date when our local star reaches its highest position over the northern hemisphere. This event has been celebrated as a seasonal ritual for millennia, leading to the construction of massive stone monuments aligned on the rising Sun at midsummer. Undeniably, our ancestors had formidable astronomical knowledge.

At the time of the solstice we experience long days and short nights – not the best time to do astronomy! But if the summer nights are balmy, it's a glorious time to go out and watch the whole sky, seeing the season's emerging constellations such as **Hercules**, **Lyra**, **Cygnus** and **Aquila**.

If you have a pair of binoculars, now is just the time to aim them at the central rectangle in Hercules: this month, the constellation is at its highest in the sky. About a third of the way down from **eta Herculis**, the star at top right, is **M13**, a globular cluster of several hundred thousand stars. It is one of the most elderly denizens of our Galaxy.

JUNE'S CONSTELLATION

Ursa Major – whose brightest stars are usually called **the Plough** – is jointly with Orion the most famous constellation. Orion's fame is clear to see: its stars are brilliant, and they make up a powerful image of a giant dominating the sky. In contrast, the seven stars of the Plough are fainter, and many people today have never seen a horse-drawn plough, from which the constellation takes its name. Some children call it 'the saucepan', while in America it's known as the Big Dipper.

But the Plough is the first constellation that most people get to know. There are two reasons for this. First, the two end stars of the Plough's 'bowl' point directly towards the Pole Star (**Polaris**), the star lying directly above the Earth's

▼ The sky at 11 pm in mid-June, with Moon positions at three-day intervals either side of Full Moon. The star positions are also correct for midnight at the beginning of

June, and 10 pm at the end of the month. The planets move slightly relative to the stars during the month.

North Pole. As the Earth spins on its axis, the stars rise and set while the Pole Star stays still – because we are actually rotating *under* the Pole Star. Locating the Pole Star is a sure way to find the direction of north. And because the Plough is so close to Polaris, it never sets, as seen from northern latitudes – and this is why it's such a familiar sight.

The Plough's seven stars are quite a rarity: unlike most constellations, several of the stars lie at the same distance and were born together. The middle five are all moving in the same direction (along with brilliant Sirius, which is also a member of the group). Over thousands of years, the shape of the Plough will gradually change, as the two 'end' stars go off on their own paths.

PLANETS ON VIEW

In the west, look out for **Saturn** low down as the sky grows dark. At magnitude +0.8, it's the brightest object in this part of the heavens; the star nearby is Regulus, marking the heart of Leo. Saturn sets at 2 am at the start of June, and at midnight by the end of the month.

Mars lies to the lower right of Saturn, setting at 1 am at the start of June, and 11.30 pm by the end. The fading Red Planet drops below magnitude +1.5 this month. From its position in Cancer in early June, Mars tracks towards Leo: on 30 June, it's right next to Regulus, with Mars slightly the fainter of the two.

WEST

Saturn
9 June
LEO
VIRGO
12 June
CORVUS
Spica
URSA MAJOR
CANES VENATICI
BOÖTES
Arcturus
CORONA BOREALIS
SERPENS
HYDRA
LIBRA
15 June
The Plough
DRACO
Zenith
M13
eta Herculis
HERCULES
OPHIUCHUS
Antares
SCORPIUS
SOUTH
Vega
LYRA
SAGITTA
Ecliptic
18 June
CYGNUS
SERPENS
SAGITTARIUS
THE MILKY WAY
Altair
AQUILA
CAPRICORNUS
Jupiter
PEGASUS
DELPHINUS
AQUARIUS
SE
EAST

June's Object Delta Cephei

	Mars
	Jupiter
	Saturn
	Moon

MOON		
Date	Time	Phase
3	8.22 pm	New Moon
10	4.03 pm	First Quarter
18	6.30 pm	Full Moon
26	1.10 pm	Last Quarter

Giant planet **Jupiter** is the brightest object of the month, after the Sun and Moon, shining at magnitude –2.7 low down in the southeast in Sagittarius. Jupiter rises at midnight at the beginning of June, and at 9.30 pm by the month's end.

Neptune (magnitude +7.9) lies in Capricornus and rises around midnight; its slightly brighter cosmic twin, **Uranus** – magnitude +5.8 – follows an hour later, in the neighbouring constellation of Aquarius.

Mercury and **Venus** are too close to the Sun to be seen this month.

MOON

The crescent Moon lies near Mars on 7 June. The following night it passes below Saturn and Regulus. The Moon lies near Spica on 12 June, and Antares on 16 June. On 19 and 20 June you'll find Jupiter above the waning Moon.

SPECIAL EVENTS

21 June, 0.59 am: Summer Solstice. The Sun reaches its most northerly point in the sky, so 21 June is Midsummer's Day, with the longest period of daylight. Correspondingly, we have the shortest nights.

28–30 June: Jupiter currently seems to have five bright satellites instead of four: the interloper is the star HD 181240 (magnitude +5.6).

JUNE'S OBJECT

At first glance, the star **Delta Cephei** – in the constellation representing King **Cepheus** – doesn't seem to merit special attention. It's a yellowish star of magnitude +4 – easily visible to the naked eye, but not prominent: a telescope reveals a fainter companion star. But this type of star holds the key to the size of the Universe.

Check the brightness of Delta Cephei carefully over days and weeks, and you'll see that its brightness changes regularly, from +3.6 (brightest) to +4.3 (faintest), every 5 days 9 hours. It's a result of the star literally swelling and shrinking in size, from 32 to 35 times the Sun's diameter.

Astronomers have found that stars like this – Cepheid variables – show a link between their period of variation and their intrinsic luminosity. By observing the period of the Cepheid and brightness that it appears in the sky, astronomers can work out its distance. Using the Hubble Space Telescope, astronomers have now measured Cepheids in the Virgo cluster of galaxies, which lies 55 million light years away.

◉ **Viewing tip**
A medium-sized pair of binoculars can reveal Jupiter's four largest moons, but you have to use them carefully. Balance your elbows on a fence or a table to minimize wobble – the magnification of the binoculars magnifies the wobble as well! You should see the moons strung out in a line either side of Jupiter's equator.

JUNE'S PICTURE

This astonishing image shows a plane crossing the face of the Sun, between two groups of sunspots. For safe viewing of our local star either project its image onto a piece of white card (through a small telescope or binoculars), or use specialist sun-gazing equipment – such as Coronado BinoMite II binoculars, which have lenses coated with a blocking sun-filter.

▲ *Robin Scagell was making a video series of solar images when he caught this sensational picture of a plane crossing the face of the Sun. He was using a ToUcam webcam attached to a 70-mm Bresser Skylux telescope, with a full-aperture solar filter.*

JUNE'S TOPIC
Midsummer's Day

Midsummer's Day is not just a date for astronomers' diaries. On the morning of 21 June, thousands of New-Agers, druids and latter-day pagans will converge on Stonehenge, to celebrate Midsummer in their own way.

In around 3000 BC, the Neolithic farmers of Salisbury Plain carefully observed just where on the horizon the Sun rose on Midsummer's Day – its northernmost rising point of the year. At the time, they dug a huge circular enclosure with a gap in the direction of Midsummer sunrise.

It was another 200 years before the stone that now marks sunrise, the rough-hewn Heel Stone, was put in place. And another 600 years passed before the farmers erected the great standing stones that make up Stonehenge itself.

Was this the world's first solar observatory, staffed with astronomers keeping a watchful eye on the Sun, and perhaps the Moon? Or was it more symbolic – a great temple to the Sun god? At the moment, no-one knows. But we can say (as two people who've been privileged to watch sunrise from the centre of Stonehenge) that our ancestors certainly knew how to create a truly awesome spectacle.

High summer is here, and with it comes the brilliant trio of the Summer Triangle – the stars **Vega**, **Deneb** and **Altair**. Each is the brightest star in its own constellation: Vega in **Lyra**, Deneb in **Cygnus** and Altair in **Aquila**.

Although the stars appear the same brightness in the sky, they could hardly be more different. Seventeen light years away, Altair is one of the closest stars to the Sun, and – at eleven times the Sun's brightness – it is quite a modest inhabitant of the cosmos. Vega lies 25 light years distant, and is fifty times more luminous than our local star.

Deneb, however, is another matter. Researchers have difficulty in measuring its distance: estimates range from 2000 light years to over 7000 light years – which means that the star must be phenomenally luminous. If it lies at the greater distance, then it is some 250,000 times brighter than the Sun.

JULY'S CONSTELLATION

Down in the sky's deep south this month lies a baleful red star – **Antares**, 'the rival of Mars' – and in its ruddiness it even surpasses the famed Red Planet. To ancient astronomers, Antares marked the heart of **Scorpius**, the celestial scorpion.

According to Greek myth, this summer constellation is intimately linked with the winter star-pattern Orion. This mighty hunter boasted that he could kill every living creature. In retaliation, the Earth-goddess Gaia created a mighty scorpion that rose behind Orion, delivering a fatal sting. The gods immortalized these opponents as star-patterns, at opposite ends of the sky, so that Orion sets as Scorpius rises.

Scorpius is one of the few constellations to resemble its namesake, though from far northern latitudes we see only the upper half. To the top right of Antares, a line of stars marks the scorpion's forelimbs. Originally, the stars we now call

▼ *The sky at 11 pm in mid-July, with Moon positions at three-day intervals either side of Full Moon. The star positions are also correct for midnight at the beginning of*

July, and 10 pm at the end of the month. The planets move slightly relative to the stars during the month.

Libra (the Scales) were its claws. Below Antares, the scorpion's body stretches down into a fine curved tail (below the horizon on the chart), and deadly sting.

Scorpius is a treasure-trove of astronomical goodies. There are several lovely double stars, including Antares: its faint companion looks greenish in contrast to Antares' strong red hue. To the right of Antares, binoculars reveal the fuzzy patch of **M4**, a globular cluster made of tens of thousands of stars. It's one of the nearest of these giant clusters, 'just' 7200 light years away.

The 'sting' of Scorpius contains two fine star clusters – **M6**, and **M7** – which we can just see with the naked eye; a telescope reveals their stars clearly.

PLANETS ON VIEW

Saturn and Mars perform a little celestial waltz low in the evening twilight. **Saturn** is the brighter, at magnitude +0.8, and is moving slowly beneath the 'chest' of Leo.

Mars starts the month next to Leo's brightest star, Regulus, and moves rapidly up and left, passing Saturn on 10 July. At magnitude +1.7, Mars is only half as bright as ringworld Saturn. By the end of July, both of these planets are lost in the twilight glow.

Jupiter is king of the night, blazing at magnitude –2.7 low in the south in Sagittarius. It's at opposition on 9 July (see July's Topic).

Having passed the Sun last month, **Venus** now begins to reappear in the evening sky. You may be able

MOON		
Date	Time	Phase
3	3.18 am	New Moon
10	5.35 am	First Quarter
18	8.59 am	Full Moon
25	7.41 pm	Last Quarter

to catch it low down in the twilight, in the northwest, right at the end of July.

Neptune and **Uranus** rise at around 10 and 11 pm respectively. Neptune (magnitude +7.8) lies in Capricornus. Uranus is in Aquarius, at magnitude +5.8.

Mercury is at its greatest elongation west of the Sun on 1 July, but it's too deep in the Sun's glare to be easily visible.

MOON

On 6 July, the thin crescent Moon lies below Saturn, Mars and Regulus. The Moon passes Spica on 10 July, and Antares on 14 July. The almost Full Moon lies near Jupiter on 16 and 17 July.

SPECIAL EVENTS

4 July: the Earth is at aphelion, its furthest point from the Sun.

On the nights of **11** and **12 July** Jupiter has a spectacularly close approach to the star HD 179478 (magnitude +7.9). In a small telescope, it looks as though the star merges in turn with Jupiter's four large moons (also known as the Galilean satellites): Europa and Io (11 July), and then Ganymede and Callisto in the early hours of 13 July.

Jupiter has a less intimate stellar encounter on **29/31 July**, when it passes the slightly brighter star HD 177120 (magnitude +6.3).

▼ *On Uxbridge golf course in Middlesex, Robin Scagell photographed this ghostly apparition of noctilucent clouds. The five-second exposure was made on Ektachrome 400 film with a Mamiya 645 medium-format camera at f/2.8.*

JULY'S OBJECT

The constellation Cygnus represents a soaring swan, her wings outspread as she flies down the Milky Way. The lowest star in Cygnus, marking the swan's head, is **Albireo**. The word looks Arabic, but it actually has no meaning and merely results from errors in translation, from Greek to Arabic to Latin.

Binoculars reveal that Albireo is in fact two stars in one. Using a telescope, you'll be treated to one of the most glorious sky-sights – a dazzling yellow star teamed up with a blue companion.

The yellow star is a giant, near the end of its life. It's 80 times bigger than the Sun, and 1000 times brighter. The fainter blue companion is 'only' 95 times brighter than the Sun.

The spectacular colour contrast is due to the stars' different temperatures. The giant star is slightly cooler than the Sun, and shines with a yellowish glow. The smaller companion is far hotter – it's so incandescent that it shines not white-hot, but blue-white.

⊙ **Viewing tip**

This is the month when you really need a good, unobstructed view to the southern horizon, to make out the summer constellations of Scorpius and Sagittarius. They never rise high in temperate latitudes, so make the best of a southerly view – especially over the sea – if you're away on holiday. A good southern horizon is also best for views of the planets, because they rise highest when they're in the south

JULY'S PICTURE

This month you may spot the rare phenomenon of noctilucent clouds. These iridescent, blue-white wraiths in the northern sky shine spookily in the twilight. Far higher than normal clouds, at 85 km up, they were once thought to be made up of dust from meteors, or even the remains of exhaust gases from the Space Shuttle. Now researchers suspect that they are composed of water ice, and may be a sign of climate change.

JULY'S TOPIC
Jupiter

Jupiter is particularly stunning this month. It's at opposition – directly in line with the Sun and Earth – on 9 July, and at its closest to the Earth this year (a trifling matter of 620 million kilometres).

The giant of the Solar System, Jupiter is vast – at 143,000 kilometres in diameter, it could contain 1300 Earths – and its brilliant clouds are very efficient at reflecting sunlight. Despite its great size, Jupiter spins faster than any other planet in the Solar System, rotating every 9 hours 55 minutes. As a result its equator bulges outwards; through a small telescope, Jupiter looks a bit like a tangerine crossed with an old-fashioned humbug. The humbug stripes are cloud belts of ammonia and methane that are stretched out by the planet's dizzy spin.

Space missions to Jupiter have revealed how active the planet is. It has a fearsome magnetic field that no astronaut would survive, with huge eruptions of lightning, and it radiates more energy than it receives from the Sun. The core is so squashed by Jupiter's mighty bulk that it simmers at 20,000°C. In fact, had the planet been 50 times heavier, the core would have been capable of sustaining nuclear reactions, and Jupiter would have become a star.

Jupiter has some elements in common with a star. It commands its own 'mini-solar system' – a family of over 60 moons. The four biggest are visible in good binoculars, and even to the unaided eye if you are really sharp-sighted). We remember a 78-year-old lady at an evening class asking, 'what are those little dots either side of Jupiter?'

These are worlds in their own right – Ganymede is even bigger than the planet Mercury. But two vie for 'star' status. The surface of Io is erupting, with incredible geysers erupting plumes of sulphur dioxide 300 km into space. Brilliant white Europa probably contains oceans of liquid water beneath a solid ice coating, where alien fish may swim...

The **Milky Way** softly wends its way overhead, and the Summer Triangle is riding high. Look inside the Triangle for the pretty constellation of **Sagitta** (the Arrow); next to it is the even more beautiful **Delphinus** (the Dolphin).

There are two eclipses to look forward to: one of the Sun on 1 August, and a lunar eclipse on 16 August. Neither of the eclipses is total as seen from the UK, but the eclipse of the Moon should make for excellent holiday viewing. It takes place just after dark, and 80% of the Moon will be covered by the Earth's shadow. Our normally brilliant Full Moon will wane to a crescent, and the obscured parts may shine with a spooky red glow, as a result of sunlight refracted by the Earth's atmosphere when the Moon moves into our planet's shadow. Alas, the best meteor shower of the year, the **Perseids**, will be affected by bright moonlight, but the shower is still worth watching from a dark location.

AUGUST'S CONSTELLATION

It has to be admitted that **Aquila** does vaguely resemble a flying eagle, albeit a rather faint one. An ancient constellation, it takes its name from the bird that was a companion to the god Jupiter – even carrying his thunderbolts for him! The constellation is dominated by **Altair**, a young blue-white star seventeen light years away, which is eleven times brighter than our Sun. It has a very fast spin: the star hurtles around at 210 kilometres per second, rotating in just 10.4 hours (as opposed to about 30 days for the Sun). As a result, it is oval in shape. Altair is a triple star, as is its neighbour **beta Aquilae** (just below, left). **Eta Aquilae** (immediately below beta) is one of the brightest Cepheid variable stars – old stars which change their brightness by swelling and shrinking. The pulsations of eta Aquilae make it vary from magnitude +3.5 to +4.4 every seven days.

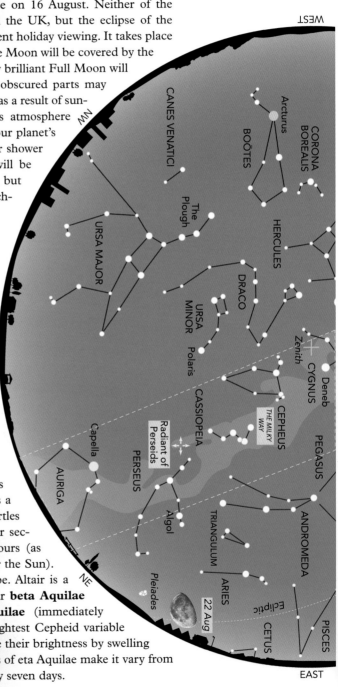

▼ The sky at 11 pm in mid-August, with Moon positions at three-day intervals either side of Full Moon. The star positions are also correct for midnight at the *beginning of August, and 10 pm at the end of the month. The planets move slightly relative to the stars during the month.*

PLANETS ON VIEW

Venus is beginning to appear very low in the northwest in the dusk, at magnitude –3.9. The Evening Star sets about 40 minutes after the Sun.

Mars, **Saturn** and **Mercury** are also skulking in the twilight glow, but being fainter than Venus (magnitudes +1.7, +0.8 and –0.2 respectively) they are not easy to spot. If you have a good northwest horizon, though, take a look at Venus through binoculars or a telescope on 13 August, and you'll see Saturn only a quarter of a degree away; while on 20 August Mercury lies a degree below the Evening Star.

On the other hand, you can't miss brilliant **Jupiter**, low in the south and shining at magnitude –2.6 in Sagittarius. It sets at around 2.30 am in mid-August.

Uranus, at magnitude +5.8, rises at around 9.30 pm in the constellation of Aquarius.

Neptune (magnitude +7.8), rising at around 8.30 pm in Capricornus, is at opposition on 15 August. The eclipsed Moon lies nearby on 16 August (see Special Events).

MOON

On 3 August the very narrow crescent Moon lies below Mars and Saturn. The Moon is near Spica on 6 August, and Antares on 10 August. On 13 August the Moon passes below Jupiter. As the last-quarter Moon rises on 23 August, it lies among the stars of the Pleiades.

WEST

Star chart labels: LIBRA, SERPENS, CORONA BOREALIS, SCORPIUS, 10 Aug, OPHIUCHUS, HERCULES, SAGITTA, Altair, eta Aquilae, THE MILKY WAY, Jupiter, SERPENS, 13 Aug, SAGITTARIUS, SOUTH, Vega, LYRA, SUMMER TRIANGLE, DELPHINUS, beta Aquilae, AQUILA, Neptune, CAPRICORNUS, DRACO, Zenith, Deneb, CYGNUS, PEGASUS, 16 Aug, PISCIS AUSTRINUS, ANDROMEDA, Square of Pegasus, AQUARIUS, Uranus, Ecliptic, 19 Aug, PISCES, CETUS, SE, EAST

Legend:
- Jupiter
- Uranus
- Neptune
- Moon
- August's Object: The Milky Way
- Radiant of Perseids

MOON			
	Date	**Time**	**Phase**
	1	11.12 am	New Moon
	8	9.20 pm	First Quarter
	16	10.16 pm	Full Moon
	24	0.49 am	Last Quarter
	30	8.58 pm	New Moon

SPECIAL EVENTS

There's a total eclipse of the Sun on **1 August**, visible from the north of Greenland, Siberia, Mongolia and parts of China. The UK will experience a partial eclipse. As seen from London, the eclipse lasts from 9.33 to 11.05 am; and at maximum (10.18 am) 12% of the Sun is obscured. For viewers in Edinburgh the Sun will appear 24% hidden at 10.17 am, with the eclipse lasting from 9.25 to 11.11 am. **DON'T LOOK AT THE SUN DIRECTLY!** (See viewing tip.)

12/13 August: this is the maximum of the annual Perseid meteor shower. You'll see Perseid meteors for several nights around the time of maximum. This won't be a particularly good year, though, as moonlight will interfere.

The evening of **16 August** sees an eclipse of the Moon, visible from the UK: though it's not total, the Moon is more than 80% covered at maximum, which occurs at 10.10 pm. The eclipse begins at 8.36 pm, and is over by 11.45 pm. During this eclipse use a small telescope to spot distant Neptune: it lies three Moon-diameters to the right of the eclipsed Moon, the faintest of a triangle of three 'stars'.

AUGUST'S OBJECT

Not so much a single object this month, but billions of them! Stars, that is – the ones that make up our **Milky Way**. It was Galileo who, with his modest telescope, first ascertained the nature of the Milky Way – 'a congeries of stars', he observed. You can do the same by sweeping the band of light with modest binoculars this month – start at Cygnus, then pan down to

👁 **Viewing tip**

If you're watching the solar eclipse this month – or observing the Sun at any other time – be careful! Never use a telescope or binoculars to look at the Sun directly: it could blind you permanently. Fogged film is no safer, because it allows the Sun's infra-red (heat) rays to get through. Eclipse goggles are safe (unless they're scratched). The best way to observe the Sun is to project its image through binoculars or a telescope onto a white piece of card.

Sagittarius and Scorpius. It's the more distant stars of our spiral galaxy that you are seeing. Because we live in our Galaxy's flat disc, perspective makes these stars appear to congregate into a band. When you look towards Sagittarius, the stars look thickest – that's because you're looking at the dense nuclear bulge of the Milky Way. The dark patches aren't voids of stars – they're huge clouds of dark dust and gas poised to form into new generations of stars and planets.

AUGUST'S PICTURE

Nothing prepares you for a total eclipse of the Sun. Although the solar eclipse of 1 August will be seen as partial from the UK, you can witness totality if you travel to China, Mongolia, Siberia or Greenland. The usually brilliant Sun is transformed into a Chinese dragon-mask with a black mouth, and – during the eclipse – the temperature drops several degrees. A truly spooky experience.

AUGUST'S TOPIC
Centre of the Milky Way

The Milky Way stretches all the way around our sky, as a gently glowing band. In reality, it is a spiral shape of some 200 billion stars, with the Sun about half-way out. The centre of the Milky Way lies in the direction of the constellation Sagittarius. But our view of the galactic centre is obscured by great clouds of dark dust that block the view for even the most powerful telescopes.

Now, however, instruments observing at other wavelengths have lifted the veil on the Galaxy's heart. Infrared telescopes can see the heat radiation from stars and gas clouds at the galactic centre. These objects are speeding around so fast that they must be in the grip of something with fantastically strong gravity. In 2002 a team of astronomers at the European Southern Observatory, in Chile, discovered a star that's orbiting the Galaxy's centre at over 18 million kph! In the meantime, radio astronomers have found that the Galaxy's exact heart is marked by a tiny source of radiation: Sagittarius A★.

Putting all these observations together, astronomers have concluded that the core of the Milky Way must contain a heavyweight black hole. The latest data from 2004 indicate that the black hole is as massive as 3.7 million Suns. When a speeding star comes too close to this invisible monster, it's ripped apart. There's a final shriek from the star's gases – producing the observed radio waves – before they fall into the black hole, and disappear from our Universe.

◀ *Robin Scagell was one of the few people to observe the 11 August 1999 solar eclipse from Cornwall – everyone else was clouded out. This photograph, taken at The Lizard, is a one-second exposure on Kodachrome 64 film, using a 1000mm f/11 mirror lens.*

The stars of summer are still with us, but are shifting westwards; replacing them are the barren constellations of autumn. But there's still a lot on view. One of our favourite stars – **Fomalhaut** – puts in an appearance low on the southern horizon this month. The brightest star in the constellation of **Piscis Austrinus** (the Southern Fish), Fomalhaut is the only first-magnitude star to feature in autumn skies. Its name means 'mouth of the whale', while some cultures call it 'the lonely star of autumn'.

Venus is starting to make a serious appearance in the west, setting over an hour after the Sun. And **Jupiter** is still looking brilliant among the stars of Sagittarius. The Moon is up to its tricks, too. On 13 September, it occults Neptune. Then – on 20 September – it moves in front of three members of the Pleiades star cluster.

SEPTEMBER'S CONSTELLATION

It has to be said that **Pegasus** is one of the most boring constellations in the sky. A large, barren square of four medium-bright stars – how did our ancestors manage to see the shape of an upside-down winged horse up there?

In legend, Pegasus sprang from the blood of Medusa the Gorgon when **Perseus** (nearby in the sky) severed her head. But all pre-classical civilizations have their fabled winged horse, and we see them depicted on Etruscan and Babylonian vases.

The star at the top right of the square – **Scheat** – is a red giant more than 100 times wider than the Sun. Close to the end of its life, it pulsates irregularly, changing in brightness by about one magnitude. **Enif** (the nose) – outside the square to the lower right – is a yellow supergiant. A small telescope, or even good binoculars, will reveal a faint blue companion star.

▼ The sky at 11 pm in mid-September, with Moon positions at three-day intervals either side of Full Moon. The star positions are also correct for midnight at the beginning of September, and 10 pm at the end of the month. The planets move slightly relative to the stars during the month.

Just next to Enif – and Pegasus' best-kept secret – is the beautiful globular cluster **M15**. You'll need a telescope for this one. M15 is around 50,000 light years away, and contains about 200,000 stars.

PLANETS ON VIEW

Venus (magnitude –3.9) is still very low down in the evening twilight, in the west, but as the month progresses the planet starts to move upwards into a darker sky. By the end of September the Evening Star is setting about an hour after the Sun.

Mercury and Mars are also hugging the same horizon as Venus. Through a telescope you may catch **Mercury** (magnitude +0.1) to the lower left of Venus during the first two weeks of September – it reaches its greatest separation from the Sun on 11 September. On the same evening, much fainter **Mars** (magnitude +1.7) is just half a degree from Venus.

Jupiter is still awesome in Sagittarius, shining at magnitude –2.4. It's setting at 1 am at the beginning of September, and 11 pm by the end of the month. The giant planet lies near the stars HD 175360 (magnitude +5.9) and HD 175501 (magnitude +7.6) – which makes Jupiter appear to have six moons, as seen through a small telescope.

Uranus reaches opposition on 13 September. You'll find it in Aquarius, at magnitude +5.7.

Its more distant twin, **Neptune** (magnitude +7.8), shines in

WEST
SERPENS
OPHIUCHUS
HERCULES
SERPENS
Ring Nebula
Vega
LYRA
CYGNUS
Deneb
Zenith
North America Nebula
CEPHEUS
ANDROMEDA
Scheat
Square of Pegasus
TRIANGULUM
ARIES
PISCES
TAURUS
ERIDANUS
EAST

SAGITTA
M15
PEGASUS
DELPHINUS
Altair
AQUILA
THE MILKY WAY
Enif
Uranus
Ecliptic
Mira
CETUS

SAGITTARIUS
Jupiter
9 Sept
12 Sept
Neptune
CAPRICORNUS
AQUARIUS
15 Sept
18 Sept

SOUTH
PISCIS AUSTRINUS
GRUS
Fomalhaut
SE

September's Object
Ring Nebula
September's Picture
North America Nebula

	Jupiter
	Uranus
	Neptune
	Moon

MOON		
Date	Time	Phase
7	3.04 pm	First Quarter
15	10.13 am	Full Moon
22	6.04 am	Last Quarter
29	9.12 am	New Moon

39

Capricornus. The Moon occults it on 13 September (see Special Events).

Saturn is too close to the Sun to be seen this month.

MOON

The Moon lies near Antares on 6 September, and near Jupiter on 9 September. It moves in front of the Pleiades on 20 September (see Special Events). On the morning of 26 September, the crescent Moon is near Regulus.

SPECIAL EVENTS

5 September: the European comet-probe Rosetta flies past asteroid 2867 Steins (see September's Topic).

On the morning of **13 September**, at 3.33 am, the Moon moves right in front of Neptune. You'll need both a good telescope, and clear western horizon, to see this very rare planetary occultation.

And on **20 September**, between 2.45 and 3.25 am, the Moon occults three stars of the Seven Sisters – the Pleiades star cluster.

22 September, 4.44 pm: it's the Autumn Equinox. The Sun is over the equator as it heads southwards in the sky, and day and night are equal in length.

SEPTEMBER'S OBJECT

Tucked into the small constellation of **Lyra** (the Lyre) – near the brilliant star **Vega** – lies a strange celestial sight. It was first

▼ From Wiltshire, Philip Perkins made a series of exposures – which he later combined – to produce this astonishing image of the North America Nebula and the Pelican Nebula (right). He used a Nikon 400 mm at f/4 on Kodak Ektapress film.

⊙ *Viewing tip*
Try to observe your favourite objects when they're well clear of the horizon. When you look low down, you are seeing through a large thickness of the atmosphere – which is always shifting and turbulent. This turbulence makes the stars appear to twinkle. Low-down planets also twinkle, but because they subtend tiny discs, the effect is less marked.

spotted by French astronomer Antoine Darquier in 1779, and described as 'a very dull nebula, but perfectly outlined; as large as Jupiter and looks like a fading planet'. Under higher magnification, it appears as a bright ring of light with a dimmer centre. Hence its usual name, the **Ring Nebula**.

You can make out the Ring Nebula with even a small telescope, though it's so compact that you'll need a magnification of over 50× to distinguish it from a star.

The Ring Nebula is the remains of a dying star – a cloud of gas lit up by the original star's incandescent core. For centuries, astronomers assumed that the Ring Nebula was a sphere of gas. But the Hubble Space Telescope has now found that it's actually barrel-shaped. It looks like a ring to us only because we happen to view the barrel end-on. Aliens observing the Ring Nebula from another perspective would undoubtedly call it something different!

SEPTEMBER'S PICTURE

The aptly named **North America Nebula**, with its companion, the Pelican Nebula, lies next to brilliant **Deneb** in Cygnus. Both are parts of a single enormous cloud of gas and dust, poised to create generations of new stars. The red glow is caused by heating from a nearby star.

SEPTEMBER'S TOPIC
Asteroids

On 5 September, Europe's Rosetta spacecraft flies just 1700 kilometres from asteroid 2867 Steins, en route for a rendezvous with Comet Churyumov-Gerasimenko in 2014. The asteroid, discovered in 1969 by N.S. Chernykh, is named after the Latvian astronomer and popularizer Karlis Steins. It's 4.6 kilometres across, and it spins every nine hours. 2867 Steins is just one of nearly 400,000 asteroids logged, although astronomers suspect that the total is over a million. Asteroids are largely found between the orbits of Mars and Jupiter, and they're almost certainly the rocky and metallic debris of a tiny world that was never able to form as a result of Jupiter's disruptive gravity. In total, their cumulative mass would only amount to 4% of that of the Moon.

Although the majority of asteroids live in the 'main belt', some cross Earth's orbit. These would pose a serious danger if they were ever to collide with our planet – as did the body, which, 65 million years ago, wiped out the dinosaurs. Astronomers are currently engaged in several programmes to track them down, and in devising schemes to divert any potentially deathly encounter

The barren Square of **Pegasus** rides high in the south, accompanied by a distinctly fishy lot of constellations swimming around the horizon. Among them are **Pisces** (the Fishes), **Cetus** (the Sea-monster), **Aquarius** (the Water-carrier), and oddball **Capricornus**, which is depicted on ancient star charts as half-goat, half fish. Lowest of all is **Piscis Austrinus** (the Southern Fish).

The evenings are now drawing in, providing glorious views of the night sky at relatively social hours – particularly after 26 October, when the clocks go back and we lose summer's extra hour of evening light.

Take the advantage of autumn's new-born darkness to pick out two of our neighbour galaxies – **M31** in **Andromeda**, and **M33** in nearby **Triangulum**. M31 (the **Andromeda Galaxy**) is easily visible to the unaided eye from a dark location – it covers an area four times larger than the Full Moon – but M33 is more of a challenge (see October's Object).

OCTOBER'S CONSTELLATION

Perseus and its neighbour **Cassiopeia** are two of the best-loved constellations in the northern night sky. They never set as seen from the UK, and are packed with celestial goodies. In legend, Perseus is the superhero who slew Medusa, the Gorgon. The constellation's brightest star is called **Mirfak** ('elbow' in Arabic) – a star nearly 600 light years away and 5000 times more luminous than our Sun.

But the 'star' of Perseus is **Algol** (whose name stems from the Arabic *al-ghul* – the 'Demon Star'). It represents the eye of Medusa – and it winks. Its variations were first brought to the attention of the astronomical community by the 18-year-old John Goodricke, a profoundly deaf amateur astronomer, in the late eighteenth century. He correctly surmised that the variations in its brightness were caused

▼ *The sky at 11 pm in mid-October, with Moon positions at three-day intervals either side of Full Moon. The star positions are also correct for midnight at the beginning of October, and 9 pm at the end of the month (after the end of BST). The planets move slightly relative to the stars during the month.*

by a fainter star eclipsing a brighter one (there are actually three stars in the system). Over a period of almost 2.9 days, the brightness of Algol's primary star appears to drop from magnitude +2.1 to +3.4.

Another gem in Perseus is the **Double Cluster**, h and chi Persei. The duo lies between Perseus and Cassiopeia, and is a sensational sight in binoculars. Some 7000 light years distant, the clusters are made of bright young blue stars – those in h are 5.6 million years old, while chi has been around for no more than 3.2 million years (compare this to our Sun: it has notched up 4.6 *billion* years so far!).

PLANETS ON VIEW

Coy **Venus** stays low in the evening twilight, towards the southwest, throughout the month. Shining at magnitude −3.9, it sets an hour after the Sun at the beginning of October, and one-and-a-half hours after it by the end of the month.

Jupiter, king of the night sky this summer, is now slipping away into the evening twilight. By the end of October the giant planet (magnitude −2.2) is setting at 8.30 pm. The star HD 177120 (magnitude +6.7) lies near Jupiter on 16 and 17 October, looking – through binoculars – like a fifth moon.

The distant planets **Uranus** (magnitude +5.8) and **Neptune** (magnitude +7.9) are residing in Aquarius and Capricornus respectively.

Saturn is climbing ever higher in the morning sky. Shining at magnitude

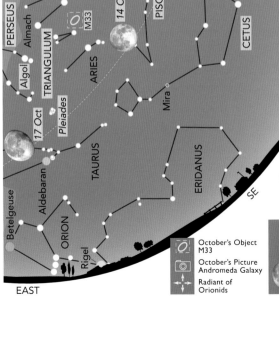

WEST

SERPENS
THE MILKY WAY
AQUILA
8 Oct
MS
Altair
CYGNUS
SAGITTA
DELPHINUS
CAPRICORNUS
Deneb
Neptune
AQUARIUS
PISCIS AUSTRINUS
Andromeda Galaxy
Zenith
Enif
PEGASUS
11 Oct
SOUTH
CASSIOPEIA
ANDROMEDA
Scheat
Square of Pegasus
Uranus
Fomalhaut
PERSEUS
Almach
14 Oct
Ecliptic
PISCES
CETUS
Algol
TRIANGULUM
M33
17 Oct
Pleiades
ARIES
Mira
Aldebaran
TAURUS
ERIDANUS
Betelgeuse
ORION
SE
Rigel

EAST

October's Object M33
October's Picture Andromeda Galaxy
Radiant of Orionids

Uranus
Neptune
Moon

MOON		
Date	Time	Phase
7	10.04 am	First Quarter
14	9.02 pm	Full Moon
21	12.54 pm	Last Quarter
28	11.14 pm	New Moon

+1.0 under the belly of Leo, the ringworld is rising at 2 am by the end of October.

Also in the morning sky, look out for **Mercury** making its best dawn show of the year. You may spot the speedy planet (magnitude −0.5) during the last two weeks of October, low in the east before sunrise. It reaches greatest elongation from the Sun on 22 October.

Mars is hidden in the Sun's glare all this month.

MOON

The crescent Moon lies near Antares on 4 October. On 6 and 7 October, the First Quarter Moon passes Jupiter. During the night of 21/22 October, the Last Quarter Moon passes just below the Praesepe star cluster in Cancer. The waning crescent Moon lies near Saturn and Mercury on the mornings of 25 and 27 October, respectively.

SPECIAL EVENTS

On **6 October**, NASA's Messenger space-probe makes the second of three close flybys of Mercury, prior to it entering orbit around Mercury in 2011.

21 October: debris from Halley's Comet smashes into Earth's atmosphere, causing the annual **Orionid** meteor shower. Unfortunately, moonlight will drown out the fainter meteors this year.

26 October, 2 am: end of British Summer Time. Clocks go back by an hour.

OCTOBER'S OBJECT

Just below the line of stars making up Andromeda – in the constellation of Triangulum – is the galaxy M33. Although M31, the Andromeda Galaxy, is generally accepted to be the most distant object easily visible to the unaided eye, some amateur astronomers claim that M33 – under exceptionally clear conditions – can be seen. This is plausible, as the galaxy is at magnitude + 5.7 (with +6.0 being the naked-eye cut-off). The galaxy's light is spread out thinly, giving very little contrast between it and the natural light of the night-time sky. But with its distance of 2.9 million light years, M33 is indeed the furthest object visible to the naked eye.

M33 is a member of our Local Group. It's a spiral galaxy, rather more ragged and unbuttoned than the Milky Way and

> ⊙ **Viewing tip**
> Around 2.5 million light years away from us, the Andromeda Galaxy is often described as the furthest object easily visible to the unaided eye. But it's not that easy to see – especially if you are suffering some light pollution. The trick is to memorize the star-patterns in Andromeda and look slightly to the side of where you expect the galaxy to be. This technique – called 'averted vision' – causes the image to fall on a part of the retina that is more light-sensitive than the central region, which is designed to see fine detail.

Andromeda Galaxy. It's also much smaller – only half the diameter of the Milky Way, at 50,000 light years across. But it makes up for its size by containing one of the biggest star-forming regions known. NGC 204 is a huge cloud of glowing gas and dust (small particles of cosmic soot) 1500 light years across (compared to 30 light years for the Orion Nebula). It is already busy creating stars, and images from the Hubble Space telescope have revealed over 200 young stars with masses between 15 and 60 times that of the Sun lurking in the mists.

If you want to see M33 properly you need a telescope. But don't use a high magnification – this will just spread the galaxy out so that it's more difficult to see. Use a low magnification on a really transparent night.

OCTOBER'S PICTURE

The Andromeda Galaxy (M33) is one of the biggest spiral galaxies known, containing nearly 400,000 million stars (almost twice the number of stars in the Milky Way). Alas, it is presented to us at such a shallow angle that we can't pick out its glorious spiral arms. In this image, its companion galaxies – M32 (top) and NGC 205 (bottom) – flank their giant host.

▼ *The Andromeda Galaxy was imaged here in a series of six 50-minute exposures from Wiltshire. The photographer, Philip Perkins, used an AP 155 EDF refractor with a Pentax 6x7 camera on Kodak GPY 400 120 format film.*

OCTOBER'S TOPIC
Return to the Moon

This October sees the launch of a space-probe which could pave the way for future human exploration of the Moon. NASA's Lunar Reconnaissance Orbiter (LRO) will go into orbit around our satellite and identify possible locations for future human exploration of the Moon. The mission is scheduled to last a year, but scientists are confident that it could extend five years longer.

In particular, researchers are keen to investigate the distribution of water on the Moon, which would be an essential resource for a possible lunar base. The probe will also undertake high-resolution mapping (looking at features just half a metre across) to help select future landing sites. And the LRO will be able to detect some of the hardware that we have already sent to our companion in space.

Piggy-backing on LRO is LCROSS – a satellite designed to watch as the upper stage of LRO's launch vehicle impacts a permanently-shadowed area of the Moon. It will look for signs of water ice in the impact plume, and then – about ten minutes later – it will itself collide with the lunar surface. Both these impacts should be easily visible to amateur astronomers, and they'll be monitored by a network of Earth- and space-based observatories.

This month, look out for two brilliant planets in the early evening sky. Venus and Jupiter are putting on a spectacular show. They're both fabulous objects to look at through a small telescope.

The first signs of winter are here; the **Pleiades** (the Seven Sisters) are starting to ride high in the night sky. This delightful star cluster is traditionally reputed to contain seven stars visible to the unaided eye – but most people can only see six. The Pleiades lie in Taurus (the Bull), which boasts a second prominent star cluster, the **Hyades**, which is fainter and wider than the Pleiades.

Orion is making his first appearance of the year. Look below the three stars of his belt for the beautiful **Orion Nebula**. Easily visible to the unaided eye, this region is undergoing an orgy of star formation – and undoubtedly, the infant stars are creating a plethora of planets around themselves.

NOVEMBER'S CONSTELLATION

Taurus is very much a second cousin to brilliant **Orion**, but a fascinating constellation nonetheless. It's dominated by **Aldebaran**, the baleful blood-red eye of the celestial bull. Around 68 light years away, and shining with a magnitude of +0.85, the star is a red giant, but not one as extreme as neighbouring **Betelgeuse**. It is around three times heavier than the Sun. The 'head' of the bull is formed by the **Hyades** star cluster. The other famous star cluster in Taurus is the far more glamorous **Pleiades**, whose stars – although further away than the Hyades – are younger and brighter.

Taurus has two 'horns' – the star **El Nath** (Arabic for 'the butting one') to the north, and **zeta Tauri** (which has an unpronounceable Babylonian name meaning 'star in the bull towards the south'). Above this star is a stellar wreck – literally. In 1054, Chinese astronomers wit-

▼ The sky at 10 pm in mid-November, with Moon positions at three-day intervals either side of Full Moon. The star positions are also correct for 11 pm at the

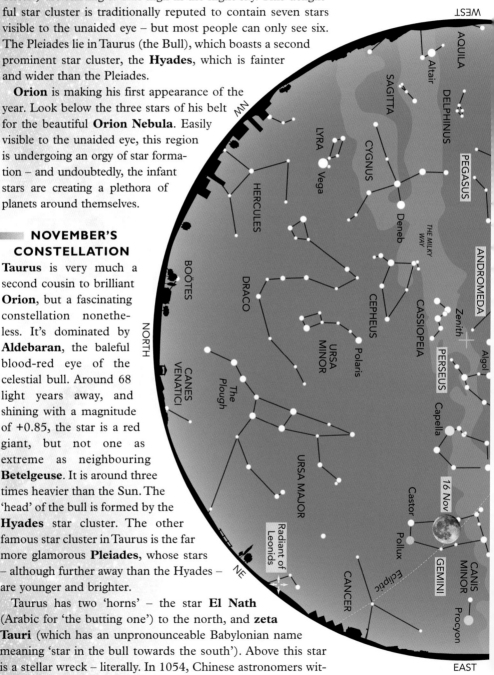

beginning of November, and 9 pm at the end of the month. The planets move slightly relative to the stars during the month.

nessed a brilliant 'new star' appear in this spot, which was visible in daytime for weeks. What the Chinese actually saw was an exploding star – a supernova – in its death throes. And today, we see its still-expanding remains as the **Crab Nebula**. It's visible through a medium-sized telescope

PLANETS ON VIEW

Venus, which has lurked for months in the evening twilight, at long last pulls away from the Sun. During November, its brightness rises from –4.0 to –4.2, and by the end of the month the Evening Star is setting three hours after the Sun.

During the month, Venus is gradually creeping closer and closer to **Jupiter**, the second brightest planet. Jupiter lies in the constellation Sagittarius, at magnitude –2.1, and it's setting by 7 pm at the end of November.

Neptune (magnitude +7.9) lies in Capricornus and sets around 10.30 pm; the Moon skims past Neptune on 6 November (see Special Events). **Uranus** lies in Aquarius at magnitude +5.8, setting at around 1.30 am.

The morning sky belongs to **Saturn** (magnitude +1.1) lying under Leo. It rises at 2.00 am at the start of November, and at midnight by the month's end. To telescope users, it will seem that the ringed planet has an extra bright moon on 14–16 November, when it passes close to the star HD 99225.

Mercury and **Mars** are too close to the Sun to be visible this month.

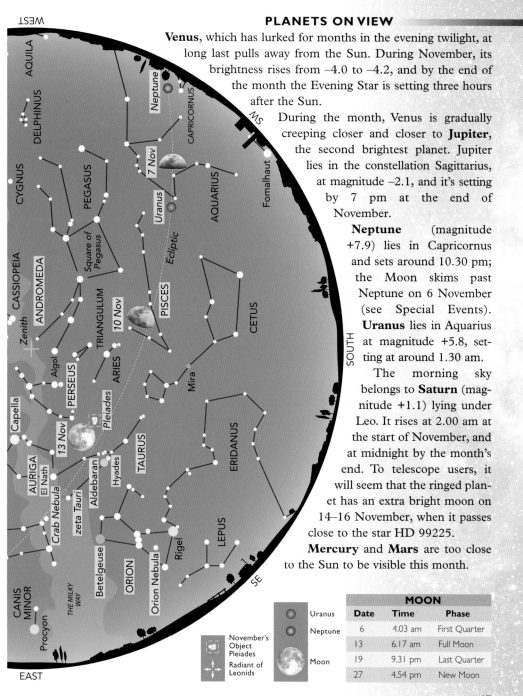

MOON		
Date	Time	Phase
6	4.03 am	First Quarter
13	6.17 am	Full Moon
19	9.31 pm	Last Quarter
27	4.54 pm	New Moon

November's Object
Pleiades

Radiant of
Leonids

Uranus
Neptune
Moon

MOON

The crescent Moon lies near Venus on 1 November, and Jupiter on 3 November. The Moon occults Neptune on 6 November and the Pleiades on 13 November (see Special Events for both). The waning Moon lies near Regulus on 19 November, Saturn in the early hours of 21 and 22 November, and Spica on the morning of 24 November.

SPECIAL EVENTS

On **6 November**, the Moon has a very close encounter with dim and distant Neptune – but you'll need a telescope or good binoculars to witness the event. If in England or Wales, you'll see the Moon skim past Neptune at 6.50 pm. People in Scotland and Northern Ireland will observe the Moon moving in front of – and occulting – Neptune between about 6.30 and 7.10 pm.

The Full Moon occults the Pleiades on **13 November**. Between 6.20 and 8.50 pm, it hides four of the Seven Sisters.

17 November: it is the maximum of the Leonid meteor shower. A few years ago, this annual shower yielded literally storms of shooting stars, but the rate has gone down as the parent comet Tempel-Tuttle, which sheds its dust to produce the meteors, has moved away from the vicinity of Earth.

NOVEMBER'S OBJECT

'A swarm of fireflies tangled in a silver braid' – this evocative description of the lovely **Pleiades** star cluster was coined by Alfred, Lord Tennyson, in his 1842 poem 'Locksley Hall', and how accurate it is. Very keen-sighted observers can pick out up to 11 stars, but most mere mortals have to content themselves with six or seven. These are just the most luminous in a group of 500 stars, lying about 400 light years away (although there's an ongoing debate about the precise distance). The brightest stars in the Pleiades are hot and blue, and all the stars are young – less than 80 million years old. They were all born together, and have yet to go their separate ways. The fledgling stars have blundered into a cloud of gas in space, which looks like gos-

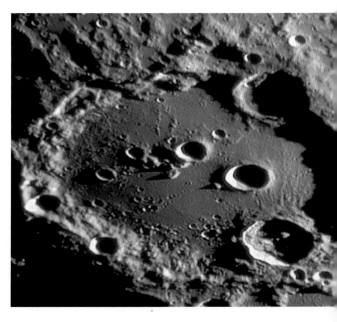

▼ *Jamie Cooper in Northamptonshire captured this image of Clavius on a video sequence, using a ToUcam webcam on a 250-mm Newtonian reflecting telescope.*

◉ *Viewing tip*

Now that the nights are drawing in earlier, and becoming darker, it's a good time to pick out faint, fuzzy objects like the Andromeda Galaxy and the Orion Nebula. But don't even think about it near the time of Full Moon – its light will drown them out. The best time to observe 'deep sky objects' is when the Moon is near to New, or after Full Moon. Check the timetable of the Moon phases in the Guide.

samer on webcam images. But they're still a beautiful sight to the unaided eye or through binoculars.

NOVEMBER'S PICTURE

Some 225 kilometres across and 3.5 kilometres deep, Clavius is one of the largest craters on the Moon – it's even visible without optical aid. Most of our satellite's large craters were created during a period of bombardment by massive asteroids 3.8 billion years ago, but the floor of Clavius – peppered with smaller craters – testifies to more recent impacts. Located in the Moon's southern highlands, Clavius featured as a lunar administrative facility in the film *2001: A Space Odyssey*.

NOVEMBER'S TOPIC
Extrasolar Planets

A revolution in astronomy has taken place during the past decade. After years of fruitless searching, scientists have discovered around 300 planets circling nearby stars.

The first came in October 1995, when Swiss astronomers Michel Mayor and Didier Queloz discovered that the faint star 51 Pegasi – just to the right of the great Square of Pegasus – was being pulled backwards and forwards every four days. It had to be the work of a planet, tugging on its parent star. Astonishingly, this planet is around the same size as the Solar System's giant, Jupiter, but it is far closer to its star than Mercury is to the Sun. Astronomers call such planets 'hot Jupiters'.

A team in California led by Geoff Marcy was already looking for planets, and soon found more. Friendly rivalry between the groups has led to a profusion of planets being found.

In addition, astronomers have found several more planets by watching for stars to dim in brightness as a planet passes in front. And one planet has even been discovered because its gravity is bending and focusing the light from a very distant star.

All these are big planets, like Jupiter and Saturn. Present-day telescopes on Earth can't locate a planet as small as our world. But all this could change. Early next year, NASA plans to launch the Kepler satellite, which will monitor the brightness of stars to detect planets passing in front of their parents. And the hope is that – one day – they will find an Earth out there.

We have a Christmas Star! The brilliant planet Venus sets four hours after the Sun (at around 8 pm), and is shining at magnitude –4.3.

And the winter constellations are conspicuously in the ascendant, with **Capella**, in **Auriga**, climbing up to the height of the heavens. Capella is actually a pair of yellow stars, with temperatures similar to the Sun – but the components are around 50 and 80 times more luminous.

Orion and his companions – **Taurus** (the Bull), with his hunting dogs (**Canis Major** and **Canis Minor**) are all sailing high in the southern sky. **Sirius** (the Dog Star, in Canis Major) is the brightest star in the sky, at magnitude –1.47. But Sirius is not intrinsically luminous: it simply lies close to the Sun, at a distance of 8.6 light years. A small telescope will reveal a companion star close to the Dog Star – appropriately named 'The Pup'.

DECEMBER'S CONSTELLATION

This month, it has of course to be Orion – the most recognizable constellation in the sky. And it's one of the rare star-groupings that really looks like its namesake – a giant of a man with a sword below his belt, wielding a club above his head. Orion is fabled in mythology as the ultimate hunter. The constellation is dominated by two brilliant stars: blood-red **Betelgeuse** at the top left and the even more brilliant blue-white **Rigel** towards bottom right.

The two stars could hardly be more different. Betelgeuse (see December's Object) is a cool, bloated, dying star – known as a red giant – over 300 times the size of the Sun. But Rigel is a vigorous young star over twice as hot as our Sun (its surface temperature is around 12,000°C), and it's more than 50,000 times as bright. The famous 'belt of Orion' is made up of the stars **Alnitak** (left), **Alnilam** and

▼ The sky at 10 pm in mid-December, with Moon positions at three-day intervals either side of Full Moon. The star positions are also correct for 11 pm at the *beginning of December, and 9 pm at the end of the month. The planets move slightly relative to the stars during the month.*

Mintaka (right) – below which hangs Orion's sword, the lair of the great **Orion Nebula**.

PLANETS ON VIEW

Venus is definitely the queen of the sky this month. The Evening Star's debut is a stunning conjunction with second-brightest planet Jupiter on 1 December, when it dramatically emerges from behind the Moon (see Special Events). And Venus (magnitude –4.3) becomes more prominent throughout December as it moves into a darker sky. By the end of the year, Venus is setting at 8 pm, around four hours after the Sun. It lies near the Pleiades on 10 and 11 December.

As Venus rises higher in the sky, **Jupiter** – magnitude –2.0 – sinks down into the twilight. By the close of the month, it's setting in the southwest at 5.30 pm, just an hour and a half after the Sun.

The last week of the year sees **Mercury** (magnitude –0.6) pop up into view in the evening sky. On 29 December, Mercury lies below the crescent Moon and Jupiter; two nights later it's a degree to the lower left of Jupiter, and one-quarter as bright.

Neptune lies in Capricornus, at magnitude +7.9, and sets at 8.30 pm. You'll find it just a degree to the right of Venus on the evening of 27 December.

Uranus is to be found in Aquarius, at magnitude +5.9, and setting about 11 pm. Around the same time, **Saturn** (magnitude +1.0) is rising in the east, in Leo.

WEST

AQUARIUS
PEGASUS
Uranus
Ecliptic
6 Dec
Square of Pegasus
ANDROMEDA
PISCES
CETUS
Algol
TRIANGULUM
ARIES
9 Dec
Mira
Zenith
PERSEUS
Algol
Capella
Algol
Pleiades
Crab Nebula
Hyades
TAURUS
Aldebaran
ERIDANUS
AURIGA
12 Dec
Mintaka
Radiant of Geminids
Castor
Pollux
Betelgeuse
Alnilam
Alnitak
Orion Nebula
Rigel
LEPUS
GEMINI
ORION
COLUMBA
15 Dec
Procyon
CANIS MINOR
THE MILKY WAY
Sirius
CANIS MAJOR
Adhara
CANCER
HYDRA
SE
SOUTH
MS

EAST

	December's Object Betelgeuse
	December's Picture Crab Nebula
	Radiant of Geminids

Uranus
Moon

MOON		
Date	Time	Phase
5	9.25 pm	First Quarter
12	4.37 pm	Full Moon
19	10.29 am	Last Quarter
27	12.22 pm	New Moon

MOON

The Moon lies near Jupiter, and occults Venus, on 1 December (see Special Events). On 16 December you'll find the Moon near Regulus, and it passes Saturn on 18 December. The waning Moon is near Spica and Antares on the mornings of 21 and 25 December respectively. Just after sunset on 29 December, the waxing crescent Moon lies near Jupiter and Mercury; and it makes another passage by Venus (though not so close) on 31 December.

SPECIAL EVENTS

At dusk on **1 December,** the Moon is hiding Venus. As the sky darkens, you'll see the lunar crescent next to Jupiter. Then, between 5 and 5.15 pm (depending on your location in the UK), brilliant Venus will suddenly pop out from behind the Moon – to complete a glorious trio of the brightest objects in the night sky.

13 December: this is the maximum of the **Geminid** meteor shower. These meteors, debris shed from an asteroid called Phaethon, are quite substantial – and hence bright. This is not a good year for observing them, though, as bright moonlight will interfere.

21 December, 12.04 pm: the Winter Solstice occurs. As a result of the tilt of Earth's axis, the Sun reaches its lowest point in the heavens as seen from the northern hemisphere: we get the shortest days, and the longest nights.

DECEMBER'S OBJECT

Known to generations of schoolchildren as 'Beetle-Juice', Betelgeuse is one of the biggest stars known. If placed in our Solar System, it would swamp the planets all the way out to the asteroid belt. And it's just one of just a few stars to be imaged as a visible disc from Earth.

Some 630 times wider than the Sun, Betelgeuse is a serious red giant – a star close to the end of its life. Its middle-aged spread has been created by the dying nuclear reactions in its core, causing its outer layers to billow and cool.

The star's vivid red colour has led to it attracting several names – including 'The Armpit of the Sacred One'!

Betelgeuse will exit the Universe in a spectacular supernova explosion. As a result of the breakdown of nuclear reactions at its heart, the star will explode – and, one day in the future, it will shine as brightly in our skies as the Moon.

DECEMBER'S PICTURE

Star-wreck: the **Crab Nebula**, in Taurus, is all that's left of a star that was seen to explode in 1054. Chinese astronomers witnessed the outburst, which was visible in the daytime sky for

▶ *The Crab Nebula, captured by Ian King with a 178 mm telescope and a CCD. The exposure time was two hours through tri-colour filters.*

◉ **Viewing tip**

Venus is dazzling this month, looking like a Christmas-tree light hanging in the sky. If you have a small telescope, though, don't wait until the sky gets totally dark as Venus will appear so bright that it will be difficult to make out anything on its disc. It's best to wait until just after the Sun has set (not before, or you risk catching the Sun in your field of view), when you'll see the globe of Venus appearing fainter against a pale blue sky.

23 days. 6500 light years away, the supernova reached a brilliance of magnitude −4 – as bright as Venus. Its convoluted remains are now spread over 15 light years of space, and are still expanding from the explosion. At the nebula's heart is a pulsar: the collapsed core of the former star, which spins at the breakneck speed of 30 times per second – emitting powerful radio waves and X-rays into the cosmos.

DECEMBER'S TOPIC
The Big Bang

Christmas is coming up, with all its associations with birth and beginnings. But how did our Universe begin? Luckily, we have some pretty firm evidence to answer that question. Firstly, the Universe is expanding – on the largest scales, galaxies are moving apart from each other. If you 'rewind the tape', you'll find that the expansion dates back to a time 13.7 billion years ago – a measurement that has only been tied down in recent years. Secondly, the Universe is not entirely cold – it's bathed in a radiation field of 2.7 degrees above Absolute Zero. All these clues point to the origin of the Universe in a blisteringly-hot 'Big Bang', which caused space to expand. The 'microwave background' of 2.7 degrees is the remnant of this birth in fire, cooled down by the relentless expansion to a mere shadow of its former self. Current observations show that space is filled with 'dark energy', which forces the galaxies apart. So the Universe is not just expanding, but is accelerating – which means that it's destined to die by simply fading away. In 100 billion years, we won't be able to see any galaxies beyond our own!

There's always something to see in our Solar System, from planets to meteors or the Moon. These objects are very close to us – in astronomical terms – so their positions, shapes and sizes appear to change constantly. It is important to know when, where and how to look if you are to enjoy exploring Earth's neighbourhood. Here we give the best dates in 2008 for observing the planets and meteors (weather permitting!), and explain some of the concepts that will help you to get the most out of your observing.

THE INFERIOR PLANETS

A planet with an orbit that lies closer to the Sun than the orbit of Earth is known as *inferior*. Mercury and Venus are the inferior planets. They show a full range of phases (like the Moon) from the thinnest crescents to full, depending on their position in relation to the Earth and the Sun. The diagram shows the various positions of the inferior planets. They are invisible when at *conjunction* and best viewed when at their eastern or western *elongations*.

> **Magnitudes**
> Astronomers measure the brightness of stars, planets and other celestial objects using a scale of *magnitudes*. Somewhat confusingly, fainter objects have higher magnitudes, while brighter objects have lower magnitudes; the most brilliant stars have negative magnitudes! Naked-eye stars range from magnitude −1.5 for the brightest star, Sirius, to +6.5 for the faintest stars you can see on a really dark night. As a guide, here are the magnitudes of selected objects:
>
> | | |
> |---|---|
> | Sun | −26.7 |
> | Full Moon | −12.5 |
> | Venus (at its brightest) | −4.6 |
> | Sirius | −1.5 |
> | Betelgeuse | +0.4 |
> | Polaris (Pole Star) | +2.0 |
> | Faintest star visible to the naked eye | +6.5 |
> | Pluto | +14 |
> | Faintest star visible to the Hubble Space Telescope | +31 |

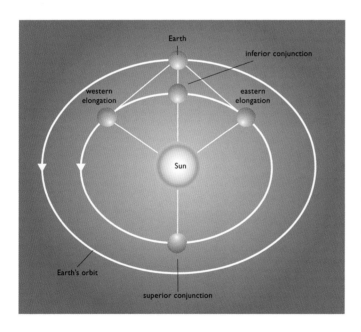

◄ At eastern or western elongation, an inferior planet is at its maximum angular distance from the Sun. Conjunction occurs at two stages in the planet's orbit. Under certain circumstances an inferior planet can transit across the Sun's disc at inferior conjunction.

Mercury

In the second half of January Mercury is at its greatest elongation (east) of the Sun and is visible in the dusk after sunset. It may just be visible low in the evening twilight again in mid May and the end of December. In late October, it is at its greatest elongation (west) and is visible in the dusk before sunrise.

● Maximum elongations of Mercury in 2008		
Date	Mag	Separation
22 Jan	−0.5	18.6° east
3 Mar	+0.2	27.1° west
14 May	+0.6	21.8° east
1 Jul	+0.6	21.8° west
11 Sep	+0.3	26.9° east
22 Oct	−0.5	18.3° west

Venus

Venus does not reach greatest elongation in 2008. In January and February it is brilliant in the southeast before dawn. It re-emerges from behind the Sun in the northwest at dusk at the end of July, and reaches its best by the end of the year. It is occulted by the Moon on 1 December.

THE SUPERIOR PLANETS

The superior planets are those with orbits that lie beyond that of the Earth. They are Mars, Jupiter, Saturn, Uranus and Neptune, as well as Pluto. The best time to observe a superior planet is when the Earth lies between it and the Sun. At this point in the planet's orbit, it is said to be at *opposition*.

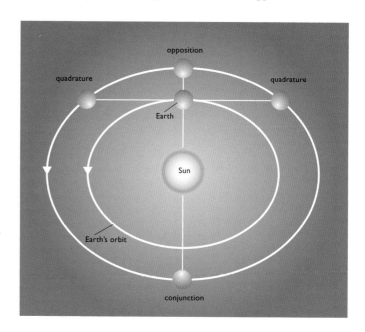

▶ Superior planets are invisible at conjunction. At quadrature the planet is at right angles to the Sun as viewed from Earth. Opposition is the best time to observe a superior planet.

● Progress of Mars through the constellations	
Early Jan–early Mar	Taurus
Early Mar–early May	Gemini
Early May–mid Jun	Cancer
Mid Jun–mid Aug	Leo
Mid Aug–mid Oct	Virgo
Mid Oct–mid Nov	Libra
Late Nov	Scorpius
December	Ophiucus

Mars

After having reached opposition on 24 December 2007, Mars is best placed for viewing at the beginning of the year. In January and February it is dazzling, high up in the night sky in Taurus but slowly fades and drops into the twilight. Its progress through the constellations is shown in the table at left.

Jupiter

Jupiter lies in the constellation of Sagittarius for all of 2008. It is best placed for observing during summer and early autumn, after it reaches opposition on 9 July.

Saturn

Saturn is in Leo for the whole of 2008. It is at opposition on 24

February and is at its best for observing from January to June and again from November onwards.

Uranus

Throughout 2008 Uranus lies in the constellation of Aquarius, so for much of the early part of the year it is drowned out by the glare from the Sun. Visibility improves during the summer and it reaches opposition on 13 September.

Neptune

Neptune spends 2008 in Capricornus. It is not visible in the early part of the year, and is best viewed in the summer. By July it is above the horizon all night, and reaches opposition on 15 August. It is occulted by the Moon on 13 September.

Pluto

Pluto has now been relegated to the status of dwarf planet. It is very faint, at magnitude +14 and difficult to locate in even the largest amateur instruments.

SOLAR AND LUNAR ECLIPSES

Solar eclipses

There are two solar eclipses in 2008 on 7 February and 1 August. The former is annular, and can be seen from Antarctica and will be partial over parts of New Zealand and Australia. The latter is total, and is visible from northern Canada, northern Greenland, Siberia, Mongolia and central China. It will be visible as a partial eclipse over southern Greenland, Europe and the rest of Asia.

Lunar Eclipses

There are two lunar eclipses in 2008 on 21 February and 16 August. The former is total and visible from the UK and most

Astronomical distances

For objects in the Solar System, like the planets, we can give their distances from the Earth in kilometres. But the distances are just too huge once we reach out to the stars. Even the nearest star (Proxima Centauri) lies 25 million million km away. So astronomers use a larger unit, the *light year*. This is the distance that light travels in one year, and it equals 9.46 million million km.

Here are the distances to some familiar astronomical objects, in light years:

Proxima Centauri	4.2
Betelgeuse	427
Centre of the Milky Way	24,000
Andromeda Galaxy	2.5 million
Most distant galaxies seen by the Hubble Space Telescope	13 billion

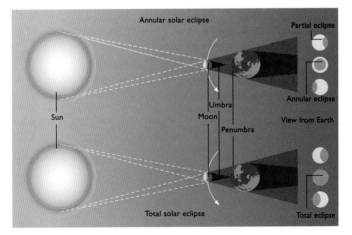

◄ *Where the dark central part (the umbra) of the Moon's shadow reaches the Earth, a total eclipse is seen. People located within the penumbra see a partial eclipse. If the umbral shadow does not reach Earth, an annular eclipse is seen. This type of eclipse occurs when the Moon is at a distant point in its orbit and is not quite large enough to cover the whole of the Sun's disc.*

Dates of maximum for selected meteor showers	
Meteor shower	date of maximum
Meteor shower	date of maximum
Quadrantids	3/4 January
Lyrids	21/22 April
Eta Aquarids	5/6 May
Perseids	12/13 August
Orionids	21/22 October
Leonids	17/18 November
Geminids	13/14 December

▶ *Meteors from a common source, occurring during a shower, enter the atmosphere along parallel trajectories. As a result of perspective, however, they appear to diverge from a single point in the sky.*

Angular separations

Astronomers measure the distance between objects, as we see them in the sky, by the angle between the objects, in degrees (symbol °). From the horizon to the point above your head is 90 degrees. All around the horizon is 360 degrees.
You can use your hand, held at arm's length, as a rough guide to angular distances, as follows:
Width of index finger   1°
Width of clenched hand 10°
Thumb to little finger
on outspread hand   20°
For smaller distances, astronomers divide the degree into 60 arcminutes (symbol ′), and the arcminute into 60 arcseconds (symbol ″).

of Europe, western Africa and all of the Americas. The latter is partial and visible from South America, Europe, Asia, Africa and Australia.

METEOR SHOWERS

Shooting stars – or *meteors* – are tiny particles of interplanetary dust, known as *meteoroids*, burning up in the Earth's atmosphere. At certain times of year, the Earth passes through a stream of these meteoroids (usually debris left behind by a comet) and a *meteor shower* is seen. The point in the sky from which the meteors appear to emanate is known as the *radiant*. Most showers are known by the constellation in which the radiant is situated.

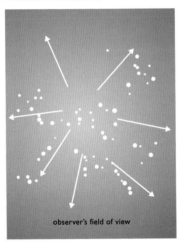

observer's field of view

When watching meteors for a coordinated meteor programme, observers generally note the time, seeing conditions, cloud cover, their own location, the time and brightness of each meteor and whether it was from the main meteor stream. It's also worth noting details of persistent afterglows (trains) and fireballs, and making counts of how many meteors appear in a given period.

COMETS

Comets are small bodies in orbit about the Sun. Consisting of frozen gases and dust, they are often known as 'dirty snowballs'. When their orbits bring them close to the Sun the ices evaporate and dramatic tails of gas and dust can sometimes be seen.

A number of comets move round the Sun in fairly small, elliptical orbits in periods of a few years; others have much longer periods. Most really brilliant comets have orbital periods of several thousands or even millions of years. The exception is Comet Halley, a bright comet with a period of about 76 years. It was last seen with the naked eye in 1986.

Binoculars and wide-field telescopes provide the best views of comet tails. Larger telescopes with a high magnification are necessary to observe fine detail in the gaseous head (coma). Most comets are discovered with professional instruments, but a few are still found by experienced amateur astronomers.

Deep sky objects are 'fuzzy patches' that lie outside the Solar System. They include star clusters, nebulae and galaxies. To observe the majority of deep sky objects you will need binoculars or a telescope, but there are also some beautiful naked eye objects, notably the Pleiades and the Orion Nebula.

The faintest object that an instrument can see is its *limiting magnitude*. The table gives a rough guide, for good seeing conditions, for a variety of small- to medium-sized telescopes.

We have provided a selection of recommended deep sky targets, together with their magnitudes. Some are described in more detail in our 'Object of the month' features. Look on the appropriate month's map to find which constellations are on view, and then choose your objects using the list below. We have provided celestial coordinates, for readers with detailed star maps. The suggested times of year for viewing are when the constellation is highest in the sky in the late evening.

Limiting magnitude for small to medium telescopes	
aperture (mm)	limiting magnitude
50	+11.2
60	+11.6
70	+11.9
80	+12.2
100	+12.7
125	+13.2
150	+13.6

RECOMMENDED DEEP SKY OBJECTS

Andromeda – autumn and early winter

M31 (NGC 224) Andromeda Galaxy	3rd magnitude spiral galaxy, RA 00h 42.7m Dec +41° 16'
M32 (NGC 221)	8th magnitude elliptical galaxy, a companion to M31. RA 00h 42.7m Dec +40° 52'
M110 (NGC 205)	8th magnitude elliptical galaxy RA 00h 40.4m Dec +41° 41'
NGC 7662 Blue Snowball	8th magnitude planetary nebula RA 23h 25.9m Dec +42° 33'

Aquarius – late autumn and early winter

M2 (NGC 7089)	6th magnitude globular cluster RA 21h 33.5m Dec –00° 49'
M72 (NGC 6981)	9th magnitude globular cluster RA 20h 53.5m Dec –12° 32'
NGC 7293 Helix Nebula	7th magnitude planetary nebula RA 22h 29.6m Dec –20° 48'
NGC 7009 Saturn Nebula	8th magnitude planetary nebula; RA 21h 04.2m Dec –11° 22'

Aries – early winter

NGC 772	10th magnitude spiral galaxy RA 01h 59.3m Dec +19° 01'

Auriga – winter

M36 (NGC 1960)	6th magnitude open cluster RA 05h 36.1m Dec +34° 08'
M37 (NGC 2099)	6th magnitude open cluster RA 05h 52.4m Dec +32° 33'
M38 (NGC 1912)	6th magnitude open cluster RA 05h 28.7m Dec +35° 50'

Cancer – late winter to early spring

M44 (NGC 2632) Praesepe or Beehive	3rd magnitude open cluster RA 08h 40.1m Dec +19° 59'
M67 (NGC 2682)	7th magnitude open cluster RA 08h 50.4m Dec +11° 49'

Canes Venatici – visible all year

M3 (NGC 5272)	6th magnitude globular cluster RA 13h 42.2m Dec +28° 23'

M51 (NGC 5194/5) Whirlpool Galaxy	8th magnitude spiral galaxy RA 13h 29.9m Dec +47° 12'
M63 (NGC 5055)	9th magnitude spiral galaxy RA 13h 15.8m Dec +42° 02'
M94 (NGC 4736)	8th magnitude spiral galaxy RA 12h 50.9m Dec +41° 07'
M106 (NGC4258)	8th magnitude spiral galaxy RA 12h 19.0m Dec +47° 18'

Canis Major – late winter

M41 (NGC 2287)	4th magnitude open cluster RA 06h 47.0m Dec –20° 44'

Capricornus – late summer and early autumn

M30 (NGC 7099)	7th magnitude globular cluster RA 21h 40.4m Dec –23° 11'

Cassiopeia – visible all year

M52 (NGC 7654)	6th magnitude open cluster RA 23h 24.2m Dec +61° 35'
M103 (NGC 581)	7th magnitude open cluster RA 01h 33.2m Dec +60° 42'
NGC 225	7th magnitude open cluster RA 00h 43.4m Dec +61 47'
NGC 457	6th magnitude open cluster RA 01h 19.1m Dec +58° 20'
NGC 663	Good binocular open cluster RA 01h 46.0m Dec +61° 15'

Cepheus – visible all year

Delta Cephei	Variable star, varying between 3.5 and 4.4 with a period of 5.37 days. It has a magnitude 6.3 companion and they make an attractive pair for small telescopes or binoculars.

Cetus – late autumn

Mira (omicron Ceti)	Irregular variable star with a period of roughly 330 days and a range between 2.0 and 10.1.
M77 (NGC 1068)	9th magnitude spiral galaxy RA 02h 42.7m Dec –00° 01'

Coma Berenices – spring

M53 (NGC 5024)	8th magnitude globular cluster RA 13h 12.9m Dec +18° 10'
M64 (NGC 4286) Black Eye Galaxy	8th magnitude spiral galaxy with a prominent dust lane that is visible in larger telescopes. RA 12h 56.7m Dec +21° 41'
M85 (NGC 4382)	9th magnitude elliptical galaxy RA 12h 25.4m Dec +18° 11'
M88 (NGC 4501)	10th magnitude spiral galaxy RA 12h 32.0m Dec.+14° 25'
M91 (NGC 4548)	10th magnitude spiral galaxy RA 12h 35.4m Dec +14° 30'
M98 (NGC 4192)	10th magnitude spiral galaxy RA 12h 13.8m Dec +14° 54'
M99 (NGC 4254)	10th magnitude spiral galaxy RA 12h 18.8m Dec +14° 25'
M100 (NGC 4321)	9th magnitude spiral galaxy RA 12h 22.9m Dec +15° 49'
NGC 4565	10th magnitude spiral galaxy RA 12h 36.3m Dec +25° 59'

Cygnus – late summer and autumn

Cygnus Rift	Dark cloud just south of Deneb that appears to split the Milky Way in two.
NGC 7000 North America Nebula	A bright nebula against the back- ground of the Milky Way, visible with binoculars under dark skies. RA 20h 58.8m Dec +44° 20'
NGC 6992 Veil Nebula (part)	Supernova remnant, visible with binoculars under dark skies. RA 20h 56.8m Dec +31 28'
M29 (NGC 6913)	7th magnitude open cluster RA 20h 23.9m Dec +36° 32'
M39 (NGC 7092)	Large 5th magnitude open cluster RA 21h 32.2m Dec +48° 26'
NGC 6826 Blinking Planetary	9th magnitude planetary nebula RA 19 44.8m Dec +50° 31'

Delphinus – late summer

NGC 6934	9th magnitude globular cluster RA 20h 34.2m Dec +07° 24'

Draco – midsummer

NGC 6543	9th magnitude planetary nebula RA 17h 58.6m Dec +66° 38'

Gemini – winter

M35 (NGC 2168)	5th magnitude open cluster RA 06h 08.9m Dec +24° 20'
NGC 2392 Eskimo Nebula	8–10th magnitude planetary nebula RA 07h 29.2m Dec +20° 55'

Hercules – early summer

M13 (NGC 6205)	6th magnitude globular cluster RA 16h 41.7m Dec +36° 28'
M92 (NGC 6341)	6th magnitude globular cluster RA 17h 17.1m Dec +43° 08'
NGC 6210	9th magnitude planetary nebula RA 16h 44.5m Dec +23 49'

Hydra – early spring

M48 (NGC 2548)	6th magnitude open cluster RA 08h 13.8m Dec −05° 48'
M68 (NGC 4590)	8th magnitude globular cluster RA 12h 39.5m Dec −26° 45'

M83 (NGC 5236)	8th magnitude spiral galaxy RA 13h 37.0m Dec −29° 52'
NGC 3242 Ghost of Jupiter	9th magnitude planetary nebula RA 10h 24.8m Dec −18°38'

Leo – spring

M65 (NGC 3623)	9th magnitude spiral galaxy RA 11h 18.9m Dec +13° 05'
M66 (NGC 3627)	9th magnitude spiral galaxy RA 11h 20.2m Dec +12° 59'
M95 (NGC 3351)	10th magnitude spiral galaxy RA 10h 44.0m Dec +11° 42'
M96 (NGC 3368)	9th magnitude spiral galaxy RA 10h 46.8m Dec +11° 49'
M105 (NGC 3379)	9th magnitude elliptical galaxy RA 10h 47.8m Dec +12° 35'

Lepus – winter

M79 (NGC 1904)	8th magnitude globular cluster RA 05h 24.5m Dec −24° 33'

Lyra – spring

M56 (NGC 6779)	8th magnitude globular cluster RA 19h 16.6m Dec +30° 11'
M57 (NGC 6720) Ring Nebula	9th magnitude planetary nebula RA 18h 53.6m Dec +33° 02'

Monoceros – winter

M50 (NGC 2323)	6th magnitude open cluster RA 07h 03.2m Dec −08° 20'
NGC 2244	Open cluster surrounded by the faint Rosette Nebula, NGC 2237. Visible in binoculars. RA 06h 32.4m Dec +04° 52'

Ophiuchus – summer

M9 (NGC 6333)	8th magnitude globular cluster RA 17h 19.2m Dec −18° 31'
M10 (NGC 6254)	7th magnitude globular cluster RA 16h 57.1m Dec −04° 06'
M12 (NCG 6218)	7th magnitude globular cluster RA 16h 47.2m Dec −01° 57'
M14 (NGC 6402)	8th magnitude globular cluster RA 17h 37.6m Dec −03° 15'
M19 (NGC 6273)	7th magnitude globular cluster RA 17h 02.6m Dec −26° 16'
M62 (NGC 6266)	7th magnitude globular cluster RA 17h 01.2m Dec −30° 07'
M107 (NGC 6171)	8th magnitude globular cluster RA 16h 32.5m Dec −13° 03'

Orion – winter

M42 (NGC 1976) Orion Nebula	4th magnitude nebula RA 05h 35.4m Dec −05° 27'
M43 (NGC 1982)	5th magnitude nebula RA 05h 35.6m Dec −05° 16'
M78 (NGC 2068)	8th magnitude nebula RA 05h 46.7m Dec +00° 03'

Pegasus – autumn

M15 (NGC 7078)	6th magnitude globular cluster RA 21h 30.0m Dec +12° 10'

Perseus – autumn to winter

M34 (NGC 1039)	5th magnitude open cluster RA 02h 42.0m Dec +42° 47'
M76 (NGC 650/1) Little Dumbbell	11th magnitude planetary nebula RA 01h 42.4m Dec +51° 34'

NGC 869/884 Double Cluster	Pair of open star clusters *RA 02h 19.0m Dec +57° 09'* *RA 02h 22.4m Dec +57° 07'*	

Pisces – autumn

M74 (NGC 628)	9th magnitude spiral galaxy *RA 01h 36.7m Dec +15° 47'*

Puppis – late winter

M46 (NGC 2437)	6th magnitude open cluster *RA 07h 41.8m Dec –14° 49'*
M47 (NGC 2422)	4th magnitude open cluster *RA 07h 36.6m Dec –14° 30'*
M93 (NGC 2447)	6th magnitude open cluster *RA 07h 44.6m Dec –23° 52'*

Sagitta – late summer

M71 (NGC 6838)	8th magnitude globular cluster *RA 19h 53.8m Dec +18° 47'*

Sagittarius – summer

M8 (NGC 6523) Lagoon Nebula	6th magnitude nebula *RA 18h 03.8m Dec –24° 23'*
M17 (NGC 6618) Omega Nebula	6th magnitude nebula *RA 18h 20.8m Dec –16° 11'*
M18 (NGC 6613)	7th magnitude open cluster *RA 18h 19.9m Dec –17 08'*
M20 (NGC 6514) Trifid Nebula	9th magnitude nebula *RA 18h 02.3m Dec –23° 02'*
M21 (NGC 6531)	6th magnitude open cluster *RA 18h 04.6m Dec –22° 30'*
M22 (NGC 6656)	5th magnitude globular cluster *RA 18h 36.4m Dec –23° 54'*
M23 (NGC 6494)	5th magnitude open cluster *RA 17h 56.8m Dec –19° 01'*
M24 (NGC 6603)	5th magnitude open cluster *RA 18h 16.9m Dec –18° 29'*
M25 (IC 4725)	5th magnitude open cluster *RA 18h 31.6m Dec –19° 15'*
M28 (NGC 6626)	7th magnitude globular cluster *RA 18h 24.5m Dec –24° 52'*
M54 (NGC 6715)	8th magnitude globular cluster *RA 18h 55.1m Dec –30° 29'*
M55 (NGC 6809)	7th magnitude globular cluster *RA 19h 40.0m Dec –30° 58'*
M69 (NGC 6637)	8th magnitude globular cluster *RA 18h 31.4m Dec –32° 21'*
M70 (NGC 6681)	8th magnitude globular cluster *RA 18h 43.2m Dec –32° 18'*
M75 (NGC 6864)	9th magnitude globular cluster *RA 20h 06.1m Dec –21° 55'*

Scorpius (northern part) – midsummer

M4 (NGC 6121)	6th magnitude globular cluster *RA 16h 23.6m Dec –26° 32'*
M7 (NGC 6475)	3rd magnitude open cluster *RA 17h 53.9m Dec –34° 49'*
M80 (NGC 6093)	7th magnitude globular cluster *RA 16h 17.0m Dec –22° 59'*

Scutum – mid- to late summer

M11 (NGC 6705) Wild Duck Cluster	6th magnitude open cluster *RA 18h 51.1m Dec –06° 16'*

M26 (NGC 6694)	8th magnitude open cluster *RA 18h 45.2m Dec –09° 24'*

Serpens – summer

M5 (NGC 5904)	6th magnitude globular cluster *RA 15h 18.6m Dec +02° 05'*
M16 (NGC 6611)	6th magnitude open cluster, surrounded by the Eagle Nebula. *RA 18h 18.8m Dec –13° 47'*

Taurus – winter

M1 (NGC 1952) Crab Nebula	8th magnitude supernova remnant *RA 05h 34.5m Dec +22° 00'*
M45 Pleiades	1st magnitude open cluster, an excellent binocular object. *RA 03h 47.0m Dec +24° 07'*

Triangulum – autumn

M33 (NGC 598)	6th magnitude spiral galaxy *RA 01h 33.9m Dec +30° 39'*

Ursa Major – all year

M81 (NGC 3031)	7th magnitude spiral galaxy *RA 09h 55.6m Dec +69° 04'*
M82 (NGC 3034)	8th magnitude starburst galaxy *RA 09h 55.8m Dec +69° 41'*
M97 (NGC 3587) Owl Nebula	12th magnitude planetary nebula *RA 11h 14.8m Dec +55° 01'*
M101 (NGC 5457)	8th magnitude spiral galaxy *RA 14h 03.2m Dec +54° 21'*
M108 (NGC 3556)	10th magnitude spiral galaxy *RA 11h 11.5m Dec +55° 40'*
M109 (NGC 3992)	10th magnitude spiral galaxy *RA 11h 57.6m Dec +53° 23'*

Virgo – spring

M49 (NGC 4472)	8th magnitude elliptical galaxy *RA 12h 29.8m Dec +08° 00'*
M58 (NGC 4579)	10th magnitude spiral galaxy *RA 12h 37.7m Dec +11° 49'*
M59 (NGC 4621)	10th magnitude elliptical galaxy *RA 12h 42.0m Dec +11° 39'*
M60 (NGC 4649)	9th magnitude elliptical galaxy *RA 12h 43.7m Dec +11° 33'*
M61 (NGC 4303)	10 magnitude spiral galaxy *RA 12h 21.9m Dec +04° 28'*
M84 (NGC 4374)	9th magnitude elliptical galaxy *RA 12h 25.1m Dec +12° 53'*
M86 (NGC 4406)	9th magnitude elliptical galaxy *RA 12h 26.2m Dec +12° 57'*
M87 (NGC 4486)	9th magnitude elliptical galaxy *RA 12h 30.8m Dec +12° 24'*
M89 (NGC 4552)	10th magnitude elliptical galaxy *RA 12h 35.7m Dec +12° 33'*
M90 (NGC 4569)	9th magnitude spiral galaxy *RA 12h 36.8m Dec +13° 10'*
M104 (NGC 4594) Sombrero Galaxy	Almost edge on 8th magnitude spiral galaxy. *RA 12h 40.0m Dec –11° 37'*

Vulpecula – late summer and autumn

M27 (NGC 6853) Dumbbell Nebula	8th magnitude planetary nebula *RA 19h 59.6m Dec +22° 43'*

LOW TECH OR HIGH TECH?

In some ways there has never been a better time to be interested in astronomy. Despite the overwhelming scourge of light pollution, which threatens virtually to blot out the heavens for much of the population, there is now a greater choice of instruments available with which to view the sky – when you get the chance. And, paradoxically, amateur astronomers are now making more impressive observations than ever before, using technology that was not available to even professional astronomers a generation or so ago.

But the high-tech revolution is not for everybody. So this article looks at the two modern approaches to amateur astronomy: the low-tech, which in effect is the same as has been with us since the 19th century, and the high-tech, in which modern electronics and optical filters have revolutionized the way we observe.

Back to basics

Many a manual of amateur astronomy recommends the beginner not to bother with a telescope, but to start observing just with binoculars. There are good reasons for this. Binoculars, unlike telescopes, have many uses and are far more widespread. They are pretty well mass-market devices. One factory in China claims to have the capacity to make 800,000 binoculars a year. The result is that basic binoculars of good quality are available for about £50, and even cheaper ones will often give excellent views – though they may lack the robustness of the more expensive models. So you need not break the bank to get started.

Binoculars will show you very much more than you can see with the naked eye, and even from light-polluted areas they will reveal stars and deep sky objects such as nebulae and star clusters that you could never view with the naked eye alone. There are no complicated mountings to worry about, and with basic binoculars no batteries to run down. They are ready for use in an instant, and indeed many advanced amateurs, who have more telescopes than they can shake an eyepiece at, own binoculars and use them regularly for a quick look or to view particular sorts of objects.

Finding objects with binoculars is an excellent way of getting to know the sky. The skills learned with binoculars will stand you in good stead when you progress to telescopes, even if you subsequently decide to go down the high-tech route. A basic knowledge of the sky can help greatly when things go wrong.

Moving on

There is a school of thought that says that you will never be happy with just binoculars, and even beginners should get a telescope for their first instrument. It's true that binoculars have their limitations: they won't show detail on the planets, and even a fairly small telescope will show you many more deep sky objects than binoculars can. If you want to progress in astronomy, a telescope is pretty much essential. But even in these affluent times, many people will consider their first purchase of a telescope very carefully. With a budget of £200 you can have a good and versatile telescope these days; in fact, you can spend half that and still get a worthwhile instrument.

Though the choice is huge, the basic decision is between a refracting telescope, with a lens at the top of the tube, and a reflecting telescope, with a mirror at the bottom of the tube. Put in a nutshell, refractors are maintenance-free and give higher contrast images, though with some colour fringing visible at high magnification in budget instruments. Reflectors have no false colour and are available in larger sizes for the same money, but the mirrors can tarnish over time and can get out of alignment after rough treatment such as in transportation. The choice is often a personal one, but in general town dwellers tend to opt for refractors, while out in the country the larger aperture of a reflector may be worth having.

One further decision is whether to go for a simple altazimuth mounting, with basic up-down and side-to-side movements, or the more complex but versatile equatorial mounting that helps you to track the stars more easily once it is correctly aligned. The fact is that many beginners find equatorial mounts hard to use, so the simplicity of an altazimuth is probably best for starters. Although the larger refractors – above 90 mm aperture – tend to be sold on equatorial mounts only, you can buy some very large reflectors on what are called Dobsonian mounts, in which the telescope is slung between a pair of arms on a turntable.

Far from being a device for beginners only, the Dobsonian-style telescope is used by many advanced amateurs because it allows some very large telescopes to be made portable and thus carried to dark-sky sites such as the annual Equinox Sky Camp held at Kelling Heath, Norfolk, every autumn. Organized by the Loughton Astronomical Society with the support of the Society for Popular Astronomy, this event attracts hundreds of amateurs who gather to observe in some of the darkest skies in England. The largest telescopes on the site are inevitably Dobsonians which have 45 or 50 cm diameter mirrors, yet can be dismantled quite quickly to be carried in an ordinary car. They may cost just as much as the highly advanced computer-controlled instruments on the site, but on a good night they can give superlative views of deep sky objects in particular. For details of this year's Kelling Heath Sky Camp, go to www.starparty.org.uk.

▲ The Sky-Watcher Startravel 80, here on a small equatorial mount, is a short-tube refractor suitable for both astro and daytime use.

▼ A basic Dobsonian telescope, such as this 8-inch (200 mm) aperture Celestron Starhopper, is a low-cost way to get a large-aperture telescope.

▲ *Giant Dobsonians (left) steal the show at the Kelling Heath Sky Camp in Norfolk. They can be dismantled for transportation.*

One thing you can't readily do with a basic altazimuth mount is take photographs through the telescope. For that you need to be able to track the celestial objects precisely and in alignment with the Earth's axis, or you will just end up with trailed images. Though limited photography is possible with some ingenuity, altazimuth instruments are basically designed for visual observing only, and you must locate the objects yourself using your knowledge of the sky. For many amateur astronomers this is part of the fun, so even in this day and age, low-tech astronomy is still popular.

Electronic astronomy

Even naked-eye astronomy has now had a high-tech makeover. A couple of years ago, Celestron introduced the SkyScout, a hand-held device which will tell you the name of any star or planet you point it at, and will help you find thousands of objects in the sky visible with the naked eye. Now rival firm Meade has brought out MySKY, a sort of hand-held sat nav for the sky, with a database of 30,000 objects and the facility to be linked to a telescope. Though actual models had not been seen at the time of writing, it remains to be seen whether these devices will become popular among amateur astronomers in the same way that in-car sat nav units have been welcomed even by those who have had no problems with reading maps.

▼ *Meade's new MySKY is the high-tech route to stargazing with the naked eye.*

And although such devices have yet to be installed in binoculars (though it's only a matter of time), modern wizardry has

already produced image-stabilized instruments which are becoming very popular with amateur astronomers. A favourite model for astronomy is the Canon 10 x 30 IS, which is now available for only £220 through a large photographic chain. Hand-held binoculars have the inevitable drawback that keeping them steady means finding some suitable surface on which you can rest your elbows or against which you can lean. But with image-stabilized binoculars you press a button and within a second or so the view miraculously settles down. Motion sensors counteract the natural small movements of your arms by moving prisms in the optical paths. And the optical quality of the Canon 10 x 30 IS is not compromised, as it offers edge-to-edge definition with a wide field of view – something that often lets down even more expensive non-stabilized binoculars. In tests, this model shows stars virtually as well as the larger 10 x 50 binoculars do, despite having an aperture of only 30 mm.

But it is the GO TO telescopes that have really brought technology to amateur astronomy, by automatically finding objects in the sky on demand. The Celestron SLT range provides basic starter scopes, both reflectors and refractors, on easy-to-use electronic mounts. To align them on the sky you set the date and time and then point the instrument at any three celestial objects in turn, pressing the Enter button each time. After that, the instrument will drive quite accurately to any other object within its grasp in the sky. Again, these are altazimuth instruments so they are not suitable for long-exposure photography, though because they will track a planet they are quite suitable for lunar and planetary photography.

At the other end of the scale are all-singing, all-dancing monsters that really require a home observatory. The precise finding and tracking abilities of these instruments, coupled with narrowband filters that help to cut through the light pollution and sensitive electronic cameras with cooled circuits to reduce electronic noise, have made it possible to take superb sky photos even from the UK. But make no mistake – though the technology is essential, it doesn't take over from expertise and skill. You can't simply go out and spend £5000 or more, and expect to get super shots on your first night out. It can take months of testing and honing of the alignment of the equipment, plus plenty of time in front of the computer processing the images, to get results which are really worth showing.

So the choice is yours as to whether to take the low or the high road to your interest in astronomy. Experience suggests that it is well worth getting to know the sky and how to use a basic instrument before plunging into the more advanced levels, so a low-tech start could be the key to a successful high-tech future.

▲ *Experienced amateur astronomer Dave Tyler checks the sky using Canon 10 x 30 image-stabilized binoculars.*

▲ *Fred Stevenson's home observatory in Amersham, Bucks, houses a 16-inch (400 mm) aperture computer-driven Meade telescope with imaging facilities.*